Dr Bill Napier is an astronomer at Armagh Observatory in Northern Ireland, and is an internationally recognized authority on the celestial hazard issue. He was one of the first astronomers in modern times to recognize that the Earth is at risk from its interplanetary and Galactic environments, and that celestial bombardment may even have precipitated the collapse of early civilisations. He is currently researching aspects of the vacuum. He has co-authored three scientific books and about eighty research papers, and is an associate member of Spaceguard UK.

'Mindblowing' *Literary Review*

Arthur C. Clarke called *Nemesis*, Bill Napier's first novel, 'The most exciting book I have ever read'.

D1024052

Revelation

Bill Napier

First published in 2000
by HEADLINE BOOK PUBLISHING

First published in paperback in 2000
by HEADLINE BOOK PUBLISHING

10 9 8 7 6 5 4 3 2 1

ISBN 0 7472 5994 1

Typeset by Avon Dataset Ltd, Bidford-on-Avon, Warks

Printed and bound in Great Britain by
Mackays of Chatham plc, Chatham, Kent

HEADLINE BOOK PUBLISHING
A division of Hodder Headline
338 Euston Road
London NW1 3BH

www.headline.co.uk
www.hodderheadline.com

This book is dedicated to Fabbio Migliorini

Prologue

At the mention of memoirs, the Minister threatens me with everything from Section Two to the Chinese water torture. Naturally, since all I want is a quiet life, I back down. To his credit, he tries not to smirk.

'You can't stop me writing a novel, though.'

The Minister turns puce but then he's known to be heavy on the port.

So here it is. Of course it's only a story, and if pressed I will deny that it ever happened. And deny it I have done, consistently, in all my conversations with those people with polite voices and calculating eyes.

To me, as a polar ice man, there's nothing odd about a tale of fire which starts in an Arctic blizzard. The planet is an interconnected whole; I measure the burning of rainforests in the thinning of the pack ice I walk on, and of fossil fuels in the desperate hunger of the ten-footers which raid our camps. The Arctic, in turn, is biding her time, quietly stoking up her revenge . . . but I digress.

The key to unlocking the secret of the diaries was Archie. My old friend Archie was the fatal miscalculation of the puppet masters. They had correctly assumed that I wouldn't understand the material I was handling, that I lacked the arcane knowledge which was the key to the secret. But if this particular puppet cut its strings, if I didn't do what my manipulators expected me to do, well, I give the credit to Archie.

We went back to the Creation, Archie and I. As boys we'd wandered around Glasgow's Castlemilk district in the days when it was run by real hard men, not the sham jessies you see now. Young buccaneers in search of trouble, which we often found. And if that seems an unlikely start to a couple of academic careers, I could tell you some juicy tales about quite a few distinguished Glaswegians. In fact our current Scottish Prime Minister . . . but there I go, wandering again.

Then there were the ladies, and then I went to Aberdeen and we drifted our separate ways until we met by chance years later at a Royal Society dinner in London. Archie the buccaneer was now a respected nuclear physicist, renowned for his work on superstring theory. I was into Arctic climate, looking for signs of trouble ahead. New Age monks, we had disdained commerce, despised the worldly, and devoted our lives instead to the search for greater truths.

As to how this unworldly pair reacted when wealth beyond calculation came within our reach, well – that's part of the story.

The rest of it has to do with blowing the planet to hell.

1

The Shadow on the Lake

Thursday, 29 July 1942

Out-of-towners. Men with an intense, almost unnatural aura about them. Come from God knows where to the back of beyond. In his imagination, the station master sees gangsters, Mafia bosses come for a secret confab.

It is, after all, a quiet branch line, and he has to occupy his mind with something.

He has no way of knowing that the three men alighting from the Pullman are infinitely more dangerous than anything his imagination can devise.

First out is John Baudino, the Pope's bodyguard. His gorilla frame almost fills the carriage door. He is carrying a dark green shopping bag. Baudino surveys the platform suspiciously before stepping down. Two others follow, one a tall, thin man with intense blue eyes. He is wearing a broad-brimmed pork-pie hat, and is smoking a cigarette. The third man is thin and studious, with a pale, serious face and round spectacles.

The man waiting impatiently on the empty railway

platform expected only Oppenheimer; the other two are a surprise.

'Hello, Arthur,' says the man with the blue eyes, shaking hands. He looks bleary, as if he hasn't slept.

'You could have flown, Oppie. A thousand miles is one helluva train ride.'

Oppenheimer drops his cigarette on the platform and exhales the last of the smoke. 'You know how it is with the General. He thinks we're too valuable to risk in the air.'

Arthur Compton leads the way to the exit gate.

The station master gives them a suspicious nod. 'Y'all here for the fishing?' he asks, attempting a friendly tone. It is out of season for the angling. His eyes stray to their unfishing-like clothes and luggage.

'No. We're German spies,' growls Baudino, thrusting the train tickets at him. The station master snaps their tickets and cackles nervously.

In Compton's estate wagon, Baudino pulls a notebook and a Colt 38 out of the shopping bag at his feet. He rests the weapon on his knees. He says, 'Do your talking somewhere quiet, Mister Compton. And not in the cottage.'

'Come on, John, it's a hideaway. Nobody even knows I'm here.'

'We found you,' Baudino says over his shoulder. He is already checking car registration numbers against a list.

Compton thinks about that. 'Yeah.' He takes the car along a narrow, quiet suburban road. After about three miles the houses peter out and the road is lined with conifer forest. Now and then a lake can be glimpsed to the right, through the trees. After ten minutes Compton goes down through the gears and then turns off along a rough track. About a mile on he arrives at a clearing, and pulls up at a log cabin. A line of washing is strung out on the verandah. They step out and stretch their limbs. The air is cool and clear. Baudino slips the gun into his trouser belt.

Compton says, 'You know what I'm enjoying about this place? The water. It's everywhere. It even descends from the sky. After the mesa, it's glorious. You guys want coffee?'

Oppenheimer shakes his head. 'Later. First, let's talk.' He leans into the wagon and pulls out a briefcase.

Compton points and they set off through a track in the woods. After half a mile they come to a lake whose far edge is somewhere over the horizon. They set off along the pebbled beach. Baudino takes up the rear, about thirty yards behind the other three, to be out of hearing: what the eggheads get up to is none of his business. His assignment is protection and to that end he keeps glancing around, peering into the forest. Now and then he touches the gun, as if for reassurance.

Compton says, 'Oppie, whatever made you come a thousand miles to the Canadian border, it must be deadly serious.'

Oppenheimer's face is grim. 'Teller thinks the bomb will set light to the atmosphere, maybe even the oceans.'

Compton stops. '*What?*'

Oppenheimer pats the briefcase. 'I've brought his calculations.'

The studious one, Lev Petrosian, speaks for the first time since they arrived. His English is good and clear with just a hint of a German accent. 'He thinks atmospheric nitrogen and carbon will catalyse fusion of the hydrogen. Here's the basic formula.' He hands over a sheet of paper.

Compton studies it for some minutes, while walking. Finally he looks up at his colleagues, consternation in his eyes. 'Jesus.'

Oppenheimer nods. 'A smart guy, our Hungarian. At the fireball temperatures we're talking about you start with carbon, combine with hydrogen all the way up to nitrogen-15, then you get your carbon back. Meantime you've transmuted four hydrogen atoms into helium-4 and fired out gamma rays all the way up the ladder.'

'Hell, Oppie, we don't even need to create the nitrogen. It's eighty per cent of the atmosphere. And we've already got the carbon in the CO_2, not to mention plenty of hydrogen in the water. If this is right it makes the atmosphere a devil's brew.' Compton shakes his head. 'But it can't be right. It takes millions of years to turn hydrogen into deuterium.'

Petrosian says, 'About one hydrogen atom in ten thousand is deuterium. It's already there in the atmosphere.'

'You mean . . .'

'God has fixed our atmosphere beautifully. He's made it so it by-passes the slow reactions in the ladder. The rates are speeded up from millions of years to a few seconds.'

'When does the process trigger?'

'It kicks in at a hundred million degrees. The bomb could reach that.'

Oppenheimer coughs slightly and stops to light up a cigarette. 'We could turn the planet into one huge fireball.'

'What does the Pope think? And Uncle Nick?' Compton is referring to Enrico Fermi and Neils Bohr, atomic physicists whose names are so sensitive that they are referred to by nickname even within the barbed wire enclave of Los Alamos.

Oppenheimer takes a nervous puff. 'They don't know yet. I want us to check it out first. We'll work on it overnight.'

Compton picks up a stone and throws it into the water. They watch the ripples before they carry on walking.

'Out with it,' Oppenheimer says.

Compton's tone is worried. 'Oppie, look at the big picture. The U-boats have just about strangled the British. Hitler's troops are occupying Europe from the North Cape to Egypt. Russia's just about finished and I'll bet a dime to a dollar Hitler will soon push through Iran and link up with the Japs in the Indian Ocean. The Germans and the Japs will soon have the whole of Asia, Russia and Europe between them.'

'So?'

'So then Hitler will be over the Bering Straits and through Canada like a knife through butter. By the time he gets there he'll be stronger than us. We have a two-thousand-mile border with the Canadians, Oppie, it's indefensible, and I don't want my hideaway to be five minutes' flying time from Goering's Stukas.'

Oppenheimer's intense blue eyes are fixed on the lake, as if he is looking over the horizon to Canada. 'That's a grand strategic vision, Arthur. But what's your point?'

'Ten minutes ago that grand strategic vision didn't bother me. So long as we won the race to build the gadget, we'd be okay. But how can we take even the slightest chance of setting the atmosphere alight? I'm sorry, Oppie, but given a straight choice we'd be better to accept Nazi slavery.'

Oppenheimer nods reluctantly. 'I've lost a lot of sleep over this one, Arthur, but I have to agree. Unless we can be a hundred per cent sure that Teller is wrong, the Bomb must never be made.'

There is just a trace of sadness in Petrosian's voice. 'I understand your reasoning, gentlemen. I'd probably think the same if I hadn't lived under the Nazis.'

2

Flesland Alpha

The new millennium

Death and destruction entered Findhorn's Aberdeen office in the form of a small, bespectacled, mild-mannered Norwegian with an over-long trenchcoat and a briefcase. He claimed that his name was Olaf Petersen, and the briefcase was stamped with the letters O.F.P. in faded gold.

Anne put her head round the door. She was being a redhead today. 'Fred, there's a Mister Olaf Petersen here.'

The red leather armchair had been purchased for a knock-down price at a fire-damage sale but it was all brass studs and wrinkles and it gave the little office a much-needed air of opulence. Petersen sank into it and handed over a little card. He looked around at the photographs which covered the office walls: icebergs, aurora borealis, a cuddly little polar bear, an icebreaker apparently stranded on a snowfield.

The card read:

Olaf F. Petersen, Cand.mag., Siv.ing. (Tromsø)
Flesland Field Centre
Norsk Advanced Technologies

'Coffee?' Findhorn asked, but he sensed that the man had little inclination for social preliminaries.

'Thank you, but I have very little time. The Company would appreciate some help, Doctor Findhorn.' Like many Scandinavians, the man's English was excellent, only the lack of any regional accent revealing that it was a second language.

'Norsk and I have done business from time to time.'

'This particular task is quite different from anything you have done for us before now. Something has turned up. The matter is urgent and requires the strictest confidentiality. We hope that you can help us in spite of the very short notice.'

Findhorn thought of the empty diary pages yawning over the coming months. Petersen was looking at him closely. 'I had hoped to take a few days' break over Christmas.'

Petersen looked disappointed. 'Frankly, I'm disappointed. You were perfect for this assignment.'

Findhorn thought it better not to overdo the hard-to-get routine. He said, 'Why don't you tell me about it?'

Petersen, smiling slightly, pulled a large white envelope from his briefcase. 'Do you have a light table?'

'Of course. Through here.'

By labelling the door 'Weather Room', Findhorn hoped to imply that further along the corridor there were other rooms with labels like 'Mud Analysis' or 'Core Sample Laboratory' or even 'Arctic Environment Simulation Facility. Do Not Enter', rather than two broom cupboards and a toilet. The light table, about five feet by four, took up much of the room. They picked their way over cardboard boxes and piles of paper. Findhorn switched on the table and pulled the black curtain over the window. Petersen opened the envelope and pulled out a transparency about a foot square. Lettering in the corner said that it had been supplied courtesy of the National Ice Center and a DMSP infrared satellite.

Findhorn laid the transparency on the table. Down the left, the west coast of Greenland showed as a grey-white, serrated patch except where sea fog obscured the outline. Someone had outlined the limit of the pack ice with a dotted line. There was a scattering of icebergs. Little arrows pointed to them, with numbers attached.

'Do you see anything odd?' Petersen asked.

Findhorn scanned the picture. 'Not really.' He pointed to an iceberg off the Davy Sound, just on the boundary between Greenlandic and international waters. 'Except maybe A-02 here. It's pretty big.'

'Unusually so, for the east coast. The big tabular bergs are usually found on the west of Greenland. They break off from the Petterman or the Quarayaq or the Jungersen glaciers, and drift down through Baffin Bay to the Newfoundland Bank.'

'So where is this one headed?'

'It's been caught up in the East Greenland Current. It may round Cape Farewell and join its western cousins or

11

it may break out into the North Atlantic. But size and drift aren't the issue, Doctor Findhorn. Take a closer look.'

There was a little dust on the transparency, overlying the big iceberg, and Findhorn puffed at it. The dust didn't blow away. He brushed it lightly with his finger but again it stayed put. He frowned.

'Try the microscope,' Petersen suggested politely.

Findhorn swivelled the microscope over the big transparency. He fiddled with the knurled knob, brought the photograph into focus.

The iceberg filled the field of view. A pattern of ripples marked its line of drift through the surrounding ocean. It was surrounded by a flotilla of lesser floes, like an aircraft carrier surrounded by yachts.

Findhorn swivelled the front lens holder. He frowned some more, puzzled.

The specks of dust had resolved themselves into rectangles, man-made structures like huts. Other, smaller shapes were scattered around.

He turned the microscope to its highest setting and increased the intensity of the light shining up through the translucent glass. And then he looked up from the microscope, astonished. 'But this is crazy.'

Olaf agreed. 'Icebergs melt. Split. Capsize. No sane individual sets foot on an iceberg.'

'But . . .'

'But a large camp has been set up on this one.' Olaf, leaning over the light table, tapped the photograph with a stubby finger. 'Yes, Doctor Findhorn, this is crazy. These small irregular shapes you see. They're men. On an iceberg

12

which could overturn at any time.'

Findhorn stood up from the microscope. The light from the table, thrown upwards, gave Petersen a slightly sinister look, like a mad scientist in an old horror movie. A vague feeling of uneasiness was coming over him. 'What exactly does Norsk want from me?'

Petersen gave a good imitation of a smile. 'First, we'd like you to fly out to the northernmost rig in our Field Centre.'

'Norsk Flesland?'

'The same. Then, from there, we'd like to fly you out to the *Norsk Explorer*, our icebreaker, which is currently about three hundred kilometres north of the rig, just on the limit of the helicopter's range. The *Explorer* will take you to A-02, which is further north again. We want you to climb that berg.'

And now it was happening again, the old, lurching sensation in the stomach. 'Why? And why me in particular?'

Petersen was still smiling, but he had calculating eyes. 'Perhaps I will have that coffee after all.'

'How you gooin ar keed?'

'Okay thanks. Just a bit nervous.'

'Yow never bin on a reeg before?' The man's voice was raised, to penetrate Findhorn's ear protectors.

Findhorn looked out at the dark sea. In the distance, lights were blazing on the horizon. The helicopter was heading directly for them.

'Nope.'

'Thought so. What's yow job?'

'I'm just visiting.'

'You joost veezeeteeng?'

Findhorn nodded. The blaze of lights was beginning to take shape. As the helicopter approached he began to make out three illuminated giants wading in the ocean, holding hands.

The Brummie was still probing. 'Not that it's any of my business, of course, yow know what I mean?'

Now Findhorn could see that their upper structures were forested with cranes and big metal Christmas trees. There were pipes and strange projections and tiny men on walkways and platforms. The arms joining the giants resolved themselves into connecting passageways. It was a city on stilts. Its lowest deck was thirty metres clear of the Arctic Ocean: the engineers had planned for a once-in-a-century giant wave. As to the icebergs, however, they relied on statistics and prayer. Against a ten-million-ton berg, Norsk Flesland might as well be made of matchsticks.

'I'm impressed,' Findhorn said.

'Ooh ar, you will be. Yow looking at something taller than the Eiffel Tower. With ten decks and three turbines geeveeng us twenty-five megawatts. We get 'alf a million barrels of crude and three hundred million cubic feet of gas every day. There's 'alf a mile of water between the reeg and the seabed and the well penetrates fifteen thousand feet of mood.'

He's close, Findhorn thought. *It's pushing six hundred thousand barrels a day, and they reach it through eighteen*

14

thousand feet of Upper Jurassic sandstone.

'But you know,' the man confided, 'for all its size, there's something keeps me listening in the dark, know what I mean?'

'A big berg?'

The man shook his head. 'A meecroscopic crack. Fatigue in a leg.'

'Which one is Alpha?'

The man leaned over Findhorn and pointed a nicotine-stained finger. 'The platform in the middle, that's Flesland Alpha, the living quarters. Beta on the left is drilling and wellhead, and Delta on the right is the gas process platform. We do twelve hours on, twelve off. They like to keep the accommodation separate. There's about fifty metres of corridor joining them.'

'What's it like, working on a rig?'

'Norwegian reegs are breell. Now on Flesland Alpha, yow've got everytheeng you want, from a ceenema to a sauwna. There's a gymnasium, snooker, leather armchairs, escalators between decks, en-suite rooms, fantastic groob. It's like the Hilton. Only the American Gulf rigs can match them, and they have the weather for barbecues. Now the Breetish exploration rigs, they're roobish. Four men to a room, recreation a grotty TV room, canteen groob worse than a motorway stop.'

'I take it you're a Brummie?' Findhorn asked.

The man bristled. 'Naeiouw. I coom from the Black Country, from Doodley, can't yow tell? There's a beeg zoo there.'

'What's your job?' Findhorn asked. The helicopter was

beginning to tilt. A long pier jutted out from Delta, and at the end of it a flame fluttered in the wind, throwing a thin orange light on the dark ocean below. Findhorn glimpsed derricks, and brilliantly lit walkways, and a confusing mass of pipes, and then the helicopter was sinking down towards an octagonal helideck, the wind from the rotors rippling water on its surface.

'Oi look after the peegs, ar keed.'

Findhorn decided against asking for a translation.

A muffled voice came over the intercom. 'There's a very high wind out there. Keep a firm hold of your baggage and watch your footing. Keep your ear protectors on.'

On deck, the wind threatened to knock Findhorn off his feet. It was cold and wet with sea spray. There was a smell of oil. Men on the helideck pointed toward a stairwell. Findhorn followed the oil men, in their orange survival suits and carrying holdalls, down metal stairs and along a short corridor. Here the air was warm. There was a queue at a desk marked *Resepsjon*; there were lifejackets to hand in, and hard hats and steel-toed boots to collect; there were ID cards to exchange for cabin and muster cards.

For Findhorn, however, the rules were being broken. The platform manager, steel grey hair poking under her helmet, was waiting. Without a word she took him by the arm and led him past the queue. There was to be no trace of Findhorn's visit to Flesland Alpha.

It was so huge that, at first, Findhorn thought he must have imagined it. Eyes straining and nerves taut, it was too easy to see non-existent structures in the whirling grey patterns of the blizzard. But then the helmsman was shouting 'Iceberg dead ahead,' and suddenly it was real, and Findhorn found himself saying, 'Oh my God.'

As it approached, the white turrets and battlements of the Disneyland castle resolved themselves into crevasses and overhanging cliffs and old meltwater tunnels as wide as motorways.

Through the big panoramic window of the bridge, wipers clicking, Findhorn and Hansen watched the ship's forecastle plunging down troughs, with black water and foam and chunks of ice swirling along the deck before smashing against the bridge and pouring over the sides. A foot of solid ice covered davits, ventilation shafts and deck railings.

Even as he watched, visibility was deteriorating. The Captain, clinging on to the engine-room telegraph, had acquired a dour, taciturn expression. His eyes, Findhorn noticed, kept straying to the ship's inclinometer. Every few seconds the clang of little bergs ran through the ship's hull.

Findhorn looked in vain for a route up the grim, lifeless structure; the cliffs were pockmarked and yet smooth; old shorelines were marked out along its length by sloping ridges. Waves bigger than houses were pounding the foot of the berg. He said again, 'Oh my God.'

'Aye,' Hansen agreed, gripping the telegraph. 'Rather you than me.'

'Ice two fifty metres,' the schoolboy called out. His face was almost buried in the cowling of the radar.

His accent had just a trace of Norwegian and he had a cool, nonchalant attitude. The giveaway was the slight tremor in his voice; that, and the grip of his hands on the edge of his desk.

'Are you sure it's the right one?'

Hansen grinned sadistically. 'This is the age of GPS, Mister. But there's one way to make sure.' A blast of sound actually shook Findhorn like a jelly. His heart jumped, and the sound of the ship's horn echoed off a hundred unseen bergs. They waited.

'Would you look at that?' Hansen exclaimed.

A tiny shape was moving at the top of the iceberg. It resolved itself into a man dressed in thick white furs. The man started to wave furiously.

'Is that Watson or Roscoe?' Hansen asked.

'Too far away to say,' Findhorn replied.

To his utter horror, he realised that the berg was swaying. The ice cliff facing them was slowly tilting over. He watched aghast as it just kept on tilting towards them. The man should have fallen off, plunging to a painful death in the icy water far below; instead he quickly scrambled back and disappeared from view. A black wave was rearing up from the foot of the berg, displacing floes as it headed their way.

As the ship entered the lee, Hansen issued more orders, all of them mysterious to Findhorn. The Captain pointed. 'There's your route up, laddie.'

Findhorn made out the thin rope ladder, now over-hanging the tilting cliff, its base immersed in the churning water. Little hunks of ice and snow were splitting away from the top of the iceberg and crashing into the sea around the ladder. Thundering echoes came from the bergs scattered around. His mouth was parched and he was beginning to feel petrified with terror.

'I'll not move in much closer, some of these beasts have a wide underwater shelf. And I'll not risk more men than necessary. Findhorn, get up there. Do your job, and get yon people down that ladder ASAP.'

Findhorn stood, frozen. 'Quickly man,' Hansen snapped, 'before she turns turtle.' A practical man, our captain, Findhorn thought, not given to expressions of good luck or similar flim-flam.

'Sub-surface ice one thirty metres ahead, captain. It goes way down.'

'Very well. This is as far as I go.' Hansen lifted a telephone and a shudder ran through the ship.

'Can't you take me closer?' Findhorn was looking at the mountainous waves between him and the berg. The ship was plunging like an elevator in free-fall and fear was distorting his voice.

'Mister Findhorn, sir. Don't push your bloody luck. I shouldn't even be here. I'm breaking icebreaker Rule Number One as it is: you can handle any two of fog, storm and ice, but if you have all three you get the hell out of it. I'm not about to tempt fate with Number Two: don't approach an iceberg closer than its height.' Hansen nodded over Findhorn's shoulder: the execution squad, in the form of Leroy, the Jamaican first officer, and Arkin, the redfaced bosun, ice club in hand and looking like a murderer.

'I've seen this happen before,' Hansen said. 'She's about

to turn turtle. And when she flips, she'll do it without warning.'

Findhorn, out of words, pulled up his fur cape. A sailor pushed the door open against the wind, and the bridge was suddenly filled with whirling snow. The man grinned as Findhorn passed.

On deck, the roar was overwhelming. A *whee!* came from overhead, from ice-festooned cables and wires attached to the masts. The snow was like stinging needles. The ship suddenly rolled. Churning black sea rose towards the deck. Findhorn overbalanced, grabbed a thick white handrail. Leroy snatched at his cape, hauled him upright. They clambered along the deck, Arkin leading and rapidly turning into a snowman.

On the lee of the ship, four sailors dressed like Eskimos were gripping the stanchions connected to the motor launch. Two of them were hammering fiercely at thick ice. Arkin climbed in, and Findhorn felt an indeterminate number of hands heaving him into the boat. Then he was gripping its side in terror as it was hoisted up on a derrick and swung out over the sea, the leverage exaggerating the ship's roll. The Zodiac slapped onto the water and Arkin snapped open the quick-release shackles, almost falling into the water as he did.

Down at sea level, the waves were immense. One loomed high over them. It hypnotized Findhorn. He watch its approach, assumed he was about to die. Instead the wave lifted the boat upwards, like a rapidly rising elevator, and threatened to smash it against the iron hull of the icebreaker; but then Arkin quickly puttered the little boat up and over its crest, towards the ice cliff. The berg seemed to have stopped tilting, but neither was it righting itself. This close to the boiling waves, the water seemed greasy. It was covered with a thin layer of frazil ice, and wisps of frost smoke outlined Findhorn's lungs and penetrated his layers of thermal clothing. The spray and snow assaulting his face were painful.

'You wan' try for the rope?' Leroy shouted, his face pitch-black against his white furry cape. Arkin was steering round an ice flow twice the size of the motor boat.

Findhorn looked at the big waves thundering off the face of the berg. The boat would smash itself to pieces if they approached too close. The ice on the cliff looked as hard as steel. Too terrified to speak, he nodded.

The rope ladder was dangling near a large cave. The water inside it was relatively calm. Arkin puttered them towards it. This close, the berg seemed monstrous. It was hissing, as the melting ice released bubbles of ancient air; Findhorn saw them sailing into the open jaws of a living entity. As they entered the cave the sea water began to churn below them, slapping powerfully off the side of the berg and drenching them with icy salt water. Arkin gripped the tiller with both hands. Then the boat was rising upwards.

Leroy shouted: 'Ice platform rising! Clear off!'

There was a terrifying hiss as the rising berg sucked in water and air. The sea churned. Arkin, eyes wide with fear, revved up the engine and swung the tiller. As they raced out from under the overhanging ice the rope ladder scraped alongside and Findhorn, in a moment of pure insanity, leaped at it. He grabbed a wooden rung and swung dizzily back under the overhang. The boat was racing clear. The noise was terrifying. He scrambled upwards, not daring to look down, but then the berg was pulling him up from the maelstrom. Ice showered from above, a fist-sized lump striking him painfully on the shoulder. He scrambled up recklessly, desperate to escape the hissing monster at his feet.

Fifty metres up, gasping for breath, he summoned up the nerve to glance down. Arkin had taken the Zodiac well clear of the berg. Small, pale faces looked up at him. The snow was closing in again and the *Norsk Explorer* was just a hazy outline. He thought of what he had just done and his whole body began to tremble.

He looked up. The rope ladder ended about twenty metres above him, tied around shiny metal pitons hammered into the ice. Beyond it was a ridge about three feet wide, an old shoreline, and on the ridge was a bearded man. Findhorn, his heart hammering in his chest, climbed up the last few feet of rope. He grabbed the gloved hand tightly and found himself hauled up on to a flat stretch of rough ice, and facing a man with a pinched nose and a worried face adorned by a five-day growth of ice-covered, grey beard. Small hard eyes peered out from behind the snow goggles. Buster Watson: Findhorn knew him from half a dozen international conferences; a pushy little egoist.

'Thank God,' the man shouted into the wind. 'Where the hell have you been, Findhorn?'

'We're lucky to be here at all in this weather. What happened to your radio?'

'We lost nearly everything when the bloody thing calved off.'

You lost the radio but not the huts?

Then Watson was shouting, 'Move it, we have very little time.' Bent almost double against the wind, he led the way across the top of the berg, along a flat plateau about fifty metres wide. Through the driving snow Findhorn glimpsed violently flapping tents and snow-driven huts. A tethered silver balloon was straining horizontally at its leash, rubbing against the ice. They passed a sonar tower whipping in the wind, firing little chirps of sound into the atmosphere overhead. The site looked for all the world like a scientific ice station.

Only the location was crazy.

Now they were passing the charred remains of a hut, a downwind line of soot marking the wind direction at the time of the fire, and the plateau was beginning to slope down. Watson led the way to a rectangular hut about twenty feet long; one of Findhorn's specks of dust. There was a surge of warm air as Watson pulled the door open against the screaming wind. Inside, a generator was throbbing. It was secured to the ice with deep steel pins. There was a smell of diesel. A shiny black cable from the generator was pinned along the ice and disappeared into a shaft about four feet wide.

Watson threw back his fur hood and took off his goggles. 'We started with a steam probe. The hole it made was a guide for a big gopher. It just melted its way down.'

Findhorn stood nervously at the edge of the shaft. Naked lights were spaced at ten metre intervals down its side and there was a long aluminium ladder, converging to a point of light far below. 'How far down does it go?'

'Three hundred feet.'

'*What?*'

'Yes. Below sea level. You first.'

3

Berg

The rungs were covered with smooth, hard ice and the spikes on Findhorn's boots meant that he had to raise his boot away from each rung before placing it on the one below.

Below about twenty feet the blizzard's scream was a whisper. At forty feet there was a sepulchral silence broken only by the metallic clatter of boots on rungs, and Watson's wheezy breathing above. The man seemed in a hurry, his boots sometimes just inches from Findhorn's head.

But then, starting at about sixty feet, Findhorn started to hear new sounds. They were coming up from below, and there were several components. There was something like an intermittent hissing. There were what might have been human voices. Most of all there was an occasional boom, so deep it was almost felt.

The ladder was tilting, a slow, pendulum-like oscillation. It had a period of maybe two minutes. Findhorn thought he could use the period of oscillation to work out the depth of the berg, started the calculation in his head, but another deep *Boom!* scattered the numbers away like crows from a farmer's shotgun. A few seconds after the boom, a blast of cold air swept briefly up the tunnel. The berg was breathing.

In the glare of the lamps, far below, Findhorn saw that the tunnel curved slightly, the ladder disappearing from view. Two hundred feet into the climb, the hissing was loud, and there was the occasional buzz of a chain saw. And then, about three hundred feet down, the shaft was opening up and Findhorn jumped onto flat ice at the end of a short tunnel. Watson pushed past and, bent double, led the way. It opened out to an amazing sight.

The cavern was fifty or sixty feet wide and as high. It was lit up by harsh blue spotlights, some on tall tripods, like a film set. Four men were directing hot, steaming water into a tunnel from a thick white hosepipe connected to a second generator. They were enveloped in the condensing fog which poured out of the tunnel mouth. Two others were shovelling icy slurry into a hop attached to the generator. In the confined space of the cavern, the noise was deafening. Findhorn's arrival created a sensation. A cheer went up, but it died out as the floor continued to tilt.

Findhorn thought, *we're under the Arctic Ocean.* He fought off a panicky moment of claustrophobia.

Watson waved his hands to encompass the cavern. 'We excavated this with hot-water cannons.' One of the men approached, chain saw swinging; in the cavern's weird illumination he looked like a troll stepped out from a Grimm fairytale. He had the wrinkled face of a heavy smoker and he was unconsciously licking his lips in fear. 'How're you doing?' he asked in a tough Dublin accent.

'Right, are we getting off this bloody coffin?'

Findhorn turned to Watson. 'How long has it been like this?'

'Since it calved. It's getting worse. In the last hour it's been tilting an extra five degrees. Look, I've a pension to collect, can we get a move on?'

'Where's Roscoe?'

'Like I said, there was an accident.'

In the circumstances, Findhorn let it pass.

'Along here. Look, we don't have much time.' The fear in Watson's voice was infectious. He led Findhorn towards the end of the cavern. They passed a tall, vertical wall with a six-inch fissure running from floor to ceiling. Findhorn was met with a strong, icy breeze as he passed the crack. To his surprise and horror, another tunnel led from the end of the cavern further down into the bowels of the iceberg. Rough steps had been hacked out of the ice. Watson started down. Findhorn almost refused to follow, felt something close to panic.

The deep, rhythmic bang was coming up from this second tunnel. At intervals along it, long metal rods had been driven into the ice, to various depths. Intense lights shone at the end of the rods, and the ice glowed a brilliant aquamarine blue from within. Each light had melted a little sphere of ice around it, and meltwater was trickling back along the rods and on to the icy floor, making a treacherous, almost frictionless surface.

But the blue glacier ice was far from pure. Stones, boulders, gravel and dust were scattered through its interior. Beyond about fifty feet, their cumulative mass acted as an optical barrier like a wall. Imbedded about thirty feet into the compressed ice, within reach of the powerful arc lamps, were larger, dark shapes. One of them was recognisable as a propellor, its blades twisted backwards. Beyond it, on the edge of visibility, was a jagged section of fuselage, still with its windows, one of them, remarkably, with its glass still intact. Two long strands of cable wound into the blackness.

A man was standing with his face to the ice. As Findhorn approached the man turned. 'Admiral Dawson, US Naval Research Office. What the hell are you doing here?'

'Just passing by. Thought you might want your life saved or something.'

The berg was levelling out.

'Thanks but we're doing just fine.'

Unexpectedly, Watson let forth a stream of profanity. 'This fucking maniac wants us here until the berg overturns. Get us out of it, Findhorn.'

Findhorn pointed at the dark shapes. 'What's that?'

'A Yak Ten. A nineteen fifties Soviet light aircraft.'

With a row of elongated bullet holes along the side of the fuselage.

'What are you trying to do, Admiral?'

'We were trying to cut towards the cabin area. Another hour would have done it, only the way this is going I don't believe we have an hour. The sonar shows more fuselage just in the dark over there. And a wing. And since you're here, you may as well come and see this.'

The berg was beginning to tilt in the opposite direction.

It was minus twenty degrees but Watson's face was beaded with sweat.

Findhorn followed Admiral Dawson further down the sloping tunnel, gripping a red nylon rope which acted as a handrail. Watson took up the rear. The tunnel was narrowing and tilting more steeply down. Findhorn had a brief vision of a grave passage deep inside a pyramid, and as they descended he felt his nerve beginning to crack. But then, a hundred feet down, Dawson stopped at a brilliant blue light. It had been driven a couple of feet into the ice and steam was hissing off it and billowing along the shaft.

Findhorn cleared a covering of frost away to reveal clear blue ice. It was a moment before he recognized the shape.

The corpse had partially mummified. Evaporation had turned it into little more than a skeleton covered with white, smooth, hard-looking flesh. Some of the flesh had transformed to grave wax. The corpse had been partially dismembered, pieces of arm being sheared off, the flesh more or less separate from the bone. Clothes had largely been stripped away. The abdominal wall was opened and the intestines, surprisingly intact, looked as if they were made of brown parchment. He found himself not a foot from a face the size of a soup plate. Dark matter had been squeezed out of the skull and the glacial drift of fifty years had spread it into a fan which stretched beyond the sphere of illumination about six feet in radius around the arc light. An eye was recognizably blue; the other, Findhorn thought, was probably round the back of the squashed

face. Teeth had penetrated the leathery skin and the jaw
had sheared sideways. The nose was flattened almost down
to the gaping mouth. The torn remains of a grey suit were
scattered amongst darker chunks of matter.

Findhorn peered closely at the hideous sight. In his
imagination, the blue eye stared back at him.

'There's another body in the pilot's seat,' said Dawson.
'No way can we reach it.'

'Why couldn't they have crashed further up the glacier?'
Watson complained.

Findhorn was peering into the ice. There was a metallic
glitter from a black, rectangular shape about four feet
into the ice. 'What's that?'

'It's what this is about, pal,' said Dawson. 'As if you
didn't know.'

The awful tilting of the berg had stopped; but neither
was the ice mountain righting itself.

Findhorn said, 'Tell your men to get out of here and
leave me a chain saw.'

Watson disappeared round a corner and returned with
the troll. The Irishman half-slithered down the tunnel, his
free hand waving a chain saw and looking like a big crab's
claw. Watson pointed his torch and without delay the man
started on the ice. The noise in the narrow tunnel was
deafening but the saw was cutting quickly into the wall,
ice spraying around the tunnel.

'Get your men out of here, Watson,' Findhorn said
again.

The berg was beginning to move again, but instead of
levelling out, the tilt was increasing. 'Oh Holy Mother of

Christ she's going,' Watson wailed, his eyes wide with fear.

The Dubliner was in to the depth of his elbows. The tunnel had levelled and was now beginning to tilt in the opposite direction.

Now the chainsaw man was in up to his shoulders.

There was a tremendous bang, deep and powerful. The berg shook. Watson shouted, 'What the hell?'

Findhorn slithered back to the main cavern, which now lay below them. A wall had split. The fissure was now a foot wide and as he looked it continued to widen with a horrible cracking noise. Men were at the shaft entrance, fighting and punching to get on the ladder. He ran back to the side tunnel, hauled himself up by the red nylon handrail.

'Abandon ship,' he called out, his voice thick with fear. But Dawson was pushing the Irishman further in.

The Irishman's feet were kicking frantically. He wriggled back out, his face grey. 'Feic this, I'm out o' here,' he said harshly. He promptly slipped, landed with a gasp on his back, and slithered down the tunnel, the chain saw tobogganning ahead of him.

'Give me your ice axe,' Dawson snapped at Findhorn, gripping the handrail.

'Don't be a fool, Admiral. She's splitting. Get out of it.' But Dawson grabbed the axe with his free hand and leaned into the shaft, hacking furiously. Findhorn, gripping the nylon rail with both hands, waited in an agony of impatience and fear.

There was another bang. The berg suddenly lurched.

'She's going!' Findhorn shouted.

The admiral was tugging at something. 'Get me out! Quickly!'

There was a third tremendous *Crash!* from the direction of the main tunnel. Findhorn's feet gave way. He thumped heavily on to the ice, tumbled into the cavern. The fissure was now six feet wide and he tobogganed down towards it. Boxes, lamps, drills, chain saws, men were slithering down out of control into its mouth. Water was surging down the shaft, carrying men with it. The lights failed. In the blackness someone was screaming, high-pitched. Findhorn, on his back and accelerating out of control, felt a freezing wind rushing past him. The screaming was now above him, receding as if it came from a man shooting upwards. From below came a deep, powerful *Bang!* like an explosion. It filled Findhorn's world: and at last he recognized it as the sound of water slamming into a cavity. He was now in near free-fall.

And then he felt a giant hand pushing him up from below, as if the tunnel was accelerating skywards, and ice gouged a painful furrow in his brow, and a patch of light grew rapidly overhead, and in a moment the approaching grey had lightened and bleak daylight was streaming into a crevasse and he was out and fifty metres up and arching through the air, arms waving helplessly. He had time to glimpse a tiny boat with two petrified faces looking up, and beyond it the misty outline of the icebreaker, and dominating all a massive, ice-speckled black wave, a malign, living entity taller than the ship, and in the seconds while he somersaulted towards the Arctic water, Findhorn knew he was about to die.

4

Findhorn's Dream

Findhorn recalled his death in great detail. Mainly, he thought what a stupid way to go.

They'd had a boozy lunch at El Greco's, Hazel, Bruce and he. The *spada* had been first class (sauce-free, grilled to perfection). They'd discussed the Matsumo contract, and had agreed it was amazingly lucrative. Over coffee and ouzo they'd wondered – out of his hearing – about the attractions of Kontos, alias 'Bonkos', the ugly Greek proprietor with the red Ferrari and the endless string of what Bruce enviously described as 'luscious bints'.

Outside the restaurant, Hazel had shouted something to Findhorn as he'd stepped onto the busy street, his head spinning with wine. He'd had only a fraction of a second to follow Hazel's shocked gaze before the Leyland truck hit him, smashing his skull onto the hard London street, a massive wheel crushing his chest an instant later.

The heart monitor sent out its microwave signal and by the time the ambulance had reached the casualty entrance at St John's, the vultures were already awaiting the formal pronouncement of death. The casualty doctor shook his head over Findhorn's smashed chest and the corpse was quickly transferred to the team with no more than a hurried signature. In their grey, sealed van, along the Mall, the body was strapped to a table. A variety of scalpels and a small saw were used to remove Findhorn's head. As they turned up Haymarket, the blood vessels attached to the body were ligatured to stem the flow of blood. At a red light, while tourists and office girls crossed in front of them, Findhorn's carotid arteries were being connected to tubes and the blood in his head was replaced by a cold, cold liquid. Around Piccadilly and up Regent Street, his head was wrapped in foil and immersed, upside down, in a vat of liquid nitrogen, causing a surge of freezing fog to flood the van temporarily before escaping through a vent into the busy street. The metal lid of the vat secured, warm air was pumped into the van and the team took off their masks, goggles and bloody gloves, and relaxed. Somebody opened a Thermos flask; a cigarette was lit; and, over the headless cadaver, the chat turned to the forthcoming match. The van headed swiftly towards the M1, its destination a large, anonymous country house tucked away in the Buckinghamshire countryside.

All this Findhorn saw as if from above, from a camera in the roof of the van.

There was a tunnel, and all that ever had been or would be was imbedded in its walls, and he was moving along the tunnel towards a tiny light marking its end, and the light grew until he found himself in a brilliant white room and he woke up, unable to move. The cold was unlike anything he had ever experienced. It was an intense pain. Something was throbbing gently in the background, like the flow of blood through his ears. The room had no walls or ceiling; it was egg-shaped, white. There was no discernible lighting but it was bright like an operating theatre. A door slid open and a nurse, twentyish, came silently in and bent over him. She was the most beautiful woman he had ever seen.

'I made it,' he said, but the voice came out as a whisper.

'Just.' Her voice was surprisingly rough.

'How long was I dead?'

'A very long time. Very long.'

'I have a body?'

She smiled. It was a strange, mechanical smile, the lips almost curling into a semicircle. 'Of course. Cloning is an ancient art. You are now thirty, perfect in physiology, and will remain so for all time. And your intellect has been boosted. By the standards of your century, you are a superman.'

'Has anyone I know survived?'

'No. Brain preservation was very uncommon in your day. It makes you a very rare specimen. We have plans for you.'

'Plans?' Findhorn felt a twinge of anxiety.

Again the strange smile. Close up, there was something not quite right about her eyes; their shape was odd. 'Did you think you would spend eternity in Paradise?'

'This cold. Can't you get rid of it? Why can't I move?'

'As I said, we have plans for you. The cold is part of it.'

A vague sense of dread began to surge through Findhorn. This wasn't the way he'd anticipated his resuscitation, not the world he'd expected to find. A thought suddenly struck him. 'You're not real, are you? A hologram?'

'Hologram,' she repeated. There was a tiny hesitation. 'Hologram. Yes, I have it, a device from your century.' Findhorn thought he detected a hint of amusement, almost mockery. 'No, Mister Findhorn, I am not a hologram.'

'But you don't exist.' A fresh horror. 'Neither do I. You're feeding impulses into my brain. None of this is real.'

'What did you expect? Space-hungry, resource-greedy people who never die? No, machines supplanted organic life a very long time ago. However we still find a living brain very useful when we can find one.'

Findhorn suddenly envisaged a computer somewhere, eternally feeding dreams into brains stored in some vast, automated warehouse. Simple economics. Much easier to tickle brain cells than re-create living, space-hungry, resource-greedy people who never die.

The throbbing was louder. It was like the engine of a ship. The cold was in his bones. It was causing him terrible pain. 'Look, this isn't what I expected. I don't want an eternity of this.' He took a painful breath and reached a decision. 'It was a mistake. Please switch me off. Let me die.'

The lips curled into a perfect semicircle. The eyes followed the shape of the mouth. She leaned over him and for the first time Findhorn saw something long, thin and metallic in her hand. 'I'm so sorry. You don't have that option.'

* * *

'What did he say?'

'He's coming round.'

'I'll tell the captain.'

Findhorn opened his eyes. The first-aid room was warm; the cold Findhorn felt came from within. He was immobile under layers of blankets. A gentle, steady throb was coming up from the ship's engine below. Leroy, dreadlocks hanging down over his brow, was leaning over him, concern showing in his eyes. The nightmare of immortality fading, he managed to whisper: 'Leroy, you're beautiful.'

The first mate's anxiety gave way to a wide grin. 'You should see my sister.'

Hansen's bearded face appeared round the door. 'Thought you were a goner.'

'What happened?'

Leroy moved aside to make room for the captain in the tiny room. 'How 'bout some nice hot soup?'

'It could kill him,' said Hansen. 'Upset his circulation and flood his brain stem with iced blood. Make it lukewarm.'

When the first officer had gone, Hansen turned to Findhorn. 'We got it.'

Findhorn nodded, almost too weak to speak.

'It was inside a block of ice. They spotted it coming out with Watson. They got you on board first, then went back for it. Took half an hour to find amongst the floes.'

'And?'

'It's in the ship's safe. The admiral seems to think it's his property. I respectfully disagree. If it hit the water it's salvage.'

Hansen pulled out a pipe and began to stuff the bowl with black, tarry tobacco. 'It cost us. The berg split clean in two. Watson, Dawson and you came out of its centre like you'd been shot out of a cannon. Three men on Watson's team never got out, four drowned in the water. Seven dead.'

Findhorn remembered. 'My God.'

'Aye. And another three died on the berg before we got there, but our American guests are being remarkably tight-lipped about that. The Leith police will sort them out.' The captain was managing to speak while lighting his pipe; he was clearly well practised in the art. 'You owe your life to Leroy. Watson, yon Admiral and you were the only ones in reach and you were all sinking down. Leroy goes for you first, but the fur gear weighs a ton in the water. Then he gets the admiral. By the time Arkin and he gets him out, Watson is gone.'

Findhorn sank back into his dreams.

The smell of frying fish drifted into the first-aid room. From below, the throbbing was stronger, more rapid. Bleak Arctic light streamed in through a porthole. The ship was rolling up and down the big waves, and each time it reached a crest Findhorn saw icebergs scattered over the sea like ships in an armada. So Hansen had probably cut west to clear the pack ice and turned south just past Jan Mayen island. But there was still drift ice; they had probably not yet reached seventy north.

Findhorn wriggled an arm from under the blankets and peeled them off one by one. He sat up; it was possibly the most difficult thing he had ever done. His wrist watch, on the table next to him, was still working and it said 7.15. That would be p.m., frying fish being an evening meal even for this cosmopolitan crew; he'd been unconscious for eighteen hours. His bladder was threatening to burst.

Ten minutes later, bladder relieved, dressed in an overlarge Aran jumper, jeans and sneakers, he presented himself at the entrance to the mess room, steadying himself against the roll of the ship.

'You raving eejit,' Hansen welcomed him. 'What are you doing up?'

'I'm after Leroy's red pea soup.'

Leroy vanished. While Findhorn was being helped into a chair he caught the eyes of the Dubliner. 'What happened to Roscoe?'

The Irishman's tone became evasive. 'There was a bit of an accident, like.'

'What exactly?'

'A sort of a fire.'

'What sort of a fire?'

'I was inside the berg when it happened.' The Irishman changed the subject. 'Ten men for a briefcase, sir. Was it worth it?'

So much for secret instructions, Findhorn thought. He was conscious of a dozen faces – Chinese, Korean, English, Norwegian, Indian and indeterminate – waiting for his answer.

Leroy stepped over the threshold. He placed crusty bread and a bowl of red soup in front of Findhorn. 'I'll know when I've opened it.'

'You won't be opening anything.' The admiral, in a light blue shirt and navy trousers, had followed Leroy in to the mess. 'The briefcase happens to be the property of the United States Government.'

'I'm fine, thanks,' said Findhorn. 'What business did you people have tunnelling in there? You were way off base.'

A blond crewman said, 'Greenland is the sovereign territory of Denmark. I expect my government may have a claim.'

Leroy clapped his hands in delight. 'Except that the berg had drifted into international waters by the time we got it. Hey, ah reckon it's finders keepers.'

Hansen was looking out of a porthole. His hair, like his beard, was nearly white, with dark streaks. Over his shoulder he said, 'Lawyers could get rich on this one.'

The admiral was in no mood for banter. 'I keep telling you people. The briefcase is American property. On behalf of the United States Government, Captain Hansen, I require that you hand it over to me now. Or take the unpleasant consequences.'

Hansen scraped at the barrel of his empty pipe. It gurgled when he blew through it. He turned and approached the admiral to within two feet. He said, 'Admiral Dawson, sir. With all due respect, awa' and bile yer heid.'

5

The Whisky Society

The *Apeiron Trader* drifted through a damp, freezing haar which wrapped itself around Findhorn's neck and trickled down to his shoulders, undercutting jacket, Aran pullover and thermal vest. Port Seton and Musselburgh drifted past a mile to port, their street lights coccooned in an orange haze.

Hansen appeared on the deck and leaned on the railing next to Findhorn, pipe smoking. 'Not a night for brass monkeys. Mind you, after your wee swim in the Davy Sound . . .'

Findhorn nodded, staring down at the flow of dark water reflecting the distant town lights. 'I'm confused.'

'Aye.' Hansen looked at Findhorn shrewdly in the half-dark. 'I've been thinking about this. What do you deduce from the following?' He raised a gloved finger. 'First. They order me to put in at Longyear Island. Why did they do that, Findhorn?'

'To transfer us over to to the *Apeiron Trader*.'

'Aye, but why? And second.' Another finger went up in the air. 'Having put us on to this glorified banana boat, and told us we're bound for Aberdeen, it does a last-minute change and comes down the coast to Edinburgh.'

'They're disorganized?'

Hansen laughed cynically. 'Norsk disorganized? No way. No, Findhorn, this is being done for a reason. Think about it. Longyear Island is about the most desolate, godforsaken hole on the planet. The transfer was carried out with only polar bears for witnesses.'

'I don't get you,' said Findhorn, but he did.

'They're trying to make sure we're not traced.'

Findhorn said, 'You've been too long at sea, Captain,' but he felt a chill: Hansen's story made sense.

'There's something in that briefcase.'

In the half-dark, the captain was looking angry. Findhorn waited, and Hansen continued: 'I've had a fax from Norsk. The crew are being put up in the Post House and flown out to their destinations tomorrow. We've been fixed up at the Sheraton.'

'Why the dour expression?'

'I have reasons. Three of them are wrapped up in sheets in the *Apeiron's* cold room. A few more are enjoying an Arctic cruise a thousand yards down in an iceberg. They'll end up in your fish fingers some day.' The wind caught little sparks from his pipe and blew them out to sea.

'What happens next?'

'Paperwork. And the Leith police and the Lloyds people and the Board of Trade and the Marine Accident Investigation Board. But not you, Doctor Findhorn, not according to my instructions. Our masters don't want you involved in these enquiries in any circumstances. They want you to disappear into the foggy night wi' that briefcase.'

'What do you think about that?'

Hansen took the pipe from his mouth and spat in the water. 'What do I think about it?' he repeated angrily. 'This just happens to be my country, bought and paid for with six hundred years of blood. I'm no' having a bunch of Eskimos telling me what I may or may not say to the lawful Scottish authorities.'

'So what will you do?'

Findhorn caught an eyeful of stinging pipe smoke, but Hansen kept puffing. 'Co-operate with the aforesaid authorities and stuff Norsk. Effing reindeer herdsmen trying to run my country.' Hansen spat again into the Firth of Forth. 'And I'll tell you somethin' for nothin'. There was some funny business went on in that American expedition.'

In the semi-dark, Findhorn could see the captain's shrewd eyes narrowed, staring intently at him. 'Just what is this about, Findhorn?'

'I haven't the faintest idea.'

'Maybe you have and maybe you haven't. And what's in yon briefcase to get the Yanks so excited?'

'Not to mention Norsk. Do you think they've fixed it so the police let me disappear into the night?'

'If they have it's an outrage. By the way, you meet with Company officials on the premises of the Whisky Society. After this little voyage, it strikes me as a damn good rendezvous.' Hansen tapped his pipe out on the railing; little sparks drifted downwind. Then he turned back to the bridge.

Leroy sauntered up and joined Findhorn at the railing.

Now they were within sight of Edinburgh Castle a couple of miles ahead and to the left, astride its basalt plug, floodlights illuminating its massive walls. The *Apeiron Trader* was slowing and heading to port, the automated lighthouse on Inchkeith Island swinging round to starboard.

'Edinburgh is a cold, cold city, mon. Time was when I had a little hot chocolate used t'wait foh me in Constitution Street. Just the thing after a long voyage. Lucinda, that was her name, a real enthusiast.' Leroy's mind was momentarily elsewhere. 'Smooth, dark skin, Jamaican, a lovely girl. But damn me, while I's in Murmansk and points north, if she doan up sticks and go back to her daddy in Jamayca, somewhere up in the Blue Mountains. He's a coffee farmer, mon, which is Jamaica-speak for abject poverty. Some day I will go there and I will rescue her from a life of pickin' coffee beans.'

'Maybe she likes picking coffee beans, Leroy. Which would you rather be, poor and warm or rich and cold?'

'But now my hot chocolate come in a mug,' Leroy complained. 'Choa man, how is de mighty fallen.'

Findhorn, his ears now painful with cold, grinned in sympathy and headed for his cabin.

There was a knock on the door. Hansen, briefcase in hand. 'From now on it's your responsibility, laddie. I take nothing more to do with it.' Findhorn nodded and took the briefcase.

He tossed it on the bed. It was black. On its side the letters LBP were printed in gold. It was in good condition and it was hard to believe that it had been under glacial ice for half a century. Findhorn tried the lock, but it was squashed almost flat. It would take a hammer and chisel to get at the contents.

Who owned it? The USA, Denmark, the Company, or Finders Keepers?

Another knock on the door, this one peremptory. Admiral Dawson, dressed for shore in a heavy seaman's jacket, and with the expression of a man anticipating a fight. The admiral nodded at the briefcase. 'Thanks. I'll have it now.'

'No way, Admiral.'

Dawson tried to push into the cabin but Findhorn put a hand on his chest and shoved. 'Hey, chum, you're a guest on this ship.'

'Get out of my way, Findhorn. That briefcase is United States property.'

'Maybe, maybe not.'

Dawson took a deep breath. He spoke softly, but there was anger in his voice. 'Look, pal, you have no idea what you're getting into here. Just forget the whole business. Hand over the briefcase and walk away. Believe me, it's in your own interests.'

'If that's a threat, can I have it in writing?'

Dawson, red-faced and grim, didn't reply. Findhorn closed the door on him.

Twenty minutes later, Findhorn was down the gangplank while it was still being secured. He had a backpack and carried the briefcase in one hand while holding the gangplank rail carefully with the other. A thrill of pleasure went through his nervous system when he felt solid concrete under his feet. There was the sour smell of yeast in the air; the Edinburgh brewers were emptying their vats. There was no sign of the admiral.

The crew began to trickle down the gangplank but Findhorn went on ahead, towards the customs shed. The Irishman, grim-faced, was standing at it as if it provided sanctuary. Two policemen were approaching him in a businesslike manner. Findhorn passed him with a nod, and then, in the shed, ran a gauntlet of keen-eyed officials; but he went unchallenged back into the dark, freezing fog.

A cluster of high-spirited young sailors passed him and disappeared into the dark; they sounded as if they had a riotous evening ahead. A police car sat on the dock, its driver watching the little flurry of late-night activity with dispassionate curiosity. Tall metal gates a couple of hundred metres ahead marked the end of the docks. More policemen, two in uniform, and more close scrutiny. A nod so imperceptible that Findhorn wondered if he had really seen it, and then he was through the gates and into the streets.

Leroy was standing in conversation with a mini-skirted girl. Beyond lay the bonded warehouses of the big distilleries; and beyond them again was Leith Walk, and pubs and restaurants and crowds and anonymity.

Findhorn walked quickly along the quiet dockside street, past the barred windows of the whisky warehouses. A taxi hooted as it passed; Leroy was grinning and waving, girl in tow. Half a mile ahead a brisk evening traffic was going around Leith roundabout. Findhorn glanced nervously behind him; the street was empty. His footsteps were echoing off the high grey walls and buildings. He broke into a trot, the backpack bouncing heavily on his back. He made it with relief to the roundabout. There were restaurant crowds here, and drunks, and young people hanging about. He turned right along Constitution Street and past the Spiral Galaxy. Close by Leith River was a high wall. Through to a little cobbled courtyard and up a flight of stairs. A man stood at the top, polite, suited, muscular.

'Are ye a member, sorr?'

'The name's Findhorn. I'm expected.'

'Aye, Doctor Findhorn, sorr. Your party's waiting for you.' The door was opened and warm air enveloped Findhorn.

It was a big old tenement room, plush red and gloriously warm after the nip of the Edinburgh haar. It was sprinkled with an odd collection of comfortable, Victorian-style armchairs and tables. Each table had a jug of water: at cask strength, it was advisable to dilute the whiskies on offer. An open fire burned cheerily in a corner and a pot of coffee was on the go next to it. There was an aroma of whisky and coffee, and the air was light blue with tobacco smoke.

The Society was crowded. A woman, at a table near the fire, caught Findhorn's eye. She was tall, about fifty, with trim, greying hair and pearl ear-rings, and was wearing a long red coat. Her companion was squat, bulky and had a far-Eastern appearance; probably Korean, Findhorn thought. The woman waved. As Findhorn approached, it became plain that the Korean's bulk was due to muscle rather than beer. He had a heavily lined face and was smoking a cigarette.

Findhorn suddenly felt uneasy.

'Doctor Findhorn? I'm Barbara Drindle, from the Arendal office of Norsk Advanced Technologies. And this is Mister Junzo Moon. I'm afraid he doesn't speak much English.' Her voice was husky and her accent was good, very good, but it wasn't native English.

Findhorn put backpack and briefcase on the floor and sat down at the vacant chair, next to the glorious heat. The woman smiled: 'After your adventures I should think you need something strong. The Society buys direct from distillers. Because of some strange quirk in the law it isn't allowed to use their brand names, which is why the bottles here are labelled by number. But you'll see a little catalogue on the bar which tells you all you need to know. What would you like?'

'A coffee, I think.' Findhorn helped himself and returned to the table.

'The Company have arranged a room for you at the Sheraton tonight. I expect you'll want to get back to your office as soon as possible.' She slid over an envelope. 'An airline ticket for Aberdeen.'

Findhorn slid the envelope back. 'No trouble. I haven't seen you around at Norsk. Which division is that?'

Suddenly, the Korean's expression was hostile, but the woman's smile didn't falter. 'The Secretariat. I work directly for Mister Olsen. And now, we'll be getting on.' She leaned down for the briefcase.

Findhorn seized her wrist. The woman was surprisingly strong.

'Do I really know you're Company? Some very persistent Americans have been after this.'

The Korean looked as if he wanted to break Findhorn's neck. The woman's smile acquired a chilly edge. She sighed, disengaged Findhorn's hand and produced a sheet of paper from her handbag:

```
TO DR F. FINDHORN.
This is to certify that Ms. Barbara
Drindle is employed by the Directorate
of Norsk Advanced Technologies. She is
to be given the documents retrieved from
the Shiva City Expedition.
```

The paper was letter-headed with the Norsk Advanced Technologies logo of an Earth held in the palm of a hand, it had all the right e-mail, telephone and postal addresses, and was signed with the neat, precise hand of Tor Olsen himself.

'Satisfied?'

Findhorn said, 'Forgive me, I had to be sure. So, you're with Olsen's office in Arendal?'

'Correct.'

She picked up the briefcase and tried the lock. Then she handed it over to the Korean. Findhorn tried to look calm while the Korean hauled at it like a bad-tempered gorilla. He finally snarled and shook his head like a dog getting rid of fleas.

Findhorn said, 'It's been under tons of ice.' Ms Drindle gave him a cool smile once again and gestured to the Korean, then headed for the exit with a wave of the hand. The Korean stood up. To Findhorn's amazement he turned out to be little more than five feet tall which, with his girth, made him look like an orang-utan. He shot Findhorn a look of pure hatred and followed Ms Drindle out.

Findhorn gave them thirty seconds, then went to the exit. A car was taking off smartly on the riverside street and he just failed to catch its registration number. Then he was briskly down the stairs and off in the opposite direction. He trotted smartly up Constitution Street and turned into the Spiral Galaxy. Once in the safety of the crowded, smoky bar, he sat down with a sigh of relief: he didn't want to be around the muscular Korean when they discovered the *Apeiron Trader*'s supply of *Playboy*s.

6

The Museum

Findhorn held onto one certainty in his uncertain world. In no circumstances was he about to take up his room at the Edinburgh Sheraton. Not with the icy Ms Drindle and her knuckle-grazing companion on the prowl.

He gave himself an hour in the Spiral Galaxy before risking the streets, feeling his lungs silhouetted by tobacco smoke. He plodded up Leith Walk, the backpack heavy on his shoulders, keeping a sharp eye out on the dark streets. Once a car stopped about twenty yards ahead of him, began to reverse. It was probably someone looking for directions. Findhorn ran off up a side road and then into the mouth of a close and stood, heart beating, for about ten minutes, before risking the streets again.

At the top of the Walk, near Calton Hill, he waved down a taxi. He took it to Newington, and trawled half a dozen anonymous B & Bs before he found one with a room and a welcome. The doorbell was answered by the lady of the house, whose long, green Campbell tartan skirt matched the hall carpet. His room was small, clean and had a deep-piled, green Campbell tartan carpet. He dropped his luggage and flopped onto the soft bed,

exhausted; the encounter with Norsk's unnerving representatives had left him drained.

He looked at his watch. It was 11 p.m. There was a
payphone in the hallway, and a directory. A television was
flickering in the lounge as he passed; some football match.
He glimpsed a few semi-comatose guests sprawled over
armchairs. He dialled through to the Sheraton and asked
for a Mister Hansen, just arrived.

It was clear from the slurring in Hansen's voice that his
liver was having to cope with something like a litre of
Glenfiddich.

'Hansen? Findhorn here. I need your help.'

'Well, well, if it'sh no' the elusive pimpernel. They seek
him here, they seek him there, they seek yon Findhorn
everywhere.'

'They? They've been looking for me?'

'Desperately. A comely wench, too, ye have hidden
depths, laddie. I'd go for two falls, two submissions and a
knockout wi' that one any day.' The captain giggled.

'She'd probably strangle you with her thighs. Will you
sober up, man?'

There was a long silence. Findhorn visualised the
captain swaying on the edge of his bed. Then: 'Whaur are
ye?'

'A few miles away. Look, would you phone Norsk in
Stavanger? I can't do it from here. Leave a message on
their machine if there's nobody there. Tell them I have the
papers they're looking for. And tell them I'll hand them
over only if given good reason.'

The silence was longer. Findhorn could almost sense

the struggle at the other end. When the captain spoke, he was clearly trying to get a grip on reality. 'Good reason?'

'Yes.'

'What the hell is that supposed to mean?'

'Listen, Hansen. Ten men died in that operation. Shiva were a hundred miles off base. They were carrying out a major tunnelling operation which had nothing to do with Arctic meteorology. There were people on that berg desperate to get their hands on that briefcase and for all I know they have a right to it. For all I know *I* am the rightful owner. I won't hand it over to the Company or anyone else until I know what this is about.'

'You won't hand over – my God, Findhorn.'

'I'm not an employee. There was no written contract, I accepted no payment. Nothing requires me to hand over material found in an iceberg to them or anyone else.'

'They'll cut off your goolies, laddie. Norsk's a giant.' Hansen struggled for an adequate description. 'A Sumo wrestler with three balls and forty foot high.'

'Phone their Stavanger office. I'll call you tomorrow.'

Back in his room, Findhorn slipped off his clothes and slid under the cold sheets. He looked at the material he had emptied from the briefcase: a bundle of letters, bound together with red tape, and about twenty small desk diaries, dark blue, each marked with a year. He opened one at random and flicked through it. It was in good condition. The binding was loose, as if someone had tried to pull it away from the pages; otherwise there were few signs that it had been under the crushing pressure of glacial ice. Water had ruined some of the other diaries, reducing the ink to an illegible smear or removing it altogether.

They were American. On the front leaf of each was written a name in English: Lev Baruch Petrosian. There were no other details. The name sounded vaguely familiar. The diary had been written up in a strange script. It looked Cyrillic but Findhorn knew the Russian alphabet and this wasn't it; neither was it Arabic. He thought it might be some Caucasian or Asian script like Persian. Scattered throughout the pages, and looking incongruous against the ancient script, were equations. There were even, here and there, phrases in English, written in a small, clear hand.

The equations caught his attention. They weren't the familiar ones of meteorology, and he didn't understand them, but he recognized the field in which they were used, and the knowledge gave him a twinge of apprehension.

He fell asleep with the bedside lamp shining in his face.

The following morning the haar had been replaced by a clear blue sky. He had bacon and eggs along with a black, coffee-like liquid, and then risked the streets, unsure whether he was in mortal danger or just paranoid.

The city centre was two miles to the north and he headed towards it, feeling increasingly nervous as he approached over the South Bridge. The Waverley railway station was below the bridge and he thought they might be looking for him there; or at the bus terminus; or the airport; or at Hertz or Avis or Budget. Or they might be cruising the streets; or they might be doing all of these things; or, he thought, I may be turning into a certifiable case of raging paranoia.

Along busy pavements to George Street. He found a business centre and started to photocopy the pages of the diaries. They were a page to a day for twenty years, two pages to a photocopy. It was tedious work. It took him an hour and a paper refill to get to 1940. For a break, he logged on to a computer and checked his e-mail. He'd been at sea for two weeks and he was faced with a long list of messages, mostly low-grade or now time-expired. The most recent, however, made him swallow nervously. It had been sent at three o'clock that morning.

> *Dear Dr Findhorn,*
> *It would be in our mutual interests to discuss the papers which you have in your possession. I do not represent Norsk Advanced Technologies. May I suggest we meet at Fat Sam's at say 1 p.m. today? Their calzone is excellent.*

He looked at his watch and did a quick calculation.

Edinburgh's George Street is stuffed with banks and there was a Bank of Scotland next to the business centre. He entered it and asked to open a safety deposit account. Outside of movies about robberies he had never seen the inside of a safety deposit. He put the diaries and the bundle of letters safely into a little steel box. Then he turned the corner to the post office in Frederick Street, where he put a label on his backpack, leaving it to be posted on to his Aberdeen office.

He emerged from the post office carrying no more than a bundle of photocopied papers: at last he was travelling light. He bought a cheap briefcase from a store with 'Sale of the Century' on a notice in its window and put the diary photocopies into it.

Now Findhorn made his way across Princes Street Gardens and up the Mound to the Edinburgh Central Library. There, in a quiet room occupied by scholars, students and a tramp getting a spot of heat, he looked through *Encyclopaedia Brittanica*. He quickly identified the script: the diaries had been written in Armenian. Then he looked up Petrosian, and it came back to him.

Lev Baruch Petrosian. A 1950s atom spy. He had vanished just before the FBI got to him. It was a long-gone scandal, the people involved now presumably old men, or dead. Findhorn thought of the blue eye, imbedded in the gruesome face, staring at him through the ice. Upstairs in the library, he flicked through *The Times* of the period. Petrosian had made it to the obituary columns and the librarian made him a photocopy.

Another short, nervous foray into the streets. He passed by a public phone booth, preferring to use one in a quiet corner of the Chambers Street museum. A grizzly bear contemplated him with small, hostile eyes. It had reared up on its hind legs, it had clawed limbs of immense power and it was displaying sharp teeth, but it was stuffed.

'Archie? Have I disturbed you?' Archie was one of those academics who led a semi-nocturnal existence, often as not turning up at his department around noon and leaving again at some strange hour of the following morning.

'Fred? How are you? Not at all, been up for hours.

Anne tells me you were heading for the north pole. Are you phoning from there?'

'I'm in Edinburgh. I hitched a lift on an icebreaker and came back early. Listen, I need advice. It involves your field of study but I can't talk about it over the phone. Can I meet you, say in a couple of hours?'

'My goodness, Freddie me lad, are you spying for the KGB or something? Okay, I've no classes this morning. I can be in George Square at eleven o'clock.'

'No. I'd like you to meet me in Edinburgh.'

There was a puzzled hesitation, then: 'Aye, okay. Meet me at Waverley station at twelve.'

'No, again, Archie. I don't want to be seen at the station. I'm in the Royal Museum in Chambers Street.'

'This has got to be woman trouble.'

'I wish.'

'Right. The museum it is. I should be there in a couple of hours.'

That was the thing about Archie. He knew when not to ask questions.

Findhorn decided to do this methodically. He'd start with transport, work his way through the armour to the natural history, and then go up to the medieval dress and the Chinese stuff on the first floor, and then points beyond.

He was about thirty, tall with long untidy hair and an untidy black beard. He was wearing an unbuttoned trenchcoat, exposing a large beer belly. The archetypal wild Glaswegian, Findhorn thought, watching nervously from the top floor gallery overhead; and a man who didn't give a damn.

Archie was looking around expectantly. Findhorn gave it a minute, but he saw no signs that his friend had been followed. Feeling like a fool, he called out and waved, and ran down the stairs past the Buddha on the first floor.

They collected coffee and doughnuts at the museum café. Findhorn led the way to a corner table and sat facing both entrances. Archie's eyes were gleaming with curiosity. 'So what gives, Fred? I've been fired up all the way here.'

'I can't tell you what this is about, Archie. Not yet.'

'Och, be reasonable! I hav'nae come a' this way for a coffee. If it's no a wumman, you're in trouble with the polis. Neither of them sounds like Fred Findhorn.'

'What can you tell me about Lev Petrosian?'

Archie raised his eyebrows in astonishment. 'The atom spy?'

'The same.'

Archie's face seemed uncertain whether to show astonishment, worry or delight. 'In the name o' the wee man, what are you getting into, laddie? Petrosian came over here as a Nazi refugee, like Klaus Fuchs. A lot of the top wartime brains did. Fuchs was the big spy in the A-bomb era, but not many people know there were others. Theodore Hall, for example, a Brit also at Los Alamos.'

'What did he actually do?'

A couple of dozen twelve-year-olds trooped boisterously into the café, carrying artist's notebooks and pencils, followed by two adults, both female. The ambient noise level went up sharply. Findhorn eyed the adults nervously.

'He was at Los Alamos twice. Don't know much about what he did. I know the first time round he was involved in a big scare. Teller got the idea that if they did manage to explode an atom bomb the fireball might be so hot it would set the world's hydrogen alight, turn the atmosphere and oceans into one big hydrogen bomb. That would have got rid of Hitler, along with the rest of humanity. Petrosian was involved in the calculations which ruled that possibility out.'

'You'd have to be very sure you got something like that right,' suggested Findhorn.

Archie was studying his doughnut closely, and knowing him, Findhorn thought he was probably analysing its topological properties. 'Aye. They kept coming back to it. Now the second time, when they were developing the H-bomb, I'm even less sure about what he did. There were rumours that the guy went off the heid.'

'In what way?'

'Let me think. Got it. It was the same again. Something about zapping the planet. But since hydrogen bombs were going off like firecrackers all through the fifties and sixties, we can safely say he was wrong.'

'Could he have found something new?'

Archie shook his head. 'Nuclear physics is understood, Freddie. There's no room for new stuff at the energy levels these guys were into.'

The adults were trying to get the pupils into a line and Findhorn thought that the teaching authority should have issued them with whips. He dredged up a distant memory, something he'd seen on a television news item. 'What about cold fusion?'

Archie's voice was dismissive. 'A fiasco. It never came to anything.'

Had the comment come from some establishment hack, Findhorn would have paid it only so much attention. But he knew Archie; okay he was one of life's iconoclasts, but he was sharp with it. The opinion commanded Findhorn's respect.

'Suppose you're wrong, Archie. Suppose Petrosian discovered something. And suppose the authorities of the day didn't want people getting curious about it. Putting it about that he went mad would be an effective cover story.'

Archie said, 'It's coming back to me now. Petrosian escaped from Canada just before the FBI closed in on him. The story is he was picked up and flew over the north pole to Russia. But there's no record that he ever arrived. The assumption was that he crashed somewhere over the polar route while making his escape.' He gave Findhorn a disconcertingly close stare. 'And all of a sudden, fifty years later, Findhorn of the Arctic leaps off an icebreaker, flips to cloak-and-dagger mode and starts asking me urgent questions about Petrosian.'

'A hypothetical, Archie. Suppose something of Petrosian's was found in the ice fifty years after it was lost. Let's say a document. And suppose that some people were very anxious to get their hands on it, would go to any lengths. The question is this: what could be in that document?'

Archie gave his friend another long, searching stare.

Then he said, 'I'm damned if I can think of a thing.'

'Archie, I may need to tap into that giant brain of yours now and then. I can see the wheels turning now. But I can't tell you more just yet.'

'Any time, day or night.'

Findhorn stood up. 'I have to go, Archie. I'm meeting some people.'

Archie's face was serious. 'Fred, you could be getting into something heavy. If you've found something out there in the polar wastes, something that people want to get their hands on fifty years after it was lost, and if that something has to do with Lev Baruch Petrosian, let me give you one piece of serious advice.'

Findhorn waited.

'Keep it damn close to your chest. And trust nobody.'

7

Fat Sam's

Findhorn looked at his watch. He had fifty-five minutes until the meeting at Fat Sam's; time enough to complete one important piece of business.

Back at the library, he pulled out a dog-eared Yellow Pages directory and ran a finger down *Translators and Interpreters*. He thought of his overstretched credit card and avoided the outfits with expensive boxes and names like 'School of Modern Languages' or 'International Interpreters', or which offered interpreters for trade missions. German and French translation figured heavily and he excluded these. That left half a dozen two-line entries. He noted their numbers.

Back to the museum. With change from the café he went through the numbers systematically. None of them had Armenian on the menu.

Back to the library. The security man at the entrance gave him a look. Now Findhorn opened the directory at *Clubs and Associations* and ploughed through working men's clubs, the Royal Naval Association, the Heart of Midlothian Football Club, Royal British Legion clubs, community associations, the Ancient Order of Hibernians, bingo clubs and Masonic Grand Lodges. From this bewildering miscellany he drew two conclusions: one, *homo sapiens* is a gregarious animal; and two, Edinburgh did not have an Armenian Club.

And he now had forty minutes.

On an inspiration he took a taxi to Buccleuch Place and asked the taxi to wait. He dithered between the School of Asian Studies and Islamic and Middle East, conscious of his one o'clock appointment and the ticking meter. He chose the Islamic at random. The building was almost deserted. He scanned a notice board, ignoring the lists of examination results and the conference notifications. There were three cards, pinned on the board. Two were curling at the edge and offered tuition, one in German, one in French. The third was new and written in blue ink:

```
Angel Translation Services
Hark the herald angels sing
Our translations are just the thing.
Peace on Earth and mercy mild
Our complete service is really wild.
We do:
German, Russian, Turkish,
Arabic, Bulgarian, Armenian.
```

It was corny enough to be a student enterprise, suggesting fees he might be able to afford. The address was in Dundee Street, which Findhorn remembered as a down-market part of the city. Again suggesting impoverishment.

The taxi passed the Fountain Brewery, a massage

parlour and a sign for Heart of Midlothian FC, and disgorged him at the entrance to a tenement flat. The interior of the close was dingy and there was a faint smell of urine. A yellow Vespa scooter was attached to the metal bannister by a heavy chain. Findhorn made his way up worn steps. On the second floor, the door on the right had a doorbell, a peephole and a card:

    R. Grigoryan
    S.A. Stefanova
    J. Grimason, aka Grim Jim

Nothing about Angel Translation Services. He hesitated, then pressed the buzzer.

Apart from the over-large gypsy ear-rings, she looked as if she was just out of bed. She was in her twenties, with dark eyes and blonde hair going dark at the roots. She held the lapels of her green dressing gown together and blinked at Findhorn curiously.

'Angel Translation Services?' Findhorn asked doubtfully.

The effect was startling. Her eyes opened wide. 'Oh my gosh! What can I do for you?'

'I'd like a little translation.'

'Romella!' she shouted, without taking her eyes off Findhorn. 'Business!' Then, 'Which language?'

'Armenian.'

'Romella! Oh, please come in. I'm Stefi Stefanova. I do Bulgarian and Turkish. She's having a bath. Are you sure you don't need some Bulgarian?'

Through a hallway with a bicycle, propped up against a table with a pile of mail. Findhorn glimpsed a final demand letter in red. Doors to left and right led to bedrooms. A pile of soft dolls was spread over a bed. A kitchen to the right was a clutter of unwashed dishes and an overflowing pedal bin. Stefi led Findhorn ahead to a small room draped with psychedelic curtains and furnished with a low table, candles and cushions, but no chairs. A football team poster was surrounded by postcards pinned on the wall along with pictures of quaint Irish cottages and dizzying snow-covered peaks. A calendar on the wall showed a hunk of half-naked masculinity flexing his pectorals for the camera.

'Did I hear you say Armenian?'

She was running a comb through shoulder-length brown hair, still damp. She was slim, although with well-rounded breasts, and quite small. She had a small round face and big brown eyes behind John Lennon spectacles. She had delicate facial bone structure and smooth skin. Silver earrings in the shape of two long cylinders hung down from delicate ears. She was wearing a plain pink T-shirt and black leather trousers, and a pair of worn Nike trainers.

'I'm Romella. Romella Grigoryan if you can pronounce it.' The accent was Scottish, melodious, with a tinge of American.

'Fred Findhorn.' They shook hands. Findhorn opened the briefcase and pulled out the photocopies. 'This is just a selection. There will be about two thousand pages in all. What do you think?'

She flicked through a few pages at random. 'The handwriting's clear enough. Some of this is pretty technical, I'd probably have difficulty even in English. But yes, I think it's okay.'

'I'm meeting some people and I'd like to leave this with you for a couple of hours. Now, there might be a couple of problems.'

She raised her eyebrows.

'I need the translation urgently. Can you take it on right away?'

She frowned doubtfully and glanced at the wall calendar. It was a good performance.

'If it's too much you could point me to another translator.' He sensed Stefi tensing at the door.

Romella smiled slightly. 'No, I can squeeze it in.'

'A verbal translation would be quickest. We'd have to go through the diaries together.'

'Okay.'

'And as I say it's urgent. It will mean working long hours.'

'Business is business.'

'There's another problem. The material is confidential.'

Romella bristled. 'Naturally, confidentiality is assured.'

'I mean, highly confidential.' Findhorn glanced at Stefi. She nodded and smiled, taking in every word with open fascination. 'We'll need a separate workplace.'

This time, the frown was genuine. 'I'll have to think about that.'

Findhorn pulled a card out of his wallet. 'You're right to be careful. Actually I'm Jack the Ripper.' She laughed, displaying a row of perfect white teeth, and read the card.

'My secretary Anne's on holiday but I can give you her home number now if you like. My father is Lord Findhorn, a Court of Session judge. He's at home too, in Ayrshire, and if you like we can phone him to confirm that I really am—'

'I wasn't implying—'

'I have to go now. We can discuss terms when I get back. That is if you want the job.'

'Unsociable hours—'

'No problem. You fix a rate.'

Taking the stairs two at a time, Findhorn wondered about another problem: how to tap the old man for a few quid.

Findhorn risked the streets again. It was a straight mile and he heard the sharp crack of the one o'clock gun just as he was turning into Fat Sam's.

A few business types were scattered around, and there was a birthday lunch in progress. Al Capone, king-sized cigar in mouth, was resting a sub-machine gun on his arm. Bogart, Dietrich and other icons of the bootleg era also looked down on the proceedings from posters scattered around the walls. In a corner, a piano was thumping out rhythmic jazz by itself, and a fat fish near the cash register kept bumping its head against the tank. A notice said it was a pirhana.

Two men at a corner table, waiting. One was tall, elderly and stooped, formally dressed in suit and tie. Findhorn could make out a large Roman nose, a blotchy skin over a skull-like face, and a slightly vacant expression which didn't fool him for a moment. The other was about forty, gaunt, with metal-rimmed spectacles, dressed in a formal suit that made him look like a Jehovah's witness. Findhorn saw them in outline: sun was streaming through a roof window, obscuring their faces.

'This place used to be a slaughterhouse,' the skull said, indicating a chair. The accent was English ruling class, Winchester, Eton or the like: a species in decline but still with plenty of bite. 'Hence the roof windows. We can move if you wish.' Findhorn shook his head. The man ordered *spaghetti alle vongole* and Findhorn took the *calzone*. The Jehovah's witness ordered nothing. They all settled for *aqua minerale*: clear heads were the order of the day.

The skull waited until the waiter was out of earshot. 'My name is Mister Pitman, as in shorthand.'

'Of course it is.' Findhorn looked at the Jehovah's witness. 'And I expect you're Mister Speedhand.'

The Jehovah's witness nodded. 'It'll do.' The accent was American.

Pitman said, 'I won't insult your intelligence by pretence of any sort, Doctor Findhorn. You hold certain documents. We represent people who are willing to pay for them.'

'Documents?'

'And please don't insult mine.'

A little bread basket arrived. 'You have a consultancy business in Aberdeen, I believe. You sell weather. You call yourself Polar Explorers to create the illusion that there is more than one of you.'

'There is more than one of me,' Findhorn complained. 'I have a secretary.'

Pitman nodded absently, trying to spread icy butter on soft bread. 'Ah yes, Anne of a thousand hairstyles. And how is your business doing?'

'I'm sure you're about to tell me,' Findhorn said warily.

'As an entrepreneur you are best described as a bad joke. You sell a few sparse grid points for commercial and military climate programmes, which make only miniscule improvements to their forecasting ability. Your turnover pays Anne's wages, and the office rent, and perhaps the coffee money. It leaves you with less profit than a street busker.'

'I could use a few more ice stations.'

The waiters had clustered round the birthday table. A candle-lit cake was presented and they burst into 'Happy Birthday to You' with the help of the piano and electrically powered black mannikins with banjos on a stage. The man waited for the cacophony and the applause to subside. 'Would a hundred thousand pounds help?'

A second-generation Sicilian waiter served up the main course with a flourish. Pitman started to poke at the little clams on his pasta. Findhorn had started on his third glass of water but still his mouth was dry. 'Enormously. But the documents, as you call them – actually they're diaries – aren't for sale.'

Mister Shorthand was concentrating on a clam, dissecting it like a zoologist. Mister Speedhand said, 'One million, then?' The American accent was turning out to be east coast, probably Boston.

Findhorn felt himself going light-headed. He looked at Al Capone, spoke thoughtfully to the gangster. 'If you offered to put a million pounds into my bank account, in exchange for the diaries, I guess I'd have to say no.'

Findhorn, dazzled by the sunlight, hoped he had imagined the look in Mister Speedhand's eyes. Pitman examined a little clam on the end of his fork. 'Someone has been talking to you.'

'No.'

Mister Speedhand said, 'Doctor Findhorn, before you find yourself in an irretrievable situation, just hand over these diaries and walk away. It's in your own interests.'

Findhorn said, 'This is fascinating.'

Pitman said, casually, 'Whoever holds these diaries is a target.'

Findhorn felt light drops of sweat developing on his forehead. He put it down to the warmth of the restaurant. 'Wrong place, wrong time. This is new millennium Edinburgh, not thirties' Chicago.'

Pitman smiled thinly. 'And you have no place to hide.'

Findhorn took a deep breath. 'If I fall under a bus, the diaries will vanish for ever.'

'Believe me, that would suit some people very nicely.'

'I could get Special Branch protection,' Findhorn said. A weird feeling was coming over him, as if he was stepping into some parallel universe: the familiar, Edinburgh surroundings were still around him, but another reality was taking over.

The thin smile widened. 'Are you a Salman Rushdie targeted by Muslim fanatics? A famous film star being stalked? You are nobody. Unless you have a high public profile, the state will save itself the expense.'

Findhorn pushed his plate away, feeling nauseous. 'You were right about the *calzone*.'

'You have a stark choice: a million pounds, or imminent death.' He stared at Findhorn with curiosity. 'For most people, the choice would present no problem at all.'

Findhorn took some toothpicks out of a dish. He started to build a little pyre but found that his hands were trembling. 'Nobody is getting these diaries until I've found out what's in them. And maybe not even then.'

A fleeting dark look; a spoiled child being denied a toy.

Mister Speedhand said, 'Doctor Findhorn, I would like you to trust me on this. You simply cannot imagine what you're getting yourself into here.'

Findhorn asked, 'You represent American interests, right?'

In spite of the sunlight streaming in Findhorn's face, he became aware of a subtle change in the body language of both men. Speedhand hesitated, and then pulled back: 'That needn't concern you. What matters is that you have just been offered an absurd sum of money for documents which you have no right to in the first place.'

'And then there's the veiled threat.'

'Was it veiled? I'm sorry about that.'

Findhorn picked off the points with his finger. 'Ten men died trying to get these diaries. I've just been offered a million for them. I've been issued with heavy threats in the event I don't hand them over. I'm sorry, chum, but until I find out what this is about . . . let's just say I'm curious.'

'Curiosity did the cat in,' Mister Speedhand said.

'I'm not a cat.'

'But do you read Armenian?' Pitman asked.

Findhorn side-slipped the question. 'Something has been puzzling me.'

The man waited. Findhorn sipped at his water and continued, 'There were no rescue vessels in the vicinity of that berg. Nothing on radar, at least. But Dawson wasn't behaving like a man about to drown. A man risking his life, yes. But not a man expecting to die.'

Findhorn waited, but the men remained impassive. 'Okay,' he finally said. 'So arrangements were in hand to rescue Dawson. What about the others?'

The older man was twirling spaghetti like a native. 'They were, shall we say, an inconvenience.'

Findhorn felt himself going pale.

'Much like yourself,' Speedhand added.

Pitman sucked up a long strand of spaghetti. 'Perhaps it will help you reach a decision if I tell you that there are other parties interested in these diaries, parties with a less friendly disposition than us.'

With a surge of self-blame Findhorn thought about the Armenian translator, and he wondered what he might be getting her into, and he wondered, *what the hell is in those diaries?*

Pitman was now attempting an avuncular tone. 'Come under our wing, Doctor Findhorn. If you really will not sell us the diaries, at least let us offer you protection, and of course a translator. Solve the riddle of the diaries, thus satisfying this dangerous curiosity of yours, and give us first refusal on the information you find.'

'The endgame should be interesting, when I hand over the information and find myself out of bargaining power. Do you seriously expect me to trust you?'

The man acquired a puzzled look. 'Of course not. But what other option do you have? Unprotected, you will last at most only a few days, perhaps hours.'

Mister Speedhand said, 'A large organization is looking for you now. You cannot use road, rail or airport.'

Pitman said, 'And the streets are very dangerous for you.'

There was a grim silence. Findhorn's toothpick structure collapsed.

'You still don't get it, Findhorn,' Speedhand said. 'We have to have those diaries. Refusal to hand them over is not an option we can tolerate.'

'And if I refuse nevertheless?'

'Without our protection, the other party will find you very quickly.' The man snapped his fingers at a passing waiter.

'Nothing is what it seems here,' said Findhorn.

Pitman's expression didn't change, but Speedhand was acquiring a hostile look.

'Take that pirhana, for instance. Actually it's a big grouper, *Serranid Serranidae*.'

'What do you want?' Speedhand asked. 'A prosecution under the Trades Description Act?'

'No. It just makes me wonder what else is on the level hereabouts.'

As the Sicilian approached, Findhorn suddenly got up and made for the exit. The men, taken by surprise, sat astonished. He ran out and turned left and left again, glancing behind from time to time, and with no plan in mind other than to lose himself. He found himself in Lothian Road. A black taxi cab appeared and he stepped in front of it. It squealed to a halt.

'Bloody hell, mate.'

'I know. Morningside.' It was the first thing that came into his head. The Morningside suburbs were full of doctors and lawyers, and big mortgages, and care homes for the well-heeled elderly.

'You'll get yourself killed, Mister.'

Not in Morningside. Nobody ever gets killed in Morningside. Nasty, rough people beat you to a pulp or knife you in Leith or Craigmillar, but that never happens to people in Morningside. They're too genteel.

'Oh my God!'

The taxi driver stared at his passenger with alarm. 'Are you okay, mate?'

'Not Morningside. Dundee Street. Can you make it fast?' A thought had suddenly hit Findhorn like a punch. *How many translators of Armenian are there in Edinburgh? And how long will it take to find Romella Grigoryan, and through her, me?*

But the Edinburgh rush hour was building up and the traffic lights were consistently against the taxi, and by the time it pulled up at the tenement, Findhorn was being torn apart with frustration. He ran up the stairs and knocked.

And knocked again.

8

Camp L

Findhorn caught a whiff of cheap perfume. He tried to sound relaxed. 'Can we go?'

'Now? Not tomorrow?'

'I'd really like to get started. We can discuss your fees on the way.'

'Can't it even wait until after dinner?'

'Please!'

Romella gave him a slow, suspicious look while Findhorn inwardly fretted. She disappeared, leaving him at the open door.

'On the way to where?' she shouted through from a bedroom.

'My brother's flat. We have to get ourselves to Charlotte Square.'

She reappeared wearing a denim jacket over her pink sweater. She handed Findhorn his briefcase.

'You're sure you're not Jack the Ripper?' She was pulling a Peruvian hat down over her ears.

'Not even Jack the Lad.'

Stefi appeared from the kitchen, wiping her hands on a kitchen towel. It was half past four in the afternoon and she was still in her dressing gown. 'Do you like shish kebabs? My shish kebabs are . . .' She kissed her fingers.

'Another time.'

'You have to eat,' Stefi pointed out.

'I just have, thanks.'

Romella said, 'Okay, let's go.'

Out to the landing. She pulled the door behind her with a click. Someone was coming up the stairs. Findhorn froze.

'Evening, Mrs Essen.'

An old crone with a plastic bag in each hand; she grunted sourly as they passed. Findhorn exhaled with relief, felt weak at the knees.

The sky was dark grey and a light trickle of sleet was promising heavier stuff to come. 'We're about a mile from Dougie's flat. You don't sound like an Armenian.'

'Not surprising, considering I'm frae Glesca . . .' she momentarily affected a thick Cowcaddens accent '. . . I was brought up for some years in California. My folks still live there, in La Jolla. Dad's a lawyer. So your father's a Court of Session judge?'

'Yes. The whole family are lawyers. If you ever see a pink Porsche driving around Edinburgh, that's my younger brother, Dougie. He's with Sutcliffe & McWhirtle.'

'I've heard of them. They're criminal lawyers, aren't they?'

'Dad thinks they're criminals who just happen to be lawyers. They specialise in finding tiny legal loopholes and turning them into gaping chasms. They'll get you off anything – if you can afford them. My sister lives in Virginia Water with a barrister called Bramfield. He's rich, she's miserable and they're both drunk whenever I visit them.'

'But you didn't go in for law. Your card says you do polar research.'

'I've broken with the family legal tradition. Result, poverty.'

'I hope you can afford my fees.'

It was growing dark and car headlights were coming on. The gloom gave Findhorn an illusion of security. They passed Fat Sam's and turned left down Lothian Road. By the time they were crossing Princes Street the rush hour was in full swing and the light sleet had turned into a freezing downpour. They trotted along slushy pavements down to Charlotte Square. Here the grey terraced flats had doors with up-market brass knockers and brass plates proclaiming private medical practices, tax consultants and law firms with bizarre names. Interspersing these were private flats with names ending in Q.C. and enormous lamps in the windows.

Shivering with cold, Findhorn turned up a short flight of broad, granite stairs. He fiddled with some keys, opened a heavy door with a brass plate saying Mrs M. MacGregor, and switched on a light.

They were met by opulence and cold. Pink Venetian chandeliers threw glittering light over a patterned Axminster carpet, a little Queen Anne table with a pseudo-thirties telephone and half a dozen stained-glass doors. Jazz players cavorted amongst spiral galaxies and naked angels on a high vaulted ceiling. Stairs at the end of the corridor curved out of sight; they were guarded by a big wooden lion, and a scantily draped Eve was eating a marble apple on the first landing.

Romella laughed with delight and surprise. 'The Sistine Chapel!'

'Dougie's into surrealism,' said Findhorn. He turned a knob on the wall and there was a faint *whump!* from a distant central heating boiler. 'He's in Gstaad just now. He skiis there over the winter.'

Into a living room with a hideous black marble fireplace, a floor-to-wall bookcase, and a faded wallpaper effect expensively created with hand-blocked Regency patterns. Light cumulus clouds floated on a sky-blue ceiling.

'Wait till you see the bedrooms,' Findhorn said. He switched on a coal-effect fire and headed for a cocktail cabinet made up to look like a Barbados rum shack.

Romella flopped down on a cream leather settee. 'The bedrooms. A gin and tonic, please, and don't overdo the tonic.'

Findhorn poured two glasses and sank into an armchair. Then he pulled the photocopies from his briefcase and put them on a glass table between them. 'There are people after these diaries. And they're looking for me. You ought to know that before you start because if you help me they might come looking for you too.'

Her low, gentle laugh was captivating. 'That must be the weirdest chat-up line ever. Certainly it's the most original I've ever had.'

'You can come and go as you please, but I'm staying here. I don't want to risk the streets more than I have to.'

'Here am I, all alone in a big empty flat with a weirdo. It's like something out of *Psycho*.' She said it jokingly but Findhorn thought there was a trace of uneasiness in her voice. 'You're kidding about people looking for you, right?'

'No, I'm serious. Maybe you want to pull out.'

'If you're into drugs . . .'

'Look, if it makes you feel safer why don't you ask your friend Stefi to come over? And Grim Jim and anyone else you want – a boyfriend if you have one. You can all stay here. There's plenty of room.'

'Okay, I'll ask Stefi. A little girl company might be good. The phone people aren't disconnecting us until tomorrow.' Romella waved a hand around. 'She'll love this. Jim's on a field trip over Christmas, he's a geology student.' She sipped at the drink. 'Are you going to tell me the real story on this stuff?'

'I am serious. There's something in the diaries. I have no idea what it is. But there are people very anxious to get their hands on them and I have been threatened. What I need is a translator to help me solve the riddle. And I have to stay out of sight while I'm about it. They're looking for me in Edinburgh and I can't risk railway stations and the like. I know I come out sounding like a mad axeman on the run from Carstairs.'

Romella was sitting unnaturally still. Findhorn waited. He added, 'I need your help. Your fees are secondary.'

'Let me phone Stefi.'

Findhorn headed for the kitchen, G&T in hand. He half-expected to hear the front door banging shut as

Romella made her escape. A thirties-style light blue refrigerator held nothing more than a bar of Swiss chocolate, a few out-of-date yoghurts and a wedge of diseased Stilton.

Romella appeared; she had taken off her denim jacket. 'I've given Stefi the story. Wild horses won't keep her away – she's a bit of a romantic. She's Bulgarian and I suspect she has Romany blood from somewhere. She promises to keep out of our hair while we're translating. She's coming over with clothes and food and stuff.'

'Brilliant.' Findhorn saw no point in hiding his relief and he grinned.

'And she loves to cook.' Romella thought of the highest number she dared. 'I think I want to charge a hundred pounds a day for this one.'

'Agreed,' Findhorn said without hesitation. 'And Stefi gets twenty plus expenses for housekeeping.'

'Well now, Fred Findhorn B.Sc, Ph.D., Arctic explorer in a hurry, why don't we get started?'

The big living room was now comfortably warm and Findhorn sank into the settee beside Romella. He passed over the copy of *The Times* obituary. 'By way of background.' She started to read out loud:

Lev Baruch Petrosian, who is presumed to have died in an Arctic plane crash, began his career by making a number of important contributions to the so-called quantum theory which underlies the modern understanding of matter and radiation. He is better known, however, as a physicist involved in the wartime development of the atomic bomb, and later in the development of the hydrogen bomb during the Cold War period. A cloud hangs over his career in that he has been suspected of espionage, although the charge was never proven. Mystery surrounds the fatal Arctic air crash . . .

She paused and looked at Findhorn, eyebrows raised.

. . . in which it is rumoured that he was escaping to the Soviet Union to avoid arrest.

The son of a shepherd, Petrosian was born in a cottage in the Pambak mountains of Armenia on 29 December 1911. His early years were as eventful as his later ones. Orphaned at an early age in the course of a Turkish massacre of Armenian Christians, he escaped as a child with an uncle to Baku on the shores of the Caspian Sea, shortly before that city fell to the Turks, allied to the Germans, in 1918. Smuggled out in a British troop ship, they reached Persia where they stayed until the end of the Great War.

His education began in a private gymnasium in Yerevan, and Petrosian soon distinguished himself as an exceptionally able student. A chance meeting with Ludwig Barth, the German physicist, resulted in an invitation to study physics at Leipzig University. In 1932 the University accepted him as a student for a doctorate, and he began work on the

*quantum theory of matter. It was an exciting time
do do physics in Germany . . .*

'In more than one way,' Findhorn suggested. 'The Nazis
were coming on stream.'

Romella picked up the thick sheaf of papers on the
table. 'And here we are. The diaries start then.'

'He must have been twenty-three. I wonder what
triggered him?'

Romella was flicking through the pages. 'A girl, maybe.
A girl by the name of Lisa Rosen.' And translating in a
low, melodious voice which Findhorn found curiously
sensual, they at last entered the strange world of Lev
Baruch Petrosian.

She was brown-haired, talkative and cheerful. The contrast
with Petrosian's withdrawn, introverted character could
hardly have been more stark.

The diaries recorded the slightly immature recollections
and emotions of a young man finding his way in a
disintegrating world. Lev's world was one of strident
voices at street corners, of unemployed men prepared to
march like robots behind swastikas and martial bands, of
professors introducing seminars with 'Heil Hitler!' and
adopting, either from conviction or self-preservation, the
attitudes and postures of the Nazis.

They also increasingly mentioned the name Lisa.

One evening, Lisa took Petrosian to a social gathering
at the house of her brother, Willy Rosen. The social
gathering turned out to be a meeting of the local student

communists. Lev politely refused the invitation to join. He attended several such meetings, arm in arm with Lisa, but always without commitment.

One snowy day in January 1933, Lisa failed to appear at the laboratory. When he visited her in her little apartment, Lev was horrified to find her in bed, her face black and blue and her eyes almost closed up. The Brownshirts had used fists and heavy sticks to break up one of the meetings. After that, it seemed to Lev the most natural thing in the world to join the communists, the only group opposing the thugs with any degree of effectiveness. On the Party's instructions, he joined in secret. He was strictly forbidden to join the Reichsbanner, the Social Democratic Party groups who fought the Nazi Brownshirts in the streets. You are too talented, he was told, too potentially valuable to the cause, to risk a knife in your ribs.

On 30 January 1933, Hitler came to power. On 27 February the Reichstag was set on fire, and a national outburst of orchestrated thuggery against communists and Jews followed. Lev, this time with Lisa, once again found himself avoiding broken glass and unruly gangs in narrow streets. On 22 September the Reich Chamber of Culture came into being and promptly set about banishing all 'non-Aryan' culture from German life. On 4 October the racial and political purity of all newspapers and their editors was assured by the passing of the Reich Press Law. On that day too, Ludwig Barth summoned Lev: 'I can no longer accept you as a student. Your background is non-Aryan; you associate with Lisa Rosen, a communist and a Jewess. You have been speaking out against the Brownshirts.'

'Is this you speaking, professor, or the University?'

'It doesn't matter; there is no prospect that the University will grant you a doctorate.'

Professor Barth's comments did no more than crystallize thoughts which were already in Lev's mind. German academic life was in free-fall, matching the descent into hell of the country outside. The universities were being Nazified, recalcitrant professors dismissed, some murdered.

That evening Willy knocked on the door of Lev's fourth-floor apartment. Lev let him in. Willy was in an excited state. 'Lev,' he said, 'you are about to be arrested. Why? For speaking out against the Brownshirts. It is the Party's decision that you must leave the country immediately.'

'And Lisa and yourself?'

'Our place is here,' Willy said, 'fighting the fascists, with what outcome who can say? But you are too valuable to lose. You must carry on the struggle for world communism abroad.' Willy gave him the name of a girl in Kiel. 'She will look after you. Now go, quickly.'

Within half an hour Lev was heaving a suitcase loaded with books and little else through dark streets. After an hour, a safe distance from his apartment, he climbed a fence and spent a freezing night on a park bench, listening to the sounds of the dark. Early in the morning he made his way to the railway station. He half expected arrest on arrival, but in fact caught a train to Kiel without incident. He half expected arrest at Kiel too, but again left the railway station unchallenged, and found his way to an address which turned out to be a taxi service. He stayed there for six weeks, never leaving the house, until it was judged safe to transport him across dark fields to Denmark. Once there, he presented himself at the Neils Bohr Institute in Copenhagen where, as it happened, Otto Frisch was looking for an assistant. He wanted to test his Aunt Lise Meitner's quirky idea that perhaps an isotope of a rare heavy element called uranium was an unstable thing, prone to spontaneous fission like an amoeba.

A few months after Petrosian's flight, a mentally unstable Nazi storm trooper by the name of Bernhard Rust became the Reich's Minister for Science, Education and Popular Culture.

Soon after that, another storm trooper was appointed Rector of Berlin University. He promptly instituted twenty-five courses in 'racial science'.

Physics became 'a tool of world Jewry for the destruction of modern science'. Einstein the Jew was 'an alien mountebank' whose prestige proved, if proof were needed, that Jewish world rule was imminent.

And while German cultural and scientific life continued to self-destruct, a great exodus of talent took place. Soon this immense flow would be turned back against the Reich, focussed on its destruction. Some of it was directed into radar, some went into codebreaking. But for Lev Petrosian, far away in the New Mexico desert, it was the Bomb.

Dear Lev,

Yes, your letter did get through on the old Geghard trading route. If you think this isn't my handwriting you're right. I'm dictating to that pious old fornicator Father Arzumanyan. He asks if he can have his arithmetic book back as you've had plenty of time to master it.

Tomas is well. So am I. So are our sheep. That's about all the news here except that I'm seeing a girl. I can't say more as the good Father would refuse to write it down. Let me just say that she has skin as smooth as a baby's bottom and a bottom as . . . oh dear, I'm being censored.

Now here's a wonderful coincidence, but also black news. Aunt Lyudmila told me her friend Karineh – the one with the nose, you remember – knew of someone who'd made it out of Germany through Denmark, just as you did. So I enquired and it turns out he's now a teacher in the Gymnasium. A man called Victor. He says he knows you from Leipzig. It also turns out he was smuggled out through the Kiel underground in exactly the same way as you, with the same Kiel girl. She must be quite something but I must stop thinking like that now I'm in love. Anyway, now for the bad news. He tells me the Gestapo have arrested your friend Lisa. He says nobody knows anything about her fate, and that this type of thing is happening all the time now.

We're all expecting war any day. I want to kill

Nazis, but who would look after the sheep? Tomas is too old to cope alone.

I love your stories about England but of course you're making them up. Tell me more anyway. And will you ever get to AMERIKA?

Your loving brother,
Anastas

Petrosian's diary, Monday, 27 August 1939

War any day.

Hoping my British citizenship application gets through otherwise I'll be an enemy alien and God knows what will happen then. Colleagues very supportive.

Newspapers full of the non-aggression pact between Nazi Germany and the Soviets. I think Russia is trying to buy time, and Germany doesn't want to fight on two fronts again. It won't last. Still, it's hard not to feel let down.

Ph.D. exam next week, Nevill Mott from Bristol the external examiner. Good choice. He's studied at Göttingen, speaks fluent German and has left-wing sympathies. He's my age and a full professor!

Wednesday, 10 October 1939

Citizenship tribunal went OK. Told them I'm full of hate for the Nazis and that I still see Lisa's broken face in my dreams. Max Born had written to confirm I was an active anti-Nazi in my Leipzig days. No mention of any communist ties, but Max wouldn't have known about that. They said I should expect category C, which will mean I'm not subject to any restrictions, Russian pact with the Nazis notwithstanding.

My first paper, jointly with Max: *On Fluctuations in Zero Point Energy*. I feel like the father of a new baby! Great prestige being linked with Max Born, who's talking about getting me a Doctor of Science at Edinburgh.

Sunday, 29 June 1940

Writing this three days after the event. A policeman knocked me up at dawn and told me to pack whatever I could carry. Taken to police station, herded with others on to the back of a lorry and taken to an army barracks at Bury St Edmunds. Then for some reason separated from the others and driven off to Glasgow. Then put on board an old steamship in pitch-black. It sailed us down the Clyde, hugging the coast going south until we reached the Isle of Man. So much for category C – I'm an enemy alien and that's that. The camp is huge. There are about thirteen hundred of us. German offensive has now given Hitler the whole of Western Europe and it can't be long before he crosses the Channel. I want to use my mathematics and physics to defeat him, but how?

I haven't even had time to contact the department.

Thursday, 3 July 1940

The general feeling amongst the internees is that the British are finished. But the British attitude, which we're getting from our guards, is baffling – they don't seem to know when they're licked.

Personally I'm not so sure they're washed up. There's still no sign of a German invasion, a month after Dunkirk. If the Huns couldn't do it then, they can't do it now. Just possibly the war isn't lost.

A big worry. Suppose I'm wrong and that the British surrender. They might have to hand over internees to the Germans as part of the deal. What would the Nazis do to people like me?

Again writing this up after the events. Taken to Liverpool on a steam packet, then herded on to the *Ettrick* with over a thousand German and Italian prisoners of war. Then out into the Atlantic. Swastika flew under the red ensign to show we're carrying prisoners but when we heard that hadn't saved the *Arandora Star* three days earlier the captain did an abrupt about turn. Now the British are putting their trust in a destroyer escort. A bad crossing made worse by having to share it with arrogant Nazis.

Saturday, 29 November 1940

We're being moved to Camp Sherbrooke to escape the Canadian winter. Sad, because we all feel settled in Camp L. I'll miss the wonderful view from the Heights of Abraham over the St Lawrence. Food and washing facilities have been much better than in England, so we've been doing rather well as enemy aliens. Spacious huts, and we could have stuck the bitter Canadian winds.

And the cultural life has been fantastic. Friedlander was even elected a Fellow of Trinity College, Cambridge last month. I've made friends with some terrific people. Hermann Bondi, Tommy Gold, Klaus Fuchs and Jürgen Rosenblum especially.

'Klaus Fuchs?' Romella asked, her brow wrinkled.

Findhorn said, 'The atom spy.'

'What about the others?'

'Some of them ring bells too. I think Bondi became Chief Scientist at the UK Ministry of Defence some time after the war.'

'Not bad going for an enemy alien.'

Findhorn frowned. 'Gold rings a bell too. Yes, got it. Bondi, Gold and Hoyle came up with the steady-state theory of the Universe. I read that in *Scientific American*. Rosenblum I don't know. Do you think the contacts are significant?'

'I'm just the translator, remember?'

'So why have you stopped?' Findhorn asked.

9

The Temple of Celestial Truth

Jesus Christ Incarnate, corporeal vessel of the soul of Tati from Sirius. Transmogrified from the world of the ethereal to that of base matter. Messenger from the Higher Level and conduit to the transcendental. And leader of the Apostles, who alone will attain Heaven.

The executioner was first to arrive. She was a middle-aged, motherly woman, of the type one might associate with coffee mornings and home-made jam. She was wearing a red anorak and a long, black skirt, and was carrying a large but featureless black leather handbag. Her taxi driver turned right at the village of Maybole, away from the traffic heading south for the Irish ferries, and drove for some miles along a quiet stretch of road along almost uninhabited countryside, towards the sea. The entrance to the Castle was blocked by traffic cones, and a notice said 'NO ENTRY DUE TO STORM DAMAGE', but a storm-swept gatekeeper removed the cones and waved the taxi in.

Heaven? The dwelling place of the Angels, located

amongst the awesome halls of the Milky Way. Its specific location, the innermost planet orbiting the white dwarf companion of Sirius.

The extraordinary proof to match this extraordinary claim? Listen to the prehistoric stories handed down by generation after generation of the Dogon, the Saharan tribe contacted by the first wave of extraterrestrials. Listen to them repeat the ancient Dogon myths that describe the white dwarf orbiting Sirius in a fifty-one-year period, a star discovered by the astronomers only last century. How else to understand this except as information given to the primitives by visitors from that binary system?

And how else to understand the Book of Revelation's 'mighty angel come down from heaven, clothed with a cloud, and his face was as it were the sun, and his feet as pillars of fire', except as a visiting UFO, glowing with the heat of re-entry, smoke and flames pouring from its nozzles?

The Castle faced the Atlantic Ocean on an isolated rocky promontory in south-west Scotland. In spite of this isolation, it was only ninety miles from Edinburgh where, somewhere within that city, the diaries were located. Cannons faced landwards from the front of the Castle but to ensure privacy Jesus preferred to rely on men who stood under golf umbrellas in glistening raincoats and spoke to each other through mobile telephones.

The south wing contained private apartments, and these had been prepared by the Outer Circles, the trainees and ordinary faithful, for the arrival of Jesus and the Inner Circle.

By nine p.m., as the evening flights from Europe started to land at Glasgow, Edinburgh and Prestwick, an unusual traffic began to flow along the narrow access road: taxis, hired executive cars, the occasional chauffeur-driven Rolls-Royce.

Jesus Christ arrived at midnight. His helicopter, glistening wet and windblown, landed on the broad lawns outside the castle, on a landing pad hastily improvised from sheets weighed down by stones and lit up by spotlights.

Prophet of Apocalypse, as announced by the Seven Angels from Sirius. How else to understand 'thy wrath is come, and the time of the dead, that they should be judged, and that thou should give reward unto thy servants the prophets, and them that fear thy name, and shouldest destroy them which destroy the earth', except as a second coming, and a call to destroy those whose unbelief is preventing the arrival of the second wave of UFOs which will transport the Apostles to Heaven?

A buffet had been laid out in the nearby stables restaurant and people ate as and when they pleased. Little groups wandered around the armoury, its walls thick with the deadly weapons of two hundred years ago; others preferred to linger amongst the columned elegance of the spectacular oval staircase. With the arrival shortly afterwards of Nan Rice, Warden of All Souls College in Oxford, who turned up in a battered old Ford Escort, the Inner Circle of the Temple of Celestial Truth was at last complete.

Because time was short, the meeting began almost immediately. The Circle had dressed in the long, black, Mandarin-collar robes which they used for formal occasions. Only Tati alias Jesus had an additional adornment, a pendant in the form of a silver Earth symbol – a cross within a circle – hanging from his neck. He was a small, stout man of about fifty with a neat, grey beard and short grey hair. A large Bible and a Pepsi were on the table in front of him.

Tata, the human transfiguration of the woman clothed with the sun and with the moon under her feet, and companion of Tati, sat next to him at the end of the table. She was tall, in her thirties, smooth-skinned and with hair swept back in a bun. She had dark, watchful eyes and a broad, somewhat lascivious mouth. Amongst the faithful, celibacy was encouraged, but there was also a discreet understanding that rank hath its privileges.

The windows of the big conference room were lashed by an Atlantic storm, and the flames in the open fire leaped and flickered in the draught. The Brothers faced each other around a square of polished oak tables littered with carafes of water, and Seven-Ups and Cokes.

'Perhaps Shin Takamara would be good enough to report on our Far Eastern concrete project.'

Shin Takamara was small, sixtyish, with a near-bald head and over-large spectacles. He had a gentle, scholarly air, and he spoke modestly, but with an undertone of quiet pride. 'I am pleased to report that we have made an excellent start. Our pilot trial, as you know, took place in Seoul in the nineties. There we induced a builder to use our sub-standard concrete in the construction of an apartment store. As you know it collapsed with the loss of five hundred lives.'

'A fine achievement,' Jesus agreed.

'How did you get round the quality-control inspectors?' The question came from Ricky Ross, the West Coast American.

Takamara smiled slightly: the American was new to the group and still learning. 'It's much cheaper, in the Korean context, to bribe an official than it is to pay for high-quality concrete. Economic arguments have a powerful influence in the tiger economies.'

'He accepted a bribe knowing that the store could collapse?' the American asked.

Takamara explained patiently. 'The concrete we used was sub-standard, but not enough to make either owner or official believe that the store would fall down. The safety margin was simply shaved away. And our engineers made sure that the air-conditioning design was inadequate for the hot Korean summer. Then, when the store changed hands a few years later, the new owners installed a new air-conditioning unit on the roof. They knew nothing about the weakened concrete. Once the unit – a thousand tons of metal – was on the roof, it was only a matter of time.'

'Not only a fine achievement, but untraceable to us.' Jesus expressed his satisfaction.

'In the last year we have created over a hundred high-rise apartments in Korea and Taiwan in a similar condition. They will all start to collapse within a few months of each other. The scandal may bring down governments.'

'Splendid. Now, our brother from Western Europe.'

Herr Bund, a stooped, middle-aged man, addressed the table. He spoke in BBC English. 'Our infiltration of Aryan supremacy groups is beginning to pay off. All they really needed was intelligent leadership. We have already incited race riots in Austria and Germany. The actual loss of life has so far been small, but a wonderful climate of fear is beginning to spread through many districts of our major cities. Give it another year and I expect the spectre of a fascist revival will begin to dominate the agenda of the European Union.'

'Congratulations, Brother Bund, to you and the West European chapel. We will follow developments with great interest.' Herr Bund smiled his satisfaction, and Jesus Christ turned to a small, weak-chinned man. 'What about the Irish question, Brother McElvaney?'

'The situation needs very little help from us. We have decided that our best course is just to stand back and let it run. We don't even need to advise on channels for the delivery of weapons and Semtex.'

Jesus frowned. 'It is not part of our philosophy to stand back and do nothing. There is no situation so bad that it cannot be made worse with judicious effort. Can't you develop it further? Perhaps even foment a civil war between north and south?'

McElvaney gulped nervously. 'We did look into such a scenario. It involved creating a series of escalating tit-for-tat outrages attributed to each other's security services.'

'Take it from the shelf, Brother, dust it down and revive it; who knows where it might lead? Let us have a detailed plan by our next meeting. And now, the United States?'

Ricky Ross could hardly contain himself. 'Of course my country is a rich source of resources for our purpose. The gun problem has spiralled out of control; crime impinges on every aspect of life; there are countless racial, economic and cultural tensions; the drug problem is overwhelming all segments of society; there is almost no sense of social cohesion; there are many small religious or backwoods groups isolated from the rest of society and hostile to federal government or any government at all.'

'A rich brew,' Jesus agreed. 'And what are you doing with it? I note there have been a few high-profile bombings.'

'I regret that my West Coast chapter can't claim credit for them. But we are spreading our message. We have already, on the internet, circulated simple cookbook recipes for creating deadly nerve gases. Our immediate hope is to repeat the Aum Shinri Kyo Tokyo subway attack, without the errors in preparation and dispersal of the sarin gas which the Supreme Truth made.'

Shin Takamara said, 'Only eleven passengers were killed, although five thousand were injured.'

'But according to expert testimony to the US Senate, if the Supreme Truth had done the job professionally, thousands would have died,' Ross said enthusiastically.

'What do you have in mind?' Jesus encouraged him.

'Simultaneous attacks in all the major cities with

subway systems. I already have a team of chemists in a ranch west of LA preparing the botulism aerosols and sarin gas. We're using hobos and drifters to calibrate the lethal toxin count.'

'I am impressed,' Jesus said. 'The Americans are a young and energetic people. The speed of your spiritual enlightenment is an inspiration to us all.'

Ricky Ross acknowledged the compliment with a broad grin.

'And now, Brother Voroshilov?'

A small, gaunt, grey-faced man nodded. His accent was hardly recognizable as that of an East European. 'With respect to my West Coast Brother, we have achieved far more in my country. In America you are plagued by specialist agents, not least the FBI. Your military machine is under control. Your judiciary is independent and more or less uncorrupt. Our judiciary and bureaucracy, on the other hand, have been almost totally subverted. And our co-operation with criminal power has been an overwhelming success, creating the greatest threat to our peace and economy. The fiscal crisis, which we have at least partly engineered, is undermining the maintenance of our strategic nuclear forces and making criminals out of our most able generals and admirals.'

'We know all this—' Jesus began.

'But I have an even greater enterprise to report. We have a nuclear suitcase operation nearing completion. I had thought to surprise our brothers and sisters with the result. However when we next meet I hope to report a spectacular success, involving a major European city.'

'You need no praise from me, Brother. Your successes speak for themselves. I can hardly wait until our next meeting.' Jesus nodded. 'And now, we come to the climax of our proceedings. Not only of our proceedings, but an opportunity which has come only once in all our history. It is a great moment for us all. Our brother from the United Kingdom will now report.'

Attention focussed on a man sitting across from Jesus. The man was about forty, gaunt, with thick lips, metal-framed spectacles and short, vertical sandy hair. He was unconsciously gripping the sheets of paper in front of him, and his cheeks were flushed. 'I have to report a temporary setback,' he said in a neutral, slightly northern accent.

Tata sensed fear in the man's face, felt her heart beat faster. Under the long oak table, her hand slid over to Tati's heavy thigh, and squeezed it tightly.

There was a heavy silence around the table. The Apostles waited.

'Our quest for the doomsday machine still continues,' he said. His voice was unsteady.

'I don't wish to interrupt,' said Jesus, 'but perhaps we should use plain language here. You were assigned to obtain certain documents. Did you, or did you not, fulfil that task?'

Unconsciously, the man's mouth was twitching. 'In plain language, I did not.'

Jesus spoke quietly. 'Perhaps you should explain the circumstances.'

Sweat was making the man's brow glisten in the light of the chandelier high above the table. He sipped nervously

at a Seven-Up. 'As you know certain facts were brought to
our attention by one of our brothers in NASA. A routine
unclassified surveillance by a French satellite had revealed
the presence of aircraft wreckage at the mouth of a glacier
in Eastern Greenland. The location of the wreckage
indicated that the wrecked aircraft was probably the one
which was intended to transport the nineteen fifties atom
spy, Lev Petrosian, to the Soviet Union, along with certain
documents.'

'Was this information classified?' Takamara asked.

'It was in the public domain, but had attracted very
little interest or attention. We had information suggesting
that the documents in the aircraft—'

Jesus interrupted, '—were the key to the doomsday
machine described by the fifth angel.'

The man gulped. 'Yes. An American scientific team,
manning a weather station on the Greenland Ice Cap
known as Shiva City, was nearby. Through a large dona-
tion by us to the Polar Research Institute which financed
the station, we were able to persuade the team, reinforced
by some of our people, to head for the wreckage. Unfortunately the glacier calved off and the Shiva City expedition found itself afloat on an iceberg. Although we had
succeeded in infiltrating the group, our Brothers went
down when the iceberg broke up. An icebreaker, however,
had by this time reached the berg.'

'A simple rescue operation?' asked Ross.

'We suspect not. The icebreaker was the property of
Norsk Holdings, the oil exploration company. At any rate
an individual aboard the ship, a polar scientist by the

name of Findhorn, acquired the documents and disappeared with them before we could get to him.'

Jesus snapped his fingers. The executioner leaned down to her handbag, pulled out a syringe and a small bottle with a straw-coloured liquid. The wooden floor creaked slightly as she tap-tapped her way across the room to Jesus. The rain battered the window, and the fire was crackling. And yet the big room was enveloped by a strange silence.

The UK brother licked his lips. His breathing was heavy.

Jesus contemplated the syringe. Then he stood up and walked over to the rain-lashed window. He was a surprisingly small man. The lights of the Castle showed a white-capped sea, merging into darkness beyond. The lights of a fishing boat were about a mile out; they were bobbing up and down: the boat was making heavy weather. Lighthouses flashed from Holy Island, Ailsa Craig and Pladda. On the horizon somewhere beyond, he knew, was Arran, but only an occasional glimpse of light could be seen in the black. Down and to the left was a boathouse; he could make out a dark figure: someone under an umbrella, talking into a mobile phone.

He turned to the UK brother. The man's face was grey. Jesus said, 'As we all know our human bodies are hosting our souls temporarily, pending our completion of the cleansing programme which the first wave initiated over five thousand years ago, when the Egyptians first worshipped our home star. That programme is to be completed within the first century of this millennium. Only by freeing the earth of its unclean souls can those of us who are the

Apostles be freed to enter the bodies which await us on our true home, Tatos, the innermost planet orbiting the white dwarf Sirius B.'

'I know this, Tati.'

'But you need to be reminded of it.' Jesus nodded to Tata. She opened the Bible at a bookmark, and read out:

And the fifth angel sounded, and I saw a star fall from heaven unto the earth: and to him was given the key to the bottomless pit.

And he opened the bottomless pit: and there arose a smoke out of the pit, as the smoke of a great furnace; and the sun and air were darkened. And there came out of the pit locusts upon the earth . . .'

Tata paused, threw a brief, mirthless smile at the UK brother and then said:

And in those days men shall seek death, and shall not find it; and shall desire to die, and death shall flee from them.'

A fanatical edge was creeping into Tati's voice. 'What does this passage describe but a cosmic machine intended for the destruction of mankind? We have always understood this prophecy. How to explain the timing of this iceberg event, if it was not caused by the Angels of Revelation? They have clearly used their powers to send the doomsday machine of this Petrosian to us. They have given us the task of fulfilling their prophecy, a task which was delegated to you. You were entrusted with fulfilling our destiny.'

Bund said, 'You have failed not only us, depriving us of our homeward journey, you fail all of the Apostles going back five thousand years to Menes of the First Dynasty.'

'And you fail the Sothic brothers and sisters who await us on Tatos,' the Warden of All Souls pointed out.

Jesus said, 'Look what you have done to us.'

The man looked as if he was about to faint. He stared wildly around the table, but saw no compassion: the faces of his brothers and sisters were uniformly grim. 'It's only a temporary setback. I can find this man. I can get the diaries back.'

The executioner had been standing quietly, away from the table. Now Jesus nodded to her. She filled the syringe slowly from the bottle, approached the man slowly.

'Please . . .' He had seen the liquid at work.

Brothers on either side seized the man's arms. The executioner held the man by the hair. He felt the point of the needle on the side of his neck, at the carotid artery. 'I can retrieve the documents,' he gabbled. 'The man hasn't left Edinburgh. My entire northern chapter has converged there. He can't set foot on the Edinburgh streets without being seen. We know that the documents are in Armenian and we're combing the city for every translator of the language.' The woman was exerting a gentle pressure with the needle; the man felt the skin about to puncture; his eyes were wide with terror. 'He'll be found within days.'

'How many days?' Jesus asked.

'Three. Three at the most.'

Jesus looked around. 'What do you say? Shall we give this wretch another chance?'

There was a murmur of agreement around the table. Tata shook her head.

Jesus looked at her, assessed the opinion around the table. 'Very well, Brother. Find this polar scientist . . .'

'Findhorn.' The voice was a croak.

'. . . this Findhorn, and the documents. Do so within twenty-four hours.'

'Twenty-four hours?' The man's voice quavered incredulously, but then his eyes went to the needle, still only inches away from his neck. The executioner was pursing her lips in annoyance. 'I will!' he whispered. 'I will!'

'One other matter.'

'Say it, Tati. Give me your instructions.'

'Findhorn's theft is an insult to our extraterrestrial fathers. Convince him of this, and have him repent, before you destroy him.'

10

Hot Air

'I believe you!'

It was a moment before he recognized Stefi: a velvet pill-box hat, glistening wet, was pulled down almost to her eyes, a *Doctor Who* scarf was wrapped around her neck and she was wearing a knee-length coat and leather boots. She was holding two large suitcases, and her eyes were shining with enthusiasm. 'I knew there was something about you.'

'Come in, Stefi.' Findhorn looked quickly up and down the street but could see nothing out of the ordinary.

'I won't be a problem. I'll keep totally out of your way.'

'Okay. Maybe I'll get to sample those shish kebabs.'

Beyond the marble Eve, on a landing as large as the Dundee Street flat, a hippopotamus peered at them through reeds. A zebra was drinking on the other wall. Unseen by it, a crocodile watched quietly, its eyes just above the water. The crocodiles on the ceiling, however, had wings and were flying in formation. The African watering-hole motif surrounding them was broken by six pastel-coloured doors. 'I'll take Dougie's room,' said Findhorn, opening a blue door. He heard Stefi Stefanova give a squeal of delight as she opened the pink door next to him. Romella took the green room across the landing.

Findhorn had a shower in a vast blue bathroom and wondered if Stefi's helpfulness would extend to buying him some underwear. When he emerged, wrapped in a bath towel, Romella was sitting on his bed with the papers in front of her, neatly sorted by years.

'Stefi's nipped out for some late-night shopping. I've left the front door unlocked if that's okay. I thought we might carry on.'

'Excellent.'

She riffled through a sheaf of the papers. 'I can't make out forty-one. It's hopeless.' Romella dropped the photocopy of the water-stained diary onto the floor. 'Before we start, what are you looking for?'

'I wish I knew. Maybe some new scientific process.' Side by side on the single bed, leaning against the ornate Mexican-imported headboard, Findhorn was enjoying the warmth of her forearm.

She picked up 1942. 'Why all this macho Arctic explorer stuff? What do you actually do?'

Findhorn looked at his new companion, and decided she was genuinely curious.

'I go out to my ice station and measure things. Cloud cover, wind patterns near the ground, most of all the way the pack ice moves.'

'Why? For weather forecasting?'

'I just do stuff like that to finance my research. What

I'm really about is testing a theory.'

'So what's the great theory?'

'I think we're heading for a catastrophe.'

'A catastrophe,' she repeated tonelessly.

'Romella, I have a confession to make. I'm not a polar explorer, I'm a mathematician. My field is instability in complicated systems.'

She laughed in surprise. 'Well, I'm gobsmacked. What's a mathematician doing at the north pole?'

'Because of something I discovered. On paper.'

'Tell me about it,' she encouraged him.

'Did you know that sea level has risen by ten centimetres in the last century? Half of that comes from melting icebergs, the other half from warming oceans.'

'Fred, I know lots of things, but not that.'

'Ten centimetres isn't a catastrophe, but fifteen metres is and I think that's where we're headed. I think that big hunks of Antarctica are about to break off. Especially the West Antarctic ice shelf, which reaches hundreds of kilometres out to sea. It's sitting on the ocean bed, barely holding onto the continent. Now a little warming to lubricate its contact with the rock and off it goes, an iceberg half the size of Britain drifting into the Pacific and melting.'

She was looking at him thoughtfully. He continued, 'Every city round the ocean rims would end up like Venice. Los Angeles would disappear, New York City would be reduced to a handful of islands and London would turn into a big lake with buildings sticking out of it. All the major financial centres except Zurich would go, and every harbour in the world would be flooded. And the map-makers would have to redraw their atlases. Can you imagine the economic chaos?'

'So why aren't you in the Antarctic drilling holes?'

'Because I think the first signs will appear around the north pole, not the south.'

'How come?'

'The way I think it will go is this. When pack ice cracks it opens up a lead – a long channel of open water. This sea water is at about minus two degrees as against minus thirty-five for the air. So heat pours out from the lead, warming the ice around it. Okay, as things are at the moment the lead will slowly freeze over again. But with global warming under way there will come a point where the leads which open up are too big to be closed again by refreezing. They'll melt more ice, creating more leads and so melting even more ice – et cetera. The ocean will suddenly dump its heat into the ice. The Arctic ice cap will just crack up and disappear.'

'The polar cap will disappear? Suddenly?'

Findhorn nodded. 'Suddenly. But that's just the trigger. The rise in sea level will add buoyancy to the West Antarctic shelf which will just lift off and float away, adding to the mayhem. Cities, islands, countries will be submerged all around the world's ocean rims. And with all that water vapour in the air, even the Greenland ice cap will start to melt. Big hunks of the planet will become hotter than the Sahara. That's why, even if you live in Jamaica or Tokyo, you should still care about the Arctic. We're all wired up together.'

'And you're out there, a lone pioneer trying to save the world. Can't you get government support or something?'

'Unfortunately my funding application was sent to Mickey Mouse, alias Sir David Milton, and that was that.'

Somebody was running up the stairs. Findhorn started.

Romella said, 'Relax, it's just Stefi. You're serious about being hunted, aren't you? Do you think this mad theory of yours has anything to do with Norsk asking you to collect the diaries?'

'I don't see any connection. Petrosian was a different sort of mad scientist.'

Stefi appeared at the bedroom door, holding a plastic bag. She looked at them and grinned slyly. Romella gave her a look and said, 'But what's it actually like, working out there? Disappearing into Arctic wastes with no TV, no fish and chips?'

'And no girls?' Stefi added.

'Imagine being inside a deep freeze day after day, sometimes with a howling wind. It can be so cold you want to weep. But there are compensations. When you fly in you see this tiny cluster of huts next to a ship and all around it is this huge expanse of ice, with long open cracks of sea water. You see these big blocks of ice, all weird sculptures and aquamarine blue. You feel as if you're on solid ground but you know you're on a skin of ice only a metre thick and the water under it goes down for two miles. Sometimes in the night you can hear the ice cracking. I've seen a hut disappear overnight. I've walked two hundred yards to starboard from an icebreaker, worked in a hut for a couple of hours, and come out to see the ship fifty yards away, aimed right at me. There's nothing like it. It's like being an explorer on another planet.'

'It sounds dangerous. All those blizzards and cracks in the ice.'

'The polar bears are the big problem. They're wonderful killing machines. They're clever, and they're especially dangerous when they're hungry.'

'Talking of which,' Stefi said. She waved the plastic bag and disappeared.

Romella flicked through the copy of the 1942 diary. 'There's some gobbledegook in here. Maybe you can make sense of it.'

Petrosian's diary, Wednesday, 28 July 1942

Our much-promised, and badly needed, long weekend.

Collected Kitty early. A joy to see her so happy. She was wearing a long green skirt and a sweater, and the Indian ear-rings I gave her. Loaded up the wagon with camping gear, but about half the car taken up with her easels and canvasses and other painting stuff. Guess what she'll be doing.

Took off eight a.m. and headed west. It was interesting to see the cacti getting smaller as we got higher and then the trees starting to appear and get bigger. Spent a couple of hours in the Petrified Forest and then on to Flagstaff. Nice town, clear air after the furnace heat of Los Alamos. Lots of pine trees around. Found a picnic place and devoured salad sandwiches and lemonade. Sky blue, air warm, and impossible to believe there's a war on. Then turned north and took a long straight road to the south rim of the Grand Canyon. It was dark by the time we got there.

Couldn't afford the restaurant prices in Grand Canyon village so decided we'd have a barbecue, which would be more fun anyway. Went to local store and bought hickory chips, charcoal, matches, firelighter, barbecue skewers, tin plates, mugs, coffee, sugar, milk, two bottles of red wine, T-bone steaks, barbecue sauces, cutlery, salt, pepper and chillies. Worked out twice as expensive as a dinner but who cares! Had a super time. Tried my party trick (reciting π to thirty decimal places). Kitty made me keep repeating it as the wine bottle went down. Think I passed the test.

Then the funny phone call. It makes me wonder how the hell they found me because I didn't know myself we were even going to be in Arizona, never mind the Grand Canyon, south rim. Went back to the store for toiletries and the phone was ringing as I entered. The storekeeper says are you Mister Miller – my code name when I travel – and I say yes. Unbelievable!! It's Oppie. Wants me to go to some lakeside cabin near a place called Escanaba, which apparently is on Lake Michigan. Over a thousand miles away. Wants me there tomorrow as a matter of 'supreme urgency'. I tell him I'm drunk and I'm here with Kitty, but he says dump her and make it anyway.

Got lost on the way back to the tent and wandered around the forest in the dark with visions of dropping into the canyon. Furious row. She can't believe I didn't phone in. Asked her if she'd run me to Flagstaff in the morning and could I borrow the train fare and she nearly hit me.

Thursday, 29 July 1942

I'll remember this day as long as I live.

I slept in the wagon, Kitty took the tent. I love Kitty to distraction and it hurts to have us quarrel. I can't blame her but at the same time can't tell her about the project.

Woke up about six. A racoon was heading for the remains of our barbecue, stopping to go up on its hind legs now and then. Ran off when I went to waken Kitty. Packed up, then zero conversation all the way to Flagstaff. Asked her to stay until Saturday and I'd try to get back and we'd still get our weekend but she took off the earrings and said, 'Give them to your Lake Michigan broad.' Felt sick.

Got to the cottage, which it turns out is being rented by Arthur Compton, also on holiday. We took a car down to a quiet beach overlooking the lake, and there I listened to Oppie's story.

Teller has been calculating the temperature build-up in the fission reaction. He finds that the heat will ignite the atmosphere and maybe even the oceans.

Arthur and Oppie both devastated. Compton says it's better to accept Nazi slavery than take the slightest chance that atom bombs could explode the air or the sea. The gadget must never be made.

Friday, 30 July 1942

Exhausted, having worked overnight on Teller's calculations. He thinks a deuterium/nitrogen reaction will take place and, the air being eighty per cent nitrogen, that we have a massive problem:

$$C^{12}(H, \gamma)N^{13}$$
$$N^{13}(\beta)C^{13}$$
$$C^{13}(H, \gamma)N^{14}$$
$$N^{14}(H, \gamma)O^{15}$$
$$O^{15}(\beta)N^{15}$$
$$N^{15}(H, He^4)C^{12}$$

So at fission temperatures two hydrogens combine with carbon to give a burst of gamma rays, the atmospheric nitrogen combines with the hydrogen in water vapour to create oxygen 15 and more gamma radiation, carrying a thumping great 7.4 Mev of energy. The O^{15} isotope is unstable and beta-decays to heavy nitrogen N^{15} in 82 seconds. A neutrino carries the energy from this clean out of the Galaxy so we forget it. But then the heavy nitrogen so created interacts with more hydrogen. It disintegrates back to ordinary carbon, creating helium and a hefty 5 Mev. It's as if the Earth's atmosphere has been created just waiting for the nuclear match. The bottleneck is the long reaction time for combining two hydrogen atoms with a carbon one. The fireball would cool down too fast to pull it off. But Teller has a trick up his sleeve. He says the two hydrogens are already there in the atmosphere's water:

about one hydrogen atom in ten thousand is deuterium.

I suspect he's wrong. If my overnight sums are right the nuclear reaction rates need one hundred million degrees to be self-sustaining. I doubt if an atom bomb will yield more than fifty million degrees. So we're maybe on the right side of hell. Nice ethical dilemmas: (i) do we have the right to risk humanity on the correctness of our calculations? (ii) with a safety margin of only two, and given a straight choice, should we take a chance on burning the world or submit to Nazi slavery?

Mentally and physically worn out. But I can't complain. Nobody's shooting bullets at me.

Saturday, 31 July 1942

Refined the calculations with the help of better cross-sections. Chance now about three in a million. Compton says this is acceptable. Oppie asked who are we to decide on behalf of humanity what's an acceptable risk. I suggest we stick a notice in the local newspaper asking the public for their opinion. They don't think that's funny.

Flew back to Flagstaff on borrowed money, in desperation borrowed a pick-up from an incredibly kind woodcutter and hammered it all the way to the Grand Canyon. Kitty gone.

'What do you make of that?' Romella asked, rubbing her forearm. 'I'm freezing.'

'An irate girlfriend, and a near-miss on vaporizing the planet. Just another weekend.'

'This formula . . .' Romella asked.

'I haven't a clue.'

'If you say so.'

'If the sums had gone the other way . . .' Findhorn said. 'What's that?' He pointed to a smudged scribble.

She tilted the page and screwed up her nose in concentration. 'It says HMS *Daring*.'

'What has that got to do with anything?'

Romella shrugged. 'How would I know? It's probably nothing.'

'I agree. Probably nothing. Forget it.'

'Standard stuff, Freddie. Teller was discovering what's called the carbon-nitrogen cycle. It's what fuels hot stars, hotter than the Sun. But nothing on Earth can approach that sort of temperature.'

It was three o'clock in the morning and they were using oblique language. Archie had said it didn't matter as he was working anyway, and Findhorn didn't believe him even slightly.

Just a chat between friends.

About nuclear physics.

At three o'clock in the morning.

Nothing unusual about that. No eavesdropper would even notice.

Could Petrosian have discovered some way of getting the necessary temperature, of locking into this cycle to create a powerful new bomb? The question came out as: 'Not even, say, a nuclear fireball?'

'Not even a nuke.'

'It's another red herring, then?'

'Extremely red. But keep digging, laddie. This gets more intriguing by the minute.'

Findhorn switched off the bedside lamp and flaked out.

11

The Gardens

'I know all about HMS *Daring*.'

Romella and Findhorn, loading up a Miele dishwasher with breakfast things, looked up in surprise. Stefi was standing in dramatic pose at the kitchen door, looking like a snow-dusted mummy.

'Well?'

She flung off coat and scarf and flopped, teasing out the moment. She pulled back a kitchen chair and put her leather-booted feet up on the table. 'At least, I know where to go to find out about it. I spoke nicely to a young man in the National Library. It's all in the Public Records Office in Kew.' She read from a little card. 'Admiralty Report Number 26/54, for instance, tells us about the ship's vibration trials. There's lots of stuff like that.'

'When were those trials?'

'1954.'

'Clever girl,' Findhorn said, 'But the diary entry was July 1942. 1954 didn't exist then.'

'Oh.'

The deflation lasted a few seconds. 'Well what about this? HMS *Daring*. British destroyer of 1,375 tons.

119

Torpedoed by a U-boat on the 18 Feb 1940 off the coast of Norway. Only fifteen survivors. He wrote his entry just four months after it sank.'

'That's it? Nothing unusual about it?'

'It was unusual for a British warship to be sunk by a U-boat, otherwise I can't see anything odd. You Brits are so proud of your Royal Navy, but Bulgaria has a navy too, you know. I could murder a coffee, especially one with two sugars and lots of milk.'

Findhorn was filling the kettle. 'We've seen nothing in the diaries.'

'But we've only gone as far as 1942,' Romella pointed out. 'Black and no sugar.'

'I need to photocopy the rest of them.'

'Where are they?' Stefi asked.

'Tucked away safely.'

'He doesn't trust us. Are you sure you want to risk the mean streets?' There was a slightly sarcastic edge to Romella's voice.

Findhorn was looking for sugar. 'I do not, but what choice do I have?'

'Okay, while you're out risking your life I'll get more girlie things from the flat. It looks as if we'll be here for some days.'

'Be careful, Romella. If anyone asks, you've never heard of me. You're not translating anything for anyone. And make sure you're not followed back here.'

Romella glanced at Stefi. 'Isn't that the most wonderful chat-up line? What do you think?'

Stefi was undoing laces. 'I believe everything Fred tells

me. He's being hunted by bad people. I'll stay here and drink coffee and hope he doesn't get caught.'

Findhorn ordered a taxi and watched for it from an upstairs window. He sat well back on the short journey to the bank, looking out at the normality on the streets and feeling foolish, as if Mr Shorthand and Mr Speedhand were receding bad dreams, with Ms Drindle and her pet gorilla even more remote and unreal.

He emerged from the bank with an armful of diaries. George Street was busy and grey, and a cold, freezing fog had descended. He walked briskly along the street, feeling exposed, and turned into the business centre.

First he phoned Archie. The call was brief.

Then he started to photocopy. The diaries went up to 1952 and after an hour he had reached 1948 and needed a break, and he phoned Archie again. This conversation was even shorter:

'Archie?'

'It's all set up, Fred.'

'Thanks.'

And Findhorn resumed the photocopying. After another hour the tedium became unbearable and he sat down at a terminal. He now had access to an antiquated, unused computer in the basement of Archie's department at Glasgow University. He thought about a password. It had to be memorable, unguessable and in no dictionary. He thought of:

In Xanadu did Kubla Khan
A stately pleasure dome decree

He took the initial letters of the first seven words, replacing the *A* by the number 1 to give iXdKK1s, and concluded it with a couple of nonsense symbols. The final password was unguessable, but mentally retrievable:

iXdKK1s!!

Assume the people behind Drindle and the Korean had access to high-speed computers which they might use in combination to approach cracking speeds of a million characters a second. A six-character password based on a combination of ten numbers would be broken in ten seconds. One based on the 26 lower case letters might take two and a quarter hours. An alphanumeric combination could be broken in forty days and eighteen hours. A password based on all 96 characters on a keyboard, upper and lower case, would occupy the computers for two years and seventy-eight days, day and night. And Findhorn's password had nine characters.

In any case, first find your computer.

The scanning was slower and even more tedious than the photocopying, and it took him well into the afternoon.

Photocopies of the diaries to 1950 were now heaped on the desk in front of him, as were the originals; but their electronic clones lay in a secret machine, accessed through an impenetrable gateway and protected by an unbreakable password.

As an afterthought, Findhorn checked his e-mail. He froze. A terse message stared at him from the monitor:

1. Seafield Cemetery, 4.00 p.m. precisely.
2. Alone.
3. Bring the diaries.
4. Contact the police and the bitch dies.

The source of the message was some Brazilian address, no doubt meaningless. He hard-copied the message. His watch said three thirty.

He phoned Romella's flat, letting it ring for a full minute before giving up. Then he rang his brother's flat. Stefi answered straight away: 'Hello?'

'Stefi.'

'Fred, thank heavens you phoned.' There was anxiety in her voice.

'What's the problem?'

'It's Romella. She should have been back long before now. And she's not answering the phone. Where can she be?'

'Stefi, stay put and don't answer the door. I'll be there shortly.' He hung up before she could reply.

In George Street, a taxi approached on cue and he took it straight to the flat. The driver was happy to park on the double yellow lines. Findhorn thought he saw movement behind a net curtain as he climbed the steps. He heard the Chubb lock turn, and then the big bolt which went into the floor, and then the Yale lock, and then Stefi's eye was peering anxiously round the door.

Findhorn handed the e-mail over without comment. Stefi gave a little scream. He dropped the diaries on the floor and ran for the stairs. 'I have twenty minutes.'

'Will you call the police?' She was running after him.

'It would take me more than twenty minutes to explain and even then they'd never believe it. And if the police get in on the act it will be the end of her.' Stefi caught up with him at the marble Eve and grabbed him by the sleeve.

'Fred, take a minute. Stop and think. What will happen to you if you go there?' She was beginning to tremble.

'Stefi, all I know is that I'm out of time.' He pulled free, ran up to the African watering hole and came back down, two steps at a time, carrying a briefcase. Stefi was standing at the front door. It was locked and she was slipping the key inside her sweater.

'What do you think you're doing?' he shouted angrily.

'Seafield Cemetery in this weather will be deserted.'

'Of course it will. Why else . . .'

'So you'll get a knife in your ribs, you idiot. If you can't think of yourself think of Romella. She's a witness. What do you think they'll do to her once they've got what they want?'

Findhorn hesitated.

'How badly do these people want the diaries?'

Ten dead; a million pound offer; a large organization hunting me. 'Very badly.'

'So. Is that not a great big bargaining chip?'

'Okay. Okay.' Findhorn paced up and down the hallway, his head bowed. Then: 'You're right, Stefi. I'll e-mail these creeps from some cyber café. We'll meet as equals in Edinburgh Castle.'

'Is that safe?'

'It's a military garrison.'

She said, 'I'll come. If you do get her back she'll need female company.'

He hesitated again. Then Stefi was saying, 'I'll stay in the background. Nobody will see you with me.'

'Hell, there's no time to argue.'

Stefi was groping around in her sweater. 'This key is bloody freezing.'

The man was about forty, gaunt, with thick lips, metal-framed spectacles and short, vertical sandy hair. He was dressed in a long black coat, the collar of which was turned up against the icy breeze, and his hands were in its pockets. He was standing next to Mons Meg, looking out over the battlements of the castle. Findhorn joined the man at the wall. Far below, office staff were criss-crossing Princes Street Gardens, looking like amoebae under a microscope. Beyond the gardens, Princes Street was festooned with decorations and crawling with traffic. 'It's a long way down,' Findhorn said.

'But at least death would be quick.' There was something odd about the man's demeanour; Findhorn couldn't specify it. 'The Castle goes back to the fourteenth century. You would think it was impregnable – who could climb walls like these? And yet it has been conquered, twice, in its long history. Once by siege, once by trickery.' The accent had a slight northern English tinge; Findhorn tentatively placed it in Yorkshire.

'Trickery is what's bugging me.'

'Yes.'

'I like it,' Findhorn said, trying to keep the fear out of

his voice. 'No false reassurances or stuff like that. I think maybe I'll be dead in a few hours and you say "yes".'

'A few hours? You are an optimist. Unless you deliver.' The man's eyes flickered towards Findhorn's briefcase. 'You have them, I sincerely hope.'

'What exactly is in these diaries?'

'If we knew that, we wouldn't need them.' The man stepped back from the wall. 'Think what we have achieved in four hundred years. Think of the damage done by a cannonball from this.' He tapped Mons Meg, the massive cannon, next to him. 'Now we have bombs the size of a cannonball which could evaporate the castle, the hill it stands on, the Esplanades and everything within a kilometre of here. Can you imagine what the future will bring?'

'Is this relevant to anything?'

A gleam entered the man's eyes. 'Oh yes, very much. God hath made man upright; but they have sought out many inventions. Ecclesiastes one, twenty-nine.'

'Oh God,' said Findhorn, 'Not a religious fanatic.'

'Take your friend. I could kill her now, by a slight movement of my finger, even although she is miles away.' He pulled a mobile phone out of his pocket and held it towards Findhorn. The little square monitor had a message, easily read even in the fading light: KILL THE BITCH.

'A touch of the button and the message is sent.' The man put his hands, with the mobile, back in the deep pockets of his coat.

Findhorn suddenly felt as if he was walking on

126

eggshells. 'Why "the bitch"? You've got something against the ladies?'

'Who can find a virtuous woman? Proverbs thirty-one, ten.'

'A woman-hater and a religious nut, all in one. I don't believe you're real.'

'Handle me with care, Doctor Findhorn. I'm real, I'm a religious fanatic, as you put it, and I am deeply irrational by your standards. And now, if you please, the diaries.'

Findhorn, dreading the reaction, unstrapped the buckles of the case and handed over a dozen sheets of paper, then stepped back to give the man a secure space. The man skimmed through the pages and then looked up sharply. 'And the rest?' His tone was suddenly harsh.

'They're not here. What you have is proof that I have them. I'm not about to hand them over without some guarantee that Romella will be released.'

'This wasn't the arrangement.'

'Not your arrangement, chum. But it is mine.'

Cold blue eyes studied Findhorn from behind the spectacles. 'You don't know who you're trying to push around.'

'The Castle's closing, gentlemen.'

The man waited until the soldier was out of hearing. 'You'll be getting her by instalments, Findhorn.'

'Start sending me parcels and I'll start burning the diaries.' Findhorn found himself getting angry, tried to control it.

'Gentlemen, if you please.'

'I'm just looking for a secure exchange. And remember

127

you need the diaries more than I need Romella. She's just a translator. She means nothing to me.'

'Is that so?' The man hissed. 'Let's take a walk down the esplanade, Doctor Findhorn, while we make a new arrangement and you explain why you're risking your life for a girl who means nothing to you.'

It was six o'clock and the rush-hour traffic was being replaced by late-night shoppers and pantomimegoers.

Findhorn turned off Princes Street down a steep path leading to the darkness of the Gardens. He cut off the path over wet grass, heading for the safety of the shadows as quickly as he could. A couple of giggling girls passed, then a drunk who wished him a Merry Christmas. Findhorn grunted in reply. He found a tree, stood in its shadow, letting his eyes slowly adapt to the dark, and waited.

And waited.

Suddenly, after half an hour, lasers began to probe the sky overhead like futuristic searchlights, coming from some point on the Salisbury Crags about three miles away. Behind Findhorn, Edinburgh vibrated with life; buses sped along a busy Princes Street; shop windows reflected the Christmas lights. He was only fifty yards from safety. In front of him, the Castle loomed high over the Gardens, its turrets and walls reflecting a pale, ghostly light.

A hundred yards to his right the Norwegian pine was draped with lights. Ahead of him two men on ladders were trying to drape a banner across the bandstand. Another was setting up chairs on the stage. Half a dozen musicians were taking instruments out of cases. There was something reassuring about the hammering and the banter. A circle of light about thirty yards in radius surrounded the bandstand; beyond this circle, shadowy forms were moving, on the limit of visibility. They were real, or they were Findhorn's imagination at work; he could not say.

It was so huge that, at first, Findhorn thought he must have imagined it. And then he realised that he had, that the towering black cliff was old lava rather than ice, that the rumble at its base was a passing Intercity train and not the thunder of waves at the foot of the berg. To his horror he realised that he had momentarily dozed; but the return to reality brought back the bitter cold and the terror.

Marooned in an island of dark shadows, surrounded by a sea of light, he gripped the briefcase with both hands and again peered into dark shadows. His mouth was dry. Now and then he looked quickly behind.

Somewhere in the dark, if the man could be believed, was Romella. She would be brought into the light of the bandstand; Findhorn would approach out of the dark with the diaries which he now held; the exchange would be made; and the parties would each melt back into the dark night.

Or so they said.

Something odd about the men on the bandstand.

A cough in the dark, over to Findhorn's right. He shrank back against the tree.

A cigarette was glowing red about a hundred yards to

the left. An occasional arc marked its passage in and out of the owner's mouth.

A torch picked out a group of three, on the bridge crossing the railway. It was the briefest flash; but Romella was in the middle of the group. The grip on his briefcase tightened.

In a minute three figures emerged into the light in front of the bandstand. Two men, one a teenage tearaway in a leather jacket, the other the religious fanatic, still in his long black coat, warmly wrapped up with a red scarf. Romella propped between them, head lolling from side to side. She was wearing a short skirt and a simple T-shirt. Findhorn thought she must be utterly frozen, perhaps even close to hypothermia. The men stood, gazing into the dark around them.

The musicians were hardly ten yards away. They were paying no attention, and Findhorn suddenly knew what it was about them. They weren't testing their instruments.

And no seating had been set up for an audience.

And the men on the ladders were taking forever to set up the banner.

He stepped out of the shadow of the tree and walked towards the three. They spotted him about thirty yards away. Romella went still.

Someone else, a small, plump woman, approached out of the dark like a ghost, and stood beside the two men. She was carrying a large, plain black handbag.

Findhorn walked into the light of the bandstand. The men were watching him intently.

Some of the musicians were climbing down the

bandstand at its far end and walking into the shadows.

Romella was shaking her head in a doped but urgent way.

12

Doomsday

Findhorn is conscious of moving shadows beyond the circle of light. He walks forward, holding up the briefcase. Closer in, he sees that the plump woman behind Romella is holding a hypodermic syringe. Romella says, 'Fred, clear off,' but her voice is slurred and barely reaches him.

He puts the case down on the frost-covered grass about ten feet from the men, and steps back. Everyone's breath is steaming in the icy air. He has never known such an alertness in all his senses; everything around him seems slow. He wonders what is going on behind the circle of light but doesn't dare to turn round.

Mister Religion leaves Romella, steps warily to the briefcase, as if he expects it to explode. He crouches down to open it and pulls out a diary at random. He pulls a small black torch from his pocket and shines it on the book, flicking rapidly through its pages. Then he shines the torch into the case and briefly counts the diaries. The lasers are flickering overhead and Findhorn feels as if he is inside some weird science-fiction fantasy.

'You can let her go now,' Findhorn says. He is judging distances.

The man looks up. 'If only life were so simple.'

'What the hell is that supposed to mean?'

'All men are liars. Psalms . . .'

'Stuff the quotes. We have an agreement.'

The man sighs. He closes the briefcase, stands up and puts the torch in his pocket. 'It's only fair, in your closing moments, that I tell you this. Miss Grigoryan is privileged. Her talents will help to solve a great mystery and enable a great prophecy to be fulfilled.'

'Prophecy?' Findhorn asked, to keep him talking.

'With her help we will be able to turn the key to the bottomless pit.' Mister Religion turns and nods. The syringe woman, and the men holding Romella, move backwards. It is as if they are on wheels. For a moment Findhorn half believes he is in a bizarre nightmare.

He hears movement from behind.

The bandstand lights switch off.

Suddenly there are only the strobing blue lights in the sky, and silhouettes against the Castle wall.

Findhorn rushes forward. He collides painfully with a dark figure who says 'Oof!' Someone from behind grabs him by the arm, shouts, 'Run, you fool! We have her.' He pulls free and sprints in her direction. He catches a whiff of Romella's perfume. She is being hauled along by the hand. Findhorn grabs her free arm; he can't make out the other party. Torches are probing dark corners. Staccato, angry shouts follow him into the dark. Someone runs past, footsteps pounding on the frozen ground. Findhorn whispers, 'Go to the left!' They run wide at the big Christmas tree, keeping away from its radius of light, towards the narrow pedestrian bridge over the railway.

Stefi, gloved and helmeted, is revving the engine of her Vespa. Seconds are lost while Romella climbs onto the pillion. She seems about to collapse. Then Findhorn is shouting 'Hold tight!' and Stefi accelerates away on the footpath, lights out. Findhorn races along the path after them, his companion following. On to a road, with lights and cars, and across it to a multi-storey car park. Footsteps pacing them from behind. Stefi's scooter is disappearing briskly round a corner, Romella clinging like a baby monkey.

The car park will have security cameras and there is is a busy street on the far side. If the Syringe People want to avoid cameras, the car park is a buffer. But now, in the street lights, Findhorn recognizes the other man: Mister Speedhand. He shouts to Findhorn and beckons towards a car, jumping into it.

Four men burst onto King Stables Road from the park entrance. Their faces are concealed under balaclavas. Findhorn knows he has no chance in a race. They spot the car, race Findhorn to it, but Findhorn gets there first and leaps in, slamming the door. It is the sort of car that has in-flight navigation and quadrophonic CD and deep leather seats and air conditioning and twin carbs, and there is a satisfying thrust in Findhorn's back as the driver takes them from zero to sixty in a millisecond. The pursuers shrink to gesticulating dots in the rear window.

Findhorn, his heart thumping, and gasping for breath, wonders about the liquid in the syringe. He looks at Mister Speedhand, and Pitman clinically studying him in the mirror, and he wonders if he should have taken his chance with the religious maniacs.

Along the Grassmarket, with its winos and bistro crowds. He thinks he glimpses a red tail light disappearing up the Candlemarket, a steep cobbled hill ending at a T-junction. The car goes up this hill. The turn, left or right, is going to be crucial. Findhorn is gasping.

Left is down the Mound, skirting the Gardens again; but it is also city centre, traffic lights, evening crowds. Right is no stopping, suburbs, countryside beyond; right is dark lay-bys, and narrow tracks winding into the Pentland Hills.

The big car turns left. Findhorn feels his legs going to jelly which is unfortunate as he intends to jump out at the first red traffic light. He sees Stefi's bright yellow scooter a couple of hundred yards ahead, wonders if Pitman has spotted it, or even if he is following it.

Down the Mound. The traffic lights are co-ordinated so that if they are green at the foot of the hill they are green all the way and he will be swept through the city and on to an unknown destination and an uncertain future.

Don't let them suspect your intentions. You are the Grateful Rescued.

'Thanks. I thought my e-mail was a long shot, especially as I just pressed the reply button. Were the musicians your people?'

'No, they were theirs. You owe us, Findhorn.' Speedhand's tone is icy, but it carries an undertone of seething anger.

'Who are they?'

'You've just lost us the diaries, Findhorn. Why should we tell you a fucking thing?'

Down the hill, the lights are at green. The cars ahead are accelerating through. Pitman is strumming his fingers on the steering wheel, studying the traffic flow, judging a system of vortices and eddies unknown to the authors of the Highway Code.

Stefi has skimmed past the traffic and she is through. Findhorn imagines that Romella, without helmet or riding gear, is being freeze-dried. The scooter turns smartly right then left, speeding up Hanover Street and out of sight.

'You didn't rescue us as an act of charity.' Findhorn's mouth is dry.

The queue ahead is streaming fast through the lights. The lights turn orange but the drivers ahead are chancing it. Pitman accelerates. The streets are packed with Christmas shoppers.

The lights are now red. Still he is going to try for it. An Edinburgh citizen, full of his rights, steps onto the road. Pitman curses and stops.

Findhorn contemplates the crowded pavements. He stays put. 'How did they find us?'

Speedhand said, 'How many translators of Armenian do you think there are in Edinburgh?'

'Okay, I'm an amateur. But I'm learning fast. What do you want from me?'

'You've just created us a mountain of trouble, friend.' The traffic flow has changed; filter traffic is turning off. It won't be long. Findhorn pretends to look out of the window but he is examining the door lock and the handle. A long stationary queue has accumulated behind them.

A horrible thought strikes him. Maybe there's a child's lock. Maybe he won't be able to open the door.

The car is an automatic. It moves off smoothly; the big engine can hardly be heard. Speedhand is saying, 'Unless you're even more stupid than I think, you've made copies of the diaries. We'll have those.' The car is slowing to turn left up Hanover Street. In a department-store window, reindeer with no visible means of propulsion are pulling Santa Claus into a snow-filled sky.

People are jaywalking. Pitman swears briefly, idles, picks up speed. Findhorn waits as long as he dares. He snatches at the door handle. The door opens; he jumps out. The car is doing about fifteen miles an hour and he staggers, almost falling, before swerving onto the pavement and muscling his way through the crowds. The car, swept along by the traffic flow, is heading up the street. He looks back and glimpses Mister Speedhand at the rear window. The man's face is out of control, full of surprise and rage. Findhorn gives him a wave but he shows no sign of Christmas spirit.

Romella emerged from the downstairs toilet after half an hour of vomiting. She was chalk-faced, apart from livid bruises around her eye and lips. She waved aside an offer of help and made her way to the leather couch.

Findhorn said, 'I'm sorry. Maybe you should just walk away from this.'

She managed a weak, defiant stare through one eye.

'Don't blame yourself, Fred. You told me the situation and I chose to think it was just a fantasy thing. You're a bit weird, after all.'

Stefi came in bearing hot chocolate.

Romella was whispering again. 'And thanks for turning up. You didn't have to do that.'

'It was the least he could do,' Stefi said. 'Look at you.'

'If you didn't turn up they were going to burn holes in me until I told them where you were. There were three of them.' She managed to pull the blanket from around her knees. 'Look at my tights!'

Findhorn obliged. 'What happened?'

'The bastards dumped me in the boot of a car and drove off. I don't know where we went. They drove for hours and I nearly froze to death.'

'They were keeping you on ice until they set up the meeting with me,' Findhorn suggested. 'They'd have killed us both, me right away. I'd have been just a braindamaged smackhead who overdosed in Princes Street Gardens. They'd have dealt with you later, once you'd translated for them.'

'When they finally let me out, it was dark and I was in a car park. My legs wouldn't hold me at first but when they did I started to struggle. They got alarmed at the noise I was making. That's when the punching began. I don't know what happened next except that they shoved me back in the boot, and next time they opened it they forced some horrible liquid down my throat. I'm sure it was just cough mixture. You know, two teaspoons only, don't overdose, may induce drowsiness.'

Romella's voice was beginning to trail off, and her eyes were beginning to swim in her head.

Stefi put the mug on the coffee table and said, 'That's enough. No more talk.'

'The car was a Mercedes 600 SL. Maybe a year old. Boot smelled new.'

They laid her out on the couch.

'Green Merc. Swiss registration, I think. Didn't get the number.'

Findhorn took off her trainers. Stefi tucked the blanket around her and switched off the lights. The room glowed a gentle red from the stove. 'She needs medical attention.'

Findhorn said, 'With bruises like that, and an overdose of medicine, a doctor would have to call the police.'

'So what?' Stefi wanted to know. 'I'm calling the police anyway.'

'Romella has a say in this. Wait until morning.'

'Any change?'

'She's breathing more easily.'

'You look like death warmed up, Fred. Get some sleep.'

Findhorn staggered off. If men were going to burst into the house waving hypodermic syringes, he hoped they would do it quietly.

Findhorn was awakened by sunlight. A voodoo mask stared at him with empty eyes, on top of a small bookcase devoted to travel books, thrillers and cricket. He looked out over the Edinburgh skyline, with its monuments and steeples. The Castle was less than a mile away, black and dominating. Stefi's yellow scooter was propped up against the wall of the back garden, out of sight from the streets. He dressed, discovering a swollen ankle, and limped down the stairs. Romella was turned towards the back of the couch and an elegant leg protruded from under the blanket; the offending tights had disappeared. Her breathing was normal. Stefi was on the armchair, head tilted back. She was snoring slightly.

In the kitchen, he found a percolator and coffee beans from a small sack stamped Blue Mountain, Mavis Bank, Jamaica. Typical Doug, he thought; no nasty instant powders for little brother. The noise of the coffee grinder was rasping in the still of the house. A couple of minutes later Romella appeared, bare-footed, hair dishevelled and with a colourful yellow and blue swelling surrounding her right eye, and a bruised lip. Her sweater and skirt were wrinkled from a night's sleep.

'The Swamp Thing,' Findhorn said.

'What?'

'An old horror movie. You remind me of something I saw in it.'

'Thanks, Fred.' She winced.

'Shall I get you a damp cloth?'

'I still feel drugged.'

Over tea and toast, Stefi turned up looking like Action Woman in black sweater and leggings. She poured herself coffee, added condensed milk from a tin and flopped down at the kitchen table.

Findhorn broke the silence. 'I had no idea things would get this heavy. I can't have you risking your lives like this.

I think you should just walk away. It's me they want, and the diaries.'

'Who are they?'

'I don't know. There are at least two groups after the diaries. One of them offered me a lot of money.'

Romella studied Findhorn over her coffee. He found her steady gaze disconcerting. 'How much money?'

'A million pounds.'

There was a stunned silence.

Stefi eventually broke it. 'A million pounds? Are you joking?'

'I'm very serious.'

'And you turned it down?' Her voice was incredulous.

'Money isn't the primary issue here, Stefi. It's not clear who really owns the diaries, if anyone. But the main thing is, I want to find out for myself what's in there. Petrosian was an atomic scientist, remember. Say he's discovered some way to make a super-bomb, or even some political secret that people don't want out. I might just want to burn the lot.'

Romella touched her bruised eye and groaned. 'Forgive me, Fred, but who are you to make judgements on things like that?'

'Diaries plus conscience equals responsibility. I had no idea what I was getting into but here I am, stuck with it. There's nobody else.'

'And suppose it's something beneficial?'

'Then I'd want to patent it first and become wildly rich.'

Stefi looked at Romella, fixed a look on Findhorn, and

spoke in a tone which allowed for no argument. 'I think you'd better start at the beginning, Mister. Spill the beans.'

Findhorn thought that maybe Stefi Stefanova had picked up some of her English from old B movies. Romella was having some difficulty drinking. She reached into a pocket for a handkerchief and patted her bruised lips. 'Yes, Fred, it's time to spill the beans.'

'You wouldn't believe a word of it,' Findhorn warned.

Stefi and Romella were giving him hard stares. He spilled the beans.

Finally Romella said, 'Right then, we should get on with it.'

Findhorn's heart leaped. 'You mean you're willing to carry on with the translation?'

'Why not? I don't like being knocked around.'

Stefi was looking reflective. 'There could be a lot of money in this.'

'Or none.' Findhorn pointed out.

Stefi said, 'Romella gets fifty per cent.'

'Ten,' said Findhorn.

'Twenty.'

'Agreed.'

'You said that money isn't the issue,' Stefi reminded him.

Findhorn nodded warily. 'Uhuh.'

'Good. So I'll settle for ten per cent.'

'For Heaven's sake, Stefi, why should you get ten per cent?'

She waved a finger at him. 'Because you need me. They

know you and they know Romella. Every time you step out of the house you both risk your necks. But me? They know nothing about me. I can come and go in safety and do research for you, like HMS *Daring*, for example.'

'Good point. You could make all the difference. I've been consulting a friend with specialist knowledge. I'll surprise him with ten per cent of whatever we end up with, which will probably be nothing.'

'How secure are we here?' Romella asked, with a touch of anxiety in her voice. 'They might find out you have a brother in Edinburgh and check up.'

'This is Doug's hideaway. Nobody knows about it. Doug has a Queen Street apartment, but as a criminal lawyer he also wanted some place he could escape to without getting phone calls or visits at strange hours from strange people. So this pad is in our Mum's maiden name – that's the MacGregor on the nameplate. And the phone is ex-directory and under Mabel MacGregor.'

Stefi waved her hands around. 'I could get to like it. All this space, and angels and crocodiles.'

Findhorn said, 'We've assembled a team, and agreed the division of spoils. It's a start.'

'One for all and all for one,' said Stefi, reinforcing Findhorn's suspicion that she learned her English from movies.

Findhorn said, 'My bet is that the value of the secret lies with whoever discovers it first. And I don't know what resources we're up against.'

Romella was dabbing her lips. 'We're in a race? So let's get started.'

* * *

Findhorn was crouching in front of the genuine coal effect Scandinavian stove with the imported Mexican fire surround, trying to understand the controls.

'There's one thing I'd love to read about now.' Romella was carefully applying a skin-coloured powder to her bruise. The photocopies were laid out on a coffee table.

'Well?'

'The first time they set off an atom bomb. How Petrosian saw it. What it was like from the inside.'

Stefi, cross-legged at the table, flicked through a heap of photocopies. Findhorn pressed a button and flames shot up. He joined Romella on the couch.

Petrosian's diary, Thursday, 12 July 1945

Philip Morrison and I took the plutonium core out of the vault at Omega. Of course it was in sub-critical pieces. We put them in a couple of valises especially fitted for the purpose. Sat them in the back seat of Robert Bacher's sedan and set off for Alamogordo, with one security car in front, one behind. Both sweating at the thought of an automobile accident. Very unlikely, but what if we got hit by a truck and the bits went critical? A weird feeling, driving through Santa Fe, a sleepy little one-horse town, carrying the core of the 'gadget' – the atom bomb. If the locals had known what was being driven through their main street!

Turned off on a dirt track and left the plutonium in a

room at MacDonald's ranch house, which had long been abandoned by the family.

Friday, 13 July 1945

Just after midnight, in MacDonald's Ranch, Bacher officially hands over the core from the University of California to Tom Farrell, General Groves's aide, along with a bill for two billion dollars.

Then we wait. Got a little sleep.

At nine a.m. Louis Slotin begins to assemble the core. He has to push the plutonium pieces together on a table to the point where they almost reach criticality. He's carrying a lot of responsibility – if he makes the slightest mistake we're dead, there's no bomb, the war in Japan takes a different turn and so does the future.

His concentration is terrific. He keeps licking his lips. You have to stare to see his hands moving at all and we're all standing like statues and screaming inside. Then Oppie turns up, practically sparking electricity with tension. This has a bad effect on everyone. Boss or not, Bacher tells him to get out. Louis completes the job.

3.18 p.m. We get a call from Kistiakowsky. The gadget is ready for the core. We carry it out on a litter and again it goes in the back seat of Bacher's sedan. We head for the tower at Trinity, Bacher at the wheel driving with extra-ordinary care.

Working in a tent at the base of the tower. The core goes on a hoist and is raised over the assembly. Lowered down into it with extreme slowness. Geiger counters rise to a crescendo as it goes in. Atmosphere unbelievable – I can't describe it. The tiniest knock could start a chain reaction.

Wind rising, flapping tent. We can't afford dust.

The core sticks. It's the heat from the plutonium, it's expanded compared with the dummy runs. The biggest concentration of eggheads the world has ever seen and not one of us thought of that. What else have we missed?

Equilibrium eventually reached and the assembly is complete by ten p.m. We leave it overnight in the tent. Groves gets some fantasy about Japanese saboteurs into his head and sends an armed guard out to it.

Saturday, 14 July 1945

Deteriorating weather. Freshening wind means the gadget sways as it's raised up the tower. Jams at one point. Eventually it reaches the top and Jerry eases it into the corrugated iron hut a hundred feet up.

Sunday, 15 July 1945

Weather getting serious. Storm clouds, high wind, thunder in the distance. What happens if Base Camp gets hit by lightning? Or even the tower?

Oppie up top, checking the connections. Alone with his creation. What thoughts are going through his head?

Eleven p.m. The General has been on site for some hours giving the weather men hell. Lightning flashing and drizzling rain. What if there's a short circuit? And what will the wind do to the radioactive dust? MPs assembled to evacuate Socorro if necessary. But Amarillo in Texas, three hundred miles away, could also get it. How do you evacuate 70,000 people at a few hours' notice?

The old rumour back again: some of the senior men are predicting the atmosphere will be set alight. Bets being taken on whether all life will be destroyed.

Truman and Churchill due to meet Stalin at Potsdam. It doesn't take much imagination to see that Truman will want a result. I imagine Oppie and Groves are under huge pressure from above.

Midnight. Can't see the Tower for mist. Heavy rain. Storms forecast to be heading this way.

Tension beyond endurance. We're all going insane with it.

Monday, 16 July 1945

Pouring rain throughout the early hours.

In the Mess Hall at Base Camp, Fermi has a new worry. He thinks if the wind changes suddenly we could all be showered with radioactive fallout. Oppie gets all distressed – he's practically weeping. Groves takes him out to the S.10,000 bunker – far too close, I thought.

Then the full force of the storm hits the tower. Lightning dangerously close. They have to postpone. At the same time the gadget has to be fired in the dark for the instrumentation to record it properly. Latest possible moment is 5.30 a.m.

Four a.m. Rain stops. Conditions to hold for next two

hours. Oppie and Groves agree to go ahead at 5.30, the last possible moment. A stream of headlights in the desert – the arming party retreating from the tower at speed.

A bunch of us are on Compania Hill, about twenty miles NW of zero point. Countdown starts at twenty minutes, then warning sirens and people at Base Camp take to trenches.

And then suddenly the sun is shining, and the hills are shimmering in the light. It's a tiny sun on the horizon, too bright to look at until it has grown into a big churning mass of yellow, and then it's floating up from the ground on a long stem of dust. The fireball turns red as it cools and at that point you can see a luminous blue glow around it – ionized air.

This is all in silence. When the bang comes it hurts my ears and then there is a long, long rumble like heavy traffic, and a strong gust of wind.

I can't describe the feeling. It's somehow threatening, as if we had interfered in a part of Nature where we had no business to be. I have goosepimples for hours afterwards.

13

Witch Hunt

Stefi said, 'I have a feeling I can't describe too. We have a piece of living history here. Can't you feel it? Is it not speaking to you?'

Findhorn stood up and stretched. 'Stefi, it's only a photocopy.'

'I'm beginning to learn things about you, Doctor Findhorn. For example, you have all the romance of a cold fried egg.'

'There's nothing in there,' Findhorn complained.

Romella said, 'He keeps coming back to this question of setting the atmosphere alight.'

'I know,' said Findhorn. He was wiggling his strained ankle. 'It preyed on his mind.'

'It's beginning to prey on mine,' Romella said.

'My nuclear physics friend says it has to be a red herring. It couldn't happen unless the bomb was so big it would zap the planet anyway.'

'This religious maniac,' Stefi asked. 'What was it he said in the Gardens?'

'I'll help them turn the key to the bottomless pit.'

'A very useful clue.' Findhorn assumed Stefi was being ironic.

She stood up. 'I'm going to speak to that nice librarian boy.'

'About HMS *Daring*?'

'*Inter alia*. I'll bring back a Chinese take-away. Byee.'

Romella had been flicking through the A4 sheets. Her face was thoughtful. 'Petrosian seems to have gotten into some sort of trouble after the war.'

Findhorn sat down on the couch again. 'Tell me the story,' he said.

At 8.14 a.m. Japanese Time, Monday, 6 August 1945, powerful shock waves ripped across Hiroshima at the speed of a bullet.

News of the explosion was flashed from the *Enola Gay* fifteen minutes after the drop, and was announced at Los Alamos through the Tech Area's Tannoy system. Oppenheimer quickly called the whole staff together in an auditorium, acknowledging the cheers and shouts like a prize fighter. Suddenly, the suspicions of the scientists' wives, that their menfolk had been engaged on something extraordinary, was confirmed. Their children learned that their fathers' work was praised by the President, that their overcrowded little Los Alamos school was being named in great newspapers. In sheer exuberance they paraded through every home in the complex, led by a band banging on pots and pans.

Three days later, Fat Man was dropped from the *Great Artiste*. Nagasaki became an inferno of flames visible for two hundred miles, and another eighty thousand dead were added to the hundred and twenty thousand of Hiroshima.

A couple of days after that, Los Alamos resounded with parties, conga lines, sirens, drunkenness and TNT explosions in the desert. For most, the doubts, the moral questions, would come later; this wasn't the time.

Over the next few weeks, depression settled over Los Alamos. A diaspora took place, as talented young men took up teaching positions in universities around the States. Few of the emigrés returned to their homelands. Fermi joined a new institute at Chicago. Oppenheimer took up his old post at CalTech but, after the daily contact with minds of scorching brilliance, and the creation of a sun which had scorched the New Mexico desert, teaching was an anti-climax. He soon accepted directorship of the Institute for Advanced Studies at Princeton, and continued to advise government on the development of the new weapons until the day came when the witch-hunters finally got to him.

Across the Atlantic the radar men, whose contribution to the victory had been even more vital than that of the atomic scientists, were likewise dispersing, and would likewise enrich scientific life in future years. Lovell, whose airborne radar had finally killed the U-boat threat, went on to create the Jodrell Bank telescope. Hoyle went on from his wartime radar work to become the most influential living astrophysicist. Bondi, an Austrian and former enemy alien, became Chief Scientific Adviser to the Ministry of Defence; and Tommy Gold, a brilliant iconoclast who had likewise fled the Nazis from Austria, would harass a complacent scientific establishment with radical new insights for the remainder of the century.

At the end of 1945 Petrosian gave up his bachelor flat. With the help of a couple of scientists' wives, he loaded cardboard boxes with Indian pottery, cacti and books, and left them in storage to be sent on. He drove his four-door Buick slowly through the weird, wind-sculpted canyons. Occasionally he glimpsed the Sangre de Cristo mountains far to the west, glowing blood-red in the light of the setting sun. The car's progress was soon marked by tracks in a light covering of snow. He reached a small house on a ridge overlooking Santa Fe; and there he stayed overnight with Kitty Cronin. The morning brought a difficult farewell.

He took Route 85 south, running parallel to the Rio Grande, before turning left, skirting the Trinity test site. Somehow Trinity was a psychological boundary. Once past it, he felt he had left one world behind and was entering another. He drove a thousand miles to Arkansas, stopping only occasionally at roadside diners to relieve himself and have an occasional snack.

Others from the Los Alamos days, and from the defeated Germany, were to turn America into a great powerhouse of science and technology; Petrosian, however, took no part in this. In Arkansas, he buried himself in a small-town community college, a position far below what his talents and reputation could have earned him. Almost wilfully, he had returned to the obscurity whence he came.

Petrosian's record as a refugee who'd worked on the

Manhattan Project was soon known locally. He had helped build the Bomb and finish the war in Japan; he had saved thousands of American and Japanese lives; he was a local hero.

Lev quickly established himself as a popular and competent teacher, with a talent for explaining difficult ideas in simple ways. He lived quietly, making only a few close friends. A few Southern girls fluttered their eyelashes at him, but he kept to himself. If asked, he would express clear opinions on anything, and soon became known as anti-segregationist, anti-religious and anti-establishment in outlook. Strangely, in this conservative backwater, these outrageous opinions merely enhanced his popularity, establishing his reputation as a slightly mad foreign eccentric. Lev nominally joined an organization for protecting academic freedom; otherwise, he stayed apart from all organized activity, political or social.

And Romella was now ploughing through year after year of diary whose pages were utterly banal. There was no hint of any drama in Petrosian's life, nothing to suggest that he had invented some new theory, found some novel means of creating energy, or thought of some way to make a super-bomb in a garden shed. He had, in effect, switched off and dropped out. Stefi was singing in the kitchen, and Romella's voice was becoming hoarse, when she said, 'And here comes the trouble.' It started one Wednesday morning in the summer of 1953.

That Wednesday morning started as an ordinary day. Lev

had developed a routine. His internal clock woke him at half past seven. He was showered and dressed by eight. Around then the mail would arrive, and he would read this over a breakfast of cereal, coffee, a boiled egg, orange juice (Florida oranges, freshly squeezed) and marmalade on toast. By nine o'clock, he was on his way to the College, a two-mile walk along a broad, tree-lined suburban road.

They announced their arrival through a letter with an unfamiliar look and a Washington Capitol postmark. With a vague sense of foreboding, he returned to the kitchen table and slit the envelope open with a breadknife. He read and re-read the contents. Then he stood up, abandoning his breakfast, and paced up and down the kitchen, his head whirling.

```
Dear Doctor Petrosian:
Your name has been raised in testimony
before the Internal Security Sub-
committee of the United States Senate
Committee on the Judiciary. This testi-
mony was taken in executive session and
publication of it has been witheld pend-
ing your having an opportunity to give
testimony. We have set Thursday, 4 June
1953 as the day when this may be
released. Accordingly, we are asking you
if you will appear at 9.30 a.m. on that
day, in room 424-C, Senate Office Build-
ing, Washington, DC. In the event that
you do not avail yourself of this
```

opportunity, the evidence will be made
public.

Sincerely yours,

Henry J. Alvarez
Chairman, Internal Security Subcommittee

Petrosian walked his standard route to the College on autopilot, scarcely aware of his surroundings. But instead of making his way to the mathematics building, he took a back path towards the Faculty of Arts and entered the corridors of the English Department. To his relief, Max Brogan was in his office.

Max Brogan was an untidy, overweight West Texan, with curly brown hair thinning on top and a double-chinned face which managed to be permanently cheerful no matter what the external circumstances. His chief claim to fame was his small, overweight wife who ran the Sweet and Tart, a culinary highspot in the little town. Today Brogan was wearing a pink, short-sleeved shirt and shorts. Pencils were sticking out of a pocket. On the face of it the friendship between Petrosian the thin aesthete, and Brogan the good-living, corpulent Falstaff, defied analysis; but a closer examination revealed a common factor: each man detected in the other, in his own way, a quiet but rock-solid individualism. The tides of fashion, whether intellectual or sartorial, ebbed and flowed in vain around these men.

Brogan was at his desk, or at least it had to be assumed there was a desk somewhere under the pyramid of books and papers in front of him. He looked up as Petrosian entered; his normally cheerful expression had a serious edge to it. 'I heard.'

Petrosian collapsed into a black leather chair. 'Anyone else?'

'Neymeier in French Literature, Sam Lewis in Liberal Studies, but what the hell it's only nine o'clock and there are bound to be plenty more. Maybe even me.'

'Why you, Max? You're as American as turkey on Thanksgiving.'

Max raised his hands. 'Maybe some writer on the reading lists I give my students, maybe I went to a party with the wrong people ten years ago. Who knows with these frigging morons?'

An old, old sensation was gradually creeping over Petrosian, a sensation he thought he had left behind twenty years ago in Germany, and fifteen years before that in Baku. It was the feeling of being a target, of being hunted by some ill-defined, implacable, malevolent force. He felt the fear in the dryness of his mouth as he spoke. 'What will I do, Max?'

'Squeal on your friends. It's a ritual. You confess and give them names, they confer absolution and move on.'

Petrosian said, 'But I've done nothing wrong.'

'I envy you, Lev. You're a single man. A man with a wife and three kids who's done nothing wrong, now that's a whole new ballpark.' Brogan shifted uneasily. Lev waited while his friend plucked up courage. Then the Texan was saying, 'Look, these guys scare me. They only need to name you and you're destroyed. Once you're on their blacklist you'll never work again.'

Petrosian repeated, 'But I've done nothing wrong.'

'But can you prove it?'

'I'm not even a communist.'

'You do your own thinking, right? You're a liberal? Maybe even a New Dealer? That's all they need, pal. They have an agenda, which is to put the American political landscape somewhere to the right of Genghis Khan.'

'Max, I've done nothing wrong.'

Max was all patience. 'You still don't get it, Lev. That's not a defence.'

Petrosian shook his head in bewilderment, and Max tried again. 'Look, Mary has a cousin, an accountant with MGM Studios. The tales he told us would make your hair stand on end. You know these people reduced the studio czars to milksops? They denounced some wartime movie as Red propaganda because it showed the Soviets fighting Nazis. Another one got the treatment because it showed Russian kids being happy. You said something, or you did something. Yesterday, or twenty years ago. Or somebody thinks you did.'

'My instinct tells me to fight these swine.'

'We got an old saying hereabouts, Lev. Those who wrestle with pigs are bound to get dirty.'

Petrosian stood up. 'Okay, Max. But I'm an old Nazi-fighter and I'll tell you this. Those who are led by pigs end up in their slimy mire.'

Back at his office, a message was on Petrosian's desk, propped up on books so that it could not be missed:

Please contact me immediately.
B. Lutyens.

Petrosian crossed the campus lawns towards the Faculty offices, his stomach churning. Janice was typing briskly on a Remington.

'The boss is expecting me.'

Normally he would have expected a smile, or a joke. But today she nodded without looking up or pausing. Lev knocked on Lutyens's door.

The Head of Faculty, Boothby W. Lutyens, was a burly, white-haired and florid-faced man. Of limited talent, his rise in the College hierarchy had a lot to do with an astute nose for office politics, coupled with an uncanny ability to say the right things at the right time. The fact that he came from a rich Southern family which had generously endowed the University was, of course, neither here nor there.

Lutyens was pouring coffee from a machine in the corner of the room. He was wearing a crumpled white suit, the trousers supported by brilliant yellow braces. He was looking grim and Lev sensed that he already knew something. He didn't offer Lev a coffee. He crossed to his desk and put his feet up. Lev remained standing, and without a word passed over the letter. Lutyens glanced at it and tossed it back. 'I have a copy.'

'What's going on?'

'What it says, Petrosian. You have questions to answer.'
Lutyens's tone was cold.

'That's not telling me much.'

'It's all you'll get from me.'

'Who are these people?' Lev asked. The hostility was baffling.

Lutyens stared at Lev over half-moon spectacles. 'Don't you read newspapers, son? It may have escaped your attention, but there's a war on. And while the Commies are in Korea spilling the blood of our boys, others right here in their own country are stabbing 'foresaid boys in the back. Infiltrating our institutions, undermining our values, getting at the minds of our young people. I imagine HUAC's questions will have something to do with your own associations in this regard. If I'd known you were a Commie I'd never have hired you.'

'What associations?'

'The American Association for Democratic Information and Freedom, a front organization if ever there was one. You evidently forgot to inform this College about your membership of that society when we offered you the post.'

'Doctor Lutyens, Americans have been forming societies for mutual purposes since America began. The process is part of democracy. The reason I belong is this: I was a student in Germany in the thirties. I saw what cowards academics are. They talk a lot of bullshit about freedom but as soon as a threat like this comes along they head for the hills. It seems to me the only safe organization to join these days is the Methodist Church.'

Lutyens puckered his lips, forming the skin above them

into tight, vertical, disapproving wrinkles. 'Watch your tone, Petrosian.'

'It strikes me that for a man to freely hold and express his beliefs is the American way. Do you have a problem with that?'

Lutyens said, 'There's a point beyond which academic freedom should not be pushed, Petrosian. We're very dependent on federal funding these days. Meaning we are vulnerable to government definitions of loyalty and politically appropriate attitudes.'

'I envy you, sir. I wish I had your moral flexibility.'

Lutyens thumped his coffee furiously down on the table. He stood up angrily, open-mouthed. Lev said, 'Can you at least tell me what testimony the loyalty board are talking about?'

Lutyens glared angrily. 'You got difficulty with your hearing? I told you, I have no more information to give. Now get out.'

Janice didn't look up as Petrosian left.

Over the next few days, subtle changes took place in Lev's professional and social life. The first time a colleague crossed the street, out of greeting distance, Lev put the apparent slight down to his own over-sensitive imagination. The second time it happened, with another colleague, he was not so sure. The third time, it was becoming clear: to be seen with Lev Petrosian was bad news. He met no overt hostility in the common room; it was just that his colleagues were polite and distant. They tended to exclude him from conversation. He was assuredly excluded from the jokes, and more than one outburst of ribald laughter, it seemed, was directed his way. In the classroom, his sophomores stared out the window more, rattled desks more, paid less attention than usual. It might just be, he thought, that the course was getting tough; but the usual banter and repartee which he shared with his students was gone, to be replaced by a sullen and hostile silence.

There was, however, nothing subtle about the unsigned note which Lev found at his feet when he opened his office door one hot, sticky afternoon. The ribbon on the typewriter was worn, and the typist was clearly unskilled. In upper-case letters, it read

```
JEWS, NIGGERS, COMMIES, YOU'RE ALL THE
SAME.
HITLER DIDN'T FINISH THE JOB.
WE WILL.
```

Petrosian found Max Brogan again in a quiet corner of the campus, seated in the shade. About fifty yards away some girls were trying out Hula-Hoops, pausing from time to time to collapse in giggles on the parched grass.

'You're looking pale,' Brogan said as Lev flopped onto the bench.

Petrosian passed over the message. Brogan's lips tensed angrily as he read it.

'What does it signify, Max?'

'*Semper in excretum, solo profundis variat.*'

'And boy, am I up to my neck in it.'

A lithe girl in tight white sweater and shorts was

gyrating her hips and Max paused momentarily. 'Lev, you need representation. I know a liberal-minded lawyer. Maybe you can plead the Fifth or something.'

Petrosian shook his head. 'I don't need a lawyer. I've done nothing wrong. And I'm not even a Communist.'

Max Brogan laughed sardonically. 'Well, that helps. You know what they say.'

'No. What do they say?'

'You don't lynch the wrong nigger, that's not the American way.'

'Don't knock your country, Max. I lived under the Nazis.'

Brogan shrugged. 'You're doomed anyway. The Board of Regents are scared shitless. I hear whispers they're aiming to buy off McCarran with a loyalty oath. That ought to shake a few professors out of their torpor. Lev, are you going to co-operate with HUAC?'

'I guess so.'

Max grinned bleakly. 'Of course you are. You're a baseball-loving, gum-chewing, God-fearing, loyal American. And you have one thing more going for you.'

'What's that, Max?'

'You're white. God help you hereabouts if you'd been born Theodore Sambo Roosevelt.'

14

Inquisition

'Hello FBI, Atlanta, this is Lewis Klein of Domestic
Intelligence, Washington. Would you connect me to Don
Dilati?' A pause, then: 'Don? Lewis Klein here . . . Fine,
thanks, and yourself? . . . It's about this guy Petrosian . . .
your very own commie, yeah. The HUAC hearings . . .
there's been a change of plan. The guy's college is holding
an internal enquiry to root out Reds and HUAC
want him shunted onto it on account of they're over-
loaded up here. Anyway, it's being held locally and I
was wondering if we might liaise with you guys down
in darkest Arkansas. We have very bad vibes about
this Petrosian. We see him as more than just a parlour
pink. We suspect he passed information on to Russia
when he worked on the atom bomb . . . Sorry, the source
is restricted. We have permission from the man upstairs
to plant the usual devices and we have a trash can
recovery order . . . What do you mean, law and order
Arkansas style, we can match you people any day . . .
'Kay, I'll come down with my team and see if we can't
stick one on him this time. I mean get something to burn
him. I'm deadly serious, that was the word, "burn" as in

high voltage . . . Sure, same to you. Good hunting.'

A local junior grade high school had been turned over to the hearings. Petrosian, feeling terribly alone, turned into the main gate and made his way to the entrance, where a black security man was sitting at an uncomfortably small school desk. The man examined Lev's letter, checked his name against a list, and waved him to the left with a sympathetic grunt. In Petrosian's lonely world, a sympathetic grunt was like a mother's hug.

A bare corridor was lined with people, mostly men, smoking, and the air was blue with cigarette smoke. Eyes, some curious, some hostile, followed his route. Black cables snaked from a window into a noisy classroom. A card tacked on the door had 'HUAC INTERVIEW ROOM' written on it in blue crayon, and another blue-collared security guard looked at Lev's letter and led him by the elbow into the room. There was a buzz of conversation as he entered. Some flashbulbs popped. Two movie cameras sat on tripods at the back of the room. The guard ushered him to a seat at the front of the classroom and then went to another one to one side of the door. Two microphones faced Lev on the desk and he thought they were unnecessary for such a small room. He found himself facing a raised dais, on which was a long desk with carafes of water, tumblers, papers and a wooden gavel. Three black, high-backed chairs were at the desk. Each had a small card in front of it: 'Mr Andrew Dodds, Board of Regents, Greers Ferry College', 'Congressman Olaf B. Yates, Arkansas', 'Senator Henry Alvarez, HUAC,

Washington'. On the wall was a blackboard which had been wiped clean, an American flag hanging limply, and next to it another door. Lev assumed that his inquisitors would enter through this second door, which probably adjoined another classroom. Hot, sticky air was circulating from an open window. The morning sun streamed across a stenographer next to the door. She had white, pulled-back hair and was sitting straight-backed in a corner, staring ahead, like a machine waiting to be started.

A couple of minutes passed. The heat was stifling and Lev's mind began to wander. He was wondering about the gavel, whether they'd transported it from Washington or borrowed it from the local courthouse, or bought it from a gavel shop, when the door near the blackboard opened and three men walked in.

They were all in their forties. Lev knew Andrew Dodds, the College representative, by sight. He was small, near-bald, with a weak, receding chin and small eyes which peered out from behind round, steel-rimmed spectacles. Petrosian thought he bore a startling resemblance to Himmler, could hardly separate the two in his mind.

Olaf B. Yates shambled in behind Dodds. The Arkansas congressman looked like, and probably was, a dirt farmer. He was a small, burly man with a rough complexion and a squat nose like a boxer's.

Alvarez was tall and stooped. He had a slightly asymmetric mouth, one corner being pulled down. It soon emerged that this corner of the mouth gave an occasional nervous twitch, which would also contract the senator's cheek. Instinctively, Petrosian felt that he could handle Dodds and the dirt farmer, that he had the intellectual edge over them; but the same instinct made him fear Alvarez, the travelling inquisitor from Washington. Alvarez had fixed a steady, hostile stare on Petrosian, as if he was reading the scientist's mind.

The man from Arkansas, Olaf B. Yates, tapped the gavel. 'This hearing will come to order in the matter of Lev Baruch Paytrojan.'

A few mysterious preliminaries over, mainly to do with the empty lawyer's chair next to Petrosian, Dodds alias Himmler fired the opening salvo. He had a methodical, clipped way of speaking and a slightly nasal, high-pitched voice which soon became irritating to listen to. 'Doctor Petrosian. It has been determined by the Attorney General, and by the Director of the FBI, that institutions throughout America are being penetrated by persons whose purposes are subversive, that is to say, broadly speaking, inimical to the American way of life. Unconstitutional means are being employed, in clandestine fashion, by these people – communists and their fellow travellers – to overthrow the state.'

From the corner of his eye Petrosian was aware that Alvarez's cheek had twitched. It was to become an increasing distraction throughout the long inter-rogation.

Dodds continued, 'They have infiltrated every level and every type of organization and institution. They have infested educational, scientific, governmental, labour and communications establishments, the latter including the entertainment world. The House Committee on Un-American Activities has been active in attempting to root out these subversive elements from American life. Young, idealistic people in educational establishments are especially vulnerable when exposed to dangerous and alien ideas. We in the Greers Ferry Community College are anxious to play our full part in this patriotic enterprise. The purpose of these hearings is to establish the loyalty to America of our staff members. Testimony has been given in closed session to this committee which may tend to call your loyalty into question. You are here to satisfy us that your loyalties do indeed lie with the country to which you now belong. Do you understand?'

Petrosian nodded.

'Please answer yes or no for the record.'

'Understood, sure.'

The Arkansas congressman asked, 'Doctor Paytrojan, where was you borned at?' The voice was almost comically hillbilly.

'Armenia.'

'That's Russia, right?'

'It is now. But Armenia is a country with its own culture, language and even script. The Armenian Church is the oldest established Christian Church. It goes back to 300 AD.'

'You don't say? But yo're still a Russian.'

'I became an American citizen in 1945.'

Dodds picked up the questioning. 'I have here the reading list you give to your sophomore students. It includes a book called *Through Rugged Ways to the Stars*, by Professor Harlow Shapley, Director of Harvard College Observatory.'

'Yes, It's on my recommended reading list.'

Dodds stared at Petrosian through his spectacles. 'Are you aware that Shapley has been co-chairman of the Progressive Citizens of America? That he has asked scientists to, I quote, "answer to a higher cause, and increase the importance of their world citizenship over their local loyalties"? What do you think he meant by that, Doctor Petrosian?'

'I know he has left-wing convictions.'

The hint of a sneer. 'You might say. HUAC have listed him as affiliated to between eleven and twenty communist front organizations.'

Alvarez interjected. He had a heavy, commanding voice, over-loud for the cramped little room and the microphones. 'Let me put it directly, sir. Do you think it right that impressionable young minds should be exposed to ideas from the minds of communists and their fellow travellers?'

'Yes.'

The answer took the panel by surprise. Petrosian added, 'But then, I'm not imposing an opinion, simply exposing students to a range of ideas.'

Alvarez changed tack abruptly. 'How are the Brooklyn Dodgers doing just now?'

It was Petrosian's turn to be surprised. 'I have no idea.'

'And the Cardinals?'

Lev shrugged, bewildered.

'Do you play baseball?'

'No, sir.'

'Football? Basketball?' Alvarez was adopting a tone of incredulity.

'No.'

'Are you physically prevented from so doing?'

'No, I'm in good health. I'm just not interested in sport.'

'Meaning you have no sense of belonging to a team. Don't you think that good American citizenship involves you in social as well as legal obligations?'

'You mean, I should answer to the higher cause of social conformity, like the communists?'

Alvarez glared at Petrosian. 'Before we go any further in this enquiry, sir, let me make one thing clear. Smart talk of that sort is unwelcome at this hearing.'

The Congressman said, 'Y'see, it's like this, Mister Paytrojan. I never knew a ballplayer who was a Communist. Good loyal Americans are team players.'

'Do you attend church?' Alvarez wanted to know, clearly rattled by Lev's defiant reply.

'No.'

'What is your religion exactly?'

'I was brought up as a Christian Armenian.'

'And now?'

'I'm no longer active.'

Mister Arkansas grinned. 'You admit to being an aytheeist?'

'Agnostic is the word. There are things in the natural world I can't explain, like why it exists at all.'

'And do you expose students to this aytheeism of yours?'

'I don't expose them to classroom propaganda of any sort, unless you consider doing your own thinking to be propaganda. All they get from me are the ideas and concepts of modern physics.'

'You have a problem with God, country and flag?' Senator Alvarez wanted to know.

'Not at all. But I also think it's my duty to make young people do their own thinking. I don't know how to do that except by exposing them to new ideas. And all new ideas are subversive to some extent.' A light sweat was forming on Lev's brow.

Alvarez again: 'So while our boys are out there in Korea meatgrinding their way back to the 38th parallel, you're back here nice and cosy telling our young people to go easy on the loyalty thing?'

'Did I say that?'

'No sir, you did not. Not in so many words.'

Alvarez leaned back. Mister Arkansas had a mock-puzzled look on his face. 'Did I hear you just admit you teach subversive ideas to students?'

'The syllabus includes some discussion of new ideas in physics. I said that all new ideas are subversive.'

'Subversive.' The congressman paused, to give the impression he was thinking about that, and also to focus attention on himself. 'Subversive. Doan that word mean undercutting the established order of things?'

'Yes.'

'And doan disloyalty involve the same thang?'

'Yes.'

'Well pardon me if I've missed somethang. I ain't had

the privilege of a higher education. It seems to me that you doan give your impressionable young students classroom propaganda but you do just happen to expose them to disloyal ideas.' A triumphant, yellow-toothed grin spread over the Arkansas farmer's face: he had outwitted an atomic scientist, delivered a crushing blow. He noted with approval the busy scribbling of the reporters.

The logic was so unbelievable that Petrosian couldn't answer it. He sat, literally speechless, until Alvarez stepped in. The senator now asked the ritual, and deadly, question: 'Doctor Petrosian, are you now or have you ever been a member of the Communist Party of the United States?'

It was expected, but still Petrosian felt his skin going clammy. 'No.'

'Nevertheless in 1946, you joined the American Committee for Democratic and Intellectual Freedom.'

'Yes.'

'Are you aware that this is a known communist front organization for the defence of communist teachers? That it has been declared un-American and subversive by this very House Committee on Un-American Activities?'

'So I heard. I didn't know that when I joined.'

Alvarez referred to a sheet of paper in front of him. 'On June 30th of 1946 you attended a party at the home of Max and Gill Brogan, who are alleged members of the Communist Party.'

'I don't remember.' Petrosian wiped sweat from his brow.

'Present at that party was Martha Haines. Are you acquainted with her?'

'Yes.' The question puzzled Petrosian. She was the local public librarian, a plump, motherly woman. He saw her every fortnight over the library counter.

'Are you aware that Miss Haines is a member of the Daughters of Bilitis?'

'The who?'

'A lesbian organization, sir. You also attended meetings at the house of Paul and Hannah Chapman, who are known to be functionaries of the Communist Party. Paul Chapman was recently dismissed from employment with General Electric as a security risk. I don't suppose you remember those meetings either.'

'I have a lot of friends from my Los Alamos days. I neither know nor care about their affiliations.'

'Yes, let's go back to those Los Alamos days, Doctor.'

A vague feeling of dread began to suffuse through Petrosian's body. 'Let me say it again. I have a lot of friends from my Los Alamos days. I neither know nor care about their affiliations.'

'One acquaintance in particular.'

Kitty! They want me to squeal on Kitty. The bastards! Petrosian wondered if they had noticed the anger which gripped his body.

Alvarez was pretending to read a name. 'A Miss Catherine Cronin. You knew this woman?'

Get the tone right. Don't get hostile, play it cool. 'Kitty Cronin. Yes, we were friends.'

'You were friends.' Alvarez was almost gloating. 'And what was the nature of this friendship?'

Picnics in the woods. Skiing. Glorious days on

mountain trails. Barbecues. Movies. Soft, hot flesh and tousled hair on pillows, and passion, and fun. And none of your fucking business. 'We were good friends.'

'How good?'

Show the bastard up. Force him to ask the intimate stuff. Make him look like the prying goat he is. 'We were close.'

Alvarez, however, seemed to sense a trap. He changed tack. 'Did you and she not meet on every occasion when you took time off from your wartime work on the Los Alamos mesa?'

'We did, which wasn't often.'

'On January 14th 1943, did you and Kitty Cronin not conduct a meeting in her house near Santa Fe? And was Klaus Fuchs, the atom spy, not also present at that meeting?'

'I don't recall. Yes I do.' Petrosian steepled his fingers in thought. 'There was a bunch of us. Dick Feynman, Klaus, someone else I can't remember. We all took off in Dick's car. It wasn't a meeting of course, that's just your way of making it sound purposeful and sinister. We just took off for the day to have a picnic and a good time. As I recall we went into Santa Fe first. Dick had arranged to pick up some girl.'

'Did you not stay overnight with Miss Cronin after the others had left?'

'The question is outrageous. A gentleman doesn't ask, nor does he tell.'

Their eyes locked. Alvarez twitched, wondering whether to make an issue of Lev's defiance. Then: 'Did you not, in the course of that evening, pass over a document to Miss Cronin?'

'No.'

It was a lie.

And Alvarez knew it.

The faces on the bench were now displaying a range of expressions from grim to angry. Petrosian felt the hostility like a physical, crushing pressure.

'Were you, at Los Alamos, a close friend of a Doctor David Bohm?'

Petrosian nodded. 'It was a small, intense, closed community. Everyone knew everyone else.'

'Let it be put on the record that Petrosian admitted to friendship with David Bohm. Are you aware that Oppenheimer has described him as an extremely dangerous man?'

'No, but it doesn't surprise me. David is full of danger-ous ideas. That's not the same as disloyalty.'

The dirt farmer again: 'Let me get this right, Mister Paytrojan from Russia. Yo're admitting you hob-nob with commies and front organizations, but still you claim you ain't red.'

'Correct.'

'Not even pink?'

Someone near the back of the room laughed.

Alvarez with a twitch: 'Doctor, I'd like to explore this curious claim of yours a little further, if I may. You are aware that the Communist Party in this country is a channel for espionage?'

'No, sir.'

The senator sighed. 'I remind you, sir, that you're under oath.'

Lev shrugged. 'I'm aware of common perceptions in this area. I have no hard evidence to support them.'

Mr Arkansas was leaning over his microphone. His voice was dripping scorn. 'I ain't been to Australia. Are you saying I shouldn't believe it exists because I ain't seen it with my own eyes? Maybe you think Australia is hearsay or sumthin?' There was some tittering from the audience, and the congressman grinned again, openly basking in his wit. Petrosian sat quietly, blinking through his spectacles.

Alvarez threw a brief, irritated glance at his Arkansas colleague. 'Doctor, the American Communist Party has been designated by the Attorney General as a subversive organization which seeks to overthrow the form of government of the United States by unconstitutional means, within the purview of Executive Orders 9835 and 10450. Given time, we could find any number of highly authoritative sources, from former communists to professors of history, who will confirm that communism has emerged as a world power with the stated goal of dominating all mankind. In the light of all this, Doctor, are you happy with the statement you have just made?'

Petrosian shook his head stubbornly. 'I don't belong to the American Communist Party and never have. I have no direct knowledge of their activities. I hear the accusations but for all I know they're the product of paranoia or mass hysteria. Or plain stupidity: there's plenty of that around.'

'Don't be absurd.' Dodds was adopting a use-your-common-sense tone. In Petrosian's mind, the identification with Himmler was becoming complete. 'Everyone knows that the Party uses conspiracy, infiltration and intrigue, deceit and duplicity and falsehood. It has infiltrated our universities, our culture and even our State Department.'

Petrosian sat quietly.

'Answer the question,' Dodds-Himmler said sharply, his eyes hard behind his steel-rimmed glasses.

'I'm sorry, I didn't recognize that as a question.'

'Were you a Communist Party member in Germany, before you fled to this country?'

'No.'

Another lie.

Petrosian wondered in near-panic what they knew, whether they had noticed his tiny hesitation. But how to explain to these morons that he had joined first for the love of a girl, and then to oppose thugs, and never out of any conviction about new world orders or similar nonsense?

Dodds-Himmler picked up a sheet of paper and handed it down to the stenographer, who seemed to be doubling as a clerk. Lev became aware of a tremendous tension in his jaw muscles. He tried to relax them, but his body wasn't obeying his brain. 'I'm now going to show you a copy of an entry held in FBI files. Mister Chairman, this is an extract from Gestapo files brought to the States in 1945, and indexed in 1948. I request that this extract be put in the record.'

'It may be made part of the record.'

'The entry is of course in German, a language in which I believe you are fluent, Doctor. Perhaps you would read it out in English for this Subcommittee. Do try to be accurate; I have an English translation in front of me.'

Petrosian read through the brief paragraph. It was a Gestapo file about him, and it was the first time he had set eyes on it. He couldn't control the trembling in his voice:

```
Petrosian, Lev, student of physics, born
29 December 1911. Subject is associated
with Communist cell active in Kiel. Was
previously active member of Communist
Party in Leipzig. In 1932 and 1933,
contacted known pro-Soviet academics
during visits to Berlin and Heidelberg.
Visited briefly the Austrian Jewess Lise
Meitner at the Nobel Institute in
Stockholm.
   Rüsselheim, RSHA IVA, Gestapo Field
Office, Kiel.
```

'The letters RSHA—' Dodds-Himmler began.

'—refer to the Central Office of Security Police,' Petrosian interrupted. 'Our paths have crossed.' Something dangerous in Petrosian's voice; Dodds backed off.

'*Associated with communist cells . . . active member of Communist Party.*' Dodds waited for Lev's response, his eyebrows raised. There was an expectant stillness in the room. Lev remained silent. 'Would you please explain the circumstances.'

'I was a student in Germany. In those days the communists were the only real opposition to the fascists.'

Mister Arkansas was displaying his teeth again. 'You don't say,' he repeated with exaggerated sarcasm.

'I ran with them for about two years. That was from 1932 to 1934. Not out of belief in their system, but because I opposed the Nazis.'

'Opposed them? By running with Communist street gangs?'

'With respect, you just don't know what it was like.'

Alvarez was passing down another piece of paper, this one like a sheet from a stenographer's notebook. 'I'm going to show you a page from a notebook left on your desk at Los Alamos on March 1945. It was drawn to the attention of the Board of Regents some weeks ago.' Petrosian's hands were trembling slightly as he took it.

'Would you confirm that this is your handwriting?'

'Yes.'

'It has calculations on it.'

'Yes. How did you get hold of this?'

'We ask the questions here. Look at the handwritten note on the top right-hand corner of the page. Mister Chairman, the actual writing was done on the page above, but the message was recovered by the FBI through high contrast photography and other techniques. Doctor, would you read it out, please?'

'Jürgen, Grand Central, 4.15 p.m.'

'This is a note to meet someone called Jürgen, is it not?'

'Yes.'

'In your handwriting?'

'Yes.'

'Who is this Jürgen?'

'Jürgen Rosenblum. A colleague from my pre-war days. I was arranging to meet him in New York.'

'And did you?'

'Yes.' Petrosian was beginning to feel faint. His back and thighs were wet with sweat.

'What precisely was the nature and purpose of this meeting with Rosenblum?'

'Why do you make it sound like something sinister? It was a simple social meeting. We have a common bond. We'd both been persecuted by the Nazis, we'd both escaped from Nazi Germany. You clearly haven't the faintest idea what that means to those of us who came through. As to the purpose of the meeting? The purpose was talk. We talked about people we knew who'd made it out, people who hadn't. We talked about science. We talked about books. We talked about the ladies. We talked and we talked—'

'Was political discussion part of all this talk?'

'Stuff like that, yes, of course.'

'I'll bet,' Alvarez said. He paused. Then: 'Did you not meet Rosenblum in an internee camp for enemy aliens in Sherbrooke, Canada, in 1939? And did you not there register with the Communist Party through Rosenblum?'

'Register? What are you talking about?'

'You know perfectly well, and before you continue with that insolent tone, sir, I ask you to remember who you're talking to. I'm not suggesting that application forms or membership cards changed hands. How was it done,

Doctor Petrosian? With a handshake in some quiet corner? A nod and a wink? An understanding that in due course you might be approached for information? Were you ever a loyal resident of America? Or have you not always been a mole, a sleeper, a Trojan horse, first in Harwell and then Los Alamos?'

'No.'

Alvarez said, 'Mister Chairman, I wish to enter the following documents in the record. They are, first, decoded extracts of messages obtained in 1939 by the British MI5 between Moscow and the Russian Embassy in London. They refer to one Leo, a GRU officer planted amongst the internees for the specific purpose of befriending refugee scientists and opening up what they call "channels of communication". The second document is an assessment by MI5 that the GRU agent in question was probably Jurgen Rosenblum.'

'Why was this Rose in Bloom allowed into America?' Mister Arkansas asked.

'The fog of war,' Alvarez replied. 'The MI5 filed their report away, and our FBI wasn't notified of their suspicions until 1943. A long surveillance failed to come up with anything until 1951. That was the meeting between Petrosian and Rosenblum.'

'Where is Rose in Bloom now?' Mister Arkansas wanted to know.

'He is living openly in New York City.' Alvarez turned his attention again to the sweating physicist. 'I'd like to get back, if I may, to the meeting you attended on July 7th at the home of Paul and Hannah Chapman.'

'It was a social evening. Their wedding anniversary, as I recall.'

'So you said. Who else attended this social evening?'

'You want me to name names?'

'You ain't a commie, right?' the Arkansas congressman asked. Lev nodded. 'So what's the problem?'

Petrosian momentarily closed his eyes. He hesitated, took a deep breath, and then said, 'Okay. Okay. Okay. I did attend one meeting of the Communist Party. There were about twenty of us present.'

The room went still.

'We were addressed by a very important Hollywood personage.' Petrosian's voice was shaky, and he was taking breath in deep gulps.

'Take your time. Tell us about it.' Mister Arkansas's eyes were gleaming. Confess your sins, my son. Unburden your soul.

'This was July 7th, just after the Chapman party. I was directed to go to Greers Ferry Park after dark.'

'Who delivered this message?'

'My –' Petrosian lowered his voice '– my controller.'

The tip-tip of the stenographer; the faint whirr of the movie cameras; something rustling in the parched grass outside.

'Your *controller*?' The congressman's voice was almost a whisper. Don't break the atmosphere. Let the confession flow. He leaned forward across the desk.

'Yes. My controller.'

'Who was this controller?'

'I've never set eyes on him.'

'How did he deliver his message?'

'It came to me by thought rays.'

A bewildered expression crossed the congressman's face.

Petrosian continued, 'There was a flying saucer in the park. It was about fifty feet across and twenty high. There was an open ramp and I went into it. I sat at a porthole and it took off. We went right up there at amazing speed but I didn't feel any acceleration. We flew over to Los Angeles to collect John Wayne. He just materialized right there in front of us, in the middle of the saucer.' There was a suppressed belly laugh from the back of the room. Petrosian continued: 'Then we went on to Saturn, which by the way is my home planet. It only took us half an hour. There we met the Leader. He was tanned with long blond hair and kind blue eyes. He told us that world domination by aliens is the only way forward for the salvation of mankind and world communism was only a step on the way and asked if we would help in this great enterprise.'

The deathly hush had been replaced by a scattering of giggles, and now laughter was surging through the room. The congressman, his face contorted by anger, was hammering the gavel. He shouted, 'I hairby cite Doctor Lev Paytrojan for perjury and contempt of these hair proceedings,' but Petrosian, mouth up against the microphone, was still testifying: 'Then the Duke gave us the low-down on how his boys were infiltrating Hollywood and influencing American minds while he acted the part of the anti-red to fool people like you. There are lots of fine Hollywood Americans in this enterprise, I'll give you that list now.'

REVELATION
___

The audience had split into two camps, half of it booing angrily, the other half laughing and applauding. The congressman was hammering the gavel sharply and shouting 'Remove this man from the microphone,' but Petrosian's voice was still coming over the uproar. 'There are three hundred names on it, people like Gary Cooper and Daryl Zanuck at the top.'

The security men, big hulks of overweight menace, were bearing down. Petrosian stood up. At the door, he glanced back at the scene of bedlam he had created. Mr Arkansas was still hammering at the desk. Dodds-Himmler was staring through his steel-rimmed spectacles at the physicist as if he had just landed from a flying saucer. The nervous twitch in Alvarez's cheek was in full swing. Half a dozen reporters were scribbling furiously.

Powerful hands gripped Petrosian's elbows. His last view of the room was the clock. The interview, it had seemed to him, had lasted a gruelling three or four hours. He was astonished to see that it had taken only twenty-five minutes.

In the corridor, Lev was startled by a sudden blaze of popping flashlights. He found himself wedged in by a scrum of reporters. He pushed his way along the corridor, answering a babble of questions as politely as he could. In the playground, near the school entrance, another movie camera had been put in place.

As he drifted towards the street, dragging the entourage, a taxi stopped and disgorged a man and woman. The man was small, round-faced and nearly bald. The woman was about thirty, with long dark hair and dressed in a long green coat. She took the man's arm and they walked unnoticed in the direction of the school. It was some moments before Lev recognized her, but when he did the reporters and the microphones and the gabble faded away, and a lump rose in Lev's throat. Their eyes met briefly as they passed. Contact was impossible. She gave a brief, wan smile and then was gone, and Petrosian thought that, apart from a little extra weight around the hips and a few wrinkles around the eyes, Kitty had changed little in eight years, and as he fought back the tears he realized that he had always loved her and always would.

'You bloody fool,' Brogan said for the fourth time in an hour.

'I'm in love with your wife, Max,' said Petrosian, smiling over at her. She raised her eyebrows and rattled a skillet onto the big electric hotplate. 'It's her crawfish pie,' said Petrosian, helping himself to more.

'Then you'd better fill up on it. You won't get any where you're headed.'

A black waitress came in through the swing door, carrying a pile of plates on each arm. 'Nummer Four wann bare an fraid aigs an oyster po-boy with dirty rice, the main in One say is yawl gone fishin for ma baked grouper, an Three doan finish their bean stew.'

'Gombee faive mins for the grouper,' Mary Brogan called back. She poured Southern Comfort into the skillet, shook it, and flames leapt towards a burned-black patch in the ceiling.

Max waved his arms. 'Some grand gesture that achieves nothing, as in zilch, as in a big round frigging zero. What the hell got into you, Lev? A good career down the tubes and maybe a year in some godawful pokey.'

'Stuffed with queers and sadistic wardens,' Petrosian suggested.

'Why did you do it, Lev? Why did you throw away your future?'

Petrosian sipped at the Coca-Cola. 'Those creeps just got up my nose.'

'Lev, maybe you can afford the grand gesture, but I have kids to get through school. And what if people start to boycott this place? All it needs is some American Legion redneck to hand out leaflets at the door and we might as well rename this place The Commie Diner.'

'Mary's not a communist, is she?'

'Come on, Lev, what the hell has that got to do with anything? Association is all it takes.' Max's expression was pained.

Lev said, softly, 'Out with it.'

There was an unbearable stress in Brogan's voice. 'Look, Lev, I'm sorry. But maybe you shouldn't come around for a while. You know – career. Mary and the boys.'

Lev nodded sadly. 'I understand fully, Max. Don't worry about it. Nothing in our friendship says you have to stand up to the bad guys like Gary Cooper in *High Noon*. I'll stay away awhile.'

The relief was palpable. Brogan extended his hand and Lev shook it silently. The Texan looked quizzically at his friend. 'I finally get it.'

'What's that, Max?'

'Your testimony to these creeps. It was the absolute truth. You really do come from Saturn.'

15

The Super

'Don't stop,' Stefi ordered.

The Chinese take-away had grown cold in the kitchen, and Romella's voice was becoming strained with the translation. Stefi had found a long, silk dressing gown with a dragon motif in one of Doug's wardrobes and was wearing it over yellow pyjamas. She was sitting on the floor with her legs folded underneath her. A black marble clock, all Victorian angels and curlicues, was about to strike one a.m.

'All this red scare stuff,' Romella asked. 'Was there any substance to it?' The swollen flesh around her right eye had developed a yellowish-green hue.

'It was before my time,' Findhorn said. 'I think the hysteria peaked in the 1950s. You know, it was a sort of *Invasion of the Bodysnatchers* thing. Your neighbour may look just like you but his mind may be under alien control.'

'Or her mind,' Stefi said. She was resting her head wearily on her hands.

'But surely it wasn't all hysteria, Fred. The communists wanted a world ruled by Moscow. And there were spies. Hell, we've just been reading about Klaus Fuchs.'

'Sure there were spies, but the witch-hunters didn't find them. Their success rate was practically zero. Imagine shooting your neighbours at random on the off-chance that one of them might be a spy. With all that misdirected effort, I suspect the McCarthy era was a golden age for the KGB.'

'What about Petrosian?' Stefi asked. 'Was he really a spy? And why are people fighting to get their hands on the diaries? Why do they want to kill you and what's in the diaries worth millions and—'

'Okay. Stefi wants her ten per cent. Read on, Romella.'

Petrosian's habits were those of a quiet and studious bachelor. In the evening he would take something easy out of the icebox and stick it in a frying pan. While it was frying he would pour himself a Martini. He would eat whatever it was, and watch whatever was on his small black-and-white television set, without paying much attention to either. The rest of the evening would be spent reading, writing or marking student exercises. On Fridays, however, he let his hair down: he ate in Mary's kitchen, and played five-stud with Max and friends until the early hours, generally winning enough to pay for the beers he brought along.

But that was before the loyalty trials. Now a barrier, invisible and yet almost tangible, had come between Petrosian and his acquaintances.

This Friday evening, having had a last supper in the Sweet and Tart, he was sipping a cold beer on his porch, a light sweat on his brow and arms. It was a sultry thirty-two degrees. Down the road, through an open window, Ella Fitzgerald was 'Eating Baloney on Coney', but she was having problems being heard over the insect night life and a distant yelping dog.

Tonight, Lev had put his normally restless mind on hold; mentally drained, he was finding simple pleasure in watching a near-full moon drift behind the willow tree in his neighbour's garden. Satchmo took it through the branches and into a starry sky. The dog was still yelping.

Around ten o'clock a big car, all whitewall tyres and tail fins and with an out-of-town number, gurgled slowly past Lev's house. Two men inside, clearly unfamiliar with the area, were scanning the street. A couple of minutes later the car returned, turned into Lev's driveway, and disgorged the two. One had short, neat hair and was incongruously dressed in a dark suit and tie. The other could hardly have been a greater contrast: he was unkempt and casually dressed, with a creased open-necked shirt and a jacket draped over his arm.

'Doctor Petrosian?'

'You look like FBI,' Petrosian said.

'Lieutenant Mercier, sir, Army Intelligence.' A badge was briefly flashed in the half-dark. 'And this is Mister Smith. Can we talk?'

'Sure.'

In the living room, hospitality was politely declined. The three men sat round a small circular table. The long-haired Mister Smith gave Petrosian a calculated smile. His affiliation, Lev noticed, was going unannounced.

Petrosian tried a shot in the dark. 'You look like an academic,' he said to Smith.

Smith kept smiling.

Petrosian finished his beer and leaned back, puzzled. 'Okay, I give up. Who are you?'

The army man said, 'This meeting is not taking place. We're not here.'

'Okay,' Petrosian said cautiously.

'And nothing said here is to be repeated outside this room.'

'There's a problem with that. I'm a card-carrying communist. Anything you say to me goes straight to Moscow.'

Mercier looked as if he was taking the comment seriously. 'We know all about the College enquiry, and we know exactly what was said at it today.'

Petrosian shook his head, mystified. 'I'll be out of work and on a blacklist within a week. What could the army possibly want with me?'

Mercier said, 'The army wouldn't touch you with a barge pole.'

'So why are you here?' Petrosian asked, baffled.

The army man reached down for his briefcase and pulled out an envelope. Petrosian's visitors watched him closely as he put down his empty beer glass and tore it open. He read the letter twice, and looked at his guests with surprise.

'Look at it from this point of view, Doctor Petrosian,' said Smith. 'As you say, you'll be out of a job within days. And once you're on that blacklist you'll never work in

America again, except maybe emptying trash cans. Try to leave America and you'll find that the State Department denies you a passport.'

'And you turn up waving this letter under my nose. Your timing is supernatural.'

Smith still had the calculated grin. 'All you need worry about are the address and the signature.' The sharp, crabbed scrawl of Norris Bradbury – Oppenheimer's successor at Los Alamos – had leapt out at Petrosian the instant he had unfolded the letter.

'And my loyalty?'

Petrosian's visitors didn't react. Lev assessed their blank stares. Then he continued, 'I think I can guess what you people are up to.'

Now Mercier raised a finger to his lips, shaking his head urgently. He mouthed the word: *Bugs.*

Petrosian looked astonished. 'Are you serious?'

'Why not? You're a suspected commie.'

'They surely have no legal right.'

The army man finally grinned. 'Oh my. You really do come from Saturn,' he said, and Petrosian wondered how on earth they had managed to bug the Sweet and Tart's busy kitchen.

Smith sat with Petrosian in the back of the car, the better to brief him as they drove through the hot night. 'By the way, my name is Griggs. Ken Griggs.'

Mercier, at the wheel of the car, glanced back. 'And I'm Mercier.'

'So we're going for the Super?'

In the half-dark, Petrosian saw Griggs give a nod. 'We're in a race, Lev.'

'I don't know if a hydrogen bomb is even feasible.'

'If the Soviets get one before us . . .'

'Somewhere in Russia there are guys talking exactly the same way.'

Mercier said, '*Pravda* regularly accuse us of planning an atomic war.'

'Are we?'

'The President doesn't confide in me. Still, if we built a couple of dozen H-bombs we could rule the world.'

'Or end it in an hour,' Griggs added playfully.

'Hey, maybe I'd rather empty trash cans,' Petrosian said.

Mercier was slowing to avoid a pothole. 'What gives with the angst? It's a simple matter of national security. The Russians are doing it, so we have to.'

Griggs said, 'The price of freedom is eternal vigilance, if you want peace prepare for war, and those who ignore history are condemned to repeat it. That'll be fifteen bucks. I charge five dollars a cliché.'

'Hey, watch your tone,' complained Mercier.

'I asked you about my loyalty,' Petrosian said.

Mercier spoke over his shoulder, 'If it was up to me you wouldn't get within a hundred miles of Los Alamos.'

Griggs said, 'The AEC operates a security clearance procedure.'

'In which case I'm back to trash cans.'

'If somebody, say like Mercier here, queries your loyalty you've had it. Doubt is all it takes and the onus is on you to dispel that doubt. You can forget about questioning evidence, the right to cross-examine witnesses and stuff like that. The procedure stands Anglo-Saxon jurisprudence on its head.'

'I don't understand.'

'But at least we have due process. You could, for example, appeal to the Personnel Security Review Board. The real purpose of the procedure is to keep HUAC at bay. Now if these monsters got their claws into you . . .'

Mercier's tone was jarring. 'These monsters just happen to be our best line of defence against internal subversion. Everyone knows the reds take their orders from Moscow. We're rooting out traitors.'

'You see what you're up against, Lev.'

Petrosian said, 'From what you guys are telling me I haven't a hope of getting into the project.'

'I'm lost.' Mercier was peering along a tunnel of light which showed only an endless, ruler-straight road. Moonlight revealed them to be insects crawling over an infinite, flat, desolate surface.

'Turn left two miles ahead. That'll take us back into town.'

'The fancy footwork is this,' Griggs said. 'The final decision on security is made by the AEC commissioners themselves. They don't have to take anyone's advice. But it's not a trick they dare to pull off more than once. I guess Bradbury sees your talents as vital to the project.'

'I'm flattered. But I might start giving secrets away to the Russians.' Sweat was trickling down Petrosian's back and his thighs were wet against the plastic upholstery.

Griggs said, 'I have to say that Bradbury wants you over the dead bodies of some of the others, Strauss especially. Still, it's like this, Lev. Our success in this project depends on our ability to attract men of talent and vision into it. These men will have all sorts of backgrounds and all sorts of viewpoints. Paranoia is a luxury we can't afford.'

'Army Intelligence are against you,' Mercier said. It wasn't clear whether he was talking to Griggs or Petrosian.

'Listen to the man, Lev, and be aware. You have no guarantee of protection. All this soft-headed liberal thinking the scientists do, exchanging information with colleagues abroad and stuff like that. It's disloyal, and it proves we're under communist influence. Therefore HUAC wants the army to take over the hydrogen bomb project. So does the army.'

'So where do I stand in this?'

'In this struggle, Lev, you're a very small fish. Take my advice and stay that way. Stick to science and keep your mouth shut on policy matters. The guy they're really after, the big whale, is Oppenheimer.'

Four weeks later Petrosian turned up at Los Alamos, having effectively vanished from Greers Ferry. After an absence of seven years, the diaries revealed no sentiment, no sense of homecoming, of loss or gain. Rather, they gave the impression of a man who had been away for a long weekend. Kitty Cronin's name was painfully absent. The pages were filled with the hydrogen bomb. Over the course of the year they became increasingly technical and

Findhorn could scarcely understand the entries. Romella began to stumble over many of the technical words. Some of them had been written in English, probably, she thought, because there was no precise equivalent in the Armenian.

Near the end of 1953, however, Petrosian's prose style suddenly changed. The entries became longer, the text became both enthusiastic and ferociously technical, and the handwriting was that of a man who could hardly write fast enough to get the words down.

By now they could hardly understand a word. But the crabbed writing, the cryptic style and the air of enthusiasm told the same story to Romella and Findhorn. The Armenian physicist was onto something.

The first such entry was on 29 November. Stefi had appeared with hot chocolate and biscuits, and Romella's voice was now slurred with tiredness.

Petrosian's diary, Sunday, 29 November 1953

Spent the day ski-ing on Sawyer Hill. Snow-plows, dead stops, jumps, lots of bruises. Cloudless day. Then did something really stupid. On an impulse I gathered up camping stuff and went to the end of Frijoles Canyon, where it joins the Rio Grande. Wonderful solitude, even the rattlers were gone. Bivouacked out. Bitterly cold.

Woke up early hours. Lay and looked at the brilliant starry sky, and with no effort on my part a thought jumped into my head. It just came. I suddenly realized that the two most awesome experiments in physics – the Casimir effect and Foucault's pendulum – are connected. Maybe it was all that talk with Bethe on ZPE. More likely it was a gift from God.

And the connection lets me solve an ancient problem: how do we know that ten minutes in ancient Greece was the same length of time as ten minutes today? We can compare metre sticks by carrying them around, but we can't transport clocks back and forth in time. Quantum fluctuations in ZPE are the answer. They give us an absolute clock, constant throughout all space and for all time.

Can we possibly have been thinking about physics the wrong way for the past forty years??!!

Okay so ZPE might not be observable because it permeates everything but changes in it surely are. If this is right, then the vacuum is a bottomless pit. The wonderful thing is that ZPE might be changed by fiddling boundary conditions, like the Casimir plates.

Leading to a fantasy thought. Could I squeeze hydrogen into small enough cavities so that low frequency ZPE is excluded and the atoms have to shrink? And so release energy? If the Coulomb barrier is overcome with a Casimir pinch, what then? Do we head for Planck energy?

Head swirling with fantastic thoughts. Can't sleep – anyway I resent the time it takes up.

Findhorn was suddenly on his feet. He paced up and down excitedly, muttering and shaking his head. Momentarily, he looked at the women wildly with bloodshot eyes. Then he carried on pacing.

'Fred!' Romella pleaded.

He paused to look at her. 'I can't tell you.'

'We're shareholders, damn you,' Stefi pointed out.

'It's too bizarre, too way out. I must be wrong.'

Stefi blocked his path. 'Try us.'

Findhorn shook his head energetically. 'You wouldn't understand. You're only a linguist.' He looked at the clock: it showed two thirty a.m. 'Stefi, I want you to get me on the next available flight to America. Not from Edinburgh airport. I'll give you my credit card number.'

'I'm only a linguist, I can't do things like that. Where in America?'

'Los Alamos. I want to nose around.'

Romella was shaking her head. 'Fred, the people you met in Fat Sam's . . .'

'. . . are almost certainly acting for the American Government.'

'And you want to put your head in the lion's mouth?'

'America is the last place they'd expect me to go. I'm gambling that my name won't be on their Immigration Department computers.'

'I'll come,' Romella said. 'The FBI must have old files on Petrosian.'

Findhorn blinked with surprise. 'You intend to just walk into the FBI offices in Washington and ask about Petrosian? You're mad.'

'As you say, Fred, it's the last thing they'd expect. They're looking for us in Edinburgh. I'm betting their right hand doesn't know what their left is doing. It's the same gamble.'

Stefi said, 'You're both mad.'

Romella said, 'You'll have to pay my fare, Fred. I'm skint.'

'Don't do it,' Stefi said.

'Give me an account number and I'll feed money into it.'

'Please can I come too?' Stefi asked. 'I've never been to America.'

Findhorn shook his head. 'You're needed here. See what you can find out about green Mercs registered in Switzerland.'

Stefi attempted a pout.

Romella picked up the photocopies and tapped them into a neat pile. 'At least tell us this, Fred. What's ZPE?'

'It stands for zero point energy. It's the lowest possible energy state any system can have.'

'I know the feeling.'

16

Cult

The first time round, it might have been his imagination.

But not the second. There it was again, a faint bump from the room directly below him. He struggled with the geometry of the house before settling on Doug's study.

Findhorn reckoned he had been asleep for about two hours.

He lay in the dark, his heart thumping, straining to hear. Long ago, the fire authorities had insisted that metal stairs should come from the top floor of the big house down to the back garden. These stairs were reached through the window in Stefi's room. Sensible to get the women and himself out, call the police from a public box.

He wriggled his feet into Doug's slippers and wrapped a dressing gown round himself before opening the door, an inch at a time. Faint light came up the stairwell.

He stepped quietly down the stairs, knowing it was against all sense. The study door was slightly ajar. Keeping about two feet back from the door, he peered in, the strong light hurting his eyes.

Romella, in a peach-colored negligée, was at the keyboard of Doug's machine, staring intently at the monitor. Findhorn couldn't make out the text on the screen, the angle was too awkward. Unexpectedly, she glanced in his direction. He pulled away and slipped back up the stairs, uncertain whether he had been seen.

In bed, he lay on his back and thought that maybe his long sojourns in Arctic environments had made him stupid, that mixing with nobody but people like himself had made him fail to appreciate the range and depth of human duplicity. That maybe the Fat Sam's people had reached Romella before he did, or that her brief captivity had turned her. Archie's words, 'Trust nobody', kept forcing themselves into his head.

They had the diaries. But they would know that Findhorn had made copies. Maybe they wanted the copies destroyed. Maybe the bandstand incident was a setup, maybe he had been allowed to escape with Romella. Maybe Romella appreciated the finer things in life, things you could do with a million pounds. All she had to do was find the files and press the delete button. Not a lot to do for a million. What did she owe Findhorn anyway?

Then he thought that maybe circumstances were making him paranoid, that there was a natural explanation, that only a heel would think this way.

He fretted for half an hour, wriggling and turning on wrinkled sheets, feeling betrayed, paranoid and guilty, sometimes all at once, before drifting into a restless sleep.

'You want to be very careful when you talk about a religious cult, Fred. The point is that "cult" is a hate word. It carries emotional baggage and people use it as a weapon to impart bad vibrations to the group they're talking about. Likewise your use of the word "nutter" shows that there's an evil intolerance at work in the murky depths of your subconscious. Most way-out systems of religious belief are harmless and deserve the tolerance—'

Findhorn interrupted, typing rapidly on the keyboard: 'Mike, I stand corrected. I'll try to be good. Still, when you have people whose aim is the destruction of human life . . .'

The signal came back on the screen: 'If that really is the aim and not something that's been ascribed to them by some hate group.'

'Does the manufacture of nerve gas and botulism toxin qualify?'

'Obviously there's a threshold beyond which you have to declare war, if only to protect those you love. Then it's PC to talk about a doomsday cult.'

'These cults exist?'

'There are thousands of minority religious groups on our register, of which a couple of dozen need watching. Even these are largely harmless or at the most a danger to themselves, through suicidal tendencies. The scary thing is that irresponsible geeks have created Internet cookbooks giving step-by-step recipes for making biological toxins, *et cetera*. Aerosol poisons plus doomsday cults are an unholy combination.'

'Mike, you're scaring me.'

Mike continued, his typing coming up rapidly and almost error-free on the monitor: 'There are features common to most of these groups. First of course is the grand apocalyptic vision. Usually they believe that a tragedy is about to hit the earth, say like Armageddon. Sometimes they think that, through group suicide, they'll escape the tragedy and be carried off to heaven, perhaps by UFO.'

'I think I read about one such group.'

'That would be the Heaven's Gate cult, a Christian-UFO group which committed mass suicide when Comet Hale Bopp came in. The body count was thirty-nine. But the belief goes back at least to the Unarians, who've been holding to the UFO thing since 1954 without harming anyone. A second feature is the charismatic leader.'

'Do these leaders have any common traits?'

'Absolutely. They're invariably a dominant male, intelligent or at least cunning, a social misfit or failure in mainstream society, and a control freak. He exerts a sort of hypnotic effect on the faithful which he uses to control their sexual, social and emotional lives.'

'You've just described Adolf Hitler,' Findhorn suggested.

'Careful, Fred. Sensitive area.'

Findhorn paused at the keyboard, uncertain whether to interrupt his old friend, now a university rabbi. Then Michael was typing: 'And another feature of the cult mentality is the accumulation of weapons coupled with a sort of paranoid belief that outsiders or governments are out to get them. They see themselves as being monitored by the FBI or other government agencies.'

'I hope they are.'

'Of course many of the cults, especially the Christian right-wing people, are themselves hate merchants. You don't want to be black, gay, communist or Jewish within a thousand miles of Christ Foremost, for example.'

'Remember Abo? He scored three out of four.'

'Let's hope he never strays into Waco, Texas. Now, do you have a specific group in mind?'

'I need to identify them but the clues are thin. The Book of Revelation seems to be central to them, they're doomsday-minded and there's a Swiss connection, I think.'

There was a pause for about thirty seconds. The study door opened and Romella came in carrying two mugs of tea. She put them down on the desk and looked over Findhorn's shoulder. Then words were coming up on the monitor at speed: 'THE TEMPLE OF CELESTIAL TRUTH.'

Findhorn felt a surge of excitement. Then his friend was typing: 'Hang on, I'm putting them on another screen. Here we are. Yes, it's not one of your big-time doomsday cults. That's the problem, some of these groups are down in the noise and the first you hear of them is when they crawl out of the woodwork with some high-profile atrocity. At its peak the Supreme Truth had forty thousand members worldwide, including thirty thousand in Russia, several of whom were engineers with access to nukes, something you might want to think about. They had assets of a billion dollars—'

'The Celestial Truth?'

'Patience, it's still downloading. This is another Christian-UFO cult, with a hodge-podge of Greek and African myth thrown in. They use prophecies from the Book of Revelation along with the sixteenth-century writings of Nostradamus to predict that world end is due any time. They can't wait for it because when it happens the resultant cleansing of sin will allow the second wave of extraterrestrials to come and carry them up to Heaven.'

'What about their organization? How are they structured?'

'I've got an organogram here, but it's all conjecture. They're thought to have regional chapters which meet to co-ordinate activities. They're highly secretive, dispersed globally, and their membership is totally unknown. They're rich, with widely dispersed assets which may total a billion dollars but nobody really knows. They run a front organization, the Tati Foundation, which supports a wide variety of causes.'

'Where are they located? On Earth, I mean.'

'Hold on. Right, they have temples in Japan and Dakota, but their main spiritual centre is tucked away in a mountain region near Davos, in Switzerland. It's a place called Piz Radönt and it looks like the devil to get to. I've got a photograph here. Hold on, I'll beam it through.'

Findhorn waited while a picture rapidly built up on the screen, line by line, overlaying the text. A blue sky appeared first, and then the tops of snowy peaks, and then the picture was showing golden, onion-shaped domes which seemed more Muslim than Christian, and finally there it was, a big white shoebox in an idyllic mountain setting. Findhorn clicked on a button, reduced the picture to stamp size, and resumed his rapid two-finger typing.

'About this world end they believe in. Is there any evidence that they'd like to speed it along?'

'Okay, here I have unclassified testimony to the Global Organized Crime Project Steering Committee, CSIS to the House of Representatives Committee on National Security.'

Findhorn hadn't a clue but let it pass.

'I'll fire it through but the essence is this. According to this testimony, NEST teams have been activated five times in California in the last two years, three of them in consequence of information pertaining to the Temple of Celestial Truth.'

'Information pertaining to. That's exceedingly vague.'

'Deliberately so, I don't doubt. They have sources to protect. The CIA has a Center for Counterterrorism, and there's an FBI equivalent for domestic stuff, and you could try them for more if you feel like wasting your time. There have also been suspicions of aerosol attacks in Germany from truck convoys, and Korean building collapses deliberately induced by poor loading and use of sub-standard concrete. But so much lousy building goes on anyway in the Far East that nobody can be sure if it was weirdo religion or just officials lining their pockets.'

'What about their leader?'

'Ah, now Freddie, there you have something very interesting.'

Findhorn waited. He read the words avidly as they came up on the monitor. 'You'll be interested to know that this particular outfit is led by a guy called Tati who just happens to come from Sirius. First time round he came to Earth in the body of Jesus. These guys are souls, you see, who just temporarily inhabit human bodies. Kind of like the Incas, who believed they came from the stars and returned to them after death.'

'When he's not being Tati from Sirius, who is he really?'

'That's what makes him interesting. Nobody knows. His background is a *big mystery*.'

'Maybe he really does come from Sirius.'

The rabbi's words came up on the screen: 'There's always that possibility.'

'Well?' Romella asked.

Findhorn was pacing up and down. 'It might be coincidence.'

'It might. Whatever you're talking about.'

'It so happens there's a doomsday cult with a centre near Davos. The Book of Revelation is one of their props.'

'Meaning what?'

Findhorn stopped pacing and Romella handed him his tea. 'I think the diaries were taken from us by the Temple of Celestial Truth. They might even be in this Piz Radönt temple.'

'Fred, don't get too excited. It's all circumstantial. Who was that anyway?'

'Mike? An old pal, a hard-drinking friend from my student days. He trained as a rabbi, did a stint in a kibbutz and came back as university pastor. He lost the use of his limbs after a motorcycle accident and now spends his time keeping up with trends in religious thought everywhere. He's become quite an authority and he makes pots of money out of it.'

'It's a compensation, I suppose.'

'I have to pull over the last batch of diaries. They're scanned into a computer. It'll take me a couple of hours.'

'Okay, I'll grab some sleep.'

'Didn't you sleep?'

'Not a lot. I was surfing the net, trying to get info on Mercedes car sales in Switzerland.'

'Any luck?'

'Sod all.' Romella left the study, looking puzzled at Findhorn's unexpected grin.

I should learn to have a little trust in people, Findhorn told himself as he tapped his way into the cookies, the record of the last five hundred keyboard instructions.

Stefi turned up in a green blouse and skirt, with a black choker and heavy eye shadow and hair freshly blonde and hanging down in ringlets. She was driving a large red Saab with cream upholstery, leaving Findhorn to wonder how close his credit card was to breaking point. She gurgled the car round to the rear lane where Romella and Findhorn tossed holdalls into the boot. She handed Findhorn a folder containing air tickets; Findhorn gave her the key to Doug's flat. Romella sat in front, while Findhorn tried to look invisible in the rear seat.

Stefi took them west, away from the city centre, handling the big car with ease. She drove through the Corstorphine suburbs and onto the M8 towards Glasgow and, beyond it, Prestwick International Airport. She took the car up to a steady eighty and Findhorn felt that he could at last safely poke his nose above windowsill level.

* * *

They slept all the way across the Pond.

'The parting of the ways,' Romella announced. She had a small green holdall at her feet and was glancing from time to time at the taxi queue on the other side of the airport glass.

Findhorn, on the other hand, was looking in the opposite direction, at the Dulles Airport departure screens. 'Would you believe I'm still weary?'

'We could find a hotel,' Romella suggested, leaving Findhorn to wonder what she had in mind.

'There's no time, Ms Grigoryan. The competition must be going flat out.'

'You still don't want to say what you've seen in the diaries?'

Findhorn rubbed his overnight stubble. 'It's too fantastic to be believable, Romella. The chances are it's nothing. I'll have to see what I can find out in Los Alamos, if anything.'

'There's something weird here, Fred. If Petrosian was escaping to Russia he didn't need the diaries to tell them what was going on. So why was he escaping with them?'

Findhorn nodded his agreement. He was still nervous about standing openly in a crowded place. 'I think I need to get to Phoenix and connect to Los Alamos from there.'

The taxi queue was shortening. Romella picked up her bag and Findhorn walked with her towards the automatic doors. She said, 'And I'll see what I can rustle up from old FBI files in Washington. I expect they're public domain by now.'

'Which leaves us with one last question, Romella. Where, in these Yoonited States, shall we meet up?'

Romella said, 'Make it some place where we can't easily be followed. Not a town like Los Alamos or Washington.'

'Sparks flew between Lev and Kitty at the Grand Canyon.'

Romella gave a surprised, sunny smile. 'What's this, Fred? Could there be romance buried somewhere in the depths of your soul?'

'I'm mad, bad and dangerous to know.' He yawned. 'The south rim of the Grand Canyon, then, just as soon as we can make it.'

'Be careful, Fred. Remember you're still a target.'

Findhorn made a face. 'Tell me about it.'

A taxi drew up and Romella turned as she opened the door. 'And don't speak to any strange women.'

17

Los Alamos

> YOU ARE ENTERING AN ACTIVE EXPLOSIVES
> TEST RANGE. AREAS ARE POTENTIALLY
> CONTAMINATED WITH EXPLOSIVE DEVICES.
> STAY ON THE ROADS. DO NOT TOUCH OR
> DISTURB ANY ITEMS. IF ITEMS ARE FOUND
> CALL THE WHITE SANDS POLICE.

The morning sun was already *hot*. The wind which gently shook the sign was tumbling sagebrush along the high desert landscape and Findhorn, feeling like a fried tomato after his six-hour taxi ride from Phoenix, was grateful for it. The cab trailed dust as it vanished, its driver weary but richer.

Two men were waiting just outside the barbed wire, next to a yellow sports car. One of them, surly, in a tan uniform with a black belt and bearing a holstered side-arm, appraised Findhorn with small, deep-set, suspicious eyes. The civilian was about thirty, tall, bespectacled, slightly stooped and had receding, balding hair. He also had stubble and the air of a man who hadn't slept overnight. A cluster of observatory domes glinted a few hundred yards away.

'Cartwright of *The Times*, I presume,' said the man. His handshake was tired, his hand clammy in spite of the dry air.

'My friends call me Ed or Eddie.'

'I'm Frank. I don't have any friends.'

Findhorn waved an arm towards the observatory domes. 'Isn't that where they hunt for threat asteroids?'

The guard looked as if Findhorn had just introduced himself as an armed terrorist.

'Hey, how did you know that?' White asked.

Findhorn smiled. 'That's another story.'

The guard wasn't returning any smiles today. 'Before this goes any further, let's see your ID, mister.' Findhorn produced passport and a hastily forged letter of authorization with a *Times* letterhead scanned in from the newspaper.

'Yes, that's one of the LINEAR telescopes,' said White, while the guard examined Findhorn's papers with an air of deep suspicion. 'Part of the Air Force GEODSS system. If you want clearance for a visit it'll take you two months and three layers of bureaucracy, and that's if you're American.'

'Listen, it's good of you to meet me down here. We're still about two hundred miles south of Los Alamos, *n'est ce pas?*'

The guard returned Findhorn's papers looking like a man who knows he's being conned but can do nothing about it. White motioned Findhorn towards the convertible Corvette, and waved his arm wearily at the receding guard. In the car, the black leather seat threatened to roast Findhorn's backside and thighs.

The little machine took off with a satisfying, sporty roar. Findhorn assumed that, this close to the ground, the alarming speed was an optical illusion.

'Sure,' White said. 'But you seemed in one hell of a hurry to write your piece about this Petrosian. And as it happens I had overnight business here.' The nature of the business went unexplained, but White added: 'We're only a mile from the Trinity Site. Now clearance for *that* . . .'

Findhorn laughed but the speedometer was showing eighty five and it came out a bit high-pitched.

Through the terracotta desert, with its wonderful pinks and purples, and distant mountains covered with snow. Past the Santa Ana Reservation, and the roadside Navajo women selling jewellery and rugs and Clint Eastwood ponchos.

Around midday, with the sun beginning to fry his brain, Findhorn was relieved to see a sign for Los Alamos.

'Most people like Los Alamos,' White was saying over a ninety-mile-an-hour wind. 'It looks for all the world like any university town. One thing about it you should remember, though.'

'The security?' Findhorn asked, his hair being pulled at the roots.

'The altitude. It's nearly eight thousand feet up. Unless you're acclimatised to that, you can't run.'

'Why would I want to run?'

White gave him a ghoulish grin. He dropped his speed, went down a gear, and in minutes they were trickling past pink and green adobe houses, and more jewellery and rugs. Near the town centre, the nuclear physicist squeezed his Corvette in between a battered yellow Oldsmobile and a string of motorcycles.

'Some people describe Los Alamos as the world's greatest concentration of nerds,' White complained. 'This is a grave injustice to Berkeley, Calfornia. But one thing missing from this community is mediocrity. It makes for a kinda skewed population.'

They were in the Blue Adobe on Central Avenue. It had walls three feet thick, and canned mariachi music, and the best air conditioning in the known Universe. Memorabilia and photographs from the Manhattan Project lined the walls. They had been lucky to find a spare booth in the crowded little restaurant. 'We have so many PhDs – the highest per capita population on Earth – that unless you're a physician you're called plain Mister. Outsiders paint us as overachievers, pressuring our kids, neglecting our wives.'

Findhorn, sensing an open sore, steered White back to the point. 'Petrosian . . .' he began.

A small, Hispanic waitress approached. She gave White a radiant smile.

'Rosa, my beautiful, what about a late breakfast?' asked White.

'For you, Francis, there are huevos rancheros, huevos borrachos or omelette.'

White translated: 'Ed, you can have eggs with green chillies, eggs with red chillies or an omelette. It comes with chillies.'

'I'll have a fried egg,' Findhorn said. On the wall opposite was a 1940s milk box from the Hillside dairy – *From Moo to You* was printed on its side. He added, 'And a glass of milk.'

'Me too,' White said. When Rosa had gone he said, 'To resume. Anything Petrosian did in the 1950s is ancient history. You're talking fifty-year-old physics. Holy moly, Ed, that was before quarks, gluons, QCD, string theory, superstrings. It was the steam age of nuclear physics.'

Findhorn mopped his brow. It felt hot to the touch. He took a shorthand notebook out of his pocket. 'How many particle types do you have?'

'Twenty-five. Everything you see around you, the whole caboodle – even the delectable Rosa – is governed by twenty-five fundamental particles. Don't ask me why twenty-five and not seven or fifteen. Nobody knows.'

'But still you have a theory for all this, the standard model. I never got beyond electrons, protons and neutrons, and of course light particles – photons.'

White nodded. 'The old timers. Use them as building blocks and you have water, CO_2, DNA, coal for your fire, brick for your house, gas for your car and medicine for your kids. The whole of chemistry comes out of combining just these four particles. Imagine Rosa as a shimmering mass of atomic particles.'

'So who needs the other twenty-one – quarks and the like?'

'You do.' White waved at the sunlight pouring in through the big windows. 'Unless you want to go around like some primordial slime, in pitch-black at absolute zero.

Sunlight depends on nuclear fusion, right? Hydrogen combining to give helium with the mass surplus going off as energy? So how do the protons – hydrogen nuclei to you – combine?'

Rosa reappeared with plates of food covered with a red dust. 'You want more chilli on that?'

'People are big on chilli hereabouts,' advised White.

Findhorn nodded, and Rosa sprinkled a generous helping over his fried egg, which, in addition to the red dust, had come with a coating of red and green chillies and a blue corn tortilla. He said, 'I recall that the intense heat you get in the middle of stars is the same as you get in an A-bomb and this heat causes hydrogen atoms to fuse together. This fusing constitutes the transmutation of elements and when that happens it releases even more heat, whence the hydrogen bomb.'

'I'm asking you, *why* does the heat make the atoms merge?'

Findhorn shrugged, and White said, 'It's a lot of stuff about an up-quark converting to a down-quark and a hip bone connecting to a thigh bone. Then you're into the other twenty-one particles. But my point is this, Ed: you don't need to know. Because Petrosian didn't know either. Like I said, they were developing the Bomb in the steam age, when people hadn't gotten beyond nuclear binding energies.'

'I'm trying to follow you,' Findhorn said. Sweat was breaking out of his brow: he had started on his egg.

White waved a fork in the air. 'What I'm getting at is that Petrosian's world is *understood*. There's nothing new to be said about it. It's been raked over by three generations of physicists and all that can possibly be known about it is known.'

The restaurant was beginning to fill up with early lunchers. A bespectacled young man sat down at the table opposite them. He looked like an outdoors type, dressed in blue denim and with long, blond hair tied back in a pony-tail. In any other situation, Findhorn would never have noticed him. 'You're telling me that Petrosian can't possibly have discovered anything relevant to modern science.'

White nodded his agreement. 'Petrosian's world was one of protons, neutrons and electrons. Any discovery he made in that area would long since have been redis-covered by someone else. There are no surprises left in the nuclear energies the Los Alamos pioneers worked at.'

'And the new particles? The other twenty-one?'

'To see the exotic stuff, the quarks and so on, you have to look at cosmic rays on the way in or go to heavy atom smashers. These machines cost megabucks and they didn't even exist in Petrosian's day. Nobody could have predicted the world they uncovered. Any idea of the Lone Ranger getting some brilliant insight that leaped across three generations of nuclear scientists – look, it's nuts. Forget it.'

Rosa was bearing down at ram speed, wielding a bowl of chilli. Findhorn, in panic, asked for coffee. It took her by surprise and she retreated back to the kitchen.

On an impulse, Findhorn tried a gamble. He studied

White closely and said, 'So how did the rumour get around?'

'What rumour?' White was looking genuinely blank.

'That Petrosian had discovered some new process.'

White's hesitation was tiny. It might just have been something to do with a throatful of Rosa's chillies. He tried to laugh, to cover it up. 'What sort of process? Where did you hear that?'

Findhorn touched the side of his nose, probed a little more. 'My source thinks there was a cover-up.'

White shook his head in annoyance. 'Sure, there's nothing like a cover-up story to sell newspapers. I suspect like the Roswell UFO incident, one or two bits of real information get distorted. Alien spacecraft, the face on Mars, energy from nothing, you name it, there's an audience out there eager to buy your conspiracy theory. And the more screwball it is the bigger your audience.' White tried a sympathetic tone. 'Look, Ed, this stuff's for our *National Enquirer*, not the English *Times*. Whoever your source is, this story about some new process has no foundation. No foundation in history, no foundation in science.'

'I'm chasing a chimera, then?'

'Absolutely.'

Findhorn tried to look convinced. 'What could have gotten the rumour started?'

White shrugged. 'You tell me.'

Findhorn gambled again. 'The process was supposed to be dangerous.'

This time White was ready. 'Your source is confused.

There was a scare in 1942 that an atomic bomb explosion might ignite the atmosphere, create an uncontrolled runaway. Oppenheimer set up a task force to check it out. Their report was codenamed LA-602 as I recall. They found that the fireball couldn't quite pull it off. Petrosian was involved in these calculations.'

White was convincing, and seemed to be making sense. *Hell*, he thought, *I'm getting into conspiracy theories myself.* Findhorn closed his notebook and said, 'Okay, Frank, thank you for that.'

'I guess you've come a long way for nothing. Look, I could get you into X-2 if you like, I have Q-clearance—'

'X-2?'

'The design group for nukes. But it's just like any other office building. Apart from the guys with the AK-47s, of course.'

'I think you've just upset our surveillance,' Findhorn said, nodding towards the pony-tailed young man, who was staring at the menu with unnatural intensity.

White grinned. 'Anyway, I don't think anyone there could help you.'

'Post-SALT, do we need Los Alamos?' Findhorn asked, breathing air in gulps. He felt his lips beginning to blister with the hot chillies.

White leaned back in his chair, steepled his hands under his chin and looked over his spectacles. 'More than ever, pal. The world is more dangerous, not less, and it's getting worse. Iran will soon be stuffed with enough recycled nuclear fuel to start a significant nuclear weapons program. Saddam Hussein and his merry men had to be bombed to stop them developing nukes. India and Pakistan have already fought three wars with each other, and now they're squaring up with nukes. Nuclear smuggling out of Russia is a deadly serious worry – it's only a matter of time before the Ultimate Truth or the Martyrs of God or the Montana Ladies' Crochet Circle rigs up some device from instructions on the Internet.'

'Surely these are problems for the FBI or CIA.'

'But without guys who know about weapons, they wouldn't know what to look for. And what about our own stockpiles? Nuclear devices deteriorate. We need expertise to keep track of that too. It's a dangerous world out there, Ed, and a complex one.'

Rosa was serving the pony-tailed young man with a plate of little tortillas stuffed with pieces of fried fish, tomatoes, lettuce, sour cream and chillies.

'If it wasn't new science, what about new technology? Could Petrosian have thought of some way to make a bomb more effective? Say by miniaturization, or avoiding the need for plutonium?'

'Let me tell you about miniaturization, Ed. Ideas for it get developed all the time but we're no longer allowed to test them. These designs are as much art as science, which is why so many bomb designers in X-2 are women. They're more intuitive. But the complexity of a nuclear explosion stretches a Cray. No way could Petrosian have leapt fifty years ahead on that one either. As for by-passing uranium or plutonium, it's not an area I can talk about, or our surveillance, whose spectacles undoubtedly contain a microphone, would choke on his tortilla boats.' White leaned forward, lowering his voice. 'But there are some things you could work out from the public domain. Like, lithium is common in rocks on Earth, but astronomers don't detect much of it in stars. Why is that?'

'I don't know, Frank. Why is that?'

White leaned forward some more. 'Because it's easy to ignite, nuclear-wise. Hydrogen needs ten or twenty million degrees. Now lithium, that needs less than a million. If you could somehow reproduce stellar—'

'Could Petrosian have thought of some way to do that in 1953? By-pass plutonium, make a nuke from rocks?'

'As a concept, quite possibly. Now if you did that, if you found some way of extracting nuclear energy using just ordinary material, that would really open the lid. But as a hazard to civilization in 1953? Where would he get even a million degrees? Lasers weren't invented until 1960. Always assuming we needed high-energy lasers to attempt the trick,' White added hastily. His tired eyes held a gleam.

'Of course. Always assuming that.'

White looked as if he was about to drop with exhaustion. Findhorn waved at the waitress. He said, 'So he didn't have lasers but he had electricity. Maybe he thought of something crazy. Take the entire power supply for New York City on a cold night. Pulse all that electricity through a microscopically thin wire. Have the wire doped with lithium and anything else you need.'

White grinned. 'Ed, that wouldn't even get you to the foothills.'

Findhorn blew out his cheeks. 'So try one of Rosa's chillies.'

* * *

Findhorn thanked White and left him heading for the Western area of town and some badly needed sleep. He took a stroll, absorbing the sights and sounds of this strange town.

White's sermon was clear. Petrosian was a wild-goose chase, a piece of history with nothing to say of relevance to the new millennium.

There was, however, a problem with that thesis. Namely, the trail of mayhem which followed the diaries. Findhorn wondered whether White's sermon had been genuine, or an attempt to deflect further enquiry. And what, he wondered, if he kept digging?

He took a cab to the Los Alamos Community Reading Room and there asked a warm, curly-haired girl for information about the post-war activities of Lev Petrosian the atom spy. Without a blink she disappeared.

And Findhorn waited. For ten minutes, his speculations becoming increasingly wild.

He was beginning to wonder whether to get out of it when a library attendant, a squat, white-haired Navajo, approached and sat down heavily three desks away from Findhorn. At least, Findhorn assumed he was a library attendant. The man clasped his hands together and stared unblinkingly at Findhorn. And then, at last, the curly-haired girl was back at his desk with a sweet smile and a black binder.

How to Make a Hydrogen Bomb.

The binder was heavy. There were research papers and there were notebooks. Findhorn started on the papers.

These were in triplicate, a top copy and two carbons. Each had a number circled at the top of it. They were abstrusely mathematical, with titles like *Quantum Tunnelling Probabilities in a Polarized Vacuum*, or *A Markov Chain Treatment of Ulam/Teller Implosion*. Findhorn could barely make sense of them, except in the broadest outline. He wrote down the titles but had the feeling that they were no more than the bread-and-butter elements of the hydrogen bomb project; the appliance of yesterday's science.

The workbooks were fatter and more interesting. There were a couple of dozen, lined and bound in blue, soft-backed covers. They too were numbered; perhaps, Findhorn speculated, to stop a potential spy smuggling his own secrets out. Findhorn started on them systematically, opening at number one, page one. The small, clear longhand writing of Petrosian was unmistakable. The notes were in English and written in ink. There was a prodigious amount of scoring out and reworking. There were lots of doodles; Petrosian seemed particularly fond of little flying saucers, reflecting the UFO-mania of the day, but there were also cows and galaxies. He did a particularly good pig, sometimes with wings. Often little cartoon bubbles would come from the mouths of the animals, and they would enclose equations, or technical terms, or cryptic comments.

With a lot of tedious effort, Findhorn found he could relate the development of Petrosian's notes to the contents of the typed papers. Here and there, in the margins, there were scribbles written in faded pencil: 'Kitty, orchestra 7 o'clock'; or 'Colloquium 2 p.m.'; or 'coffee, beans, oil, milk'; or 'proofs deadline NOW'.

In the late afternoon, one doodle in particular caught his eye. It was a little cartoon showing Albert Einstein smoking a pipe. A long stream of smoke from the pipe connected three large puffs of smoke, like clouds, over Einstein's head.

The date was Monday 30 November, 1953. The day after his diary recorded his high excitement.

The first puff showed a picture of a ship. Little bubbles were coming from its propellor. Next to it was written: 'HMS *Daring* 1894.'

The second showed a sort of golfball with a dozen legs sticking out of it. Next to it was written: 'Chase & Henshal'.

The third contained only the letters 'ZPE'.

Findhorn contemplated that. He copied the quirky little picture into his notebook.

Towards the evening, with his head reeling, Findhorn closed the last of the notebooks and sat back with a sigh and a stretch. The library attendant, if such he was, hadn't moved for the entire session. Findhorn returned the heavy binder to the curly-haired girl with the smile, and emerged into the warm evening air and a streetful of nerds returning from work on bicycles, skates and four-wheel trucks loaded with skis.

Findhorn now hired an RV with an unexpectedly throaty roar on a one-way drop. He drove south, with the lights of Santa Fe twinkling in the distance. The Jemez Mountains were still in sunlight to the west, and they were glowing blood red. His mouth was still burning. Ahead, Santa Fe was like a big Mongol encampment on a hillside, its lights a myriad of campfires.

Petrosian had been hiding something. He had been careful to erase all mention of his overnight inspiration from his daytime workbook, and all signs of the excitement which he confided to his diaries. It was as if there had been two Petrosians. And yet the little doodles were the windows to his soul. They were mind games, Petrosian at play. A purposeful play.

Findhorn struggled with the bizarre images: HMS *Daring*, 1894; a golfball with legs; ZPE. And they danced in his head with other, darker pictures: city-destroying fireballs; blazing oceans.

He looked in his rear mirror, and the hairs on the back of his neck prickled. The headlights were still half a mile to the rear, as they had been since Los Alamos.

He thought that it had to be coincidence, that jet lag and tension were bringing out some mild paranoia, that the claustrophobic atmosphere of security pervading Los Alamos made you think that way, that there was no possible way for White or anyone else in the States to connect Cartwright of *The Times* with Findhorn of the Arctic.

He thought all of that, and he congratulated himself on this triumph of pure reason over primitive, irrational fear. And he put his foot down.

18

The Venona Files

The cost of doubling back, taking nonsense routes and side roads on the two hundred mile journey from Santa Fe to Flagstaff was eight precious hours. It left Findhorn screaming with frustration. It was late afternoon by the time he reached the entrance to the wooded camp site at the Grand Canyon, but at least he was sure that he was not being followed.

He drove past the entrance just the same.

Five miles on he slowed down, did a U-turn on the empty road and turned back, wondering if everyone on the receiving end of surveillance ended up with galloping paranoia. On the way back to the canyon not a vehicle passed him, in either direction.

The trees and ground were lightly dusted with snow. The Mather Campground was bigger than he had visualized and he hoped that finding Romella, if she was here, wouldn't turn out to be a major headache. There was a light scattering of cars and tents amongst the trees, and he nosed the camper around the roadways lacing the site. He wondered where, fifty years earlier, Petrosian and Kitty had stayed. There was no sign of Romella, and no telling which if any of the handful of vehicles around was hers. He parked in a quiet spot – the nearest car was a made-in-Japan, four-wheel-drive effort two hundred yards away, all gleaming chrome and hideous purple. He put diaries, laptop and notebook into a backpack rather than risk leaving them in the van. He stepped out, took a moment to stretch and fill his lungs with cool, pine-scented air, and then walked briskly along a path towards a little cluster of shops he had passed earlier. He headed east along a trail skirting the rim from Mather Point.

Findhorn had seen the photographs often enough; but the reality still impressed. The scale was inhuman, too large to absorb. He leaned over the low parapet and traced the path of a little trail far below. He thought he would like to do it some day but he couldn't see a way out of the fix he was in and he might not manage it before he met his assassins.

A few people – families, couples, individuals – were scattered around. They were doing normal things: taking photographs, sitting on the low wall, looking out over the vista, eating. Findhorn looked at them all with deep suspicion and wondered if he would ever recapture his lost innocence. He walked off, exploring the unfamiliar surroundings, looking into curio shops and restaurants with names like Hopi House, Bright Angel Lodge, Lookout Studio, Verkamp's Curios.

There was no Romella.

Then he wandered west to Hermit's Rest, and back along the tracks interspersing the tree-scattered camp site. He was now shivering in the cold air. Hopelessly restless, he returned to the Canyon rim and again looked out over the great pink scar. Heavy, snow-laden clouds were coming in low and the air temperature was plummeting.

He turned in the direction of Bright Angel Lodge and a caffeine hit. With a pile of dollars at the ready, he phoned through to the Edinburgh flat. It would be around noon.

A male voice answered.

'Dougie?'

A pause, then, 'Fred!'

Findhorn's younger brother. 'Hi, Dougie, you're back early?'

'Too much snow, the skiing was lousy. Hey, am I glad you phoned! I got home in the early hours to find guess what . . .'

'Stefi Stefanova. I'm sorry, I hope you don't object.'

A pause, then, 'Object? The day I complain to coming home and finding a blonde stunner in my flat . . . I just wondered if she was an impostor or something.'

'No, she's genuine.'

'And under a grilling from me, I find you've had two wenches staying with you.' There was a wicked chuckle. 'I'm highly impressed, but this isn't the big brother I know at all.'

'Come on, Doug, it's business.'

'Business? If the old man gets to hear of this . . .'

'Translation business, you total idiot. Listen, has Stefi explained things?'

'Not a thing. I don't think she really believes I'm me.'

'Put her on.'

A minute later a nervous voice came over the telephone. 'Fred?'

'Stefi, you can relax. That's my brother Dougie, he's just come back early from Gstaadt.'

The relief in her voice was unmistakeable. 'Oh thank goodness. I suppose I should move out now. No, he's shaking his head.'

'Stefi, you can trust Dougie absolutely, except maybe at bedtimes, if you see what I mean. Now, business. Can you find out what happened to HMS *Daring* in 1894?'

'I think so. What's that about bedtimes?'

'I'll phone you later today. And it's okay to tell Dougie the whole story provided that he wants to hear it. Remember he's a lawyer, he may not want to know about it.'

Dougie came back on line. Findhorn said, 'Dougie, Stefi has a story to tell that you'll hardly believe. There could be a huge amount at stake, or nothing at all. The only thing is, you may not want to become privy to information which might compromise your position as a pillar of the legal community. Anyway, it's up to you.'

Findhorn could practically feel his brother straining at the leash. Dougie was saying, 'My God, Fred, get the hell off the phone so I can quiz this woman.'

'I'll be in touch.' Findhorn sipped at his coffee and thought that, knowing Little Brother, it wouldn't be long before he was looking for ten per cent.

ZPE. Zero point energy. The lowest possible energy state, the energy of empty space. But how much energy was that? A fantastic thought jumped into Findhorn's head. Could you get at that energy, whatever it amounted to? Could you somehow mine the vacuum?

Now Findhorn was beginning to remember the cosmologists' claim: that the Universe was created *ex nihilo*, that the Big Bang itself was a fluctuation in the vacuum. The ultimate free lunch, they said. The Creation was God's industrial accident, a vacuum fluctuation that had gotten out of hand.

And Petrosian, that November night in 1953, had become very excited about zero point energy.

Something was beginning to connect.

At a table in the Lodge, Findhorn wrote down some barely remembered numbers on the hotel stationery. In the beginning was the erg, about the energy of a small, falling feather. At a million grams to a ton, a fifty-ton express train moving at one hundred kilometres an hour carried – he did the sums – two hundred million million ergs, or two followed by fourteen zeroes, or 2×10^{14} ergs. He doodled a little more and finally wrote out a small table:

a falling feather	1 erg
a gram of dynamite	10^{11} ergs
a bullet	10^{11} ergs
an express train	2×10^{14} ergs
a naval gun	5×10^{15} ergs
the Hiroshima bomb	8×10^{20} ergs
a medium hydrogen bomb	4×10^{22} ergs
solar output (one second)	4×10^{33} ergs

| energy to evaporate Atlantic | 4×10^{33} ergs |
| energy of a moving galaxy | 2×10^{59} ergs |

So the energy coming out of the Sun, if suitably concentrated, would evaporate the Atlantic Ocean in one second. Not many people know that, he told himself with satisfaction. He hadn't known it himself until now.

Then he remembered the figure he was after. The Planck energy, the ultimate energy contained in a cubic centimetre of vacuum. He added to his little column:

| energy per cc of vacuum | 10^{93} ergs |

He looked at the scribbled number, compared it with the others he had written. He thought: no, no way.

The number looked at him, hypnotizing him. 10^{93} ergs. Per cubic centimetre. He ran from it, crossed quickly to the reception desk. The girl was very friendly, very smooth, very American. 'I need to do some e-mailing. Can I plug in somewhere?'

'Sure. Use the office. Round here.'

```
Archie - As a matter of top priority I
need to speak to the best people going
about the vacuum, about the energy it
contains, and about the possibility of
extracting energy from it. Can you
recommend anyone? Or even fix something?
I'll phone later.
```

Findhorn ordered another espresso and sat at the table. The afternoon sun briefly peeked out from below heavy cloud, changed its mind and disappeared again. He wrote out a one and followed it with ninety-three zeroes. Findhorn looked at it. It wasn't a number, it was a battering ram. It was power beyond imagination. It was the heat of God's forge.

'Hi, Fred.'

Findhorn's heart leaped. She was in a cream-coloured designer fleece with black jeans and black leather boots. The fleece was open and beneath it Findhorn glimpsed a Rennie Mackintosh necklace and a nicely rounded black T-shirt with an 'I Love ET' motif, complete with a picture of the cuddly alien. Somewhere she had taken time off from the mayhem to have her hair styled in a boyish cut. A casual black bag was draped over her shoulder. The bruise over her eye was well down and she was trying not to look too pleased to see him.

Findhorn caught a light whiff of expensive perfume. 'Hi, Romella. Any problems on the way here?'

'Nope. If there was surveillance I missed it.' She tapped her bag. 'I've got some goodies.'

'Would you like to walk?'

'Later. I haven't eaten since yesterday. And I'll want to spread some papers out, but not here.'

'Okay, let's visit the grocery store and go back to my car. You're sure we're safe here?'

At last she smiled, a sly, mischievous smile. 'Am I safe from you?'

At the little table in the RV, Romella produced a thick

wodge of papers. The bottled-gas stove was bringing a pot of water to the boil and the little blue flames were warming the air. 'The FBI people couldn't have been more helpful,' she said.

Findhorn nodded at the papers. 'I can't wait to get into this. But it'll surely take all night.'

'Yes. It's almost their entire take on Petrosian.'

'Almost?'

'There are deletions, allowed under the Act. Where national security is involved, or innocent people still alive might be compromised in some way, they delete things.'

'Okay. I guess we now have about everything we're going to get.'

Romella pulled off her Muscovado boots with a sigh and kicked them into a corner. The Berghaus fleece was dropped on the floor, and she lounged back on a low, maroon-coloured sofa. The water was beginning to simmer and the windows were steaming up. Irrationally, the steamed windows gave Findhorn a cocooned, protected feeling, as if they somehow kept out a hostile world.

'I got three things out of the FBI,' she said. 'But first why don't you tell me how you got on at Los Alamos?'

He moved over to the cooker, tore open a packet of spaghetti and rattled plates onto a work surface. He poured olive oil into a little bowl, chopped basil into shreds with a gleaming kitchen knife and added it to the oil. He started on the pine nuts, chopping them finely. 'They think he was mad. No way could he have found anything they haven't. And they have fifty years of high energy physics since Petrosian to back them up.'

'What's your gut-feeling, Fred?'

'There's a cover-up.'

Romella said, 'Wow.' She tucked her legs under herself, gave Findhorn an astute look and said, 'And what about Petrosian's secret? You have the look of a man who's onto something.'

Findhorn was grating a little hard lump of Parmesan cheese. 'You must be CIA. How else did you get all that help from the FBI?'

'You're wrong, Fred. I work for Alien Abductions. You should know that, you've hardly taken your eyes off my T-shirt.'

'Sorry. It's the ET picture, I assure you.'

She laughed. 'Which would be damned insulting if true. I forgive you, Fred, you're just back from ten years at the north pole. And I notice you haven't answered my question.'

Findhorn was adding spaghetti to the boiling water. 'This will take a few minutes. Keep talking.'

'I think not.' She was looking in a compact mirror, gently prodding the bruise around her eye with her little finger.

'What?'

'Fred, I've come bearing three gifts. I want something in exchange. Tell me what you're onto.'

Findhorn stopped stirring. Romella's voice was cold. 'You don't trust me, do you?'

She snapped the compact lid shut, started to pull on her boots.

'What are you doing?' Findhorn asked in alarm.

'Enjoy your spaghetti.' She slipped into her coat, picked up her casual bag and slid the camper door open.

'Romella!' He grabbed her arm in panic. 'I can't do this on my own.'

She kissed the air next to his cheek. 'Goodbye, darling.' Then she was out and flouncing through the snow towards the chrome and purple monster.

'I surrender, damn you. I'll tell you everything.'

She turned, already shivering in the thin cold air. Findhorn was holding his hands together in an attitude of prayer. Inside, he closed the door, took her coat off, helped her off with her boots and said, 'I'm beginning to think that Petrosian thought of some way to extract energy from empty space. The amount of energy involved might be huge. Please don't leave me.'

'Energy from empty space? You surely don't mean from nothing?'

The water was spilling over the pot. Findhorn turned the gas down. 'I can't tell you more just yet. I'm waiting for Stefi to tell me what happened to HMS *Daring* in 1894. Now it's your turn.'

'You're telling me the truth,' Romella declared. 'That is so crackers that you couldn't make it up. Okay. First, the Venona files.' Findhorn opened his mouth, and Romella said, 'These are transcripts of Soviet secret messages covering 1940 to 1948. They tell me about three thousand of them were partially decrypted. I got copies of about a hundred relating to Los Alamos.'

'Do they mention Petrosian?'

'Maybe. We'll have to dig. Second, transcripts of FBI

interrogations of scientists during the McCarthy era, especially those involved in the hydrogen bomb project. Petrosian included; they had a go at him more than once. And third, we have the FBI surveillance reports on Petrosian.'

Findhorn paused from his cooking. '*The Times*' obituary claimed that Petrosian spied for the Russians.'

Romella patted the heap of papers in front of her. 'The trail to Petrosian's secret is somewhere in here, Fred, if it's anywhere. Some clue that will lead us there.'

The RV was now warm, and the air was light with Diorissimo and pesto. Findhorn popped a cork. The evening promised a heady mixture of spaghetti *al pesto*, Valpolicella and espionage, and who knew what else.

TOP SECRET UMBRA VENONA
NEW YORK/MOSCOW
YOUNG is currently in charge of a group at CAMP-2, and has handed Beck a report about present activities at the CAMP along with a list of the key personnel in ENORMOZ. There is still no indication of when FUNICULAR will be operational. Beck considers that it is almost impossible 88746 62354 76234 cultivate QUANTUM.
CHARLES, QUANTUM and BILL OF EXCHANGE are travelling to PRESERVE and will meet with VOGEL and TINA.
ALEKSANDR

'Is that before or after decryption?' Findhorn wanted to

know. He lifted a strand of spaghetti from the saucepan with a fork.

'Say you have a message. You look up the words in a codebook, a sort of dictionary which replaces each word by a four-figure number. Then you group all these numbers into sets of five. Then to each set of five you add another five-figure number which you take from a one-time pad. It can only be read by the guy at the other end holding the same one-time pad. The Russians kept each and every one-time pad under permanent armed guard. And because you use each page from the pad only once, the code is unbreakable.'

Findhorn gave a satisfied grunt. '*Al dente*. But it was broken nevertheless.'

Romella was sipping red wine. 'Partly. After a few thousand hours, a few million dollars and one or two nervous breakdowns.'

'How come?' Findhorn was using a fork and spoon to heap pasta onto plates.

'In late 1942, when the Russians were under pressure from the German invasion, somebody blundered. They duplicated the one-time pads. As soon as you do that you create patterns. It was just enough for some very clever people to get into parts of the messages. Another thing was that the Finns, who were fighting the Russians, overran a Soviet consulate in December 1941: The NKVD had to quit in a hurry and they left behind four codebooks which were only partially burned. One codebook was for diplomatic messages, one was for the NKVD – that's the old KGB – one for the GRU, that's Soviet Military

Intelligence, and one for the Naval GRU. They sent the stuff to Sweden to avoid the risk of recapture. The Swedes were of course neutral but they knew damn well that if the Russians took Finland they'd be next in line. So the codebooks ended up in America.'

He spooned pesto sauce onto the plates and sprinkled *parmigiano* over it. 'So what's the significance of Venona?'

'To the Americans and the Brits? It was a dream come true. It gave a picture of the depth of penetration of the Soviet spy apparatus in every sort of place. It caught big spies like Klaus Fuchs, it uncovered the Cambridge Apostles like Philby, Burgess and McLean, and it electrocuted the Rosenbergs. And it caught hundreds of small fry worldwide.'

'Presumably the numbers here are bits of code that nobody has been able to break.'

Romella nodded with her mouth full. Then she said, 'You may be a human relations disaster, Fred, but you can cook. The names are cryptonyms, jargon used by the GRU and NKVD. Take "Charles". That refers to Klaus Fuchs. "Bill of Exchange" is Oppenheimer, "Camp-2" is Los Alamos and so on. The FBI gave me a list. So, the message translates to:

"Theodore Hall is currently in charge of a group at Los Alamos, and has handed Beck a report about present activities there along with a list of the key personnel in the Manhattan Project. There is still no indication of when the Bomb will be operational. Beck considers that it is almost impossible blah blah cultivate Quantum.

"Fuchs, Quantum and Oppenheimer are travelling to the Argonne Radiation Laboratory" – that's in Chicago – "and will meet with Vogel and Tina." '

'Who are "Quantum", "Vogel" and "Tina"?' Findhorn asked.

'Nobody knows. "Vogel" and "Tina" were a husband-and-wife spy team. "Vogel" was also known as "Pers".'

'That must narrow things down.'

'You can play detectives. It's like Jack the Ripper, about two dozen suspects and every one made to sound plausible. Some people named a physicist called Rudolf Peierls, apparently on the grounds that his wife Eugenia was Russian and they were friendly with Fuchs. MI5 took Peierls's security clearance away after the war. Unfortunately for the amateur detectives, the US gave Peierls the medal of freedom in 1947 and the UK gave him a knighthood in 1968, and the accusation was eventually shown to be ridiculous.'

Findhorn said, 'Okay, so we'll never know if Petrosian was a spy.'

Romella looked doubtful. 'I disagree. We have one big advantage over the FBI.'

'Haven't we just?' Findhorn said. He waited while Romella sucked up a long strand of spaghetti. Then she continued, 'Yes. If we can collate something in the diaries with something in the Venona files . . .'

'Let's go through them, match the dates with diary entries, and see if we can make a connection.'

Romella flicked through the FBI files with her free hand. 'It'll take for ever.'

Findhorn topped up her half-empty glass. 'We can get drunk while we're at it.'

The first connection came two hours later, in a short, cryptic message from Aleksandr, the New York *rezident*. By now, enveloped in the warm air of the RV, and with the gas still burning, drowsiness was beginning to overtake them. While Findhorn, propped up against a wall, read the FBI files, Romella was sprawled out on a couch, translating the Armenian text at the corresponding dates.

TOP SECRET UMBRA VENONA
NEW YORK/MOSCOW
On 14 January CHARLES, ANT, QUANTUM and spell Feynman endspell 28312 81241 49775 visited spell Kitty Cronin endspell 65324 76385 76349 automobile.

'Hey.' Findhorn was suddenly alert. 'Kitty Cronin.'

Romella sat up. She picked up the little blue 1943 diary and flicked to 14 January. She scanned the entry rapidly and her face lit up. 'Fred, listen to this:

Another of those rare days off.

Klaus, Dick and I had an early start. Met up at the East Gate and took off in Dick's car. He had some girl lined up in Santa Fe, who turned out to be a brassy blonde called Halina, terrific looker but utterly brainless. Klaus's sister Kristel was down from Cambridge. A thin, nervous sort of girl. Picked them both up near the Post Office, then up into the hills to collect Kitty.

Spent an exhausting day on Sawyer Hill, learning to ski. The brassy blonde surprised us all by being very good at it, although with a skirt that hardly covered her knees she must have been frozen to the bone.

In the evening, back to Kitty's, starving and frozen. She had a table made up for us. Cold roast chicken, plenty of wine, milk, bread and apples. Nectar! Later, Dick went off with the blonde, Klaus and his sister. The round trip must have used up his gas allowance for the month.

Stayed over at Kitty's. Both of us bruised in awkward places!'

'Okay. "Charles" is Klaus Fuchs. Who's "Ant"?'

Romella shuffled papers. 'I've an FBI dossier on her someplace. Here we are.' She skimmed the pages. 'Kristel Fuchs, younger sister of Klaus, alias Kristel Heineman. Unhappily married with three children. She lived in Cambridge, Massachusetts. Later diagnosed as schizophrenic, recovered, married again and had another three kids.'

'Was she a spy?'

'It says that Fuchs used to meet his contact, Harry Gold, alias "Goose", in Kristel's home. But there's no evidence that she knew what was going on.'

'Okay,' said Findhorn, 'We have Klaus and Kristel Fuchs, Dick Feynman and Kitty Cronin in the Venona message. And we have "Quantum".'

'And we have Klaus and Kristel Fuchs, Dick Feynman and Kitty Cronin in Petrosian's account of a picnic held on the same day. And Petrosian.'

Findhorn drew up two columns on a sheet of A4 paper:

KLAUS FUCHS	=	CHARLES
DICK FEYNMAN	=	?
BRAINLESS BLONDE	=	?
KRISTEL FUCHS	=	ANT
KITTY CRONIN	=	?
LEV PETROSIAN	=	?

He said, 'So the question is, where do we place "Quantum"?'

'We can forget Kitty and the blonde,' Romella said. 'Kitty wasn't part of the Manhattan Project and the blonde was just a casual pick-up.'

Findhorn blew out his cheeks. 'And Feynman was an all-American kid from the Bronx. He's never been a suspect. In that case the chances are that Petrosian was "Quantum".'

'Hey, we've found something. If that's right, he probably wasn't a spy. At least, Beck considered he couldn't be cultivated as one.'

'So why the hell was Petrosian fleeing to Russia with useless diaries?'

Romella said, 'It's hot in here.' She started to slip off her dark, lace-topped stockings. She stretched, and ET stretched along with her. 'Okay, Fred, let's call it a day.'

Then, eyes full of innocent enquiry, 'I was wondering about the sleeping arrangements.'

Findhorn looked across at the purple and chrome, made-in-Japan monster a few hundred yards away. Light flakes of snow were drifting past the window and the sky was now dark grey.

'Is that vile thing yours?'

'The purple people eater? Yes, I've rented it.'

'It's going to be a cold night. You could freeze to death in it.'

'So what do you suggest?' Romella asked.

'I'll lend you a blanket.'

'You know, Fred, there's a sort of purity about my hatred for you. It's undiluted by any other emotion. It has the intensity of a laser. Can't you feel it? Or are you made of stone?'

Findhorn's face showed bewilderment. 'Two blankets, then.'

19

Foucault's Pendulum

Findhorn trudged shivering along a track lightly dusted with snow and the prints of a small, clawed animal. A thin, red-nosed zombie was lurching into the men's toilets, carrying a towel and toilet bag. In Babbitt's, a couple of sleepy campers, all skip caps and quilted body warmers, were drifting along the meat aisle. Through bleary eyes Findhorn found milk and picked up a cereal called Morning Zing.

A tall, round-faced girl at the counter was stacking newspapers. 'You the yellow RV?'

'Uhuh.' Findhorn struggled with unfamiliar coins.

'This was faxed through for you.'

Back outside the store, Findhorn read the message:

```
I got this from a naval architecture
book but I haven't a clue what it means.
If you want more I could go to Kew and
look at the Admiralty Reports they keep
progress books ships logs etcetera.
   In 1894 high-speed sea trials of the
British destroyer HMS Daring revealed
```

severe propeller vibrations which were attributed to the formation and collapse of bubbles, a phenomenon known as cavitation. This phenomenon has now been widely studied and is important in many underwater applications. A related problem was discovered during the First World War, when the need to detect enemy submarines led to the development of high intensity subaqueous acoustic sources. It was realized in 1927 that such intense underwater sound produces cavitation. An extraordinary discovery was made in 1934, namely that when the bubbles collapse they produce visible blue light. The source of this light remains a mystery to this day. One possibility, suggested by the Nobel prizewinner Julian Schwinger, is that a dynamic Casimir effect is at work, that is, that zero point energy is being extracted from the vacuum. A bubble in water is a hole in a dielectric medium and the speed of collapse is extremely . . .

Findhorn shouted 'Yes! Yes!' and did a brief war dance on the sidewalk. A fifteen-year-old girl scuttled off in alarm, clutching milk. He skipped to the end:

```
Your brother's nice and we're getting
on fine. Told him the story and he wants
you to phone him urgently.
Love
Stefi
```

Findhorn did a subtraction and found that it was nearly four o'clock in the afternoon in Glasgow. Even Archie would be up and about by now. He went smartly back into Babbitt's, fed a heap of nickels into the call box and dialled through. He had almost given up when there was a sort of moan from the other end of the line.

'Archie?'

A moment, and then, loud and clear, 'Fred, lad.'

'I've woken you up.'

'Not tae worry.'

'Look, the time has come to pick that giant brain of yours.'

'About?'

'What's the connection between Foucault's pendulum and the Casimir effect?'

Another long silence. When he spoke, Archie's voice was serious. 'You're into some heavy stuff here, Fred.'

'A pendulum is heavy stuff?'

'It's awesome. You want ten years' worth of frontier science in a five-minute call?'

Findhorn stayed silent. There was the sound of running water in the background, what sounded like a female voice, another long silence, two nickels' worth, and finally Archie was saying, 'This is desperate, you appreciate. Let's go back to Foucault's pendulum. You probably know about it. This was an experiment carried out in 1851 inside the Panthéon in Paris. This guy Foucault suspends a heavy iron ball from the dome by a wire two hundred feet long and sets it swinging. A pin at the bottom of the ball scrapes the surface of a tray of sand, so that the direction of swing gets traced out in the sand.'

'A straight line.'

'Except that over the hours the direction of this straight line shifts. It moves clockwise, at a rate that would have it back to its original direction in thirty-two hours . . '. Leave the shower running, sweetie.'

'I know the experiment.'

'Then you also know the shift is just a human perspective because we're a lot of self-centered bloody apes and we have to bend our minds to see the real picture which is that the pendulum isn't shifting, we are. The tray of sand was doing the turning. The Panthéon, the sand tray, the watching Parisians, they were all spinning, carried round on a rotating Earth. The swing of the pendulum was fixed in space. It's constant in relation to distant galaxies.'

'Why is this awesome?'

'Och, use the stuff between your ears, Freddie.'

'I'm trying.'

'Don't you see, Fred? The pendulum's telling us that somehow its inertia is fixed by intergalactic space. What's a child's swing, or the sway of a ship, but glorified pendulums? It means all of local dynamics, say like the damage done when you walk into a lamp post, is under the control of distant galaxies. You either see that as slightly strange or you're brain dead . . . Of course I know your name, it's Heather.'

'Okay, so our frame of reference for dynamics is the whole Universe.'

'Aye, laddie even down to the dance of atoms.'

Findhorn counted five nickels. 'Keep going.'

'Now, out of the blue, Findhorn of the Arctic is asking me also about the Casimir effect, which by some strange coincidence is also telling us something about the energy of the Universe. In this experiment you take two flat plates and hold them very close together. You have to do this in a vacuum to get rid of air pressure, and you have to make the plates microscopically flat. When you do that, when you put the surfaces of these flat plates very close together but not touching, a force acts to push them together . . . Cut that out, will you, Helen?'

'You mean a force like gravity?'

'I do not. Gravity comes from matter. This force comes from empty space. It's caused by energy contained in empty space, which we call zero point energy because it's irreducible. There's no way you can get rid of it. Some enthusiasts will tell you this ZPE is the bedrock of the Universe and that everything you see, including us, is just low-energy froth floating on the surface of a deep ocean of vacuum energy.'

'That seems a bit fantastic.'

There was a chuckle at the other end of the line. 'Mother Nature is not required to pander to your limited imagination, Fred. Paradox or not, the Casimir effect proves that empty space is a vast store of energy. And since I'm not as dumb as I look, my guess is you're asking me these questions because Petrosian thought he could link the two. Maybe he saw this zero point energy as the common factor, the magic door between the local and the cosmic.' There was a brief, curious crackle on the line. 'Now there's a sorcerer's trick for you. To find the key to the magic door. To pull down energy from galaxies. Awesome . . .'

'Archie, I think I want to speak to Aristotle.'

'He's dead.'

'Aristotle Papagianopoulos, at the University of Patras.'

There was a long silence, and then: 'Papa the Greek. I wouldn't.'

Something negative in Archie's voice. Findhorn was suddenly alert. 'What's the problem? I understand he's a world authority on fundamental physics.'

'Oh aye, he makes Hawking look like the school dunce.'

'So?'

'For a start it's easier to get an audience with the Pope. I've never been close enough to touch his robe.'

'But suppose I do get an audience?'

'He'd have no time for you, Fred. He's the most arrogant pillock since Louis XIV.'

'I'd be wasting my time?'

'Absolutely.'

'I'm going anyway. I have to try.'

'Don't be daft—'

The last coin ran out.

Findhorn put the receiver down. A feeling of unease

had suddenly enveloped him. It took him some seconds to identify the cause.

It might have been an altruistic wish to steer him away from an embarrassing encounter, or even a touch of academic jealousy.

But whatever, Archie had been trying to control him.

There was a note for him on the RV steering wheel: *Stuff this camping lark. I'm having breakfast at the Bright Angel Lodge and I think I've found something.*

20

FBI

Romella was sitting at a big panoramic window with the early morning sun throwing an orange-red light on the top of the canyon walls. The Colorado River far below was still in gloom. This morning she was in Levi's, cuff boots and an Aran sweater, and Findhorn wondered where she kept her store of clothes. The long silver earrings, he noticed, were back. Coffee cups and a plate of biscuits were on a low table in front of her, along with a few sheets of photocopied typescript.

There was a serious edge to her expression. Without preliminaries, she handed over a sheet of paper. 'Read this.'

```
SECRECY ORDER
(Title 35, United States Code 1952,
sections 181-188).
NOTICE: To Dr Lev Baruch Petrosian, his
heirs and assignees, attorneys and
agents.
You are hereby notified that your
```

application has been found to contain material, the disclosure of which might be detrimental to national security. Accordingly, you are ordered not to publish, construct or disclose the invention or any information relevant to it, either verbally, in print, or in any other manner whatsoever, to any individual, group or organization unaware of the invention prior to the date of this order, but to keep the principal and details of the invention secret unless written consent is first obtained from the Commissioner of Patents.

You are expressly forbidden to export all or any part of the invention described in your application, or any material information relating to the invention, to any foreign country or foreign national within the United States.

Breach of this order renders you liable to penalties as described in Sections 182 and 186 of 35 U.S.C. (1952).

This order should not be construed to mean that the Government intends to, or has, adopted the aforementioned invention.

Findhorn looked up. 'Wow!'

'He invented something.'

'Which the United States Government suppressed.'

Findhorn stood up and walked over to the big window, to give himself time to take in this new information. The sunlight had crept a little way down the canyon, and a light mist was rising from the snow on the trees along the south rim. A little group had started on the downward trail. Findhorn counted five adults and two children. He turned back and sat down at the table. Romella was rubbing her thighs, clearly enjoying the warmth which the sunlight was now bringing. He said, 'You know what this means, Romella? We're looking for something which the US government doesn't want us to find.'

She nodded. 'Yes. We're in hostile territory. Maybe we're even spies.'

'Do they know we're here?' Findhorn wondered.

Romella said, 'I don't want to find out the hard way. It might be a good idea to get out of America as quickly as possible.'

'How did you get this?' Findhorn asked, waving the paper.

'Didn't I mention that my old man is an attorney?'

'In La Jolla, not Washington.'

'Still, Grigoryan, Skale and Partners have connections, and Dad will do anything for her little girl except part with his money. So, when I went to the Patent Office to search under Petrosian, a smooth path had been prepared for me. Otherwise . . .' She tapped the papers in front of her. 'And then I went to the FBI and did exactly the same.

252

Dad tells me there's freedom of information and there's Freedom of Information. To get the right sort of freedom you sometimes need a little arm-twisting.'

'So you turn up on Dad's doorstep and say, hey, I want to get material on Lev Petrosian the atom spy, and he said, sure Romella, I'll fix it for you. Didn't he ask any questions?'

'Dad gave up on me long ago. I think he sees me as slightly eccentric, like Mother.'

'Romella, for a woman, you've done brilliantly. We now know there's some machine at the focus of this.'

'The bad news is that somebody's been asking for the same material as us. It's some legal office in Switzerland, acting on behalf of a client.'

'Switzerland,' Findhorn repeated.

'Switzerland,' she confirmed.

Findhorn poured coffee and sat back with a sigh. 'I have to get to Greece as quickly as possible.'

Romella raised her eyebrows, but asked no questions. 'And I want to get the hell out of here before the system catches up. But read the FBI stuff before you go.'

Show: 18. Tape: 3142.

7 November, this is Agents Miller and Gruber, we are with Doctor Lev Petrosian. Um, this is (non-interview dialogue).

Q. Doctor Petrosian, thank you for agreeing to speak to us. This is really just a routine enquiry and I'm sure you'll be able to satisfy us.

LP. Sure. Go ahead.

Q. You're entitled to have an advocate present if you wish.

LP. Okay, but I don't see the need.

Q. Of course we know that, um, we know that your work here at Los Alamos is highly classified and we can't, um, enter into any aspects of that.

LP. Fine, yes, I'm glad you appreciate that.

Q. Uh, it's really what might be called your extra-mural activities. In particular you took a week's leave over the period beginning 15 June this year.

LP. That's right, I did, yes.

Q. Which you spent in New York City.

LP. About three days, yes. Then I did some walking in the Appalachians.

Q. What was your business in New York?

LP. It's like I said, I was on vacation.

Q. Did you, uh, during your stay there, did you, uh, meet a man called John McGill on the steps of the American Museum of Natural History?

LP. Not that I recall.

Q. Did you hand over an envelope to the aforesaid John McGill?

LP. No.

Q. I'm now about to show you a series of photographs. Would you examine these, please, and can you identify the parties?

LP. Well yes, that's me, obviously, and that's the guy called McGill. I guess you've been following me around.

Q. You admit to having met him?

LP. Yes I did, well there's the evidence I guess. I'd forgotten all about that.

Q. I'm sure of that, sir. Now, can you explain the circumstances of that meeting?

LP. It's coming back now. He's a journalist. He has a lot of contacts or so he tells me, and being a journalist that would make sense. He said he could put in a word for me about an enquiry I was making.

Q. About?

LP. About a lady.

Q. Yes, a lady.

[Interjection by Agent Miller:] So who's the dame, buster?

[Non-interview dialogue between agents Gruber and Miller]

Q. Sorry about that, sir. Would you like to tell us about the lady?

LP. A German girl I knew pre-war. Her name is Lisa. Or was. I wanted to find out what happened to her, whether she came through.

Q. How were you introduced to McGill?

LP. It was through a man called Jürgen Rosenblum. We met in 1941 in Camp Sherbrooke, that was an enemy alien camp in Canada, before they sorted out who their friends and enemies really were. Jürgen and I met by chance again a couple of years ago.

Q. Does the address 238 West 28th Street mean anything to you?

LP. No.

Q. Would it surprise you to know that John McGill's real

name is Andrei Sobolev and that his working address is 238 West 28th Street and that this is the address of Amtorg, ah, otherwise known as the Soviet Trade Delegation?

[Silence]

Q. Sir?

LP. Yes, I'm shattered.

Q. What was in the envelope you gave him?

LP. Well it wasn't nuclear secrets if that's what you're thinking. It was information about Lisa which might help to trace her. Her friends pre-war, the university classes she attended and so on.

Q. Did you have an emotional attachment to this Lisa?

LP. It was a long time ago.

Q. Yes, sir. Would you like to answer my question?

LP. I can't say what my feelings are now.

Q. [Agent Miller]: Were you screwing her, for Christ's sake?

[Gruber to Miller]: Shut up.

LP. There was another woman in the meantime but that broke up. The war did funny things to some of us not that King Kong here would understand that even if I could explain it. Lisa was a link to my past.

Q. Has it occurred to you, um, huh, sir, did you think, has it occurred to you that if you had an emotional attachment to this Lisa, and she was found alive and well in the Soviet sector, that you would become a prime target for Soviet blackmail?

LP. No. I guess I'm a bit naive about stuff like that.

Q. [Agent Miller]. Or (expletive) smart. Maybe there were

atomic secrets in that envelope and the dame story is a cover.

Q. During that vacation, did you have any other business in New York or elsewhere?

LP. No.

Q. Did you visit the, were you at, did the Soviets, did you, er, visit the Soviet consulate during your vacation?

LP. Oh God, I did, this must look very bad. Yes I did.

[Agent Miller]: Here we (expletive) go again.

LP. I have a brother in Soviet Armenia. I was trying to get an exit visa to let him visit here. I've saved enough money that I could pay for his air fare. I haven't seen him in twenty years. He's all the family I have.

[Agent Miller]: Another frigging weak link.

LP. Not at all. Army Intelligence have known about Anastas from day one.

Q. One last thing, Doctor Petrosian. May we have permission to search your flat?

LP. No, I don't want you to do that.

Q. Why not?

LP. Because there are things in it I'd rather you didn't find.

Q. Um huh. Thank you for your co-operation, sir. Have a good day.

Findhorn was looking puzzled. 'Things he'd rather they didn't find?'

Romella said, 'Maybe the diaries. But keep reading.'

Q. Thank you for agreeing to assist us in our enquiry, Mrs Morgenstern.

KM. That's okay, glad to help. What's this about?

Q. You are acquainted with Lev Baruch Petrosian?

KM. Is this about Lev? Yes, I've known Lev a long time.

Q. And how long is that?

KM. Over a decade now. We met in Santa Fe in the early forties.

Q. When he was working on the bomb?

KM. I know that now, but I didn't know it then. Why are you asking about Lev?

Q. What exactly was your relationship with Doctor Petrosian?

KM. We were friends.

Q. Close?

KM. Yes.

Q. Was it an intimate relationship?

KM. I'm sorry but I don't think that's any of your business.

Q. Then Petrosian went off to the South.

KM. Yes, and we sort of lost touch. He came back to Los Alamos in the fifties.

Q. By which time you were married.

KM. Yes.

Q. [Agent Miller] To Mr Morgenstern.

KM. Got it in one.

Q. When you met Petrosian again in the fifties, did you resume your friendship with him?

KM. Yes.

Q. [Agent Miller] Were you lovers?

KM. You've got a damn nerve.

Q. Mrs Morgenstern, how much did Doctor Petrosian

reveal to you about his work at Los Alamos, either in the forties or fifties?

KM. Not a thing. It was secret work. Of course everybody in Santa Fe knew there was some secret army work going on but we never had an inkling of what it was.

Q. Did he ever talk about Russia?

KM. No. We talked movies, not politics. Wait a minute, yes, I think he said something about how he admired the fight the Russian people were putting up. That was during the war.

Q. He made pro-Russian comments?

KM. I suppose you could put it that way.

Q. Did he ever talk to you about his family?

KM. No.

Q. Did you know he had a brother in Soviet Armenia?

KM. No.

Q. Did he, at any time, ask you to post documents or letters?

KM. No.

Q. [Agent Miller] You're lying, lady.

KM. Maybe a postcard or something.

Q. [Agent Miller] Maybe a big fat envelope now and then?

KM. I don't want to answer any more questions.

Q. How long did this passing of documents go on? [Silence]

Q. Let me put it like this, Mrs Morgenstern. Is Mister Morgenstern aware that you and Petrosian are having an affair?

KM. That's outrageous. We are not.

Q. [Agent Miller] You want to hear a nice juicy tape?

KM. You bastards.

Q. How many letters did you post, Mrs Morgenstern?

KM. I have nothing more to say to you people.

Q. On 21 June last, did you drive to Niagara Falls with Lev Petrosian and another man?

KM. I told you, I've nothing more to say.

Q. What was the other man's name?

[Silence]

Q. [Agent Miller] Here's an even better (expletive) way to put it. Espionage could get you thirty years, maybe even the chair.

KM. I want to speak to my lawyer.

Q. Mrs Morgenstern, we can all save ourselves a lot of trouble here if you will just answer the question.

Q. His name was Railton or something. I'd never met him before.

Q. Is this the man? [Subject shown photographs of Jürgen Rosenblum.]

KM. Yes that's Railton.

Q. What did you talk about?

KM. Just anything. The things people talk about on a pleasant afternoon's drive.

Q. [Agent Miller] We got some pleasant pillow talk Mister Morgenstern might like to hear.

KM. Would you do a thing like that?

Q. We're not concerned with your private life, ma'am. Just so long as we know what was said on that drive.

'Now hold on. There's something peculiar here.'

'What do you mean?' Romella asked.

'Rosenblum was a Soviet spy, right?'

She flicked through some pages. 'Yes, one of a string of couriers used by the Soviets in the fifties. Fuchs used to pass on secret papers to a guy called Tommy Gold in the forties, but by this time Gold was doing thirty years.'

'So if Petrosian was handing over secret papers, why was he giving them to Kitty? Why not Gold in the forties and then Rosenblum in the fifties?'

'Maybe she was a courier too.'

'So why didn't the FBI charge her?'

Romella raised her hands expressively.

KM. It was just a drive into the Santa Fe hills. We talked about nothing in particular.

Q. [Agent Miller] And where was Mister Morgenstern at this time?

KM. Chicago. On business, or so he said.

Q. The documents you passed on: where did they go?

KM. It was always the same. Some address in Turkey.

Q. Can you be more specific?

KM. I paid no attention. A place called Igloo or Iguana or something. I can't say any more.

Q. Who was it addressed to?

KM. It was a shop. Some unpronounceable name. He said his sister worked there.

Q. There is no record that Petrosian has a sister. Does that surprise you?

KM. I told you, he never talked about his family.

Q. On that drive on 21 June, were Rosenblum and Petrosian ever out of hearing?

KM. Just once, when I had to attend a call of nature.

Q. Was there discussion of Petrosian's work at Los Alamos?

KM. No. There was one thing.

Q. Yes.

KM. Will you give me that tape? [pause] On the way back from my call of nature, there was some sort of altercation. Railton was sort of animated, and Lev was shaking his head and I'm sure he said, 'No, I won't do it,' something like that. They shut up when I got near.

Q. Can you think of anything else they said?

KM. No.

Q. Anything at all, then or later? Please take your time.

KM. It was all just day-in-the-country talk after that.

Q. Is there anything else you would like to tell us?

KM. No. There is nothing else.

Q. Thank you for your co-operation, Mrs Morgenstern. Have a good day.

KM. About that tape.

Q. What tape is that, Mrs Morgenstern?

Romella looked up from the transcript. 'He was sending messages through Kitty.' Their eyes locked. 'I wonder what sort of messages he was sending, Fred.'

Findhorn said, 'Whatever, they were going to a place in Turkey called Igloo.'

'Or Iguana.'

'So half a century ago he maybe sent something to

some unknown address in some unknown town, and it's never been heard of since.'

Romella said, 'I'll bet Kitty Cronin knew all along where it went. And she may still be alive.'

Findhorn looked at Romella incredulously. 'Are you serious? That has to be the coldest trail on the planet.'

'Do you have a better idea?' Romella asked, seething. 'I'm going to try and work out what Petrosian discovered myself.'

Romella laughed and spluttered, clattering her coffee cup on the table. The desk clerk looked up sharply.

'Okay, Mizz Grigoryan, but we're living in desperate times.'

She patted her bruised lip dry with a paper napkin. 'I suppose two magnificent idiots are better than one. Talking about time . . .'

Findhorn stood up. 'Yes. We must be almost out of it. The other side have more expertise and more money. And they have another advantage over us: they know what they're after.'

'I fear we're beginning to lose it.' She tapped the papers on the table into a neat pile. 'Where will we meet up, Fred?'

'Somewhere on the planet.'

Romella nodded thoughtfully. 'Agreed. Somewhere on the planet.'

21

Revelation Island

Findhorn, in a strange city, was nervous of wandering Washington's streets after dark; but neither did a late night stay in Dallas airport terminal promise an evening of fun and sparkle. With about eight hours before the Athens flight, he booked into the Hilton on the grounds that if he was going to go bust he might as well do it in style. In a hotel room the likes of which he had seen only in movies, he plugged in his laptop. There was a lot of junk mail, and a message from Romella.

> Fred - Something has turned up. Cancel
> your Greek trip and meet me tomorrow.
> I'll be in the Holiday Inn in San Diego.
> Confirm receipt of this message immedi-
> ately. Romella.

He frowned, ran a jacuzzi for two, undressed, re-read the message and then slipped into the churning water. He wondered why she wasn't staying with her parents in La Jolla, which was practically a suburb of Dan Diego. After half an hour of troubled thought and underwater pummelling, he walked dripping to the telephone and called the Holiday Inn, San Diego. A room had been reserved for a Ms Grigoryan, for the following evening. He replugged his computer, carried it to the tub and balanced it precariously on the edge, and typed:

```
I've cancelled Athens. Arriving San
Diego late tomorrow. Fred.
```

He pressed return and lay back. He tried to let the warm jets relax his muscles but disturbing thoughts forbade it. Then he typed 'foo', followed by 'iXdKK1s!!' The Glasgow computers were protected from the outside world by impenetrable firewalls; but Findhorn was now inside that world. In every direction there was still a mass of forbidding gateways; but Archie had always been careless. Findhorn typed 'cd home/amk/mail', entering Archie's electronic mailbox and feeling like a thief. He changed to the inbox directory, the store for messages which Archie had received. The most recent of these had arrived only half an hour ago. It said:

```
I've cancelled Athens. Arriving San
Diego late tomorrow. Fred.
```

He skimmed through Archie's e-mails of the last few days, feeling sick and betrayed.

It was still dark but Findhorn was hit at the aircraft door

by warm, perfumed Mediterranean air. Athens airport seemed to be one vast dormitory for backpackers. The old hands had found quiet corners and were stretched out unconscious in sleeping bags; others, in varying degrees of comatoseness, were propped up against walls or check-in desks, holding paper cups or cigarettes.

Findhorn caught a bus which rattled him and half a dozen sleepy travellers rapidly into the city centre. He recognized the Acropolis on a hilltop, ghostly in the pre-dawn light. Venus blazed down in a dark blue sky, but dawn was breaking rapidly, and by the time he had navigated his way to the railway station it was daylight. Surprisingly at this hour, the platform was choc-a-bloc, and when the train arrived Findhorn was swept on board in something like a rugby scrum. He found himself squeezed between a young, hairy German and his ferociously fit girlfriend, wearing identical T-shirts and shorts. There was no question of reaching his reserved seat and he watched the flat-roofed white houses of the Athens suburbs trundle past, giving way to open countryside, until a ticket inspector looked at his ticket, shook his head, gabbled something, and put him off at a level crossing in the middle of a flat expanse of parched vineyards.

Findhorn watched the train disappear over the horizon.

The sun was getting hot.

And every minute he stood on the track was a minute gained by the opposition.

After an hour of increasing frustration a large car with dark-tinted windows stopped at the crossing and disgorged a small, stout man carrying a shopping bag, with a jacket draped over his arm. The car took off. The man looked at Findhorn curiously and said something incomprehensible. Findhorn, unsure what to expect, said good morning. They stood in silence, waiting. In ten minutes another car stopped and disgorged a little fat woman, and then there was a steady trickle of cars and vans, and at last a train approached on the horizon and Findhorn once again found himself bundled uncomprehendingly on board, wondering if his non-appearance at San Diego had yet registered and, if so, what the enemy would be doing about it.

This train was almost empty, and it was excruciatingly slow. The sun was intense through the carriage window. Glancing out at one point, Findhorn was surprised to find himself looking down the funnel of a ship: they were on a narrow bridge over the Gulf of Corinth, linking mainland Greece to the Peloponnese peninsula. Past Corinth, the train ambled along the most spectacular coastline Findhorn had ever seen, bounded by cliffs on the left and a turquoise sea on the right. By the time the train trundled into a station called ΠΑΤΡΑ, it was noon and Findhorn was headachey and sticky.

He wandered randomly, followed awhile by a scraggy black mongrel which appeared from a cloistered walkway and trotted behind him before being distracted by a smell in an alleyway. He found himself in a spacious square with slender palm trees, a sundial, and a scattering of tavernas and pastry shops. A few deep-wrinkled locals watched him curiously over tumblers of white wine. He tried 'University' in three languages and got a fair amount of gabble but no directions. He wandered through the swing doors of a hotel and tried out the three languages again on a cheerful, dark-eyed girl and she finally drew a map and waved her hands expressively.

Half an hour later he saw the low, white buildings of the university on a distant hill, beyond the edge of town. Across the campus and into a cavernous atrium; a hook-nosed, dark youth who steered Findhorn towards the physics faculty office; a rotund woman with a hint of a moustache with enough English to say that Professor Papagianopoulos is away; a two-day conference on the subject of Space, Time and Vacuum; on the island of Patmos; in the Cyclades, a good distance away. Go back to Athens and fly to the island of Kos and then take the ferry to the sacred island; the sail takes four hours and at the time of year the sea can be rough; the conference is for registered participants only; you are most welcome.

Screaming internally with frustration, Findhorn managed to organize a taxi to the bus station, and an air-conditioned bus had him back in Athens by mid-afternoon. To his surprise he found that his credit card was still good for a flight to Kos. The sun had meantime vanished behind grey, drizzly clouds. There was a long, slow swell which had the ferry yawing from side to side. It was infinitely less fearsome than his icebreaker experience of a week ago, but something in his ear seemed to be in resonance with the sway. At least the ferry was quiet and he was able to retch quietly in the lavatory without frightening the passengers.

Four hours later, the engine note changed and the heaving moderated. Findhorn, feeling like death, half-crawled up the ferry stairs to find that the ship was sailing into a calm harbour under a thundery sky. The water was reflecting the lights of a village, and a massive fortress monastery crowned the hill behind it.

Findhorn now staggered past fish taverns, cafés and tourist shops, most of them shuttered and closed. He found himself wandering up steep little alleys with tiny churches, grand mansions and dazzling white cubic houses clustered around the Monastery of St John. He had no idea where he was going or what he was doing. There was a sudden heavy downpour of rain but he was past caring. Here and there he would cross a little square opening into a stunning view over the Aegean.

There was a two-storeyed villa, with a sign on the wrought-iron gate which might have meant rooms to let. Exhausted, wet and despairing, he pressed the bell and waited. A female voice on the intercom said something incomprehensible, and he said, 'I want to rent a room.' The gate opened with a click, and he walked into a small courtyard decorated with ferns and small trees. A woman looked down from a verandah. She was in her mid-thirties and wearing a plain blue dress, and she waved him in with a smile.

Dripping wet, he entered a well-equipped kitchen stuffed with Chinamen. Three were clustered round pots steaming on a cooker, two were setting a table and a sixth, an older man, was sitting on a kitchen chair, balancing it on two legs while drinking red wine straight from a bottle. There was a flurry of greetings. The eldest man paused, his mouth at the bottle. He stood up, smiled, bowed politely, and said in a deep voice and excellent English, 'Are you here for the conference?'

The Chinese delegation seemed to know where they were going, and Findhorn drifted with them through the narrow wet alleyways. In a square no larger than a tennis court, they drifted into a small hotel. A notice on an easel said *Space, Time and Vacuum*. A buzz of conversation was coming from the left and Findhorn wandered into a room with about thirty people, mostly male, milling around. A glance told him the story: the suit count was low, the beard count was high. This was an academic conference. An array of name badges was laid out on a long table and a couple of women were taking bundles of notes, ticking names off against a list and handing out the badges. There was a crowd around a third woman in a corner, who was checking name badges and handing over small blue rucksacks from a heap.

Without rucksack and name badge, Findhorn knew, he might as well have the word 'Intruder' branded on his forehead. In a dining room beyond the registration desk, tables were layed out with glasses of wine and plates with canapés, cheese and tomatoes. He wandered into this room and picked up a glass of white wine. The room was buzzing but he caught only snatches of conversation. He drifted, trying to look inconspicuous as he checked name badges. He spotted the name *Aristotle Papagionopoulos* from about ten yards, across a temporarily clear stretch of room. Aristotle's head was thrust forward, and he was listening intensely to a bald, bespectacled Englishman. His face was wrinkled; intense brown eyes spoke of a fanatical intelligence but, at the same time, a certain dissociation from the real world. Findhorn, not knowing what he would say to the man, gently pushed his way forwards, mentally bracing himself for the Ari Papa experience.

'Good evening, Doctor Findhorn.'

Findhorn turns, spills wine. The Revelation Man, Mister Mons Meg himself. Archie is at his side, wearing a white linen suit with the jacket over his arm. There is sweat under Archie's armpits and his bearded face is red with astonishment, dismay and consternation.

The expression on the Revelation Man's face, on the other hand, is approaching beatitude. 'And welcome to Patmos. This tiny island has been called the Jerusalem of the Aegean. If God spares you the time, you should enter through the walls which protect the Monastery, and see its extraordinary treasures: Byzantine icons, sacred vessels, frescoes over eight hundred years old, embroideries over a thousand. There are wonderful illuminated manuscripts and rare books.'

'Any old diaries?' Findhorn's voice is shaky.

Mr Revelation laughs. 'Patmos is where Saint John the Theologian, under divine inspiration, wrote his Book of Revelation. Is this not, then, the most fitting place on earth to contemplate John's vision of the Apocalypse?'

Findhorn takes a fresh look at the conference attendees.

The biblical vision springing to his mind is Daniel in the lion's den.

22

Papa the Greek

Findhorn tried to stay calm. Without a word he turned away and pushed towards Papagianopoulos. The Greek was still listening to the Englishman, but now with a sceptical, irritated look.

Findhorn interrupted the conversation. 'I want to learn about the vacuum.'

Papagianopoulos didn't falter for a second. 'But to understand the vacuum, you must first understand time.' His strongly accented speech made him unmistakably Greek.

'My name is Cartwright and I'm a science reporter for *The Times in London*. May I call you Papa?'

'No, I am Aristotle, if you must be familiar at all. May I introduce my colleague, Professor Bradfield?' Bradfield was tall, nearly bald, dressed in a heavy dark suit and tie, and with a face beaded with sweat. He announced himself as John Bradfield from the Rutherford-Appleton laboratory. He had a limp, two-fingered handshake.

Papagianopoulos said, 'I can best describe Professor Bradfield as an excellent guide for beaten paths.'

'Beaten paths are for beaten men,' Bradfield said. 'And

am I beaten? By some fringe eccentric from the Balkan hinterlands?'

Findhorn deduced from this exchange that the two men were friends. He said, 'I shouldn't be here. I've gate-crashed. I'm writing up an article on the nature of the vacuum and I want to speak to the best people going.' Experience had taught Findhorn that the way to an academic's heart was flattery, laid on with a trowel.

Papagianopoulos nodded his approval of Findhorn's judgement. 'You have come to the right person.'

'It's noisy in here. I'd be pleased to take you to dinner someplace where we can talk.'

'I'll join you,' said Bradfield. 'I can correct my colleague's errors.'

'An interview with *The Times* is worth a little yapping at the heels. But the dinner, Mr Journalist, is mine. I have friends on this island.'

Archie approached and mumbled something. 'By all means join us,' Findhorn said.

Aristotle glanced at Archie's name badge and nodded indifferently. 'At this time of the evening there is a cool breeze in the hills. I suggest we enjoy it.'

They followed Aristotle out to a small, tinny Fiat parked in the square, patches of bare metal showing through the blue. Findhorn glanced back. Mr Revelation was at the hotel entrance, gloating happily. Archie and Bradfield squeezed into the back. The air was humid and there was a smell of cats. Aristotle rattled the car out of the square and took it along a quiet road lined with trees and limestone outcrops. It eventually turned inland and wound its way steeply up into the hills. Near the top of a rocky summit they drove into a village – or at least a cluster of four or five houses – and stopped.

A black Alsatian, plainly dead, lay stretched out on a dusty track. Even in the dying light they could see flies swarming around it. An old woman, on a rocking chair under the shade of a tree, watched the visitors while knitting with effortless skill. The track went round to the back of a low, whitewashed house and Aristotle led the way. As they approached, the dead Alsatian jumped up and trotted off.

They sat on kitchen chairs round a small garden table at the back of a house. There was a cooking smell and dishes were clattering. Bradfield compromised his standards by removing his jacket, although the Brasenose College tie stayed tightly round his neck. The garden was bounded by a low limestone wall and fell steeply away. They sat under overhanging vines. A thin, stooped man emerged from a kitchen door with a white paper tablecover which he spread over the table. Aristotle seemed to be known and there was an exchange of noisy Greek banter. The man vanished and reappeared with big hunks of bread, goat's cheese and herb-sprinkled tomatoes, and two carafes of cold white wine.

Findhorn looked over the parched, stony land falling steeply away, and the dark sea glittering beyond; the sun was a large, scarlet ellipse just above the horizon, shining through thunder-laden clouds. He thought that the scene had probably changed little in thousands of years, and that in California or Nice a house with a view like this would set you back a million bucks.

He spoke to Bradfield. 'Thanks for sparing me your time.'

Bradfield said, 'Glad to help.' Even gladder to see his name in *The Times*, Findhorn suspected.

Aristotle waved his hands expansively over the darkening landscape. 'This is a magic place. Greece is where the nature of matter and the vacuum were first discussed, six hundred years before Christ. It was here that my namesake, the other Aristotle, argued that a pure void does not exist in Nature. His insight was lost for two thousand years. It was the twentieth century before the particle physicists discovered that the vacuum is indeed a sea of seething particles and radiation. We are therefore in the most natural setting on Earth for this discussion.'

Findhorn fired the opening shot. He sailed as close to the truth as he dared. 'I'm trying to check these persistent stories about Petrosian, the atom spy. You may have heard of them. The story that he had found some way to extract energy from empty space.'

Bradfield gave Findhorn a quizzical look. 'I don't recall any such tale.'

'Could there possibly have been anything to it?'

The Englishman tried not to smirk. 'Of course not. Some very strange ideas come out of America from time to time. Especially from that era, there were what I would describe as peculiar mental phenomena. Flying saucers, psychokinesis, the Red menace and so on. I believe they were all psychological responses to 1950s anxieties about a thermonuclear holocaust.'

'You dismiss it, then?'

Bradfield continued, 'I have a problem, Mister Cartwright. Because my views belong to the mainstream of physics I'm too easily portrayed as a sort of Establishment spokesman. I feel like the Sheriff of Nottingham against Robin Hood here –' Bradfield glanced briefly at Aristotle '– but in fact the consensus of opinion in physics is against the idea that empty space holds any significant energy. Opinions to the contrary have been expressed by a small, noisy clique of outsiders. I expect that's what has triggered your enquiry. However, you ought to know that these people carry little influence with the scientific community.'

The waiter came out carrying an oil lamp, which he placed in the centre of the table and lit with a cigarette lighter. Aristotle pointedly ignored Bradfield, speaking to Findhorn. 'Fashions come and go in science as elsewhere. The only opinion which matters is that of Mother Nature.'

'We get a lot of crank science in our field,' Bradfield countered smoothly. Aristotle visibly tensed.

Findhorn tried to deflect the rapidly growing animosity. 'I read something about the Casimir effect and zero point energy. What are these things? And just how much energy are we talking about?'

Aristotle produced a biro, moved a plate of bread aside and started to scribble on the tablecover. 'The vacuum is filled with a light of unimaginable intensity if we could only see it. Let me first write down its intensity.' Then he wrote an equation in a large, extrovert scrawl: $I_v = K v^3$. Findhorn tilted his head to read the equation. 'Remember

I'm a mere journalist. You'll have to explain.'

The Greek tried a joke. 'Even journalists can read. I_v is the intensity of this light at a particular frequency v. K is an extremely small number.'

'Which would therefore make the intensity of the light extremely small,' Findhorn pointed out. 'What is K anyway?'

Aristotle scribbled down 6.14×10^{-57}. 'For the innumerate, this is 6.14 divided by the number one followed by fifty-seven zeros.'

'K is as near to zero as makes no difference,' Findhorn said.

Aristotle was patient. 'But look at the other term, young man, the v^3. The equation also tells you something else, namely that the intensity of this light increases with the cube of its frequency. No matter how tiny K is, its smallness is always overwhelmed at a sufficiently high frequency.'

'Okay, so we're immersed in a radiation field of tremendous intensity.' Findhorn broke some bread, dipped it in his wine. He'd seen people do this in movies. 'Why doesn't it just fry us? I don't even see it. Space is black.'

Aristotle waved his arms to encompass the sky; a slightly fanatical tone was creeping into his voice. Or maybe, Findhorn thought, it was just Latin dramatics. 'Does a fish at the bottom of the ocean feel the weight of a ton of overlying water on every square centimetre of its surface? Do you feel the atmosphere bearing down on you, a kilogram compressing every square centimetre of your body? You do not. Because it pervades you. Only differences in pressure can be felt. You cannot feel the crushing atmospheric pressure, but you can feel a light breeze on your cheeks.'

'You're telling me that we don't see this vacuum light because we're pervaded by it.'

Aristotle nodded again. 'It is everywhere, in the retinae of your eyes, in your gut, in the spaces between your atoms.'

'So how do we know it even exists?'

'If you were in a submarine, with no pressure gauge, how could you tell if you were under the ocean?'

'Tell me.'

More dramatics. Aristotle was now squeezing an imaginary submarine between the palms of his hands. 'By the tiny shrinking of its steel hull. A shrinkage of a few millimetres would let you infer the existence of a huge ocean pressure outside. In the same way there are subtle manifestations of the vacuum radiation. Tiny shifts in the expected energy levels of atoms. Miniscule forces acting between flat plates in a vacuum. The merest hints of this shadow world. The rest is inference. But we have no plumb lines to explore the ultimate depths of this ocean of energy. It is *terra incognita*.'

'And how does this relate to zero point energy?'

'ZPE, my journalist friend, is the energy of the vacuum, that is to say, the energy of this radiation field. It is a remnant of the Creation, and it is vast beyond comprehension.'

'And the Casimir effect?'

'So intense is this radiation, at the highest frequencies,

that wherever there is the slightest shadow, the difference in intensity creates a pressure. This is what happens with the Casimir effect. The plates shield each other, however slightly, from the surrounding vacuum radiation. The differential pressure of the light forces them together.'

Bradfield interrupted the dialogue. His voice was carrying an undertone of annoyance. 'Don't let my colleague's enthusiasm sweep you along, Mr Cartwright. The best experiments have produced less Casimir force than the weight of a paperclip.'

Aristotle said, 'Beh!' dismissively. He scribbled some more: $F = Cd^{-4}$. 'This is the force pushing the plates together. You see the closer the plates are, the better they shield each other, the bigger the push. The force increases with the inverse fourth power of their separation d. It is true that experimental limitations have put a wide separation between the plates in the laboratory and the measured force is small. But put them ten times closer and they would feel ten thousand times the force. One hundred times closer and the force is multiplied by one hundred million times.'

'A thousand times closer and you'd crush that submarine,' Archie suggested. His sweaty, red face had a strange, almost feverish look. Findhorn thought it was something like greed.

'But how could we get at all this power?' Findhorn asked. 'What did Petrosian see?'

Bradfield again, the irritation becoming open. 'What power? It doesn't exist. There is no vacuum energy.'

Archie was looking puzzled. 'But Professor Bradfield,

you've just told us that people have measured the force between the plates.'

'They have measured *a* force. But it's all interatomic. The atoms feel it when they are close to each other.'

'It has nothing to do with the vacuum?'

Bradfield was emphatic. 'Nothing. The vacuum is empty. Ideas about extracting energy from it belong with anti-gravity devices and astral projection.'

Findhorn asked, 'Can you prove that?'

Bradfield held out his hand at arm's length. 'I see my hand. No distortion, no bending of light, my hand is just there.'

Findhorn looked baffled. 'That's proof?'

Bradfield said, 'Correct, Mister Cartwright. Energy has mass. Mass exerts gravity. If the vacuum carried as much energy as Papa here claims, the Universe would be far more massive than the astronomers tell us. It would collapse in on itself under its own weight. The cosmos would be the size of a golfball.' He waved his hands around, in a parody of Aristotle. 'Some golfball!'

Archie was scribbling with Aristotle's pen. 'I get your point. Even with the tiny energy already measured in the lab: you couldn't see distant galaxies.' He leaned back, frowning at Aristotle. 'There's already a contradiction between the lab and the telescope.'

Bradfield managed to sip his wine while nodding agreement. 'A blatant one. And Aristotle knows it. Vacuum energy extraction belongs with perpetual motion machines and cold fusion. It's nonsense.'

'The nonsense is entirely Professor Bradfield's.'

Aristotle's face was flushed. 'Gravity is just a mutual shielding of atoms from the ZPE. The zero point energy cannot shield itself from itself. It cannot exert a gravitational force and does not, therefore, collapse the Universe.'

Uninvited, plates of soup were approaching, balanced on the waiter's arms. Findhorn found himself looking at little fish, and octopus tentacles immersed in a thick, tomato-red juice. Bradfield looked at his plate with something like alarm. The Alsatian reappeared and settled down with a sigh, out of kicking range but within throwing distance of scraps.

Aristotle said, 'Pepper? The undeniable fact is, Mister Cartwright, that numerous small atomic effects can be explained – can only be explained – if the vacuum contains radiation whose intensity increases without limit as we go to higher and higher frequencies. Its energy must approach infinity.'

Bradfield was being smooth again. 'Not everything that appears in an equation has physical reality. This ZPE is nothing more than a computational trick.'

Aristotle dipped bread into his fish soup. 'We progress. My colleague now admits that ZPE is a unifying explanation for a wide range of atomic phenomena. The Americans – or is it the British? – have an expression for this. If it looks like a duck, it walks like a duck and it quacks like a duck, then we call it a duck, not a computational trick.'

Archie was prodding a tentacle with his fork, as if he expected a reaction.

Findhorn said, 'This is getting over my head.'

'Perhaps you need more retsina, my friend,' Aristotle suggested, pouring it.

Findhorn thought the wine bore some resemblance to paint stripper, but he sipped it anyway. 'How much energy are we talking about?'

Aristotle speared a fish with his fork. 'The zero point energy shapes molecules, even determines the internal structure of atoms. The material world is a froth floating on the surface of a deep ocean of vacuum energy.'

'Give me a number.'

Papa tossed it out casually. 'There is enough energy in a volume of space the size of a coffee cup to evaporate the world's oceans.'

Archie's eyes gleamed. Bradfield said, 'Ugh!' Whether in reference to the soup or the Greek's claim was unclear.

'But that's vast,' Findhorn said lamely.

'You must have considered the implications of a source of infinite energy, easily tapped,' said Aristotle.

'Cheap electricity. The end of starvation. Water in the desert. A world of plenty.'

Aristotle burst out laughing. 'Cheap super-bombs, more powerful than nuclear weapons and much easier to build. Economic collapse. Massive unemployment. Social chaos. And, somewhere, the emergence of another Führer to rescue the situation.'

Findhorn tried again. 'How could you mine this energy, Papa? How could it be done?'

Aristotle pushed his chair back and stood up, carrying his plate. The Alsatian jumped up expectantly. The waiter exchanged exuberant Greek with Aristotle. No money was changing hands and Findhorn let it go. 'Simple. Think of some simple way to make the vacuum decay. To change the ground state of the neutral vacuum.'

Bradfield looked as if he was in pain.

'I don't understand these terms,' Findhorn said in frustration.

'Forget mechanical devices like parallel plates. Go atomic. Look for a system which shimmers in the vacuum energy, like a crystal with complex resonances on the quantum scale, allowing it to achieve the impossible, like a momentary reversal of time's arrow. Work on that.' Aristotle stood at the kitchen door. 'There is one problem, I believe, with any attempt to engineer the vacuum. Petrosian may or may not have thought of it.'

Findhorn waited. Aristotle finished his dramatic pause, and continued: 'We would be toying with something we know very little about.'

'You mean . . .'

'Now, Mr *Times* journalist . . .' was there, Findhorn wondered, a tiny hint of scepticism in Aristotle's tone? '. . . I have given you time, vacuum, cosmos. It is everything you need for your newspaper article.' There was a brilliant blue flash, and seconds later Zeus roared angrily around the hills. 'We should return.'

'One last thing, Papa,' Findhorn said.

Aristotle waited.

'Who were Chase and Henshal?'

In the near-dark, Aristotle looked blank. Bradfield looked blank. Archie looked blank. And so, finally, did Findhorn.

* * *

'I guess you were surprised to see me,' Archie said. The air was oppressive, and his brow had a light coating of sweat. He kept glancing through the kitchen window towards the courtyard.

Findhorn poured them both more wine. 'The surprise was entirely yours, Archie. Still, you've had time to think up a plausible story.'

Archie blew out his cheeks, took a gulp. 'You're too effing bright for plausible stories. I may as well tell you.'

'You must have come out here like lightning, after you sent me that phoney message.'

Archie hesitated. Then: 'Aye. How did you know it was false?'

'You almost had me fooled. Your mistake lay in those intermediate addresses between Angel Lodge and my Aberdeen one. You mis-spelled digital.com as digitil.com. It meant the e-mail header had been typed in manually by someone covering his tracks. And by this time it had twigged that every time I contacted you something bad happened shortly afterwards.'

Archie stayed silent.

Findhorn was suddenly angry. 'People are trying to kill me.'

'That wasn't part of the deal.' Archie's gaze still kept flicking towards the window.

'You hurt me, Archie. You were the one person on this planet I thought I could trust.'

'Aye, well, we all have to grow up.'

'Why?' Findhorn asked, although he knew the answer.

Archie looked at Findhorn. His eyes were red-rimmed. 'You're a fool, Fred. If this Petrosian was really onto something then a fortune isn't the word for it. Imagine having a patent for some device that gives the world free energy.'

'You heard Papa the Greek. It could blow up in your face. So grab the money and stuff the risks?'

'Fred, you're holding something that could make you richer than Croesus. I've had it with poverty, I do not recommend it. I want more out of life than slogging my guts out, trying to educate a generation of third-rate students who don't give a damn. I just wanted to be up there with the people who made it. A piece of the action, was that so bad?'

'Some action.' Findhorn paused, then suddenly asked: 'What's your connection with these religious nuts?'

Archie shifted uncomfortably. 'You don't know what you're up against.'

'Are you and Romella in it together?'

He was sulking like a child.

'If Bradfield is right there's no zero point energy and this Casimir thing is just interatomic forces.'

'Aye.'

'Aye, spoken like a no.'

Archie sipped at the wine with every sign of disliking it. 'Bradfield conveniently forgot to mention one thing. These atomic forces he was spoutin' about. They're caused by ZPE in the first place.'

'You mean . . .'

'They're just part of the effing vacuum energy. He also

286

slightly misled you about a small noisy clique of outsiders. The people who believed in ZPE also laid down the foundations of modern physics. People like Einstein, Planck, Feynman and Bethe.'

Feynman and Bethe. Names in Petrosian's diary: he had worked with them at Los Alamos. 'So what's your gut feeling, Archie?'

'My money's on the Greek.' Then, 'Fred, there's something I have to tell you.' Archie refilled his tumbler and took another long draught. He screwed his face up with disgust. 'Effing turpentine.'

'You need that stuff to screw up your courage?'

'I'm supposed to invite you over to my hotel for a late drink. It's a kilometre away and between here and there, there are lots of dark alleys. And there are lots of nice wee coves for late night swimmers to drown in and I don't suppose the forensic science in this neck of the woods is world-beating.'

Findhorn felt as if spiders were crawling up his back. 'I wondered how they were planning to do it.'

'Revelation Island. Jerusalem of the effing Aegean.' Archie shook his head. 'Get off it, Fred. Get out of it as fast as you can.'

'I've been thinking of nothing else. But there's only one way off Patmos, and that's the ferry in Skala harbour.'

'Do you hear me? Get out of this house. Vanish. Sleep out in the open. Then come straight down from the hills and onto the ferry when it's crowded. And never, never be alone between here and the nearest airport, not for a second. It's your only chance, Fred.'

'What about you?'

'I'll tell them you went looking for a place in Oriko, to be close to a beach. It's the best I can do for you.' For the first time in the evening Archie looked directly at his friend. The man's eyes were dark with despair. 'I failed you, Fred. I'm sorry. But for a few days there I had a wonderful vision of freedom.'

Findhorn had a better idea. In the early morning he emerged, freshly shaven but cold and smelling a little of sheep dung, along a track leading into Kampos, the northernmost village of the island. In one little shop he bought black shoe polish, in another some safety pins, scissors and a few yards of black cloth. Then he disappeared back up the track. It took him two hours of experiment before he was satisfied, and he had trouble with the dark eyebrows, but the men on the quayside paid no attention to the woman in sunglasses, dressed head to toe in the traditional black, who climbed the gangplank onto the morning ferry.

The taxi driver fully justified the fearful reputation of all Greek taxi drivers and Findhorn, having just escaped with his life, thought it would be dumb to end up wrapped round a lamp post. He arrived at Athens airport drained and in a state of nervous exhaustion. He just caught a flight to Heathrow, changing at Paris, and found himself a quiet, clean bed and breakfast in Cricklewood, as far from Central London as the Underground would take him.

He bought a burger and ate it in his room, watching

some nondescript quiz game on television while his mind whirled around the day's events. *I came close. I now know the stakes. But I'm no nearer Petrosian's mechanism.*

He telephoned nobody, checked no e-mails. In no way could he be traced here. Nothing could touch him. He was secure. Absolutely safe. Yet again, he thought, pure reason triumphs over irrational fear.

And he jammed a chair up against the door handle.

23

The Traitor

Jürgen Rosenblum was wearing a long overcoat, with a fur collar which was turned up, protecting his ears from the snow-laden, icy wind. He was stamping his feet and staring glumly at the window display. Assorted dummies were dressed in tropical beachwear against a backdrop of palm trees and sun-drenched beaches. They were lounging in physiologically improbable attitudes around a motor boat, underneath a notice which said 'Sparkle with Speedo Swimwear'.

He looked up, saw Petrosian and grinned. 'Hey, old friend!'

'Well,' Petrosian answered in German, taking his hand, 'you look like a snowman. How's life?'

Rosenblum grinned some more. 'It's hell, but we proleteriat have to keep plugging away towards a socialist society.'

Petrosian said, ' "Onward our heroes march to victory," ' and Rosenblum gave him a quizzical look.

Rosenblum took Petrosian by the arm and they walked along the streets, facing into the bitter wind. Petrosian felt his ears in pain. 'So, what's this about, Jurg?'

'Not here. Let's take a walk.'

They crossed into Central Park and headed north. There were ice skaters on a pond and children playing around snowmen. Rosenblum nodded at a woman walking a small frozen terrier. Once past her, he said, 'Lev, you're about to be arrested.'

'*What?*'

'This is on a need to know basis, Lev, and one thing you don't need to know is the source of my information. Let's just say that I have a New York friend who has a New York friend.'

There was nobody close to them, but Petrosian spoke quietly. 'I know I was bugged at Greers Ferry. And the FBI wanted to know about Kitty and me.'

'We should speak in English, Lev. German draws attention. You've been bugged for a year now. And you were under surveillance for almost two years during the Manhattan Project.'

'How do you know this?'

'Lev, like I say, don't ask. But a warrant for your arrest will be going out today. Maybe it's already out.'

'What's the charge?' Petrosian was looking bewildered.

'Espionage.'

Rosenblum watched his friend's shocked reaction with clinical interest. Then Petrosian managed to say, 'They've got it wrong.'

'I know that. Don't ask me how I know it,' Rosenblum added hastily.

'Maybe if I just spoke to them.'

'Sure.' The tone wasn't even sarcastic. 'I'm getting

frostbite in the butt, let's find a café.'

Petrosian said, 'Since you know so much, Jurgen, maybe you know what case they've got against me.'

'Some of it goes back to the Manhattan. They know you handed documents over to Kitty.'

'They were just letters.'

'Why didn't you use PO Box 1663 at Santa Fe like the rest of Los Alamos?'

'I can't say.'

'You'll have to say if it comes to a trial.'

'I know it looks bad.'

'It looks terrible.'

They turned out of the park. The paths had been cleared of snow but more was falling from the sky. They walked along North Broadway. Rosenblum gave his friend time for the information to sink in, didn't disrupt his train of thought with conversation. He steered him into a warm café and sat him down at a window table before returning with a tray. He distributed cappuccino and bagels between them.

Rosenblum dipped his bagel into the cappuccino. A man appeared on the other side of the window, his collar turned up and hat pulled down almost to his eyes. He stood with his back to them, flapping his arms together. Rosenblum looked at him with a mixture of suspicion and alarm.

'Jürgen, that happened a decade ago. If they were going to do anything they'd have done it then.'

'Wrong, wrong, wrong. Then was war. They took a chance on you out of sheer necessity. Now is different.

They have new stuff on you, evidence that will convince any jury.' Rosenblum kept glancing at the man on the other side of the window.

'How can they have? I haven't done anything.'

'You were seen entering the Soviet Consulate in New York on several occasions.'

'I have a brother in Armenia. I was asking about the possibility of getting an exit visa for him and his family. The FBI quizzed me about that.'

'Were they satisfied?' A middle-aged woman approached the man. They linked arms and scurried off. Rosenblum visibly relaxed. He took a nibble at his bagel.

Petrosian said, 'I think so.'

'They were not. However that's not why you're about to be arrested. Twenty-four hours ago a long telegram was sent from the consulate to Moscow, not in their usual cryptogram which is unbreakable, but in an old GRU effort which Arlington Hall cracked years ago. It mentions you by name. It says you've supplied wonderful new, detailed information about the Los Alamos work which they'll be sending out by pouch. It's cleverly meshed with stuff they know the Americans already know if you get the general meaning. It delivers you to the executioner with vaseline on your skull and electrodes on your balls. You're the walking dead, Lev. And you have no place to hide.'

Petrosian felt himself going pale. He pushed his plate away. 'For a friend, Jürgen, you're the most treacherous bastard I've ever met.'

'Hey.' Rosenblum's tone was that of injured innocence.

'Don't shoot the messenger. I'm your pal.'

'I'll report this conversation to the FBI.'

'Who'd believe it? Would you if you were a fed?'

'Why not?'

'You have two ways of leaving this country, Lev. You can take the Rosenberg route.' The Rosenberg spies had gone to the electric chair only the previous summer. Petrosian was beginning to feel faint. 'Or you can be flown out in style, in your very own private aircraft. The Soviet Union would welcome a man of your talent and creativity. You'd lead a privileged life. But there's an entrance fee.'

'I'll bet there is.'

'All the information you can give about the Super.'

Petrosian shook his head sadly. 'From time to time I wondered about you, Jurg. And now all sorts of little things fit into place.' He leaned back in his chair, examined Rosenblum's face curiously. 'Tell me, what does it feel like, being a traitor?'

'I wouldn't know, pal, I'm a patriot. Only my loyalty isn't determined by accident of birth, or history or geography. It goes to the whole human race, not this or that tribe. I hated history and geography at school. All those battles and king lists.'

'Which school was that?'

'Come on, Lev, this is for the greater good. I'm your lifeline. Just what was in those letters you handed to Kitty anyway?'

'You don't need to know. Maybe I'll take my chances with the American judicial system.'

Rosenblum displayed yellow teeth. 'The courts go on the evidence before them. What else can they do? You got evidence to say you've been set up? Anyone can say they've been set up, if the courts were to start buying that, without evidence, every hood in the country would just have to turn up and declare they'd been set up and nobody would ever get convicted of nothing, you want to go to the FBI and say "I've been set up but I can't prove it," and they'll say, "Oh, that explains all this evidence pal, sorry to have bothered you"?'

'Calm down, I'm the one with his life on the line.'

'I need an answer. Take ten seconds.'

'I've had a bellyful of repressive societies.'

'This is a free society? McCarthy is Snow White and HUAC are the Seven Dwarfs?'

'What are you offering me, Jurg? Uncle Joe and the Soviet Union?'

'You'd rather be toast in Alcatraz? You want to fry in your own fat, hear yourself sizzle sizzle like bacon in a pan? Savour the aroma of fried Petrosian?'

'No.'

'Is that a yes or a no? Your ten seconds is up, Lev. For a man who has no choice in the matter you're taking a helluva time.'

Petrosian put his face in his hands. 'It's true, I don't have a choice.'

Rosenblum grinned. 'I take that as a yes. What tribute can you bring to the Motherland in exchange for your salvation?'

'I can't go back to Los Alamos. They'd arrest me.'

Rosenblum waited.

Then Petrosian said, 'I've kept a diary for twenty years. Everything I've done about the atom bomb and the Super is recorded in them. I can give you my diaries.'

'But like you said, you can't go back for them.'

'They're here in town. I moved them out of Los Alamos when the FBI started to poke around. After all they amount to a gross breach of security. They'll tell your scientists in the gulags where we're at, the complete state of the art.'

'What gulags? That's just Western propaganda. And the scientists will need technical stuff.'

'The technical stuff is there in summary. Deuterium-tritium reaction rates, implosion geometries, everything. And every significant conversation I've had. It's a complete record of the hydrogen bomb's development from the Los Alamos perspective. And there's even some stuff from Livermore.'

Rosenblum nodded happily. 'That sounds like your entrance fee. I'll put it to them. Hey, old pal, cheer up. You're about to start a new life in a socialist paradise.'

'I can't last long here. Your friends have forty-eight hours to get me out of the country. If they haven't fixed me up by then, I'll give myself up to the FBI.'

Rosenblum scribbled down a number in a diary, tore out the page and handed it over. 'You're a tough negotiator. Call me tomorrow morning. You'll have to avoid the dragnet until then.'

Petrosian managed to smile. 'I've done that sort of thing before.'

'Hey, it's good to see you happy. So have I.'

The snow was becoming blizzard-like. Petrosian watched Rosenblum scurrying towards a subway. He turned in the opposite direction, walking briskly north, ignoring the bitter cold. He had no clear intention in mind other than to retrieve the diaries and find, somewhere in the United States of America, some place safe and warm to sleep.

It was dark by the time Petrosian stepped off the bus at the Trinity Cemetery. He made his way along ill-remembered streets, navigating as much by his internal compass as by landmarks. Eventually he recognized the house, a white, wooden affair with a short driveway in which an old Ford was parked. The snow on the path was pristine; there were lights in the house.

Ant opened the door. She looked at Lev with surprise, and then a worried look came over her gaunt face. 'Kristel, hello. I've come to collect my briefcase.'

He heard the voices, low and businesslike.

She was stalling them.

He grabbed jacket, coat, briefcase with diaries. In the kitchen he put a finger to his lips and tiptoed out in exaggerated fashion. The children, mystified, suppressed giggles.

Quietly out the back door. Through the back garden. Over the fence, through the garden of the neighbour to the rear. Turn left, past Kristel's street. A Buick was parked at her front gate. Petrosian turned smartly right, taking a narrow lane with garbage cans; an old metal fence with a child-sized gap; trees beyond. He squeezed through the gap and was into a stretch of lightly wooded parkland. He walked through it to another street, out of ideas, aware only that he had to get as far away as possible.

He bought a ticket at the railway station and waited in an agony of impatience on the platform. Early morning businessmen began to turn up; he kept well away. The Pullman, when it turned up, was half empty. It sat at the platform for an excruciating ten minutes while he watched the entrance and wondered how they could possibly fail to check on something as obvious as a railway station. He thought they probably would check on the station; his photograph would be recognized by the clerk; and they would be waiting for him at the other end, a simple act which would culminate, a couple of years on, in his blood boiling and flames shooting from his mouth.

The train took off but Petrosian kept his eye on the station entrance, his imagination seeing men rushing onto the platform at the last second. The morning commuters started on their newspapers; regulars exchanged nods or greetings; someone started on an interminable story and ended up speaking to himself. Nobody even glanced at Petrosian and he marvelled that his inner fear was attracting no attention. The train ambled along the line for about ten minutes and then came to a halt. Commuters poured on. Nobody got off. Petrosian, his nerves at breaking point, pushed his way through the incoming passengers and jumped off the train just as it began to move away.

The ticket collector, a young, stooped man with a black waistcoat, looked at his ticket in surprise.

'Change of plan,' Petrosian explained.

'You want a rebate?' said the man.

'No thanks.'

'Won't take more'n five minutes.'

'I'm in a hurry.'

'Hey, it's worth four bucks fifty, Mister,' the man complained to the retreating figure, while Petrosian inwardly cursed the attention he had drawn to himself.

The word will be getting around. I daren't use public transport again.

As a middle-sized town in the State of New York, Poughkeepsie would have a taxi service. But taxis have radios. Petrosian visualised himself in the back seat of the taxi when his description came through; visualised the affected nonchalance of the driver as he pretended not to recognize it as that of his passenger; the man's fear that he might be murdered; the coded message to the office; the FBI men closing in.

I daren't use a taxi.

The briefcase was the killer. Look for a man carrying a medium-sized black briefcase. He thought of ditching it, abandoning the record of his last fifteen eventful years. But the diaries were also his passport. Without them, he was doomed.

Change the briefcase? It was too early. The shops were still closed. And for that matter, the streets were too quiet and he was still only ten minutes away from Kristel's house and he had effectively shouted 'Come and get me!' at the Poughkeepsie station.

Hire a car?

Certainly sir, just wait here a moment while I check availability and incidentally, since you fit the description which has just come through, make a quick telephone call.

Stay put? Hide away in some quiet park as he had done in Leipzig?

Leipzig was overnight, and a major city. This was early morning in a small town. Staying put would just give them time to close the net. He walked the main street in despair, lugging the briefcase which shouted, rang bells and blew whistles, with Rosenblum's phrase 'toast in Alcatraz' filling his head.

24

Executive Lounge

Sunshine. And cappuccinos in little hill-town bars, and buzzing little motofurgonis carrying big flagons of wine. Clattering dishes and noisy Italian chatter. Monasteries in Greece, and creepy religious fanatics, and treacherous friends and strangulation in dark alleys. Findhorn woke up, the lurid pastiche from his dreamworld fading for ever. Grey London light peeked under the curtains and his watch said eight a.m. He dressed quickly, trying to put his mind into gear as he stumbled down the stairs. Past the dining room, where a few Italian tourists were enjoying a full English breakfast, adding a notch to their cholesterol counts. He skipped breakfast, settled with the lady of the house, a plump, grey-haired little woman, and headed out in search of a business centre, a cybercafé, anywhere to plug into his e-mail.

There was a new message, a single telephone number with an American code. He thought it might be New York and if so it would be three in the morning. He dialled through.

'Fred?' She sounded excited.

'Where are you?'

'La Guardia, in New York. I'm just about to board Concorde.'

'What?'

'Relax, Fred, your brother's financing me. Stefi and Doug are coming down from Edinburgh. We're all going to have a council of war at Heathrow in three hours. Where are you?'

Findhorn had to look around for a moment. 'London.'

'Terrific, we gambled on that. I'll see you in three hours, then. We'll rendezvous at the Pizza Hut in Terminal One.'

'The Pizza Hut. You'll probably get there before me.'

'Doug wants you to phone him as soon as you can. Must fly – ha ha.'

Findhorn dialled Doug's Edinburgh flat. 'Dougie?'

'Fred, you're alive. Okay listen, we're just leaving for the airport.'

'Romella explained. I'll see you shortly.'

'Yes, but listen. I've been working hard on your behalf. I've been into the green Merc question etcetera and I've got things to tell you.'

Findhorn smiled. Little Brother was psyching himself up for the financial pitch. 'I look forward to hearing it.'

'And I'm picking up the tab from here on.'

'All right, you greedy little sod, how much are you in for?'

'Thirty per cent of the action. I'm taking a risk, it could be thirty per cent of zero.'

'A risk? You don't know the meaning of the word. I've been climbing icebergs, avoiding assassins . . .'

'But, Mister Bond, do you have the shekels to keep going?'

'Without the diaries this thing would never have flown. Ten per cent.'

'Flown? Without me you've crash landed. My legal contacts are refreshing the parts other people can't reach. And there's my flat, a safe house if ever there was one. Twenty-five per cent.'

'I don't need you,' Findhorn lied. 'Twenty.'

'Done. See you shortly.'

In the event Findhorn was the first to reach the Pizza Hut. After his second coffee he got up and prowled around restlessly, wandering through the Sock Shop, the Tie Rack, Past Times and Thorntons. In W.H. Smith he browsed aimlessly. The blurb on one book, *Nemesis*, proclaimed that 'This may be the last thriller you ever read'. He put it back hastily; it threatened to be prophetic.

He was on his third coffee when Stefi and Doug emerged from the airport crowds. She was wearing a white fur coat and Findhorn marvelled at how she could do it on her post-graduate income. Doug bore little physical resemblance to Findhorn, except for a slight roundness of the jaw, inherited from the paternal line as far back as the family photographs went. He was shorter than Fred, stouter, had hair which was, surprisingly for a young man, already beginning to thin, and had thick black spectacles. He was wearing a pinstripe suit and a long dark Gucci trenchcoat, and was carrying an expensive-looking tanned leather briefcase.

Stefi pecked Findhorn on the cheek.

'Breakfast, quick,' said Doug.

Findhorn let them get on with hash browns, fried eggs and sausages without disturbing them. A family of five spread themselves over two adjacent tables, spilling drinks and squabbling. The children had runny noses, and the parents seemed to have given up on the discipline thing.

On their second coffee, Romella turned up with an overnight bag. A light blue greatcoat was draped over her shoulders, she was wearing a plain white blouse and a short black skirt, and she was looking ragged. Findhorn introduced his brother.

'Okay,' said Findhorn, 'shall we confab here?'

Romella waved away the menu which Doug proffered her. 'If you like. But I can get us into the BA executive lounge on my Concorde ticket.'

There was a rapid exodus.

'Me first,' Findhorn said. 'I've discovered the nature of the Petrosian machine.' And he told them about the energy of the vacuum, how it might be nothing or vast beyond comprehension, and how Petrosian had found some way – or thought he'd found some way – of tapping into it, and that it might be the dawn of a new world or, depending on unknown physics, the end of it. He told them about the near miss with the atom bomb and how he thought that Petrosian's mind had been sensitized to instability by the experience. And he told them how he, Findhorn, was worried about instability in complex systems too, although in a much smaller way and in a different field. And he told them that he had failed to find the secret, the actual mechanism whereby Petrosian believed the vacuum energy could be tapped.

Stefi was wide-eyed. 'I'm overwhelmed, Fred. If you're right, and this is some machine for getting energy from nothing, it could turn the world on its head.'

Doug was open-mouthed. 'The financial possibilities are unbelievable.'

'Remember the caveat. It would need to be examined for stability.'

'Stefi and I think we know who kidnapped Romella, and who's lying behind the effort to get the diaries. And what you're telling us fits beautifully with what we've found. It provides the motive.'

'Surely it's the Temple of Celestial Truth?'

'I think they're just stooges. I believe they've been triggered by a much more powerful outfit.'

Findhorn felt his scalp prickling slightly. He leaned forward. Doug pulled a square white envelope from his briefcase. He glanced surreptitiously around the lounge before handing it over. 'These were taken by security cameras in the Edinburgh Sheraton. Anyone you recognize in them?'

The lens was wide-angle and gave a full view of a hotel corridor at the cost of a slight distortion of the field. Little numbers in the top right hand corner of the black and white pictures recorded the time. Findhorn flicked through the first half-dozen, recognized nobody. Numbers seven through eleven amounted to a series of stills; they recorded an inebriated man emerging from an elevator, standing in a confused attitude, making his way to a door, vanishing.

The time on the last picture was 23.47. Edinburgh pubs closed at eleven thirty.

'Captain Hansen,' said Findhorn.

The next photograph was marked 01.07. The elevator had disgorged a man and a woman. The man had a broad-brimmed hat, a long coat and sunglasses, none of which could disguise the small, bulky frame. The woman's face was likewise adorned with dark glasses but it was long, it had a turned-down mouth and the the same grim demeanour. She too was wearing a long coat which reminded Findhorn of something he'd seen in a movie about Wyatt Earp.

The next few stills showed them moving along the corridor, stopping at Hansen's door, the door opening although Hansen was out of view, and then, again, a blank corridor. The last two pictures were marked 05.33 and showed the same pair in the corridor, and then standing at the elevator, and then gone.

Findhorn closed the folder and slid it back. 'These are the people who tried to get Petrosian's briefcase from me. They claimed they were Norsk officials.'

'And they were in Hansen's room for over four hours.' Doug passed over another envelope. 'Here are some police photographs.'

'How did you get hold of them?'

'Santa popped them down the chimney. And this is the preliminary autopsy report. It's a rough draft and very technical, but it gives you an idea of what they were doing during those hours.' Findhorn flicked through the photographs. He felt himself going pale. 'The wire you see is telephone cable. There's evidence that he was gagged, I suppose to stop him screaming. The burn marks around his genitals suggest that they were using the room's electricity supply in some way. There are also pinhole marks around his stomach suggesting the same – look at plates three and four. And they drove things under his fingernails before they took them off – plates seven to ten. You don't want to look at the rest of it. Professor Hillion did the actual autopsy. His preliminary conclusion is that Hansen's heart gave out.'

Doug took the pictures and folder back from Findhorn's shaking hand.

'Why?'

'They were trying to find you, Fred.'

Findhorn said, 'These people weren't employed by Norsk. They said they'd come from Arendal. Norsk doesn't have an office in Arendal. I should know, I lived there for a year.'

Doug nodded. 'Norsk's head office is in Leiden.'

'I didn't know that.' Findhorn was unsettled, the images of Hansen were filling his mind.

'It's fairly standard, Fred. Lots of European companies have head offices with Netherlands addresses except that they're not really in the Netherlands. They're in the Dutch Antilles, Aruba to be precise, which is an island north of Venezuela.'

'You mean . . .'

'Norsk is owned by an offshore company. Find the owner of that offshore company, and you find the real power behind Norsk. Places like Aruba and Nassau act as black boxes. Officials in these offshore havens often adopt a *laager* mentality when it comes to enquiries about fiscal, tax and even criminal matters. It's all but impossible to penetrate the flow of cash in, through and out of them. However, you'll be glad to learn that your little brother not only knows people who know people with corruptible contacts in these places, the aforesaid people owe your little brother one or two favours.'

'You're surely not talking about criminals?' Romella asked, mock-innocent.

Doug's expression was pained. 'Clients, Romella, please. Anyway, I now know who really owns Norsk.' He gave a lawyer's pause, as if to let the fact sink in with the jury. 'And this knowledge has allowed me to identify your friends in the Sheraton photographs.'

Doug sipped at a tonic water and asked, 'What do you know about the Japanese Friendship Societies?'

Findhorn shook his head, and Doug continued: 'They're gangsters, the *sokaiya* in Japanese. They're a specialist branch of the *yakusa*. Originally they made their money by threatening to disrupt the annual meetings of large corporations unless they received large payoffs. It seems this was a legal activity in Japan until 1983. Anyway, I imagine payoffs continue to this day, legal or not. But now enter Darwinian evolution. A very strange relationship has grown up between the corporations that they used to prey on and these parasites. Now the corporations hire them to make sure nobody asks awkward questions at shareholders' meetings.'

'I have a horrible feeling,' Findhorn said.

'Aye, Fred. The nasties you met in the Whisky Club belong to a clan known as the *Genyosha*, the Dark Ocean Society. They're connected with a group known as Matsumo Holdings. Now the *Genyosha* have a track record. Their methods of friendly persuasion include limb breaking, finger amputation and the like. Rumour has it that the more stubborn shareholders have had a joyous early reunion with their ancestors.'

Findhorn said flatly, 'Look, Norsk asked me to get the diaries from that iceberg. Why didn't they just send regular company officials to collect them and be done with it?'

'Fred, I can think of only one explanation. Matsumo Holdings wants to do you harm.'

Findhorn blew out his cheeks. 'As in a joyous reunion with my ancestors?'

Doug nodded. 'It seems to be enough that you've been in contact with the diaries. And now, with this vacuum energy business you're telling us about, it all begins to fit.' He pulled a thick, glossy brochure out of his briefcase. 'I've dug up a group profile for Matsumo Holdings.'

'A group profile?'

'Yes. Matsumo took over the Fuyo group last year.'

'Means nothing to me,' said Findhorn.

'Don't get alarmed, Fred, I know you have the commercial acumen of a Tibetan monk. I'll keep it simple. The Fuyo group is centered round the *zaibatsu*.' He raised his eyebrows interrogatively, and Findhorn looked blank. Doug said, 'Right,' in the tone of a man about to climb a steep hill. 'The *zaibatsu* were a pre-war conglomerate of companies. The US occupation forces broke them up because of their support for the Japanese military during the war. But the Japanese ran rings round their US masters.'

'How?'

'The power centres in Japan have always been linked by secret societies. The industrialists carried on wheeling and dealing as before but without a formal legal identity. This post-war group – a *keiretsu*, or conglomerate of companies – had the Fuji Bank at their core. The group included Nissan, Yasuda Trust and Banking, the Marubei Corporation and Yamaichi. With the Matsumo takeover the group now includes the big four Japanese brokerage houses – Nomura, Nikko, Daiwa and Yamaichi Securities – as well as another major bank, the Dai-Ichi Kangyo.'

'So Matsumo are big. I'm impressed.'

Doug took another sip at his water. 'I'm glad you're impressed, Fred. Because these are the people who want you dead.'

Findhorn wondered whether, in that case, there was any place on earth where he would be safe.

Doug's expression was grim. 'And now we know why.'

Findhorn looked at his brother. 'As you say, I'm as streetwise as a Tibetan monk. Explain.'

Stefi said, 'It comes down to the people who asked you to get the diaries.'

'Norsk Advanced Technologies?'

She nodded. 'The child of Matsumo.' Stefi opened a thick, glossy booklet, the Annual Report and Accounts of Matsumo Holdings, English version. Its front cover showed a montage of famous Far Eastern constructions. Findhorn briefly recognized the four-kilometre Akashi

Kaikyo suspension bridge, and the fifteen hundred foot tall Petronas twin towers of Kuala Lumpur: the world's longest and the world's highest.

'Fred, Matsumo Holdings may be huge, but they're vulnerable to something. They've been taking a massive gamble. Look at this list.' Under the heading *Principal Group Companies*, Stefi's fingernail scanned down a list with names like Energy America, Hickson Oil, Seafield Oil, Shell Africa, Expro-Borneo and Fortune Exploration.

'Oil. It's been Yoshi Matsumo's obsession for the past five years. He's sunk his organization's future in it,' Stefi said. 'Partly they've been doing this through acquisitions, partly through creating new oil exploration companies. The big spender is Norsk Advanced Techs – which we know to be ninety per cent Japanese. Look here at Matsumo's three-year summary.' She turned the pages to *Profit and Loss Account*. 'Norsk are into deep ocean oil exploration. As of 31 March they had fixed assets of 34 billion sterling, liabilities of 13 billion, and creditors' amounts falling due of 14 billion. All that risk, all that cash going out.'

Findhorn said, 'That sort of money is bigger than the GNP of some countries. They're taking a massively expensive gamble.'

'But it looks as if it's succeeding,' Stefi continued. 'The field they've discovered in the Norwegian sector is huge. Now the cost of getting oil out from under the Arctic is beyond the means of a little country like Norway, but it seems there's been a little horse-trading.' Stefi put a finger to his lips, as if she was about to reveal some great secret.

'But they need oil prices to stay high. If, hypothetically, oil prices were to take a steep plunge any time within the next few years, the consequences would be horrific. It would bring Matsumo Holdings down. The knock-on effect would collapse Far Eastern economies like dominoes, and the effects would be felt in the West. And something even worse.' Stefi paused dramatically.

'Tell me.'

'Mister Matsumo would be at the apex of this apocalyptic disaster. Think of his personal humiliation.'

Findhorn groaned.

Stefi said, 'Yoshi Matsumo can't afford you, Fred. He absolutely must bump you off before you get to the secret.'

'This is unreal. Nobody does a thing like that.'

'Fred, grow up.' Stefi's smile had an edge to it. 'There's a rumour that the war in Chechnya a few years ago was fomented by the Matsumo group to push up the price of oil. If they can engineer something like that, what's an Arctic explorer?'

Doug said, 'Half the industrialists in the world would kill to get this process, the other half would kill to destroy it. Think of oil companies like BP, Exxon, Shell being bankrupted overnight. Car manufacturers and all their tributaries going into recession. Look at the mass unemployment that would follow.'

Romella said, 'You're speaking from the perspective of the rich twenty per cent of humanity. What about the billion people who are short of water? What about fertilizer, infrastructure and medicine for the Third World? Free energy would let people distil sea water and pipe it to desert regions, and create nitrate fertilizers from the air.'

'Or Semtex,' said Stefi. 'Think of massive terrorism on the cheap. The population explosion, the imbalances in power that would result in the Middle East. It would suck everyone in.'

Doug's eyes were gleaming behind his thick spectacles. 'There are fortunes to be made here. Huge fortunes.'

Findhorn said, 'Hey, this is fun. Only without Petrosian's machine we're out of the game, and we don't have Petrosian's machine.'

Romella yawned and stretched. 'Be nice to me. I know where it is.'

25

Armenia

Romella said, 'You were right about the old Geghard trading route. The merchandise went out that way after the war.'

A thrill ran through Findhorn. But now she was saying, 'There's a downside. The competition got to Kitty first.'

A teenage maneater, all eyeshadow and false lashes, entered the executive lounge, carrying a small suitcase. She stared openly at Findhorn, and Findhorn shot her a suspicious look.

Romella continued, 'It's weird. They got to Kitty less than an hour before I did. The poor woman got quite confused. So did I.'

'So where exactly were the messages going?'

Romella beamed. 'Not Turkey. Armenia!'

'You think he was sending them to his brother?'

'Almost certainly. And it wasn't atomic secrets or he'd have given them to a courier like Harry Gold or Rosenblum.'

Findhorn said, 'Hey, maybe it *was* just letters.'

'Maybe, but Kitty remembered the last thing Petrosian

sent out just before he disappeared. It was a thick envelope and she thought there was something about it. She remembers, after all those years.'

'Okay, it's our best shot, not to mention our only one. Now all we have to do is find Lev's brother, if he's still alive.'

Romella said, 'We'll need visas.'

Doug said, 'It sounds as if we're neck and neck with the competition. If they travel out via Heathrow you might even be on the same plane. They could be in the terminal now.'

Stefi giggled nervously. 'But surely not in this lounge.'

Findhorn shook his head. 'No chance. It's too unlikely.'

'Much too unlikely,' Doug agreed.

They looked around, suddenly aware. A gaggle of white-haired ladies were sharing some scandal three tables away; a couple of Japanese businessmen were sharing a joke over hot chocolates; otherwise the lounge was quiet.

Findhorn was looking at a departures screen. He said, 'Blimey! Where's the Armenian embassy?'

Doug and Stefi were standing, cold and impatient, at the entrance to Terminal Four. Findhorn was barely out of the taxi when Doug thrust tickets into his hand. 'It's boarding now, Gate Fourteen. Miss it and the next flight is in two days. Run.'

'Good luck!' Stefi called after the retreating figures.

In Terminal Four, a harrassed official jabbered into a handset as he hustled Findhorn and Romella through the security and passport controls. They were joined by a large American in a green check suit who trailed them, puffing, through long corridors, and then they were straight onto the aircraft, with a burly stewardess hovering at the door.

Findhorn settled in at a window seat, and Romella's boarding card took her to a seat near the rear of the aircraft. The Tupolev had the air of discarded Soviet rolling stock. It reeked of kerosene and had worn carpets and rickety chairs. And open luggage racks: it was an aircraft designed for the flat Russian steppes, without steep banking turns in mind.

The American, with thick spectacles and a green jacket, slumped down next to him. Fat arms overflowed into Findhorn's space and a *New York Times* spread itself around.

'Bin to Armeenya before?'

Findhorn shook his head, trying to get the right degree of surliness.

'Still full of commies. Y'on business?'

Findhorn turned up the surliness a fraction. He mumbled without looking up from the in-flight magazine. 'Touring.'

'Armeenyan women are the pits. They got no class and no deodorant.' The American picked his nose and spread his elbows some more.

The air conditioning wasn't working, and the aircraft sat on the tarmac for half an hour while the air grew stifling and Findhorn's shirt and pants became sticky with sweat. A baby exercised her lungs mightily, and the hostess prowled up and down the aisle like a prison warder. Finally the three jet engines howled, died, howled, died and on the third howl thrust them along the tarmac and into the blue sky with a take-off angle like a Lancaster heading for Dresden.

Somewhere over the English Channel, the American tried again. 'By the way, don't let the lousy upholstery fool you. This is one extremely strong aircraft. It's made from girders.'

Findhorn grunted happily.

'Not so sure about the maintenance, though. I hear some of the ground crew haven't been paid for months.' The American started on the in-flight magazine, leaving Findhorn to examine the rivets on the wing.

There was a long, sweaty wait on the tarmac at Amsterdam and it was dark by the time the Tupolev touched ground in Armenia. In Findhorn's highly strung state, it seemed to come in at a hell of a speed. Yerevan Airport was a massive, concrete, solid structure, unadorned with the shops and restaurants of Western airports. Findhorn and Romella joined the queue trickling one at a time through a short passageway. An overhead mirror gave the uniformed girl a view of the passageway as she flicked through his visa and forged passport. She fixed a puzzled stare on him, and went through the documents again, slowly. He tried to look casual while his insides turned to jelly. Then she had stamped his passport and he was through and wondering why, if Armenia was an independent country, the immigration officials were Russian.

A bus with a cracked windscreen took a handful of passengers into Yerevan, along pitch-black streets lined with brightly lit market stalls. Beds were made up at the side of the stalls: it seemed that the owners slept *al fresco* beside their merchandise.

The Hotel Dvin was another massive tribute to the Soviet concrete industry, and there was another queue as names were checked at the reception desk and passports were taken. The noisy American was making a big thing of being a regular visitor, calling everyone by their first names in a deep, loud bass. Findhorn tried to get away at the elevator, but the man caught the door as it was closing. A woman at a desk seven flights up gave each of them a key. Romella had the room opposite; at least the American was further down the corridor. Findhorn tossed briefcase and holdall onto the bed and opened the balcony doors. He looked out over a dark city, letting the delicious, cool wind blow over him for five minutes. Then he slipped quietly out of his room. He returned two hours later, rattled and frustrated, had a quick shower and flopped into bed. He slept badly.

In the early morning Findhorn found himself looking out over the same scene he had seen in former Soviet bloc countries from Poland to Slovakia. A jumble of shacks, corrugated iron roofs, piles of rubble. A couple of mangy dogs prowled around, and a cock was crowing from somewhere inside a tree-packed garden. To his right the snowy peak of Mount Ararat, seventeen thousand feet high, floated in the sky, its base hidden in a blue haze. Around half past seven women with plastic bags began to emerge along unpaved tracks, and a few identikit cars trailed exhaust smoke along the potholed road.

Findhorn had a breakfast of grated beetroot, hard-boiled eggs, carrots and coffee. There was no sign of either Romella or the American. The girl at the reception spoke good English. She was courteous, had plenty of class and no need of deodorant. 'I'd like to hire a car, please,' said Findhorn.

'I've fixed it.' Findhorn turned. Romella, breathing heavily, as if she had been running.

'How are we for time?'

'Assume we're out of it.'

'I don't trust that American.'

They waited without conversation in the big, drab foyer. The American appeared, still in green jacket and trousers, with a small black bag over a shoulder. 'Hey ho!' he waved in passing. 'What did I tell you about the women?'

After ten minutes a small man with Turkish features and a Clark Gable moustache appeared. Romella gave her instructions with the help of a hand-drawn map. Then Findhorn and Romella were ushered into the back of a black Mercedes.

'I thought we'd start at the Geghard Monastery.'

'That letter from Anastas?'

'Yes, transcribed by some priest. The Petrosian family must have been known to people there.'

'Except that the priests are almost certainly long gone, along with Anastas.'

The driver was fiddling with the ignition. The engine

coughed into life. He paused to light up a Turkish cigarette, and then took off without bothering about such refinements as rear mirrors, signals, or looking over his shoulder. He took them through earthquake-ravaged streets and past drab high-rise slums bedecked with washing. Twelve flights up, someone had knocked a hole in the side of the building, presumably to get fresh air into his flat. Children and dogs played in the dust. The sun was up and the air was getting warm.

Then they had cleared the city and were onto a steeply climbing road, with a good surface, and the traffic was light. Soon they were passing through mountainous country with high open vistas and steep gorges lined with fluted basalt. To Findhorn, the country had a vaguely biblical look about it. Away from the pollution below, he noted that Mount Ararat was in fact connected to the ground rather than floating in the sky. The road was deserted. After an hour of driving, Romella checking landmarks against the map, they passed a couple of girls carrying water in big Coke bottles, pushing a donkey ahead of them. Then there were calves at the roadside, drinking at a pipe flooding the road with water.

Mountains rose steeply on either side of them and the road became winding. Romella said, 'We should be there soon,' and in another fifteen minutes the road ended at a dusty little square with a couple of coaches and half a dozen parked cars. A trio of men in traditional dress welcomed them with a short, frenetic number played on drum, bagpipes and flute, and they walked up a steep, cobbled path past a handful of women selling sticky sweets and little brochures. The monastery was partly built into striated, precipitous mountainside.

At the arched entrance, Romella said, 'This may call for some delicate treatment. Remember Armenia was communist not so long ago and people don't necessarily open up.'

'I can take a hint.' He left Romella to disappear along a cloister, and strolled around the sparse, earthquake-cracked structure for about twenty minutes before taking a side door in a wall, and climbing a narrow track which wound steeply upwards. He sat on a rock and looked down on the monastery. Their driver was leaning against the side of his car, chain-smoking. A handful of tourists were wandering around the courtyard. The women with the sweets just sat. Presently Romella emerged, looking around her, and Findhorn climbed smartly back down the hill.

In the car, Romella said, '*Gna aya chanaparhov tas kilometr u tegvi depi zakh.*' It was the first time Findhorn had heard her speak Armenian.

She sat back in the car and said, 'It's our lucky day. Lev's brother is not only alive, he hasn't moved house in his entire life. Lev and Anastas were brought up in a shepherd's cottage not far from here.'

They drove back about ten kilometres before Romella tapped Clark Gable on the shoulder and issued another volley of instructions. The man grunted. In another kilometre, around a corner, was a track leading to what looked like a shepherd's cottage. They turned along it, bumping over rough ground, past a tethered goat, and drew to a halt beside a dirty grey Skoda.

Out of the car, they stretched their legs. Flies were everywhere.

The man who opened the door was over eighty. He was white-haired and stooped, with a white moustache and deeply wrinkled skin. But his dark eyes were alert, and full of curiosity. Findhorn spoke in English, Romella translated into Armenian. They first established that the old man was in fact Anastas Petrosian, and they had hardly started when the shepherd waved them in. Inexplicably, Clark Gable seemed to think the invitation extended to him. He wandered into the room, his eyes taking in everything.

They sat in a small, cluttered room around a rough-hewn table. The room smelled of pipe tobacco. A small, ancient bureau was covered with photographs: a young woman and children, separately and together, a young man, a near-Victorian photograph of an elderly couple. The shepherd disappeared into a kitchen and reappeared with bread, cheese, four tumblers and a bottle containing some golden liquid.

'First,' said Findhorn, 'forgive me, but I don't speak Armenian.' There was an exchange between Romella and the old man. The shepherd smiled, as if the idea of a foreigner speaking Armenian was crazy. 'I'm a historian,' Findhorn lied. 'I'm interested in the life and works of your brother, Lev Petrosian.'

The old man's eyes opened wide with astonishment. There was an outburst of gabbling between him and

Romella. Findhorn let it run its course. 'During the war, and just after it, your brother wrote some scientific papers, I mean articles. I know that when he was in America, he sent some of these to you for safe keeping. I am writing a history of that period, and I would very much like to know what became of these documents. Did they reach you?'

The old man said nothing, but his wrinkled face had acquired a tense expression.

Findhorn tried again. 'I don't want to take these papers away. I only need to read them for my historical research. If you have these papers, I would be grateful to read them. In your presence, without removing any. Or if you gave them to the authorities, please let me know where they went.'

Silence. The shepherd might have been mute. He certainly had no talent for disguising his thoughts: suspicion was plainly written over his face.

Findhorn sipped at the liquid. It was a first-class cognac. 'I know it was a very long time ago, but the Bomb was a watershed in the history of the world. Others have changed history with swords and armies, but your brother and his colleagues did it with mathematics and physics. Everything about that time has to be known. Especially I want Lev's contribution to be recorded for posterity, everything he did to be understood. He musn't be allowed to sink into obscurity, eclipsed by Oppenheimer, Teller, Fermi and the rest. His papers have been missing for fifty years and you are the link. For my research, and for the memory of your brother's achievements, I would be grateful to see them.

You're the only person alive who can help me.'

The shepherd moved to a dresser and opened a drawer. They waited expectantly. Out came a jar, and a pipe was filled with dark tobacco. He puffed slowly at it, and a blue billowing haze began to drift round the little room. Then he returned to the table and spoke to the driver, who started to shake his head aggressively. A lively conversation followed.

Finally Romella turned to Findhorn: 'The old man says he doesn't possess such documents. He's lying. That fool of a driver is antagonizing him. It's some political thing.'

Findhorn assimilated this, and Romella continued: 'He's also telling us that even if he had them, possession would have been dangerous in the days of the Soviet Union. He'd have been expected to hand them over to the authorities and even then he might have ended up in a gulag. I think he's afraid, his mind is still set in the old ways.'

'He thinks he'll get into trouble if he admits to having them?'

Romella nodded. 'That's my interpretation.' But an angry exchange was going on between Clark Gable and the shepherd. Then the old man was on his feet again. He crossed to the dresser, opened another drawer, and turned with a medal which he laid on the table with a flourish. The driver made a remark, clearly insulting, and the shepherd replied in a withering tone of rage and contempt.

Findhorn sat bewildered, trying to make sense of it. But the bottom line was clear. If the old man had the Petrosian documents, he wasn't about to admit the fact. 'Okay, we're getting nowhere. Forget it.'

'What?'

'We're upsetting him.'

'Excuse me? Fred, would you keep your eye on the ball? Somewhere in this house, within yards of us, is a document which would make the Count of Monte Cristo look like a case for social security. It'll revolutionize the future. And you want to give up on it?'

The shepherd and the driver were now snarling angrily at each other. Findhorn raised his voice over the noise. 'He's scared of the authorities.'

'So let's threaten him with them.'

'He probably thinks we are the authorities and this is a sting. Look, Romella, this is out of control. He just needs reassuring that we're okay people. Let's clear off and try again later without that idiot driver.'

Romella looked at the angry exchange and reluctantly nodded her agreement. She tapped the driver on the shoulder, and said something to the old man in a conciliatory tone.

The driver made some remark to the shepherd which had the effect of further infuriating the old man. Romella said, 'Get out!' sharply in English, and turned to the door.

Clark Gable's driving was jerky and erratic, and he muttered and growled to himself all the way back to the Hotel Dvin. Findhorn felt queasy and decided to skip lunch. Romella agreed with surprising readiness, given the urgency, and Findhorn stretched out on his hotel bed, letting the breeze blow in through the open balcony door.

He had lain on the bed, dozing, for a good hour before a simple but shocking possibility occurred to him. It came in a half-dream, based on an old made-for-TV movie about the Count of Monte Cristo. The half-dream had all the costume pieces and the wigs and the absurd haughty faces of both sexes, but the man playing the Count was a woman, Romella, and Findhorn suddenly opened his eyes and stared at the flies on the ceiling and realized that his travelling companion might not be averse to a little private enterprise followed by a lifestyle which put the Count of Monte Cristo in the shade.

He knocked on Romella's door and had the familiar sinking feeling in his stomach, and he put the hour's delay down to his Calvinistic upbringing, the constant tendency to assume the best of humanity in the face of overwhelming evidence to the contrary.

A taxi, hastily summoned at the front desk, took him back out of the city, Findhorn directing from memory. An hour later, turning into the stony track, his heart sank when he saw a small blue car parked beside the shepherd's Skoda. He motioned the driver to stop about fifty yards back from the cottage. The lack of a mutual language gave the driver no means to express his surprise other than by exaggerated eye movements.

It was late afternoon and the little living room now looked dull. A smell of burnt cooking now overlaid the aroma of tobacco. Otherwise the room was much as Findhorn had left it except for a few grey bricks which had been removed from above the stove and were lying on the floor in amongst chips of plaster and dust. The cavity so revealed had about the same dimensions as Findhorn's safety deposit box in Edinburgh. It contained a legal-looking document which to Findhorn looked like a will or property deeds. It also contained a small bundle of banknotes, neatly tied by string. Whoever had raided the cavity had not been interested in the money.

Findhorn picked his way over the man's corpse – the face and tongue were purple and the eyes, bulging from the ligature round his neck, were staring at the ceiling – and found a bread knife in the kitchen. A pot of beans had almost boiled dry and Findhorn switched it off. Back in the living room, he used the knife to cut a small handful of white hair from the shepherd's head. He put this hair in his shirt pocket, used a handkerchief to wipe clean every surface that he had touched. He raised Romella gently from her chair by the elbow.

His first thought had been that she had strangled the man, but he quickly put the absurdity out of his mind. She clutched him for some moments, desperate for secure human contact. He said, 'Better dry your eyes.' Then they were out, Findhorn closing the front door with the handkerchief, and taking her by the hand. The driver was leaning against the side of his car, about halfway through a cigarette.

The American was drinking beer in a quiet corner of the big entrance foyer of the Dvin. Findhorn returned the man's wave, keeping on the move. He took the elevator to the seventh floor with Romella, quickly gathered up his worldly goods. They headed down the stairs just as the elevator door was opening and checked out, retrieving their passports.

They flew back in a shiny new Airbus, the flagship of Armenian Airlines. It had, he knew, a service contract, state-of-the-art navigation, microchips with everything. Canned music soothed him, and the hostesses were smiling and elegant and smelled delicious. His safety belt worked and the toilet door locked.

He looked down at Ararat, the biblical mountain, and the white-capped Little Caucasus Range; beyond them, in a light haze, was Georgia and the endless expanse of the Russian Federation. London was only four hours away. He regretted that, in his haste to flee the assassins, he had taken the first and only flight to Heathrow instead of going via Paris or Amsterdam or Coonabarabran or Outer Mongolia.

Findhorn downed two bloody marys, but the images of violent death wouldn't go away. He stopped himself asking for a third.

It wasn't just that the bad guys had won the race for the secret.

It was also that he was a loose end; he could talk. And even with the deficiencies of the Armenian telephone network, his flight number would by now be known, arrangements would by now have been made.

'Why did you go back?' he asked.

Her eyes were still red. 'Isn't it obvious? Three of us were a threat, especially that idiot driver. I thought if I went back alone I could talk to him gently. Fred, he was still warm to the touch. It was horrible.'

It was practically their first exchange of words in three hours. He squeezed her hand.

It would, perhaps, look like an accidental encounter, something as innocent as a shared taxi with a stranger. Or they might use someone he knew and trusted.

Beside him, Romella stared morosely out of the window, and Findhorn wondered.

26

Escape

Like Newton's apple, it took a collision to jog Petrosian into a new thought. He mumbled an apology to the man with the newspaper, watched him as he hurried off, and then turned into the newsagent's.

And he didn't even have to buy a newspaper: there were a dozen cards stuck on a pin-board, and one of them said:

Pierce-Arrow V12 Model 53 Roadster 6500 c.c. whitewalled tires servo-assistid breaks resently resprayed padded dash new chrome bumpers spots recent overhaul 50000 miles $500 o.n.o. ask for Tom.

The apartment door was opened about two inches. A dark eye surveyed him suspiciously. The girl, he thought, had beautiful eyelashes.

'Hi. Can I speak to Tom?'

'Maybe he ain't hair.' There was a scuffling sound from the rear of the flat. Petrosian glimpsed a naked black youth running between rooms. The girl said, 'He doan get up at this time, mister.'

'It's about his car.'

'He get up for that.'

The door closed.

It was opened again two minutes later by the youth tucking a shirt into his jeans, who sauntered out of the building to a builder's yard, Petrosian in tow.

And there it was, spare wheel attached to its side, a running board along its length, new chrome bumpers and painted a gleaming black.

'How does it run?'

'Like a dream, mister.'

'I mean, is it reliable?'

'Hey, I ain't never had a day's trouble with it.' The youth was a picture of injured innocence. On the other hand he wasn't offering a trial run.

Petrosian pretended to examine the car. The tyres were bald, and a patch of canvas was beginning to show through one of them.

'What's the mileage?'

'Fifty thou.'

Petrosian looked inside. The driver's seat was sagging and pedals were worn smooth; he estimated that it had done four or maybe five times that distance.

'You're asking for five hundred dollars?'

'Yassuh, faive.'

No time to waste haggling. But if I don't haggle it looks suspicious.

'Okay. But make it four.'

'Hey, I's a poorist, I cain't make charitable donations. I need four seventy five for this piece of luxury.'

'Four twenty-five, then.'

'Done for four fifty, mister. Cash, right?'

Anastas's air fare, Petrosian thought.

'Jürgen?'

'Hey, old pal.'

'They're onto me.'

'Don't say another word. Just listen. It's fixed up for tomorrow night, ten o'clock.'

Petrosian's voice was filled with dismay. 'Tomorrow? I won't last that long.'

'I said just listen.'

'All right, where?'

'A place you know, Lev, a lake where you once thought the planet would overheat. Now my phone's tapped and your call is being traced. So get off the line and get the hell out of there.'

Jesus. 'Thanks, Jürgen.'

'A night and a day, Lev, just hold out for a night and a day.'

'What about you?'

'I got a four-minute start on them. If I don't make it, say hello to the Motherland for me.'

There was a faint, peculiar click on the line. But Petrosian was on Interstate 93, and merged with the heavy evening traffic flowing towards Boston in less than a minute.

'It has been set up?'

'Yes, sir.'

'Nothing can go wrong?'

'Absolutely not. The Corporation need have no fear.'

'You had better be right, for all our sakes. Tonight, I will pray for his soul.' The Chairman sipped at his white wine with satisfaction. 'A good Orvieto is hard to beat, unless it is a better Frascati. And what about his secret?'

'He has been carrying a large briefcase around since he fled. It never leaves his hand. It will of course disappear along with him.'

Something in the man's body language. The Chairman said, 'Was there anything else?'

'There is one thing, a small item.'

The Chairman went still. In his long experience of life, it was small items which brought empires crashing down. 'Well?'

'Within the last hour, I'm told that the FBI have picked up his trail.'

'Yes?'

'He is very close to the Canadian border. If he crosses it . . .'

The Chairman continued: 'The FBI will have no jurisdiction.'

'Precisely, sir. They would have to cross the border illegally.'

The Chairman relaxed. The man worried too much; a line on a map was indeed a small matter. 'I will speak to Mister Hoover. But be assured, he understands the force of necessity.'

Exhausted, Petrosian saw the lights of a small town.

He had to eat, had to drink, had to sleep.

He had taken the Pierce-Arrow V12 Model 53 Roadster with whitewall tyres six hundred miles east while the faint engine tap gradually intensified until it turned into the deafening clatter of a crankshaft trying to tear loose. The Pierce-Arrow was a twenty-year-old car and bound to attract attention; in Petrosian's case, a Pierce-Arrow with a big end hammering out over the countryside was an invitation to the electric chair. Somewhere past Grand Rapids he had finally lost his nerve, turned off the highway onto some rural road, and driven the car for another fifty miles until steam began to pour out of the overheated engine. He drove it, without lights, as far as he could take it into a wood, and ditched it.

He wished he'd taken the time to look for a Model T.

There was one piece of good fortune. Through the trees, he could see Lake Michigan sparkling in the distance.

There were no buses that early and Petrosian could only have cleared off on foot or by train. The New York express had just left by the time they got to the station and it had taken a lot of phone calling to cover the halts. It was another half-hour by the time a dim-witted young railway-man at Ploughkeepsie identified Petrosian: the spy, they assumed, must have a cool nerve to get off at the adjacent station.

A saturation search of the town revealed no sign of the spy; neither had he taken a bus, called a taxi or hired a car. However, a trawl of early morning shops had turned up a newsagent who recognized him. The man had entered his shop, looked at the cards on the wall and left without buying anything. He'd only noticed the guy because he looked a bit foreign and had seemed in an agitated state.

One of the cards advertised a car for sale. Tom Clay, a local delinquent, denied any involvement in the liquor store heist the previous week and informed them that the Colt 45 in the drawer was being held for a friend. However he readily admitted to selling the Pierce-Arrow to a weirdo with more money than sense.

By the time an APB had been issued, the spy could have been anywhere within a hundred and fifty mile radius, which encompassed such conurbations as New York City, Boston and Philadelphia. Common sense dictated that he would by now have ditched such a conspicuous car and be on a Pullman or a Greyhound to anywhere. It was therefore a wonderful piece of good fortune that a routine tap on his controller, Rosenblum, turned up a brief conversation with Petrosian. The trace told them that he was in all probability heading for Boston.

Except that the spy knew the call was being traced. Therefore unless he was really stupid – and the agents had to assume that an atomic scientist wasn't – he would be heading in some other direction. This being the north-east of the United States, he had somewhat limited options. He might head for Portland, Concord or Albany, or of course he could be trying for Canada, across the border to Montreal. The St Lawrence River was a barrier which could only be crossed at a handful of places, such as Sherbrooke or Niagara Falls.

There was one further piece of information: he had a

rendezvous at a lake. In that case he would be heading west, towards one of the Great Lakes. He would then be on the I–90 which, being a toll road, meant that he would easily be picked up, say at Syracuse or Buffalo.

As the hours passed and no news came in, it became increasingly likely that he had slipped the net. But the information about the lake was so clear that it had to be assumed he was by now on one of the towns or villages bordering Lakes Superior, Michigan, Huron, Erie or Ontario.

'A lake where you once thought the planet would overheat.' It might be weird, but it had a vaguely nuclear sound about it. Maybe somebody in the AEC or Army Intelligence could shed some light, maybe even some of his longhair colleagues would help assuming they weren't all bleeding-hearted commies.

They had until ten o'clock tomorrow to catch this guy.

The briefcase was like a lead weight, no matter which hand he held it in. He wandered along the main street, keeping an eye out for police and attracting the occasional curious glance from passers-by. The door of a neon-lit bar opened as he passed, and he was enveloped in a wonderful stream of hot, beery air. A spicy food smell reminded him that he hadn't eaten all day. Further along the street he passed a hotel. He caught a glimpse of the dining room. A couple of blond children were watching delightedly as a waiter poured flames over their steaks. Then the door had swung shut and he was tramping on through the snow.

He had the money, US dollars. He too could eat a steak

diane flambé; he too could spend the night in a warm, comfortable bed.

It was much too dangerous. The FBI could be checking hotels in the area. Even by walking on the main street, with suit and briefcase at this time of night, he was taking a terrible risk. But to stay out overnight, in some park, was to risk death by exposure. Already the bitter cold seemed to be numbing his spine.

Near the edge of the town, the shops and bars petered out. There was a dark lake, reflecting lights from the far shore. An esplanade ran alongside it, and on the side away from the lake was a scattering of terraced houses and waterfront hotels. A couple of hundred yards ahead, a pier projected out. A cluster of motor boats and yachts was moored alongside the pier, the masts of the yachts swaying gently.

The oldest urge of all – the urge to survive – brought a desperate thought to Petrosian's mind.

This far from town, the road was deserted. He crossed to the waterfront, climbed over a rail and walked along the pebbled shore, to be invisible from the houses. At the pier he climbed up slippery stone steps and walked along it, looking down at the moored vessels.

Petrosian knew nothing about boats. He guessed that the motor boats would be started by ignition keys and that the owners would keep these at home. His eye was drawn to one of the yachts; in the dark it seemed blue. 'The Overdraft' was written on its side. Suddenly the cold and exhaustion were just too much to bear and Petrosian went down the smooth, treacherous steps, gripping the rusty handrail to keep balance, and then he was on the yacht.

There was nobody in sight. There was a little trapdoor and a steep flight of stairs. Down these, he groped around, adjusting his eyes to the dark. There was a strong smell of diesel. He could make out, from the little frost-covered portholes which lined the walls, that the cabin curved inwards. As his eyes adapted to the dark he could make out a sofa, cupboards, a galley, and the door to another little room which he assumed was a toilet.

A galley meant a stove and heat. He scrabbled through drawers and found a near-empty box of matches. Experimenting, he soon had propane gas hissing on a ring. He struck the first match. It promptly fizzled out. Suddenly realising there were only two matches left, he took great care with the second only to find the phosphorus head splitting off with a fizzle.

The last match was now the most important thing in Petrosian's universe. He struck it carefully, firmly but not too harshly. It lit, flickered, started to die. He tilted it, cupping his hands round it, brought it to the hissing gas. There was a pop and the gas lit, throwing a blue light around the little cabin. Petrosian was too weary to laugh or cry.

At the front of the cabin were two bunks, built into the side. There were folded sheets, and wooden planks, and cushions. In a minute Petrosian had made them into a bed. He flopped on the edge of it, watching the gas flame as if it hypnotized him.

In a minute the cabin had warmed. He threw off his

suit, just had the presence of mind to turn off the gas, slid between icy sheets and in moments fell into the sleep of utter exhaustion.

27

DNA

Past the passport control, Findhorn looked warily at the humanity in transit around him. He steered Romella towards a quite corner. She looked at him in surprise but said nothing.

Findhorn licked dry lips. He said, 'Ten men on the berg. Then Hansen. And now Petrosian's brother. Twelve dead and I'm on Matsumo's hit list. Maybe even the CIA's, if they kill people. I don't see any way out of this. What's my survival time, Romella?'

'Fred, don't crack up now.'

'Somebody has Petrosian's secret, and we haven't a clue about it. Where does that leave us?'

Romella stayed silent, and Findhorn continued, his stomach knotted. 'And where do you come into this, Romella? Have you made an alliance with someone?'

'It's not the way it looks,' Romella said. She added, 'Fred, you have to trust me.'

'Why?'

He found the coolness in her voice disturbing: 'You have no other choice.'

Two armed policemen were strolling at the far end of

the terminal. Findhorn found reassurance in the sight. 'There may be people here who want to do me harm.'

She put her arm in his. 'We can lose them.'

Three taxis and an hour later, they found themselves a small table in the Black Swan near Egham, overlooking the Thames. Findhorn came back with coffees. 'We've lost the game, right?' It was his first remark since the airport.

Her face was grim. 'How can I put this gently? If we have, you're dead.'

Findhorn stared.

She poured the coffee. 'How can Matsumo be sure you haven't worked out the Petrosian secret from the diaries, enough to put a patent together? He almost has to erase you some time in the next day or two. What choice does he have, Fred? Believe me, you're being intensively hunted.' She scanned his face closely. 'By the way, *have* you worked out the secret?'

Over Romella's shoulder, he saw an elderly couple clambering out of a motor launch at a lock. They were doing things with a tow rope but didn't seem very sure of themselves. A small black mongrel on the cabin roof was watching them with interest.

'And where do you stand?'

She was spreading butter on a scone. 'I'm a translator.'

'I want to trust you.'

Romella stayed silent, then said, 'You're keeping something back.'

'It's true.'

She took a bite at the scone. 'Fred, why did you cut a piece of hair from Anastas?'

'Petrosian wasn't on that plane.'

Romella froze, coffee cup halfway to her lips.

'There were two bodies in that wreckage. The pilot's body was at the controls, and the other body wasn't that of Petrosian.'

'Don't worry, Fred, I'll look after you. I'm beginning to like you.'

'The body in question was blue-eyed. Petrosian was trans-Caucasian, an Armenian with Turkish and Persian ancestry. His eyes would have been brown.'

'And you've been keeping this to yourself from day one?'

'I also kept back a corner of a diary cover. It has dried blood on it. And here, as you say –' he tapped his top pocket '– I have a clip of hair from Anastas Petrosian's body. I'm going to try for a DNA comparison.'

'Fred, how did you see inside that iceberg? There were lights, right?'

'Yes, arc lights. And there was a torch. His face was a foot away from mine.' The memory of the hideous face came back to Findhorn.

Behind her round spectacles, Romella's brown eyes were a picture of scepticism. 'Doesn't ice look blue in a strong light? Maybe it was playing tricks on you.'

'Some day I'll write a book about what ice looks like and what it does. Meantime the eye was blue and that wasn't Petrosian. I don't know what happened on that

342

Canadian lake. But somehow Petrosian's diaries climbed on board and he didn't.'

'Maybe they threw him out over the north pole.'

'My bet is he just vanished into the woods. Maybe he made a deal with the Russians. Atomic secrets – maybe *his* secret – in exchange for a new identity. They were fooling the FBI into thinking he'd vanished behind the Red Curtain. The old Petrosian dead, the new one starting a fresh life.'

She acquired a thoughtful look. 'Let's go along with your fantasy for a moment. Do you propose we search for one man who's been missing for fifty years, somewhere on the planet? Someone who'd been given a fresh identity and is therefore totally untraceable? Who's probably now dead? And if he's alive and we find him, what then? Do you think he'll just reveal all, assuming he's not totally gaga by now?'

Behind Romella, the motor launch, the couple and the dog were sinking below eye level. The dog was yapping excitedly, tail wagging. Under the table, her foot rubbed against his leg.

'Hello, is that the Hsü Clinic?'

'Yaais.' Middle-aged female, stockbroker-belt English. Findhorn visualised heavy-frame spectacles, hair tied up in a bun, a disapproving mouth.

'I want to check up on the relationship between two people.'

At first, Findhorn thought he had been switched over to a machine: 'Thank you for calling the Hsü Clinic your requests are treated in strict confidence results from our state of the art AB1377 automated DNA sequencer have been accepted as evidence of identity in over a thousand United Kingdom court cases you may post or call in personally with samples the procedure takes about three weeks we can confirm paternity with 99.99 per cent confidence in most cases or non-paternity with absolute certainty our terms are cash in advance.'

'I have biological samples from both.'

'Yaais. What is the nature of the relationship to be tested paternity is two hundred pounds everyone else three fifty except zygotic twins which we can do for a hundred pounds plus VAT.'

'Brothers.'

'Is this for an intended legal action?'

'No, it's purely personal, for a family tree enquiry. From one party I have a small sample of hair, from the other I have a square centimetre of dried blood from a fifty-year-old book.'

A brief silence, and then the machine switched back to human mode. 'Oh my good life! Are we in Agatha Christie territory, then?'

'Nothing so dull.'

Another pause, while Ms Stockbroker assessed this answer. Findhorn filled the silence by saying, 'I need the answer by tomorrow.'

'Most of our clients need it by yesterday. The waiting list is six weeks.'

'Tomorrow will do.'

The voice acquired a frosty edge. 'DNA sequencing is a

skilled and time-consuming process and the results may have medico-legal consequences the sample preparation alone . . .'

'I'll call in later today with the samples and a thousand pounds cash.'

'I look forward to that, sir. You should have the results by this evening. You did say *two* thousand pounds?'

Romella found an Internet café in Staines. A handful of men and women, mostly young, were typing at terminals: a couple of female students on a project, a legal type peering at some turgid document, a schoolboy scanning a job list. She sat down next to a young man wearing earphones who, his face a caricature of intensity, was travelling through labyrinths, encountering strange and hostile creatures which he destroyed by tapping at the keyboard at amazing speed. She logged in to a search engine and typed 'holocaust + survivors'. Within minutes, as Romella clicked her way through infinitely darker labyrinths, she found herself sucked into a world more lunatic and unreal than that of her troll-fighting neighbour. She emerged, disturbed, into the sunlight an hour later, and took comfort in the normality of her surroundings, the shops, the bridge over the Thames, even the heavy afternoon traffic. She caught a red bus into central London and a tube to the Elephant and Castle. By the time she reached the address she had found on the Internet, it was dark, she was cold, and London was experiencing its first flurry of winter snow.

* * *

And by the time Findhorn emerged from the Leicester Square crowds, it was almost ten o'clock and Romella was frozen to the bone.

He dispensed with social preliminaries. 'Petrosian never got on that Russian plane. How did you get on?'

'Apart from being propositioned three times in the last hour? It was pathetic. The bulletin boards were the worst. You know, somebody in Romania asking his sister, last seen in Dachau, to get in touch, as if he hopes that some eighty-year-old granny will be surfing the Web . . .'

'Romella, calm down. It's all in the past.'

'I've always seen it that way. But for some people the pain's still here, right now.'

'Okay. Let's get you some place warm.' Findhorn took her by the arm and guided her towards the nearest cinema. 'Where are you staying tonight?'

'With you. Please.'

A surge of excitement went through Findhorn, quickly followed by a feeling of guilt brought on by the thought that to agree would be to exploit her unsettled state. 'We'll talk about that. And you can tell me what you found.'

'We'll talk about it? With men like you, Fred, how do we win our wars?'

They sat at the back of the cinema, and for two forgetful hours ate popcorn and drank orange juice, while warmth seeped into their bones and the Son of Godzilla rampaged through New York streets.

28

The Archivist

'There are no lists, there is no central registry. But depending on the time and money available to you, there are several places you could start looking,' said the archivist.

'Money isn't a problem,' Findhorn said, 'time is.'

'Some people have been trying to trace survivors for sixty years.'

'We have about sixty hours. Maximum.'

The archivist's mouth showed disapproval. 'If this were a subject for jokes, I would say that is a very bad one.'

'We have to try,' Findhorn said.

'What can possibly make the quest so urgent?'

'You don't want to know.'

The archivist looked at Findhorn curiously. Then, 'Which camp was she sent to?'

'I don't know.'

She sighed. 'If you could tie down the date on which she was transported, you might find some information in Nazi archives, say the ones held by the USA in the Berlin Documentation Centre, or by the French archive in the *Wehrmachtauskunftstelle*, which is also held in Berlin.

347

The Nazis liked to document everything. In fact they were quite meticulous.'

'Is there really no central point for information?'

She smiled tolerantly, to smooth the sharpness in her voice. 'What did you expect, a survivors' coffee club? If you had a few months to spare, I might have suggested that you go to Europe. You could have tried the Rijksinstituut voor Oorlogsdocumentatiae in Amsterdam or the Centre Documentation Juive Contemporaire in Paris. There is the Weiner Library only a couple of Underground stops away from here. In the States there is the Center for Holocaust Studies in Brooklyn as well as the Simon Wiesenthal Institute in Los Angeles, and there are centres in Washington and Chicago. Or of course you could have tried to gain access to the archives of Yad Vashem in Jerusalem.'

Findhorn's experience of information retrieval was search engines on the Internet, specialist librarians with a same-day response time, huge centralized databases with point-and-click access. The impossibility of the task was beginning to sink in.

The archivist was still talking. 'You will find two things in common about all these places. One, the staff are understanding and sympathetic. Two, names are jealously guarded. The pain is private to those who survived, not something for public intrusion. And as I said, there are no formal lists of survivors, only people who chose to share their memories with these places.'

'The flying time alone—' Romella started to say.

'—is the least of your worries. The procedures for

gaining access to documentation are often cumbersome and time-consuming. A letter of introduction is always helpful.' The archivist leaned back in her chair and looked at them over steepled hands. 'What information exactly do you have about this Lisa Rosen?'

Romella said, 'She was a student at Leipzig University in 1933, when she was aged about twenty. She was arrested and disappeared in 1939.'

The archivist's eyebrows were raised expectantly. She fingered her gold necklace, waiting. Then she said, 'And?'

'That's it.'

She shook her head, almost amused. 'Let's try anyway.'

They were in a room stacked with filing cabinets, tapes, discs, books, papers and a computer with printer and scanner attached. She led them to a cabinet, pulled open a drawer marked R–S and began on a card catalogue.

It produced ten Lisa Rosens.

'Understand these are ten who survived, emigrated and chose to tell their stories to us. The great majority of Lisa Rosens simply did not survive. This alone tilts the odds heavily against you. Of those who did get through, most emigrated to Israel or the States, not here. And most of those who came here have kept their stories to themselves or their families, or at most shared them with small survivor groups.' She paused, looking at them with a degree of sympathy. 'Even in the unlikely event that she survived, in all probability she will never be found. And you will certainly not trace her in three days.'

'We have to,' said Findhorn.

Romella looked through the cards. 'None of them fit.

Munich, Berlin, Dryans, wherever that is. Oh, here's a Leipzig, a girl who survived Theresienstadt.'

'Twelve years old at liberation,' the Archivist pointed out.

'What about Willy Rosen, her brother?'

There were nine Wilhelm Rosens. None of them fitted.

'Okay,' Findhorn said with a tone of finality. 'Thanks for your trouble.'

She took them through a room with three busy secretaries and walls covered with blown-up photographs of pyramids of hair, of human-packed cattle trucks, of skeletal creatures in striped tunics. At the exit she said, 'You could try Leipzig itself, perhaps tracing contacts through the University admissions records. 'I've known people make surprising progress with telephone directories.'

They stepped out of the door, stunned, and found themselves in a cold London morning, sixty years in the future. They made their way to a tube entrance. Businessmen were queuing to buy newspapers. Two old men at a bus stop were having a spirited argument over some football match. The street had a trattoria, a café, a video shop, an amusement arcade, closed at this early hour. There was an air of unreality, even triviality, about it all. Reality lurked behind the camera-protected door they had just left, in the mementos and the papers and the whispered tales on the tapes. In spite of the sunshine, the air was sharp and cold.

Romella found a telephone booth and insisted that Findhorn stay out of earshot. She spoke earnestly for a couple of minutes while Findhorn flapped his arms for warmth. Then she put down the receiver and they started to walk briskly towards Piccadilly. 'Okay. Doug wants you to phone him. He thinks he's onto something with the green Merc. I've started Stefi on the Leipzig problem. To save time I'm going straight there.'

'You go to Leipzig. I'm heading for Japan.'

They were on a pedestrian crossing. She stopped, looking at Findhorn in astonishment. 'You're mad.'

'Matsumo and I may make an alliance. He wants this thing killed.'

'You want to bet your life on that?'

A blue Mazda hooted impatiently. They moved off the road. Findhorn said, 'If you'd sunk twenty billion dollars looking for oil in the Arctic, would you want your investment undercut with a free energy machine?'

'Killing Petrosian's secret isn't in the deal,' she said angrily.

'The deal is irrelevant. I'm beginning to think that whatever Petrosian discovered could set the planet alight.'

Romella's face was grim. 'You don't know that for sure either. What right do you have to take a decision that could affect the whole planet?'

'What right do I have to pass it on? Petrosian didn't. This is contingency planning in case we have to move fast. First we need to find the secret.'

'I'd mention the fortune it could make you except that you'd start flaunting your damned principles.'

A sudden shower of freezing rain was sending Leicester Square pedestrians scurrying in all directions. They carried on, oblivious. Findhorn said, 'It's Mission Impossible, Romella, but somehow you'll have to find Petrosian within forty-eight hours if he's still alive. By that time I should be back from Kyoto and we can take it from there.'

Romella's next comment was like a blow to Findhorn's stomach. 'If you're going to kill the secret, you'll have to kill whoever is holding it.'

'I know.'

'You can't do it, right?'

Findhorn stayed silent. 'But it's okay to hand the job over to someone else.'

The silence was painful, but Romella pursued the point ruthlessly. 'You need somebody killed, Fred? The Whisky Club people can do that. You don't need to deliver yourself to Matsumo's gangsters.' Romella waved at a taxi. 'You'll end up in the Sea of Japan.'

The taxi had completed a U-turn in the busy street and was pulling up on a double yellow line. Fred said, 'He needs me as an ally.'

She shook her head. 'And once you're of no more use to him?'

'Don't think I haven't sweated over that. But what else can I do? Look, take me to that cybercafé in Staines. It's practically on the way.'

Findhorn, attuned to subtle intonations in his brother's voice, knew immediately that Doug had something to say. 'Fred? Have I got news for you! How many green Mercs were sold in Switzerland over the past eighteen months?'

'Two? Five thousand?'

'A hundred and sixty. And how many of these were 600 SL's?'

'Ten.'

'Eighteen. The cars were sold to a couple of lawyers, a rich widow, one over-the-hill actor, two restaurateurs etcetera. And one was a company car registered to a Konrad Albrecht, General Manager of a firm called Rexon Optica in Davos.'

'Davos? Isn't that—'

'It is, not far from the Temple of Celestial Truth. Rexon Optica specializes in making holographic guidance systems for a variety of NATO SAMs as well as for the Mark Three Eurofighter.'

Findhorn's silence was so long that Dougie had to ask, 'Are you there, Fred?' Then Findhorn said, 'This is desperately thin.'

'There's more. I've been using a PI firm—'

'Dougie, I'm catching a plane.'

'Okay, bottom line. Konrad Albrecht also has a ranch in Dakota where, surprise, surprise, the cult just happens to have its other main temple. He has a flat in Monaco and a holiday home in the Southern Uplands, which, surprise cubed, is where he's been staying over Christmas, complete with the company car.'

'Are you tying him in with the Temple?'

'He could even be their leader, Tati. Nobody outside the cult has seen him.'

'Doug, I have to fly. I need one more thing from you.'

'What's that?'

'A burglar. I'll call you tomorrow.'

Dougie was starting to splutter but Findhorn put the receiver down.

Findhorn's e-mail was brief and went to the Head Office, Matsumo Holdings, Chairman, for the attention of:

'I will be in London, Heathrow, in thirty minutes, and will then take the next available flight to Kyoto. I do not know which flight that is. Can I be met? Findhorn.'

They hardly exchanged a word during the taxi ride. Black and white images from the past kept flickering in and out of Findhorn's mind like old newsreels, interspersed with fantasies involving Japanese gangsters and the Sea of Japan.

Terminal Two was packed with Christmas travellers. Check-out queues straggled across the floor like big snakes. They scanned the flight departures. As if by some psychic force, the screen threw up an early afternoon flight for Osaka, courtesy of KLM. Findhorn said, 'Osaka's not too far from Kyoto. If there's a seat, that's my bus.'

Romella was looking worried. 'I just hope we meet again, Fred.'

Findhorn grinned nervously. 'That sounds like a line from a wartime romance.'

'Where will we rendezvous, in the event you survive your meeting with Matsumo?'

'Leave a message on my e-mail. But remember it will probably be read by others.'

'Be very careful, Fred.' Without warning she put her arms round his kneck and kissed him voluptuously on the lips, pushing her pelvis hard up against his. Then she pushed him away and she was gone, melting into the crowds, and Findhorn stood flushed and disturbed, with his heart pounding in his chest.

At the KLM desk, a cheerful blonde Dutch woman said, 'Ah, Mr Findhorn, you were expected and there is a message for you,' and she handed over a ticket along with a typed message attached by a paper clip: 'A room has been reserved for you in the Siran Keikan, Kyoto.'

Siberia – black, vast and surreal, was overhung with mysterious curtains of red and green which had been shimmering for hour after hour in the sky above. The 747 had trundled along like a hedgehog crossing a car park, skirting the Arctic Circle on its route to Japan. Findhorn sipped his gin and tonic and looked in vain for lights thirty thousand feet below. He wondered what it was like on the ground; toyed playfully with fantasy images of a forced landing in the frozen tundra, starving passengers eyeing each other hungrily, timber wolves beyond the circle of light around dying embers; and he thought he would probably, in that situation, stand a better chance than he did now. He finished his drink, gave his legs a business-class stretch and yawned, while the big aircraft flew him at ten miles a minute towards Yoshi Matsumo and the Dark Ocean Society.

Stefi had performed a minor miracle . . .

There was a light drizzle as the aircraft touched down at Munich airport. Romella took a bus into the city centre. She watched schoolchildren horsing around, a young couple in brightly coloured clothes on bicycles, women with shopping bags pausing to chat. Between the sheer happy normality of it, and the lunatic world in which she had been immersed a few hours previously, she could make no connection whatsoever.

. . . she had picked up on an Armenian survivor called Victor . . .

Taking her cue from the twin-domed Frauenkirche, she walked north through the Ludwigstrasse before turning right onto the Maximilianstrasse. Light blazed from decorated department stores and the streets were busy with last-minute Christmas shoppers.

. . . who had known not only Petrosian and Lisa . . .

She had expected high-rise flats British style, awash with graffiti and urine and, following the directions, was surprised to find herself inside a small shopping mall. She entered a lift with a young couple and a pink baby asleep in a pram, and emerged on a corridor with deep pile carpet on the floor and expensive fabric on the walls.

. . . but also another mutual friend from their Leipzig days . . .

Number five was directly opposite. There was a small peephole and a nameplate. It said Karl Sachs, and she hoped that her acting ability would be as good as her German.

. . . whose name was Karl Sachs, a retired Jewish doctor who now lived in Munich with his wife.

The man who opened the door was wrinkled, white haired, with a light blue cardigan and pince-nez spectacles.

He gave a cautiously welcoming smile and said, 'Miss Dvorjak?'

Kansai Airport was like any other big airport except that it was also a big, rectangular island in the sea, connected to Osaka city by a long, narrow umbilical cord. There was no reception committee. With some difficulty, Findhorn found a train to Kyoto. It arrived when the timetable said it would. It was spotlessly clean, smooth and silent. The 'guards' were shapely young females who turned to smile and bow as they left each carriage. Findhorn thought about the UK railway system and returned their smiles.

The map showed the line passing through Osaka and Kyoto, but from the window there was no way to tell where one city ended and the other began: he was travelling through a megalopolis, a city made of cities. At Kyoto railway station he decided against heroism and hired a cab. He said, 'Siran Keikan,' and settled back.

In the hotel itself more shapely females bowed and shuffled and treated his cheap overnight bag like the Ark of the Covenant. He had a shower in a tiny bathroom, slipped into the hotel dressing gown and flaked out.

The representatives of the Friendship Society came for him at eight o'clock the next morning. There were two of them. They were polite, if economical with the friendship. They were young men in dark suits who either did not, or chose not to, speak English. Findhorn sat alone in the back of a big air-conditioned BMW which swept him quietly along the Shijo-Dori, past tall office blocks and expensive-looking department stores with names like Takashimaya and Fuji Daimaru, past swastika-covered shinto shrines and cyclists on pavements. Then they were out of town and onto a winding road, with trees on the right and a big expanse of water on the left.

The Friendship man turned and waved his hands at the lake. 'Biwa,' he barked.

Findhorn said okay and declined the offer of a Lucky. They passed a long, spectacular suspension bridge which looked familiar, and he remembered it as the one he had seen on the cover of Matsumo's Annual Report. Then they were into hilly, tree-covered territory, and the car was passing a middle-sized town, with wooden single-storeyed houses crowded together in narrow, cable-strung streets, and then there were flooded fields and tea bushes.

Some miles beyond the town, the car slowed and turned off up a hilly road. The driver turned into what looked like a cement works. Findhorn glimpsed the flickering blue of TV monitors through the slatted blinds of the big windows. Then the car was through the works and winding up a narrow, tarmacked path with a lawn on either side, interspersed with small manicured trees and wrestlers, holy men and geisha girls, laquered and life-sized.

The house was a simple one-storied affair. It comprised half a dozen or so simple buildings, all glass and unvarnished wood and verandas and pagoda-like roofs, linked by sheltered walkways and hump-backed bridges over still water, and surrounded by paths through lawns interspersed with miniature trees and stone lanterns. Through some tall trees Findhorn glimpsed what seemed to be a small golf course. A gardener with a long fishing net was scooping up leaves from a pond. He paid Findhorn no attention.

The car stopped and Mr Friendship opened Findhorn's door with a scowl. A middle-aged woman, in a traditional kimono and heavy-framed spectacles, was standing at the top of a flight of wooden steps. As Findhorn approached she smiled, bowed, said, '*O-agari kudasai*' and, to Findhorn's embarrassment, dropped to her knees, untied his shoe laces and slipped his feet into brown slippers.

There was a large, scented atrium, almost bare of furniture apart from a couple of low chairs, some vases with flowers, and a pedestal a few feet ahead of him. The pedestal had Kanji script written down it, and it was topped with a bust of a severe-looking, bald-headed character. And in case anyone had missed the point first time round, Matsumo stared down severely in oil from the wall on the left. Findhorn was suddenly struck by the resemblance to Ming the Merciless in an old Flash Gordon movie he'd seen as a boy. In the circumstances, the comparison brought him no comfort.

The woman led the way past the pedestal to a sliding paper door, and bowed as Findhorn entered. He had hardly noticed the Friendship Society men until they closed the door behind him.

The room was furnished with little more than a low table, on which a few magazines were neatly piled. There were no chairs, but thin, square cushions and tatami mats were scattered around the floor in a geometric pattern.

Delicate scents came from flowers in vases occupying the corners of the room. The walls were paper screens. One wall was taken up, floor to ceiling, by a bookcase, the opposite one by a number of unusual paintings.

Findhorn, tense and sensing danger, looked at the nearest one. It was a rectangle about four feet long, filled with what looked like half a dozen big whorls. They were light blue. Some were overlying others, partly obliterating them, while others seemed to merge, the lines at their edges running parallel. Here and there little thin fingers of lines tried to squeeze through their big brothers. As he looked, Findhorn began to make sense of the patterns, to detect a strange mixture of harmony and clashing, order and chaos. It was both peaceful and, as he looked, increasingly hypnotic.

'You are looking at the rolling waves of the sea.'

Findhorn turned, startled.

The gardener, alias Yoshi Matsumo.

Findhorn said, 'I thought I was seeing fingerprints.'

Matsumo's expression didn't change. He spoke in good Oriental English. 'How can I put this delicately? To understand the painting one needs, shall we say, a certain sensitivity, I suppose you could call it an awareness of artistic form. The painting is in the traditional style known as *Nihon-ga*. It is by Matazo Kayama, from Kyoto. He is a master of the style.'

Matsumo hadn't bowed, offered to shake hands, smiled or said *O-agari kudasai*. His words were polite; but his expression was that of a man who has just disturbed a burglar.

REVELATION

Matsumo continued, 'You have come a very long way, Findhorn-san. I believe you would benefit from a very long rest.'

Findhorn thought that maybe Matsumo's English wasn't perfect and that he didn't mean it the way it sounded.

29

Matsumo

'Look down there, young lady.' The doctor's hands waved over the city. 'And tell me what you see.'

Sachs and Romella were standing on a verandah, wine glasses in hand. They were high above a long main road, with car headlights drifting along in both directions; it was now almost dark. The Alps, low in the distance, formed a background to the church-scattered skyline. The sound of clattering dishes came from the kitchen.

Romella looked over the skyline of the mediaeval city. 'A stunning view. A lot of busy traffic. Big department stores. Hordes of people doing last-minute Christmas shopping.'

Sachs said, 'I look down and I see ghosts. It was along the *Ludwigstrasse* that the Brownshirts used to march, behind row after row of swastikas. There were children in Bavarian costumes, there were brass bands pounding out old Bavarian marching tunes. I feel a sense of dissociation.' His English was excellent, if accented. 'Somehow I'm just not part of what you see, the ghosts are my reality. But you can't understand what I mean.'

Maybe not.

362

He continued, 'Anyway, your interest is not in my life's journey, but in that of this Lisa woman. She survived.'

She survived! A thrill ran through Romella. 'How do you know?'

The old doctor smiled. 'I met her. It was through the grapevine, as I think you call it nowadays. She had been a good communist at the University, like me, as well as being Jewish. An acquaintance in medical school had heard of a survivors' group based in Leipzig – a handful of people, you understand. I made contact, and there she was, the only one of the group I knew. We swore to keep in touch, and have done so ever since.'

'She's still alive?'

'And happily married. We write to each other every year.'

Romella tried to keep the urgency out of her voice. 'I'd be extremely grateful if you could arrange a meeting.'

The doctor frowned; Romella held her breath. Then he was saying, 'Forgive me, I'm neglecting my wife. Misha, you should have called me. Why don't you sit down, *fraülein*, while I do my duty in the kitchen?'

The Friendship reps stood one on either side of the bathing-room door, presumably to intervene should Findhorn attempt to drown Yoshi Matsumo.

Findhorn sat chest-deep in the wooden tub, his clothes ostensibly removed for ironing but in reality, he suspected, to search for electronic devices. He was sweating in the painfully hot water, and any movement was painful. Steam billowed around the little room.

Matsumo, his expression openly hostile, contemplated Findhorn. 'I ask myself, did this man cross Asia to apologize in person for his theft of the Petrosian papers? He did not. Well then, has he come full of contrition, ready to give them to me? He has not. There are no papers in your luggage, nor did you deposit any between Kansai and Hikone.' He sipped at a small glass of saki and continued: 'There remain two possibilities. He has come to negotiate a sale with me, or he has come to blackmail me with the documents. On either count, I admire your courage if not your intelligence.'

'You're wrong on both counts. I'm here to propose an alliance.'

Matsumo's eyes peered into Findhorn's, looking for a trick. 'For what purpose? Why do you imagine I would possibly make an alliance with you?'

'Our interests coincide, at least momentarily. The secret has been taken from me.'

'What?' Ripples of hot water spread out from Matsumo. 'Who has taken the papers?'

'They were stolen from me by a man from Sirius.'

Matsumo's expression didn't change. Findhorn continued, 'The same man who intended to steal the process from you.'

'And have you identified this man from Sirius?'

'I have. He's an industrialist. And I have reason to believe he's assembling a team of engineers to announce the process and discuss the construction of a prototype machine. As soon as his engineers know about the basic process, the secret is out and can't be put back.'

'You see what you have done with your stupid theft?'

Findhorn ignored the angry comment. 'I intend to indulge in a little industrial espionage, in the hope of finding the where and when. I suspect that the meeting will take place somewhere in Switzerland, and that it will be held very shortly.'

Matsumo barked something. One of the Friendship men slid open a panel door, and they left. Shortly the woman, who Findhorn presumed to be Matsumo's wife, came in with towels. She was followed by a girl of about eighteen, dressed in the traditional kimono, carrying Findhorn's clothes, neatly ironed and folded. Matsumo's wife crossed to a circular paper panel door and slid the two halves open. Cool air drifted into the room and Findhorn found himself looking out over the garden, where a low table had been set next to a gingko tree. Matsumo climbed the steps out of the tub onto the tatami floor. He was pink up to his chest and had a wrinkled, drooping stomach and white pubic hair. His wife began to pat him dry with a big white towel. Findhorn, feeling acutely embarrassed, climbed out and wrapped a towel around himself, declining the girl's offer of help. The girl tried to keep a straight face.

Lunch comprised mixed *sashimi*, raw squid and salmon cut into rose shapes, with thick slices of tuna, served on heavily lacquered square plates. A sea bass, garnished with daikon radishes and lemon, stared mournfully up at Findhorn. The ladies had vanished and the Friendship bodyguards were standing motionless a discreet twenty yards away. Lake Biwa sparkled below them, and Findhorn followed the wake of a powerful hydrofoil out to a central island, on which he could just make out a clutter of shrines.

'As you are a Westerner, I assume that you are driven by greed,' Matsumo said. 'You must suppose that by telling me where I can retrieve the secret, you will be given a share of future profits from it.'

The air, cool after the scalding tub, was refreshing. Findhorn said, 'The process may be dangerously unstable. It might cause disaster on a planetary scale. It has to be strangled at birth.'

Matsumo's face registered no surprise. Findhorn continued: 'Maybe the risk is at the one per cent level, maybe it's one shot in a million. But the potential profits are vast and the man from Sirius is willing to take the slight chance.'

'And you object to this?'

'If the risk was his alone, fine. But he's taking a chance with the future of life on Earth in return for personal gain. Four billion years of evolution being gambled on the turn of a card. And if we're alone in the Galaxy . . .'

'Now I understand. You seek the Petrosian document in order to destroy it for altruistic reasons.'

Findhorn was finding the sea bass a bit awkward. 'As do you, for reasons of commercial greed.'

Matsumo's hostile expression was gradually giving way to something approaching respect. 'So. You have been investigating my company's affairs.'

'Uhuh. Especially Norsk Advanced Technologies.'

Matsumo studied Findhorn's face closely. He grunted. 'Either you are, as you would have me believe, an idealist intent on saving the planet, or you are a very clever buccaneer.'

'Let me guess the sequence of events. When the aircraft wreckage was exposed, you found yourself in a race with the Americans to get to it. You didn't want an open conflict with them and and so you asked the religious fanatics to do the job for you. You got them onto that expedition, intending the diaries to end up on your icebreaker. What was the inducement, Matsumo-sensei? A substantial sum of money?'

Matsumo remained silent.

'So far it's been all take and no give. Tell me what happened. What's your connection with the man from Sirius?'

Matsumo resumed his surgery with chopsticks. 'In the course of my long career one or two people have addressed me in that tone. Sadly, misfortune came their way.' He neatly pulled skin away from flesh. 'I knew the rumours about the slight risk of instability of the Petrosian secret but gave them no credence. How could any machine be so destructive? But I also knew that the Temple of Celestial Truth fanatics, with their distorted vision of reality, would believe it because they wanted it to be true. They would see the diaries as the route to a doomsday machine. That was the real inducement for them. The agreement was that they would acquire the diaries and give them to me, and I would then build them the machine.'

'Except that you had no intention of honouring the agreement. You intended to destroy the diaries,' Findhorn suggested.

'And the fanatics.'

'Let me guess some more. The leader of the cult double-crossed you. He no more believes it's unstable than do you. And he no more intends to hand over a fortune-making machine than he really believes he's from Sirius.'

'That would seem to be the case. I admit to a miscalculation. The man would seem to be a total fraud. I do not pretend to understand the psychology of religious leaders. However, you say that you have learned the identity of this wretch?'

'Is it possible to eat a fried egg with chopsticks?'

'Of course.' Matsumo snapped his fingers. The girl appeared with steaming white rice in delicate porcelain bowls. She set the plates out, brushing her arm lightly against Findhorn. She was wearing jade green eyeshadow and her eyes were accentuated by heavy black eye liner, and she gave Findhorn a slow, almost insolent, sultry glance. Matsumo caught the look and said something sharply. She scurried off, giggling behind her hand.

'If you are a clever buccaneer, you too will try to double-cross me at the first opportunity,' Matsumo said. 'Strangling the process at birth: you understand the implications?'

Findhorn nodded, the old familiar feeling creeping into his stomach. 'The industrialist in question has read the document. To kill the knowledge, you have to kill the man.'

'Not *I*, Findhorn-san. *We*. Only if you share the guilt can your future silence, and hence my security, be assured.' Matsumo was skilfully separating the spinal cord of the raw bass from its flesh. 'You must join my ninjas in the enterprise.'

'Oh God.'

'Are you prepared to do this?'

'To become a murderer? What choice do I have?' Findhorn heard the words from his own mouth, could hardly believe he was speaking them.

'And then there are the engineers.'

'They should be left alone. My man won't have dared to spread the process around. Security is everything. He'll announce the process at his meeting with them, probably cut them in on the profits to ensure their secrecy.'

Matsumo paused, flesh from the dead fish hovering at his mouth. 'That is what I would do. Then we had better get to your man before he meets them. If we wait until the meeting, everyone at it must be killed.'

'I'm having to grow up fast here,' said Findhorn, putting his chopsticks down.

'The morality of killing worries you, especially as we are not even in a war. But think, Findhorn-san. If you do not kill this wretched man, he will build a machine and risk the planet for personal gain. What morality is there in doing nothing to stop him taking that reckless chance? Your choice is this. Kill a man, or do not kill him. If you do, you become a murderer. If you do not, you connive in risking the termination of life on Earth.'

'I suspect you've been through this sort of consideration before.'

Matsumo shrugged. 'Most men never pass beyond the moral simplicities to be found in a western. Their minds are shaped by ignorant clerics and Hollywood producers. But the world belongs to men who understand the limitations of the morality tales.'

'I love it. Your powers of self-delusion. The way you put a cosy gloss on murder.'

Matsumo changed the subject. 'The girl who has been with you. She is not just a companion for cold nights.'

'She's been helping me with the diaries.'

'Come, Findhorn-san, she is more than a translator.'

Findhorn shrugged. 'I don't know who she represents. For a while I thought she had sold out to the Celestial Truth.'

'She is dangerous. She will try to steal the secret from both of us. Therefore she too must be disposed of. It is equally demanded by the logic.'

'The lady's not disposable.'

Matsumo didn't reply. But then, Findhorn thought, he doesn't have to.

'Of course as a Party member I had privileges, but it wasn't too long before I became completely disillusioned with the system. It was corrupt from top to bottom. The Party finally gave me permission to emigrate to Canada and I took it. I practised there for thirty years, in a little town called Kapuskasing.'

'That explains your excellent English.'

Sachs shook his head sceptically. 'You're too kind. I have a thick German accent. Anyhow, with children grown up and dispersed over three continents, we decided to return here. Misha's surviving family are Bavarian.'

'More potatoes?' They were practically the first words Misha had spoken. A small, rotund, domestic woman, she seemed content to let her husband do all the talking.

Romella smiled and patted her stomach. 'No, thank you.'

'You are too skinny,' Misha scolded.

'I will telephone Lisa now,' said Sachs. 'Forgive me, but you understand that we all preserve each other's privacy. I will explain that you are writing a thesis about German universities in the 1930s and would like to speak with her. I am almost certain she will say no. Please wait here.'

Sachs disappeared into a corridor. Romella waited some minutes. When he came back, the man's face was negative. 'I am sorry. She is very old, like all of us now, and although she still has a sharp mind, she does not want to relive that part of her life. She sends her apologies and wishes you luck with your thesis.'

Romella nodded. Sachs showed surprise at her apparent lack of disappointment and she cursed herself as a lousy actress.

The point of the visit had been achieved. The rest of the meal was spent in inconsequential conversation. She left an hour later, sincerely wishing them every good fortune and leaving an unopened bottle of wine on the table.

The compartment in the train back to the airport was quiet. She took the little van Eck monitor out of her handbag and switched it on. It worked! The number Sachs had dialled came up on the little screen. Romella quickly noted it down, for fear that the unfamiliar device, hastily purchased in the spy shop near Burlington Arcade, would suddenly crash. It was a UK number but she didn't recognize the city.

At Munich airport, she phoned through to International Enquiries. The address was in Lincoln but it wasn't in the name of Lisa Rosen.

Neither was it in the name of Lev Petrosian.

It was, however, in the name of one Len Peterson.

There were no available flights between Kansai and Europe before six-thirty the following morning. Findhorn refused the offer of a lift to Kyoto and instead took the hydro out to the sacred island in Lake Biwa. At the top of a few hundred steps he took in the Buddhist shrine, the burning joss sticks and the breathtaking view. He thought he could see Matsumo's home, sunlight glinting off the windows. Then, with darkness falling, he took the Keihan to Kyoto and wandered the crowded, brilliantly lit streets. More than once, without any visual evidence, he thought he was being followed; but he put the sensation down to his overstressed nervous system.

Away from the centre of town Findhorn followed a crowd and found himself on a path lined with paper lanterns. Yet another shrine, this one small. A mysterious ceremony was taking place, involving chanting priests, flutes, tinkling bells and sonorous drums. Feeling like an alien from another planet, he bought a coke at a stall and made his way back to the hotel.

He sat in a small office while the manager obligingly

typed in a password on a computer. There were two new
messages on his e-mail:

> *Petrosian is alive and I know where he
> is. Meet me at Branston Hall, 5 miles
> out of Lincoln.*
> *Romella.*

Findhorn's brief burst of elation was abruptly cut short by
the second message:

> *We have a mutual task to accomplish.*
> *Reply to this address with a rendezvous.*
> *Barbara Drindle.*

30

Lev Baruch Petrosian

They found the flat close to the Westgate, near the Toy Museum and within sight of the Castle. Findhorn followed Romella up the stairs, trying not to notice her well-shaped legs. There were three doors leading off the top landing. The right-hand door had a handwritten card in the nameplate holder: *L. Peterson*. Findhorn and Romella looked at each other. Then Findhorn took a deep breath and knocked.

The delay was so long that it began to seem there was nobody at home. But then there was a noise from inside, and the door was opened by a white-haired woman with deeply wrinkled skin. She was in her eighties, and was a little stooped, but smartly dressed in a grey cardigan and long blue dress. She was wearing a gold necklace. 'Yes?'

'Mrs Peterson? My name is Fred Findhorn, and this is Romella Grigoryan. I wonder if we might have a word with your husband?'

Her voice was frail but clear, well-spoken but with just a hint of some foreign accent. 'You're not the telephone people.'

Findhorn patted his briefcase. 'We want to return some lost property.'

She frowned suspiciously. 'I did not think we had lost anything.'

'It was lost a long time ago.'

There was a hesitation as the woman absorbed this startling information. Then she opened the door further and said, 'You had better come in, then.'

She left them in a large, airy drawing room. The furniture was old but of good quality. There were no photographs. One corner of a bay window looked out over the city, framed by cathedral and castle. The other corner looked across at a flat whose windows were covered with stickers and pennants.

The man who entered the room was also white-haired and wrinkled. He had a grey pullover and rather shapeless flannels. His skin was brown, through heredity rather than suntan, and his eyes were dark and intelligent. He looked at his visitors with curiosity. His voice was quiet and clear, with just a trace of American. 'Sit down, please.' Findhorn and Romella shared a couch.

'Would you like some coffee?' Mrs Peterson asked at the door.

'Yes, thank you,' Romella said for both of them. 'Can I help?'

'I can manage.'

Mr Peterson sat down on a worn armchair opposite the couch Findhorn and Romella were on. 'Lost property, you said?'

It was the moment Findhorn had both dreaded and

anticipated. He opened the briefcase at his feet and pulled out the A4 sheets a bundle at a time, placing them on a low coffee table between them. He handed one bundle over at random; he had written '1945' on a transparent cover with a black felt tip pen. 'These are only copies, I'm afraid. But I think I know where the originals are held.'

Mr Peterson took spectacles from a shirt pocket and slowly put them on. He did not immediately open the document. He held it in both hands, looking at the date. His hands seemed a little arthritic. Then he gave Findhorn a long, disconcerting stare, a strange expression on his face. Finally he opened the diary and slowly flicked through the pages.

The sound of a kettle being filled came from the kitchen.

He stopped at a page halfway through the 1945 diary. 'That was some day. I remember it like yesterday: *At nine a.m. Louis Slotin begins to assemble the core*.' He looked up. 'He was a Canadian. Poor Louis was killed at Los Alamos not long afterwards, doing much the same thing. He put two sub-critical bits of plutonium just a fraction too close. There was a burst of radiation. Very brief, but enough.'

'Biscuits?' Mrs Peterson was asking at the doorway.

'No, thanks. Are you sure you don't want some help?' Mrs Peterson shook her head and left.

'So . . .' Peterson said, waiting for Findhorn.

'They were found last week, in the wreckage of a Soviet light aircraft near Greenland. I'm a polar meteorologist.'

Petrosian, alias Peterson, sighed. 'After fifty years. I'm supposed to have died in that crash. How did you find me?'

'A survivor called Victor led us to Sachs, and Sachs led us to you.'

'I suppose it was a bit of an obsession, all this diary writing. You know I keep a diary even to this day. I have a cupboard full of them. Of course I have nothing of consequence to write about these days. Not like Los Alamos, or Germany in the thirties. And I'm glad of the fact, if only because I find it hard to hold a pen. And who will be interested enough to read them after Lisa and I are gone?'

'You have two customers right here,' Romella said quietly.

'Coffee won't be a minute,' said Mrs Peterson, putting a tray on the table. It had milk, cups and sugar neatly laid out, and she had given them biscuits anyway.

Petrosian waited until she had left the room and said, 'This will be a terrible shock to my wife. Partly because it revives a past which she prefers not to remember. Different survivors handled their pain in different ways. Lisa's way was to put the past firmly behind her. To blot it out if you like. Her only contact with those days is an old friend in . . . ah, you say that is how you found us?'

Romella said, 'It wasn't Herr Sachs's fault. I tricked him. I got him to phone Lisa and recorded the number electronically. It was probably an illegal act.'

'And of course, there is the destruction of our life

together. Do you think they will send me to prison at my age?'

Findhorn was shocked. 'That is not our intention. We're not here in any sort of official capacity.'

Romella added, 'We intend no harm to your wife and yourself.'

'We're the only people alive who know your identity. And we intend to keep it that way.' As soon as he had spoken, Findhorn remembered Petrosian's brother Anastas. He hoped Lev wouldn't ask about him.

'What then?'

Findhorn did not feel ready to ask the question. 'There is something which puzzles me, sir.' As a rule he didn't 'sir' anybody, but in the presence of this man it came naturally. 'It's about your escape from Lake Michigan. You weren't on that Russian plane, but of course the diaries we have don't cover that event. What happened, that night?'

Petrosian leaned back in his chair. The smell of coffee was drifting through. 'Well now. That too was some day. Or rather, some night.'

Petrosian was wakened by the rhythmic slap of water on the side of the yacht. Grey light was streaming through the little portholes. Suddenly afraid that the boat owner might appear, he rolled out of the bunk and climbed up the steps to the galley door. It had frozen in place. He put his shoulder to it without success, then retrieved a bread knife and finally managed to prise the door open with a loud crack.

The yacht was six inches deep in overnight snow. The lake, however, had not yet frozen, although the surface was dotted with thin floes and the little waves had a turgid, almost treacly look about them.

The holiday cottage, where he assumed the pick-up would take place, was on the opposite coast of the lake, about a hundred miles over the horizon to the west.

The abandoned car might or might not be reported within hours.

They might or might not think to search a boat.

The owner might or might not turn up.

His appearance on a public highway, conspicuously lugging his suitcase, would seal his fate. Unless they hadn't yet started looking hereabouts.

He could sail the boat across the water. He'd never sailed a small boat in his life. Its loss might go unnoticed for days, or the owner might live in one of the houses a hundred yards away.

All imponderables, on which his life came or went.

By about three a.m. it had become clear that the spy, if he was indeed heading for one of the Great Lakes, had slipped off the main highways. There was nothing to be done until daylight.

Dawn was a somewhat nominal concept as it brought little more than a grey gloom to the landscape. However, as the day progressed, police patrols in a score of little towns bordering the Great Lakes reported no sightings of the black Pierce-Arrow car. It began to look as if the lake referred to had been a minor one, like Mooselookmeguntic or the Richardson Lakes, or Moosehead or First Connecticut. They all skirted the Canadian border. They were all in remote and inaccessible places. Or maybe they were fooling themselves and the spy's rendezvous was further south, say Lake Winnipesaukee in New Hampshire. Despair began to settle round the FBI team like a descending mist.

The team's musings were interrupted by excellent news around mid-morning. Forestry workers had reported an abandoned car to the local police. It had been driven off a narrow track deep into the woods. It was a Pierce-Arrow with whitewall tyres. Its number plate told them that Tom Clay was the legally registered owner. A place called Ludington, a small town on the shores of Lake Michigan, was within sight of the car.

They as good as had him.

The early afternoon, however, brought no reports from hotels, boarding houses, restaurants or cafés. This was odd because firstly the guy had to eat, and secondly, if he'd stayed out overnight he would now be as stiff as a board. It was known that he had money; he had emptied his account of nearly a thousand dollars a few days previously, and Tom Clay had reported that the spy paid for the car out of a fat wad of notes.

A boarding house enquiry produced one sighting. The proprietor had seen nothing, but one of his resident ladies had mentioned, over breakfast, a man behaving oddly. At around ten o'clock the previous night she had just happened to be looking out of her upstairs window. She had seen a man with a briefcase climb over the railing directly opposite the house, and disappear out of sight below the embankment wall. There was a perfectly good sidewalk, and if he was taking a stroll, why carry a briefcase? She had kept looking and thought she had seen movement on the pier a few minutes later. It was sufficiently odd that she mentioned it to her other friends over breakfast. Was he a spy or something, she asked the FBI agent, her eyes gleaming, and the proprietor had tut-tutted politely.

God bless old ladies and net curtains everywhere. He was either heading north to Manistee, or he had found a boat. Any attempt to hitch a ride on that quiet road at that time of night, at twenty below, would have saved the state the cost of the high voltage electricity. Therefore he must be in one of the boats, not a hundred yards away from them.

He wasn't, but he had been. His footprints were still on the deck and the owner was a New York construction worker who hadn't been near the place for three months. Unfortunately the footprints went back into town and soon merged with those of the pedestrian populace at large. And by the time they found that the early morning ferry to Kewaunee was still sailing, it had already crossed the Lake and disgorged its passengers.

Petrosian was shivering violently and glad of the fact.

Somewhere, maybe in a *Reader's Digest* article in some waiting room, he'd read that you're in trouble when you stop shivering. It meant the body had run out of the energy it needed to shiver.

Shivering is a heating mechanism. Hold onto that.

He was also frightened.

There were two hazards to be avoided, an imminent death through exposure, and a delayed one through electrocution.

He looked into the dark woods. There were probably moose and timber wolves, and beavers in the frozen ponds. So far, however, there had been only a deathly stillness. As the evening progressed the clouds had thinned and the temperature was plunging downwards. A three-quarters moon was rising.

He looked at his watch for the tenth time in an hour. It had little luminous numbers and hands, and as a man who knew about radiation he had made sure the luminescence came from electron transitions and not radium.

He hadn't eaten for thirty hours.

So what? Survive the night. Then worry about your belly.

Having just looked at his watch, he did so again. It was twenty minutes to ten. The lights of a small town reflected off the water some miles to the south. Three point two miles to be exact. An hour's walk for a fit man with a briefcase on a good surface. Longer for a physical wreck who hadn't eaten for thirty hours and who peered fearfully into the dark woods between every step.

Petrosian had watched a solitary angler on a jetty, wondering in alarm if he intended to fish overnight. Around eight o'clock, however, the man had packed up his estate wagon and driven off through the forest track, having had no luck. Now Petrosian was left in a silence broken only by the gentle lapping of waves on the shore just beyond the road.

There was a roaring log fire, and a hot plate of chilli con carne, and a woman with Lisa's wonderfully curved body and a warm, loving expression, and yet at the same time with Kitty's long legs and slim face and blonde hair. The warmth from the fire was penetrating his bones and he sank into the deep pile of the rug, and he yielded to the overwhelming urge to sleep, and he found himself lying in the snow, face down, with no recollection of having fallen. He had lost feeling in the toes of his left foot, wondered if they would have to be amputated, had a brief, panicky vision of losing his leg.

At first he wondered what had wakened him, and then he heard the faint engine sound, coming from the direction of the lake. At first he thought it must be some ship, but as it grew in intensity he recognized it as the sound of an aircraft. He rolled over, managed to get onto his hands and knees, and then with an effort staggered to his feet. He tugged at the briefcase, but it now seemed to be full of bricks. He started to drag himself through the snow, falling and picking himself up, steering around bumps and hollows.

And now he could see it through the trees, a small dark shape, its propeller scattering the moonlight. It was maybe a couple of miles out.

And there was a car, approaching swiftly from the direction of Kewaunee.

Petrosian stopped about twenty yards back from the edge of the track, hidden in the trees. The plane was low and seemed to be heading directly for him. The car was maybe a couple of miles away and closing fast.

The engine noise dropped in pitch, sounded almost like a cough. Then there were twin sprays of water, bright in the moonlight, and the engine was revving up and the aircraft was taxi-ing towards the jetty. Petrosian, in an agony of indecision, held back.

The engine of the little aircraft died. The door opened and a man stepped on the float. He was gripping the wing with one hand and holding something in the other. It looked like a coil of rope. He was looking into the trees, seeming to stare directly at Petrosian. Then, suddenly, the car was driving over the pebbled shoreline, its headlights momentarily flooding the plane and the pilot. Petrosian, terrified, dropped the suitcase and braced himself to run into the woods.

The driver of the car was out and running along the jetty. The pilot threw him a rope. There was an exchange of conversation in Russian. Petrosian recognized one of the voices, tried to run forwards, fell, couldn't get up. By the time he got to his feet the driver was half-crawling along the wing, a leg dangling in search of a strut, the pilot holding him by the arm while the little aircraft tilted and swayed dangerously.

And then they were in, the door was slammed shut and the propeller was revving up, and Petrosian was stumbling along the jetty like a drunk man, waving and shouting hoarsely.

The engine died and the door opened.

'Hey, Lev!' Rosenblum shouted in pleasure.

'I have them. The diaries.'

'So where are they? Bring them here!'

Petrosian stumbled back into the dark, returned with the briefcase. Rosenblum was halfway along the wing. He threw the coil of rope. Petrosian caught it and pulled, and then he was heaving Rosenblum off the wing and onto the jetty. It took up all his remaining energy.

'Thought you hadn't made it, old pal. The shoreline's crawling with feds. This is it?' He lifted the case, grinning, his spectacles reflecting moonlight.

'They're all there, Jürgen.'

Rosenblum reached into his inside pocket. For an insane moment Petrosian thought he was about to be shot. But then Rosenblum was handing over an envelope and saying, 'Passport, driving licence, birth certificate etcetera. They've even given you a life history if you want to use it. You're born again, Lev. Look, we can probably squeeze you in. You sure you want to do it this way?'

Petrosian nodded, took the envelope, looked at it stupidly.

'The car's yours, you've owned it for years. The key's in the ignition. Now take it and clear off fast. And excuse me if I get the hell out of here. The Motherland awaits her revolutionary hero.' They shook hands.

Just before he closed the door, Rosenblum waved and shouted, 'Get moving, Lev! Go to Mexico or someplace.' And then the propeller was revving up, and the aircraft was accelerating over the water.

In the life-saving warmth of the car, Petrosian took a last look over the lake. But there was little to be seen; only a decaying wake scattering the moonlight, and shadows.

31

Instability

Petrosian smiled sadly. 'The diaries were useless, you see. They had no information which could have helped Stalin to develop the Super. But I told my treacherous friend Rosenblum otherwise and he accepted them in exchange for a new identity for me. They were my passport to freedom. Thank you for these copies. They will be wonderful reading for me.'

Romella asked, 'Why did you suppress your discovery? It could have made you rich.'

'And conspicuous. Anyway, rich to what purpose? We are happy. We are comfortable. We have everything we need.'

Findhorn chipped in. 'It could have brought you scientific honours.'

Petrosian almost laughed. 'Ah! So I am talking to a scientist! Einstein once told me he wished he'd been a woodcutter. I came to understand what he meant. We have never been happier than when Lev Petrosian died in that air crash, and Leonard Peterson the antiquarian bookseller married Lisa Rosen the tutor of German. The key to our happiness has lain in our anonymity.' He looked at them, suddenly wary. 'Which brings me to the question of why you are here.'

Romella tried to say it kindly, but the words were harsh. 'We may have to take away that key.'

Lisa came in with a large coffee percolator. She had a slight stoop. She placed it on the tray and said, 'Have you seen the table mats, dear?'

Petrosian said, 'Lisa, I wonder if you would leave us for a while?'

She looked at him, suddenly alert, and then at the visitors. 'What is wrong?'

'Nothing,' said Petrosian.

'Then why are you looking like that?'

'It's nothing to worry about, Mrs Peterson,' Romella lied. Lisa left, trailing scepticism and worry.

'I think I understand. Your purpose is blackmail.' Petrosian's accent was acquiring a Germanic tinge. 'You wish to extort the secret of the process from me in exchange for your silence.'

Findhorn poured coffee into delicate white cups. 'The secret is already in someone else's hands. Milk?'

'No! That is terrible! But how can that be?'

There was no avoiding it. Findhorn said, 'The diaries led some people to your brother Anastas.'

'Anastas? He wasn't harmed?'

'No,' Findhorn lied. 'I saw him briefly myself.'

Petrosian's face showed relief. 'And how is he?'

'He was well when I left him. Still working, I think. He has a little Skoda and he smokes a pipe. We shared a very good Armenian cognac. Unfortunately his house was robbed, and documents taken.'

Petrosian seemed to be talking half to himself. 'My vanity has created this problem. It was such a wonderful discovery, but I should have strangled it at birth. First I tried to patent my discovery. Only when they turned it down did I realize I was up against huge commercial interests. I even began to feel that my life was at risk.'

Petrosian's mind was momentarily elsewhere. Then he continued, 'Then I realized that the process had uncertainties, you see, it might just possibly be dangerous. I therefore decided to hide it against the day when it would be examined by a community more knowledgeable and enlightened than that of the nineteen fifties.'

'So you sent it to your brother through the Geghard trading route?' Romella asked, pouring milk for herself.

Petrosian showed surprise. He sipped at his coffee, and added a spoonful of brown sugar crystals. 'I am amazed at what you have found out.'

'We also know you sent letters to your brother through Kitty Cronin. But we don't know how.'

'Ah, Kitty.' His mind seemed to wander. 'Is she still alive?'

'And well,' said Romella. 'She married a businessman called Morgenstern. They were divorced after fifteen years. There were two children. She moved to some place in the Colorado Rockies and opened a shop selling mountain climbing equipment.'

A smile briefly softened the tension in Petrosian's face. 'She loved mountains.'

'She retired ten years ago and now she's living with her daughter in Miami.'

'I am glad life went well for her. Kitty's sister-in-law worked in the Turkish Embassy in Washington. My letters went there. They were delivered uncensored to an address in Igdir, a little town in Turkey. From there it was easy. My father was a shepherd, and Anastas continued in that style. In the Gegham mountains we knew every track between Lake Sevan and the Turkish border. The Geghard bazaar existed long before the war. It was a clandestine trading route. We used it to bring in cheese, coffee and other good things from Turkey, and barter them at Garni and Geghard. So far as I know the war merely enhanced the flow. To have been caught . . . well, they shot children too.'

Findhorn said, 'We're here because we want to know why you suppressed your discovery. It wasn't just for personal reasons.'

Romella held out the plate of cream biscuits to the old man, but he shook his head. 'I am not sure how much to tell you.'

'Perhaps I can help,' said Findhorn. 'I suspect that the process is unstable. If you can persuade me that it is, I'll try to have it stopped.'

'Perhaps you will. Or perhaps you have failed to recover the secret and wish to trick a simple old man into giving you it.'

'You must consider that possibility,' Findhorn said. 'After all, we're total strangers.'

Petrosian stood up and walked over to the big window.

'I was almost unmasked once. It happened in Oxford, not long after the war. I saw a man in the Causeway giving me a very strange look. It was some seconds before I recognized Rudolf Peierls. I had to keep walking towards him. But of course I was dead by then, and I simply passed him without giving the slightest sign of recognition. To this day I am not sure whether he recognized me.'

'Did anything come of it?'

'Yes. I launched my antiquarian book career here in Lincoln rather than Oxford.'

'Regrets?'

'None. I never kept up with the scientific literature, at least not at research level. But my career as a seller of old books has put me in contact with some of the finest minds who ever existed. My best friends speak to me from many countries and many centuries.' He turned back from the window and sat down. 'You can thank them for the decision I have made. You see, without them, I would not have the insight into the human soul which I believe I have. I choose to trust you, and hope that my friends are not letting me down. I will tell you about the process.'

Findhorn gave Romella a look. She said, 'I'll give Mrs Peterson a hand. Technical stuff gives me a headache.'

Romella took their hired Rover towards the A1. They drove into a pleasant little market town called Retford, looking for signs for the dual carriageway, and promptly got lost in a maze of one-way streets.

'Open my handbag,' she said.

Findhorn retrieved the large black bag from the back

seat. It held a jumble of what Findhorn assumed was the usual women's stuff, including a small bottle of the Diorissima perfume which was driving him mad; and two folded sheets of paper.

'Look at the papers. Dad's been using some heavy pressure. He fired them through this morning and he's dying with curiosity.'

There were two documents. The first was rubber-stamped 'CIA Restricted Release':

```
TO: DIRECTOR FBI
FM: DIRECTOR CIA
OUT: [            ]
FROM: [           ]
DATE OF INFO: 7-12 JULY 1953
SUBJECT: TRAVEL TO MEXICO OF MRS K.
MORGENSTERN
1. On 7 July a usually reliable source
reported that Kitty Morgenstern née
Cronin planned to take a vacation in
Mexico City in the near future. You will
recall that during the war she was
suspected of transmitting documents
containing atomic secrets, given her by
Lev Petrosian, to the USSR.
2. Another usually reliable source has
reported that Mrs Morgenstern stayed at
the home of Edward Ros while in Mexico
City. Edward Ros is a well-known left-
wing journalist.
```

3. During this stay, they were visited
by a man whose description is remarkably
close to that of Dr Lev Petrosian. You
will recall that according to our field
agents Dr Petrosian attempted to escape
to the USSR from the Canadian border in
a Soviet light aircraft. This aircraft
was   clandestinely   shot   down   on
Presidential orders by the USAF over
Greenland.
4. Although unconfirmed, the above
report leads to the conjecture that Dr
Petrosian was in fact not on board
aforesaid aircraft.
5. The above information was obtained
from highly sensitive sources and should
not be disseminated further.

DISTRIBUTION: LEGAL ATTACHE

In the absence of sensible comment, Findhorn said,
'Blimey!' He turned to the second sheet. It was marked
'Official Dispatch' and was heavily deleted.

POUCH Air
DISPATCH NO. ⬚
CLASSIFICATION ⬚
TO: ⬚
FROM: ⬚
SUBJECT: (Dr) Lev Petrosian

1. You will, of course, recall the investigation of subject which you conducted at our request in 1949–51. You will recall that on several occasions subject met a known Soviet agent, J. Rosenblum, as well as Soviet Embassy officials (his cover story, that he was enquiring about friends and relatives behind the Iron Curtain, could not be broken).

2.

3. Subject was recognized on several occasions in Oxford, England, after his supposed attempted escape to the USSR. He now lives with Lisa née Rosen, a German Communist who survived the concentration camps. He has established a bookselling business in Lincoln, England.

4. MI6 surveillance of said bookshop has so far revealed no evidence of contact with known or suspected Soviet agents. On 23 August,⬚⬚⬚⬚⬚⬚, the wife of ⬚⬚⬚⬚⬚⬚, was in the city of Lincoln but no contact was made.

5. Subject has no further access to classified material.

6. In the light of the above, and the difficulty of using VENONA, wiretap and

similar material in open court, we have
decided not to seek extradition or
prosecution. The British MI6 have been
informed. His illegal entry to the UK
will be ignored as he may be a useful
trap should the Soviets wish to use him
on any future occasion. The Home
Secretary concurs.

COORDINATING OFFICER

At last they were through the town and heading
west. Findhorn looked out at the flat agricultural land.
Ahead of them, a small aircraft was dropping slowly
towards some airfield hidden by trees. 'So Lev and Lisa
have been in hiding for fifty years, and there was no
need.'

'We can't tell them that.' Romella was slowing for a
tight corner.

'Agreed. We leave them to hide in peace. I wonder
about the blanked-out stuff.'

'Don't push your luck, Fred. I was lucky to get even
that.'

A few miles ahead of them, streams of lorries were
marking out the line of the A1. Romella was looking
thoughtful. 'You've reached your decision on the Petrosian
secret.'

'It needs a stake driven through its heart.'

'What? Why?'

'It's too dangerous. It could work like a dream or it could evaporate the planet.'

'What are the odds?'

'A hundred to one it would be okay. Maybe even a thousand to one.'

'One chance in a hundred of oblivion versus a near certainty of ending up richer than Bill Gates. I might take a chance on it, Fred.'

'I might give it a try too. At an individual level it could be a gamble worth taking. But not if you're risking the whole of humanity. There are people out there who don't give a toss for anyone but themselves.'

'And Albrecht is probably one of them,' she said. Ahead, a tractor was trailing a machine with long, swaying metal prongs. She slowed, edged cautiously past. 'Duty obliges us to hand this over to the authorities.'

'We have a higher duty, Ms Grigoryan. To the greater good.'

'That was pure Rosenblum. You have an anti-authoritarian streak, Fred. But who the hell are we to make a decision like that? We have to send it upstairs.'

'There's nothing I'd love more. Unfortunately my conscience is right here in the car with me, not upstairs. Someone out there would take that one per cent chance.'

She shook her head in disagreement.

They were now on a long, straight stretch of road. 'I guess the Romans were here,' Findhorn said, to break the tense silence.

The junction with the A1 was about a mile ahead.

Romella was frowning. 'The deal is that we find Petrosian's secret.'

'So let's stick to that.'

'But, Fred, we don't even know where the document is.'

'It's probably in Albrecht's hands by now. My guess is he's poring over it in some hideaway, about to summon his engineers. We have to reach him before they do because the moment they've gone over it, it's out. He'll start on a patent application. I reckon we have less than forty-eight hours.'

'But you now know the principle of the thing. Can't you beat him to a patent – assuming in your infinite wisdom you decide the risk is worth taking?'

'No chance. The mathematical details would take weeks to work through before you even started on the engineering aspects.'

'Have you thought this through, Fred? Say we find Albrecht. What do we do about him? By now he knows the secret.'

Findhorn, anticipating Romella's next words, had the sensation of a trapdoor opening in his stomach. She was slowing down as they approached the junction.

'Are you up to murder, Fred? Would you kill for the greater good?'

Findhorn was biting his thumbnail. 'Matsumo asked me the same question.'

'Fred, a man in his business acquires enemies. He probably hides from Mossad, the Palestinians, the Iraqis, the Iranians, the Mafia and the Salvation Army. He's an elusive man. How can we possibly discover where he is?'

'The Celestial Truth might know. The information might be in their Swiss headquarters.'

The Rover had stopped at the junction. The A1 was a solid mass of traffic, streaming north and south like anti-parallel lava flows. It took a second for the implication of Findhorn's remark to sink in; when it did, Romella turned to him open-mouthed. 'Are you serious? Break into the Temple?'

'It'll have to be tomorrow. We're out of time.'

'You're raving, foaming-at-the-mouth insane.'

'Decision time, Romella. South to Whitehall, or north to Dougie's?'

There was a momentary gap in the flow of southbound traffic. In the north lane, lorries were effectively blocking the carriageway and leaving a stretch of empty road in front of them. 'Oh, bloody hell,' Romella said, swinging the Rover smartly across the road and into the northbound carriageway.

Findhorn said, 'I put it down to my charm.'

32

Piz Radönt

Findhorn came out of the Glasgow sleet into the warmth and chatter of a crowded pizza parlour. Waiters were whirling around the tables, the plates balanced on their arms defying gravity. A young Sicilian in a tuxedo led Findhorn to a table, lit a candle. Findhorn, indifferent to what he would eat, ordered spaghetti and clams.

His free hours in Glasgow had left him emotionally battered. Miss Young, the white-haired departmental secretary, had looked at Findhorn with open-mouthed dismay when he had called in. He knew it when she scuttled off to collect Julian Walsh, the prim-mouthed, fussy little head of physics, and he knew it when Walsh came in the door looking like a funeral undertaker.

Archie had been on vacation, and had stood too close to the edge of the Isthmus of Corinth. It's a steep man-made gorge, in Greece, you know.

I've heard of it. Did anyone see him fall?

No. You're surely not implying that he jumped? The prim lips had twitched anxiously: the eyes had worried about departmental scandal, pressure of work, sharp questions at next month's faculty meeting.

Oh no, nothing like that. He'd been pushed. He was a path to the Temple of Celestial Truth, and much too dangerous to be left alive.

Findhorn had kept the last bits to himself, and Walsh's lips had relaxed, he had grown expansive. He will be missed. His second-year lectures on solid-state physics were a model of clarity.

Findhorn followed the spaghetti by a phoney *zabaglione*, made with cheap sherry rather than *marsala al'uovo*, but the house saved money and the punters didn't know the difference. He emerged into an Argyle Street drizzle.

The next twenty-four hours, he knew, were going to be the most difficult and dangerous in his life.

He wandered off reluctantly to find a taxi, his whole body suffused with a sense of dread, the spaghetti and clams lying heavy in his stomach.

'I'm dying. I can feel myself slipping away.'

'Shut up, Stefi. Let Joe do his job.'

'I tell you I'm freezing to death.'

'At least be quiet about it.' Findhorn turns to the man crouching behind the boulder. 'What do you see?'

'Gie's a minute.' The man shifts his position slightly, and taps the brass eyepiece of the telescope. 'A big dog. It looks like an Irish setter. No, it's a Doberman.'

Findhorn says, 'That's bad news.'

'You might put it that way. Here, have a peek.'

The man stands up, rubbing his thighs and flapping his arms. Findhorn crouches down, fiddles with the focus. Under the high magnification the image in the Questar is rippling slightly as cold air drifting up from the valley far below mingles with the colder air at three thousand metres.

A fence nine feet or so high encloses about four acres of rocky, sloping ground in the shape of a square. In the centre of the square is a large rectangular building, glowing red in the light of the setting sun. A kilometre beyond it, and separated from the building by an immense grim chasm, a restaurant sits atop an adjoining peak like an illuminated flying saucer. In the telescope Findhorn can just make out that restaurant and building are joined by a cable and that a trio of small cable cars are slotted into a concrete station underneath the restaurant. The cable disappears round the back of the rectangular building and Findhorn cannot see where it ends.

The building has four turrets, one at each corner, and golden domes surmounting each turret. There are windows on two levels, about a dozen on each of the two sides Findhorn can see. The roof is steeply sloping and white with snow, the eaves projecting out over the walls. A massive, arched double door shimmers in the field of view, and above it is a large wooden circle enclosing a cross: the zodiacal Earth sign, and the adopted symbol of the Temple of Celestial Truth. In front of the big door three people are in conversation. They seem to be dressed in long black robes, but at this range it is impossible to make out any features. The Doberman is sniffing around their ankles.

'What do you think, Joe?' Findhorn asks.

'It gives me the creeps.'

'I mean . . .'

'I don't like the look of it. It's high risk.'

Findhorn glances at his watch but it isn't necessary. Already they are in the gloomy shadow of a big mountain and the temperature is plummeting. The Temple is still in red sunlight, but long black fingers are creeping towards it.

'Point of entry?'

The man nudges Findhorn aside, looks through the eyepiece of the powerful telescope again.

'They've gone in. I can't see the dog. Point of entry.' He pauses thoughtfully, a general studying the terrain. 'The flat-roofed building to the left.'

'The one with the helipad?'

'Aye. We can approach using these rock outcrops as cover, then snip through the wire and into the wee building, if it's empty, that is.'

'Then?'

The man stands up and starts to fold away the Questar. 'Then it gets difficult. A first-floor window if we're lucky. If not it has to be the roof.'

Findhorn thinks about the high, steep, snow-covered roof. He says, 'Stefi, you get back to the car.'

'No, I'll stay here. If you get lost I'll flash the torch.'

'Okay, people, let's go.'

'I don't think so,' the man says.

There is a stunned silence. He says, 'It's far too risky.'

'We have a deal. Ten thousand pounds to get us in and out undetected. Tonight.' The steel in Romella's voice takes Findhorn by surprise.

'Lady, yon perimeter fence and the dog are telling us something. These people are security minded, a fact which I do not like one little bit. There could be all sorts of nasty surprises in there. I don't know what you lot are into, but with my record, if I'm caught I go down for ten years.'

'Can't you do it?' Findhorn asks.

The man bristles. 'I can, but I'm not into kamikaze. You didn't tell me to expect a set-up like yon. I'm telling you this one is pure insanity.' He waved a hand towards the big building a mile away. 'It's no' exactly some suburban bungalow with PVC windows.'

Romella says, 'Twenty thousand pounds. And if you can't do it we'll get someone else.' *Except that we're out of time to get anyone else.*

Greed and prudence are battling it out in the man's head. Romella adds, 'Just as soon as we get back to Glasgow.'

Joe is balancing the odds. Cold is penetrating the marrow of Findhorn's bones. Then the burglar is saying, 'There's a showroom just up the road from where I live. It has a sweet wee Alfa Romeo in it, two-plus-two, open top, flamenco red. A fabulous bird trap. It costs twenty-six.'

'Get us in and out, undetected, and you'll be driving it tomorrow morning.'

In the near-dark, Joe is still weighing the odds. Then

he exhales heavily and picks up his rucksack: 'Okay, okay. But if I give the word, don't ask any questions, just run.'

They cut left, leaving Stefi shivering behind the rock. They plough through deep snow and skirt boulders, taking a meandering path through hollows. Findhorn assumes they won't be seen in the dying light, at the same time imagines dark faces watching them from every window. It is a difficult, tiring walk. As they approach, it seems increasingly unlikely that they can have avoided detection. Snatches of Mike's typed words run through his mind, form a disturbing pastiche: '... accumulation of weapons ... paranoid ... aerosol attacks ... body count ...'

About two hundred yards from the fence, in the shelter of a massive, glacier-scored boulder, Joe motions them to a halt. The sun is still touching the top of the domes but otherwise the grounds are dark. Most of the windows are lit up, but, as they watch, shutters are closing over them. He rumbles around in a rucksack, produces night-vision binoculars, props his elbows on the boulder, scans the building. 'Bleedin' lights, can see eff all.' Then he is rumbling again in the bag. He distributes black silk gloves. 'Put these on. Now single file, follow me, and no talking.' Findhorn brings up the rear, his nervous system jangling and his feet painful with cold.

About thirty yards out, close to the perimeter fence, Joe stops. A light wind is freshening, and whistling gently through the fence, which is topped with barbed wire.

He produces a flat slab from his bag. 'Best fillet of steak. Cost me nine francs.'

'You got off light.'

Then Joe looks again through his binoculars, and, like a discus thrower, hurls the steak over the fence. A minute passes. Then he whispers, 'Run!' and in seconds they have covered the thirty yards to the wire. Strong wirecutters make a low gap in the fence and then they are through, crawling, and up against the rear wall of the flat building. Findhorn's heart is thumping in his chest. Romella is panting.

Joe stands up and tests a window. It is unlocked. He titters. The window squeaks loudly as he opens it and he curses quietly. Findhorn cringes. And then they help each other through the gap. There is warm air, and a smell of chlorine. The lights from the main building throw a ghostly glow through the cavernous swimming pool, and ripples of light are shimmering over the roof and walls from the water.

They creep past exercise bikes and treadmills, which, in the faint light, look like mediaeval instruments of torture. At the swimming-pool door, Joe uses a small flashlight to examine the lock. 'Kid's stuff,' he declares. His voice echoes. Romella holds the flashlight while Joe gets busy with a Swiss army knife. He uses its detachable toothpick and the long, thin awl-like blade.

Joe opens the door a couple of inches. The warm air from the swimming pool makes an instant mist with the outside cold. Directly ahead of them is a patch of black shadow where the round turret joins the wall. 'Move fast,'

Joe whispers. They run, bent double, across thirty feet of exposed ground to the shelter of the shadow, leaving tracks in the deep snow. There is a narrow, dark window in the turret, about ten feet above the ground. It is protected by heavy internal shutters.

They pass the Doberman, lying in the snow. It raises its head momentarily. There is a dribble of froth at the side of its mouth and its breathing is noisy. Findhorn feels bad, hopes the animal will be okay.

Joe gives instructions in sign language and Findhorn finds himself supporting the burglar on his shoulders. After a minute the discomfort turns to an ache, and after another minute the ache is approaching pain, but then the weight is off his shoulders and he looks up to see Joe heaving himself in through the window.

Minutes pass.

Suddenly the perimeter lights come on. For a panicky moment Findhorn thinks they have been detected, has a brief fantasy image of klaxons sounding and jackbooted German guards shouting '*Achtung!*' But the seconds pass, and there is only the whistle of the wind through the fencing, and Romella and Findhorn squeeze into the dark corner, as far as possible from the ocean of white light around them, while the hammering in their hearts subsides. There is the faintest hiss from above. A thick, knotted rope is dangling down. Findhorn goes first, turns to pull Romella unceremoniously in as she clambers over the windowsill.

Then Joe is quietly closing the window behind them. He stuffs the knotted rope back in his rucksack.

They are on a wooden spiral staircase, devoid of carpets, pictures or any sort of decoration.

Voices.

They go down the wooden stairs on tiptoe. Joe is carrying his rucksack, as if to drop it and run at a moment's notice. There is a heavy, partially open wooden door. Joe waves Findhorn and Romella back, takes a look. Then he is rummaging in his rucksack. They drop their heavy jackets on the steps and wriggle into long, black theatrical robes which add to the miasma of unreality already enveloping Findhorn. Romella is struggling with a camera, looping its cord round her neck while trying not to make it bulge under the robe. Joe stuffs things into pockets and inside his shirt.

Out into the warm, carpeted corridor. Findhorn catches a whiff of hot food. At the end of the corridor is a broad flight of stairs. Along and to the right, an open double door from which comes a buzz of conversation and the clatter of dishes and cutlery. To reach the stairs they will have to pass this door. They follow Joe, stepping warily along the corridor.

A man and a woman appear at the top of the stairs. Joe, Romella and Findhorn huddle together, as if talking. Findhorn realizes that their costume pieces are all wrong, they are too black, the collar isn't right. The man and woman, heads bowed and hands in their sleeves, are down the stairs and walking towards them. They pay the trio no attention and turn into the refectory.

Joe passes by the open door. Findhorn dares a glance as they pass. He glimpses four long dark tables, with about a hundred faithful in all. There is a raised dais and a lectern with a backdrop of heavy curtains. They pass unnoticed, climb the stairs, find themselves on a landing with two corridors leading off.

One corridor leads to a chapel, ablaze with candles. Silver flying saucers hang from its ceiling, suspended on chains. A mother-ship the size of a large chandelier, lined with portholes, dominates them all. The chapel walls are covered with paintings: Jesus with open arms, saints with halos. These are interspersed with blow-ups of the Roswell alien, the face on Mars, the Belt of Orion, a star map showing the track of Sirius as it snakes across the sky. A feeling of uneasiness overwhelms Findhorn, as if he is in the presence of evil. He can't analyze it, tries to shrug it off, but the feeling persists.

They retreat. Joe points to a double door. 'This has the look of a private apartment,' he whispers.

Findhorn nods his agreement. Light is shining under the door. Joe drops to his knees, starts to use some tool on the lock. Romella stands guard at the top of the landing. A gust of laughter comes up from the refectory.

Then the door clicks open and they are in a hallway, which, for sumptuous excess, rivals Dougie's flat. Its walls are lined with tapestries. They step onto soft carpet, their path illuminated by reproduction oil lamps on the walls.

Voices, coming from an open door ten metres to their right. Joe creeps along, peers into the living room, pulls his head back. Findhorn admires his nerve. Then Joe looks again, and turns to them with an expression which somehow combines fear, horror and anger all at once. He waves them past the room.

It is empty. Marlon Brando, looking noble in a toga, is addressing a Roman lynch mob in a Nebraska accent, his words sub-titled in German. A walnut-topped desk is heaped with a disorganized clutter of revolvers, automatic pistols and cardboard ammunition boxes. About a dozen small orange cylinders are lined up against a wall. The words SARIN GAS are stencilled on them. Findhorn guesses there is probably enough of it to wipe out a small city. Joe's complexion is waxy. He hisses, 'What have you people got me into?'

Half a dozen doors lead off from the hallway. A faint blue light is shining under one of them. Joe goes down on his knees at the door and from a pocket pulls out what looks like a thin strip of coiled wire. He is visibly trembling. He uncoils the wire and slips it under the door. At the other end is an eyepiece and he holds this to his eye while wiggling the wire. Then he sighs with relief, and they are into a large empty study. The blue light comes from three small television monitors on a desk at the window. The monitors are showing the outside grounds. The front of the swimming pool is clearly visible: they had crossed in full view of a camera. Joe raises his hands to his cheeks, mutters something about Never Again.

Joe rewinds a video tape and presses the play button. Then he crosses to the shuttered window and pulls the heavy velvet curtains closed. 'Right, do your business and be quick about it. If we're caught . . .'

Quickly, Findhorn switches on the computer. It requests a password. Someone with Tati's secrets is unlikely to leave a password scribbled on some notepad and he wastes no time guessing. Romella is skimming through papers on another desk. There is something about the eight worldly dharmas: fame and infamy, praise and insult, gain and loss, pleasure and pain. She goes through the drawers, holding a flashlight in her mouth. One contains only maps. The other has pens, pencils, scrap paper. The third drawer is locked. She takes the torch from her mouth and hisses softly at Joe.

The burglar goes down on his knees, looks closely at the lock in the torchlight and produces the Swiss army knife again. 'Simple tumbril,' he whispers in a shaky voice; Findhorn wonders why everyone is whispering in this big, empty apartment. Joe closes his eyes in concentration. He hardly seems to be moving the thin blade. But then, as if by a miracle, the drawer slides smoothly open.

Romella lifts the contents out, puts them on the desk and switches on a desk lamp.

Findhorn becomes aware that his gloved hands are shaking. They begin to go through the papers.

'Footsteps?' Romella asks.

They freeze.

Another dog. The bark is deep, of the type associated with a pit bull or a big hound. It is directly below the study window. Then there is the scrunch of boots over snow and a rough male voice.

'They've found the Doberman.' Joe's eyes are wild.

A door slams in the wind. Brilliant lights come on outside, finding chinks in the window shutters.

Joe runs out of the room. For a moment they think he has abandoned them. But then he is back. 'The gymnasium roof's lit up. Come on, we're out of here.'

'No.'

'*What?*'

Romella takes the camera from around her neck. Findhorn holds the papers in place while Romella clicks, a page at a time. He notices that her hands, too, are unsteady.

The distant chop-chop of an approaching helicopter.

Joe is wringing his hands, pacing up and down. 'Right, people. Let's go.' He is thinking of the guns and the sarin gas, senses that capture will be a terminal event.

The helicopter is getting noisy. Findhorn says, 'Now the address book.'

Joe cuts loose a stream of obscenity. Now the helicopter is roaring mightily. The shutters rattle, and a moving light flickers through a gap. Romella and Findhorn are still photographing. Then they hear the engine dying and the whoosh-whoosh of the freewheeling rotor.

And then the sound of voices. Maybe four or five people. Joe is performing a sort of war dance, silent and frenzied.

Footsteps, heading for the front of the house. *They can't help but see our tracks in the snow*, Findhorn thinks in desperation.

Romella says, 'Okay.' Hastily, she returns the papers to the drawer.

'Lock it,' says Findhorn.

'There's nae time, ye eejit.'

'Lock it if you want to collect your money.'

Joe is on the edge of violence. He kneels down with his knife, fiddles with the lock. The pit bull is going crazy, its deep bay freezing Findhorn's blood. Somebody is speaking interrogatively in German.

Switch off the table lamp. Open the curtains. Exit the study, along the hallway to the landing. Findhorn gives Joe a look. Joe relocks the apartment door.

Halfway down the stairs, Joe turns and sprints back up, almost colliding with Romella. He tries a door at random: a broom cupboard. Joe squeezes in and Findhorn bundles Romella after him. The faithful are chanting, approaching the stairway. Desperately, Findhorn tries another door. It is locked, and the next and the next. He hauls open a door just as the first of the faithful reach the landing, finds himself in another apartment. He just has time to see them, dressed in long black gowns, male and female side by side, led by a bald-headed male of about fifty looking like a bespectacled Bruce Willis. The man is leading the chant in a tenor voice, each line being echoed by about half the faithful. Findhorn stands petrified in the dark room as the procession moves solemnly along the corridor, inches from him.

The procession passes. Joe opens the door, looking hunted. Findhorn opens his. The faithful are disappearing into the chapel, two abreast. One of them, a small, middle-aged woman, looks back, gives them a puzzled look. In the corridor, Joe bows his head and clasps his hands together inside the wide sleeves of the robe. He is trying not to run. The chant is now in English, fading as the line enters the chapel:

*Come to us, Blessed of Tatos, release us from the
shackles of Earth
Come to us, Blessed of Tatos, carry our souls upwards
to Sirius
Come to us, Blessed of Tatos, enfold us in your arms
May we hasten your Coming by our earthly deeds
Blessed of Tatos, come to us
Blessed of Tatos, come to us.*

They reach the spiral staircase. Joe whispers, 'Right, for Christ's sake, let's get out of this nut house.' He opens the window. They are now bathed in the lights of the helipad. There is a ten-foot drop. Romella goes first, risking a broken ankle. Findhorn follows without hesitation. Joe drops his bag, which lands in the snow with a thud. He balances precariously on the windowsill, knees bent, closing the window. The stairwell light comes on. He hasn't a second to position himself and has a simple choice: a stunt-man-type jump, or a drop of sarin on his skin. He jumps.

Away from the turret, they find themselves in full view of a man with a rifle over his shoulder. He is speaking to the pilot. Joe says, 'Come,' and they walk across the snow, heads bowed and arms in sleeves, towards the swimming pool, Romella with rucksack and jackets over her arms. The rifleman pays them no attention whatsoever.

Into the enfolding cloak of darkness, beyond the perimeter lights; disoriented, looking for Stefi's torchlight. Joe stays behind, crouching down at the fence. He is closing up the gap and taking the time to do it well; he wants his two-plus-two open-top, flamenco red bird trap.

Findhorn will settle for a toilet.

33

The Raid

In Doug's Davos hotel bedroom, with white peaks framed by the window, Findhorn plugs into the big television screen rather than the cramped little monitor of his laptop. Doug, in an armchair, has Stefi on his knee but doesn't seem to mind. Romella is sitting cross-legged on the double bed while Findhorn, on the edge of the bed, flicks through the items from Albrecht's locked drawer:

- A letter from Mr Tedesco, President of the Society for Information Display. Can you spare one of your senior staff to give a seminar on Advanced Cockpit Displays?
- A long, technical letter from an Andrew Roper, of the UK's MOD, requesting an evaluation of an exciting new development in night-vision goggles (paper enclosed).
- A letter from Colonel Herzberg of US Army Aviation Center, Fort Rucker. Confirming that he will be bringing his team to Davos next month to discuss the new gun system. Secretaries will co-ordinate diaries. Issues to be discussed include survivability, combat effectiveness, human factors engineering, visionics,

horizon technology integration, reliability, ASE equipment interfacing. Something has been scrawled over it. Findhorn recognizes the word 'Rosa'.

- A newsletter, described as 'The Key to Unlock the Glory of the Last Days'. Something about the Rewards of Giving. It reads like a scam for the gullible.

- A love letter, or at least a lust letter, from a lady in Boston called Zoë. Romella translates: something about a Nile cruise, an obscure joke about an Italian football team, and the hope they can repeat the experience some time.

- A letter from the Curator, L'Annonciade, St. Tropez, reiterating the gallery's gratitude for the loan of the Klee and confirming that it would be insured for $7,500,000 (seven point five million US dollars) while being exhibited.

- An invitation from H. Silver and Associates, Advanced Systems Division, to attend the fourth HSA Conference on Attack Helicopters in London, England. Attendance fee £1,495 (+17.5% VAT).

- Somebody from Hull with a visionary new aircraft design which he will reveal in exchange for a fifty per cent share in future profits; the letter is handwritten in biro on lined paper and has a three-up, second-flat-on-the-left address; the spelling is atrocious.

- An address book, small, black and shiny. Findhorn flicks on to the next item.

- A bill for SF 24,310 for installation of an Aga (four-oven, pewter) from Tamman & Sons, Zurich. It is addressed to a Herr W. Neff and has an address near

Blatten, Brig, Valais, Switzerland. There is a photocopy of a cheque for that amount, signed by H.W. Neff and drawn on an account in Brig, Switzerland.

'Hey,' says Romella.

'I think so too,' Findhorn replies. 'Who is this Mister Neff, and why should Albrecht be paying for his Aga?'

'Is Neff in the address book?'

Findhorn skims through the electronic copy. There is no Herr Neff.

On the screen, Findhorn displays the last item, a photocopied letter. It has been written in German, with a thick-nibbed fountain pen.

Stefi is running her hands absent-mindedly through Doug's thinning hair. She says,

> 'My darling Zoë
> Thank you for your wonderful letter. Agreed I can't compete with twenty-four Italian footballers but at my time of life I've learned that what counts is quality. I'll be in Morocco for the first two weeks in January. It will be business but I'm sending the Pirate on ahead and hope to put in a few days of sin and debauchery on the high seas. If you can stand the heat, why don't you join me? I'll pay the fare over as usual. Reply to me at Optika and mark it "Personal".
> Your loving
> Konrad.'

'I wish I was fluent in twenty languages.'

Stefi seems not to have heard. She is studying the letter closely. 'Go back to the Neff letter.'

Findhorn studies the signature on the cheque, flicks forward again to the love letter from Konrad. Different signatures, but written by the same hand, even with the same thick-nibbed pen. He claps his hands together. 'Well done. Ms Stefanova. Herr Neff and Konrad Albrecht are one and the same.'

Stefi beams. 'Yes, I think we've just struck gold.'

'Albrecht's hideaway. Someplace near Blatten in Switzerland. Could he be there now? With his engineers?'

Romella pulls the telephone onto the bed beside her. 'Put that letter from the US Army back on screen.'

Findhorn obliges. She says, 'That scrawl. It says *Rosa*.'

'Okay, he has a secretary at Davos called Rosa.' He puts the address book on screen again, flicks through its pages. He has a sense of excitement, like a hunter closing in on a quarry. There is a Rosa Stumpf, with a Davos address. Romella dials through, surprises Findhorn by speaking in fluent German. Findhorn hears a young woman's voice, with the sound of children shouting in the background.

Romella puts the phone down, turns to Findhorn. 'I said I was from Fort Rucker and needed to contact Albrecht urgently. She gave me his ex-directory number.'

She dials Albrecht's home number. Frau Albrecht answers. My husband is walking the dog. You have missed him by five minutes.

He is not away, then?

Who is this? Suspicion in her voice.

This is Colonel Herzberg's secretary. I'm phoning from the States.

He will be here in two hours' time with a colleague. Then they are going off someplace to discuss a business matter. Thirty-five years and Konrad has never before missed Christmas at home. Do you wish to call back in say three hours?

No. It will wait, thank you.

Ach! And at Christmas too. But he will be back tomorrow.

Merry Christmas. Goodbye.

And you may never see your husband again.

Romella says, 'He's summoning his engineers. We're out of time.'

Findhorn types into the Internet, throws up a map of Switzerland. Davos is on the far eastern edge of Switzerland. Brig is about halfway between Geneva and Davos. Blatten is a tiny village high in the Bernese Alps. A track lies beyond it, a thin line winding into the mountains. Instinctively, Findhorn knows that Albrecht's hideaway is somewhere up there. 'I need to contact Matsumo's killers.'

Romella says, 'You'll need your translator.'

The killers are waiting for them at Geneva Airport. Ms Drindle is wearing a heavy fur coat and a sort of Cossack hat. Dark trousers protrude below the coat. The sun-glasses, Findhorn presumes, come from her camera-shy nature. The Korean's face is similarly adorned but he has a black trenchcoat and hat which makes him look like a small, fat jazz player.

There are no handshakes or words of welcome. Findhorn and Romella follow them into the cold air. 'You drive,' Ms Drindle instructs Findhorn. 'Keep strictly to the speed limit.' The car is a black, four-wheel drive Suzuki with French number plates. Findhorn takes the wheel. Romella sits beside him. He has to think carefully about changing gear in a car with a left-hand drive. He takes them carefully through Geneva and over the Mont Blanc bridge, which for some reason is decked out with the flags of the Swiss cantons. The big water jet is off but the paddle steamer restaurant is doing Christmas lunches. He follows the signs for Thonon and is soon taking them along flat white countryside with Lac Léman to their left. He is acutely aware that until now the people in the rear of the car have been trying to find and kill him.

Conversation is zero.

They are through the tongue of France which borders the south of the lake, and back into Switzerland, before Drindle speaks in her mannish voice. 'Tell me how you would go about it, Findhorn.'

The road looks as if it has just been cleared of snow but already a thin fresh layer is beginning to form. Findhorn is driving with excessive care.

'I'm too sick to think about it.'

'Do so anyway.'

Findhorn mumbles, 'Knock on his door and blow his head off.'

In the mirror, he sees Drindle give a quick nod. 'Actually

that can work. At least with proper planning and in the right circumstances, such as a quiet suburban area. It has the crowning merit of simplicity.'

'There has to be an alternative to this.'

'Name it.'

Findhorn exhales deeply and shakes his head; he's been over it a thousand times.

Drindle continues, almost leaning over Findhorn's shoulder. 'There are three essentials in an operation like this. Planning, surprise and invisibility. You must leave not the slightest trace of your presence, apart from the corpse itself.'

'Don't try to make this sound like a legitimate military operation, Drindle. You're just a murderer.'

Her voice is icy. 'You are in no position to make facile moral judgements.'

Findhorn has no answer.

How much the Korean understands is unclear, but in the mirror Findhorn sees the man giving him a long, hostile stare. Findhorn turns and looks into the small, bloodshot eyes. He says, 'Screw you.'

The snow is getting heavy. Romella, to deflect tension, says: 'I just hope we get through.'

Findhorn hopes they don't.

'We're about a hundred kilometres from the Simplon Pass,' she adds, unfolding a map.

An old-fashioned Beetle trundles past, its spiky tyres glittering like chariot wheels.

'Consider this car, Findhorn. Foreign plates, four-wheel drive, snow chains, nothing unusual. But we will be off the main highway, climbing a very steep road with no ski slopes or other tourist attractions at the end of it, a road which leads only to the chalets of the rich scattered over the mountainside. We will be noticed.'

'It's Christmas. People have visitors.'

'Good. But what do we do with the car? Park it outside Albrecht's house? What would you do if you were Albrecht, with a trillion dollar secret and a host of enemies, if you saw a strange car waiting unexpectedly outside your empty home?'

'Run a mile.'

'Precisely. Therefore the car will not be there. We will find an empty woodshed, or even park it in his own garage. In this weather there will be no traces in the snow of man or vehicle.'

Findhorn says, 'I think I'm going to be sick.'

Ahead of them they see an oasis of light underneath a blanket of heavy grey sky. At the boundary of the town there is a blue notice with a list of passes which are *offen*, *ouvert*, *aperto* and open. Findhorn notes that the Simplon Pass is one of them and that it's the quickest escape route from Switzerland once the deed is done. Romella tells him to turn left.

He turns left and finds himself on a road running parallel to a railway station. There is a row of bright red carriages with *Zermatt* marked on their sides. There is a bridge, and Findhorn turns onto it and they drive over the white, tumbling River Rhône, and then he is immediately onto a steeply climbing hill. He drops gear.

And he drops gear again: the road begins to climb seriously. He uses low gears and extreme care.

Picture-postcard chalets, all snow-laden roofs and glittering Christmas trees, are scattered over high white slopes. It seems incredible that there are houses up there. He sees no signs of a road up to them. Grim, icy giants watch his progress through gaps in the clouds. Brig becomes a glow far below them.

They crawl into a small village. There is a handful of cars and a cable car station. Far above them, a little blue cable car is disappearing into the clouds. Findhorn stops their vehicle and they step out, their breath misting in the freezing air. Drindle walks over to a cluster of post boxes. They scan the names. Herr W. Neff lives in a house called *Heya*.

They split up. Findhorn finds himself wandering along narrow streets, barely a car width. Snow is piled high on either side. There are neat wooden chalets with verandahs and red shutters, and dates and names painted in white Gothic script on their walls. Part of the village is given over to big wooden huts standing on thick wooden stilts. Some are filled with wood, others with hay. He passes a church whose small, crowded cemetery is outlined under a metre of pristine, fluffy snow. There is an air of orderliness about everything. There is, however, no *Heya*.

A one-track, potholed road leads out of the village: the thin, black line on Findhorn's map. He looks at it, trying to follow its route up the mountain. Here and there he glimpses stretches of the road. Romella is flouncing through the car park snow. She is wearing blue jeans and leather boots; Findhorn thinks there is something vaguely eccentric about the combination of Peruvian hat and Doug's duffle coat. He points upwards. 'I don't think it can be done.'

She looks up. 'You could be right.'

'What the hell are we doing here?'

'I'm beginning to wonder.'

The killers appear and they settle into the car. Findhorn takes off, leaving the square and taking the car onto the track. He is gripped by fear within the first two hundred yards. It is almost impossible not to skid, and within half a mile the metal barriers have petered out. He glances briefly away from the road, finds himself looking down on the roofs of chalets far, far below, and experiences a surge of terror. In the car, there is dead silence.

After about a mile the road worsens. The snow becomes deeper, and he has to negotiate a series of tight hairpin bends with nothing between the car and thousands of feet of air. His jaw aches with tension, his hands are sore with gripping the steering wheel and a dull ache has developed in his gut. Above them, a massive white cloud is billowing down the mountainside like an approaching avalanche.

At last, in a state of quiet terror, Findhorn sees an Alpine villa on the edge of his vision: he doesn't dare take his eye off the track. A final bend and the road levels, terminating at a square of open, flat ground. They step out. Findhorn is weak at the knees. To him, the altitude is incredible. They are looking out over white Alpine peaks and the air is pure and cold. He catches a whiff of wood smoke. Boulders as big as houses are scattered around. A forest of snow-laden conifers lies above them and there is a rough track into the trees. Far across the valley, clouds are pouring down between peaks like a vast waterfall.

The chalet is marked *Heya*. It is about fifty yards back from the square and is reached by a steep path. There is no garage, but there is a Saab in the square, and tracks in the snow where another vehicle has taken off recently. The winter supply of wood is piled high at the side of the chalet, which has a wooden verandah with little flower boxes. The roof is under a metre of snow and projects out over the house. The upstairs shutters are closed. A small Christmas tree is set to the side of a big downstairs window, its lights brilliant in the gloom.

'This guy likes seclusion,' Findhorn says. He is shaking all over.

'Which suits our purpose nicely.' Drindle is opening the rear door of the Suzuki.

'There might be a housekeeper,' Romella suggested.

'If there is, so much the worse for her.' Drindle is pulling what looks like a squat shotgun out of a holdall. The Korean is balancing a pistol in each hand, as if he is weighing potatoes. He ends up stuffing one in each trenchcoat pocket.

'There shouldn't be, not with secret discussions about to take place,' Findhorn hopes. In spite of the cold air he feels little beads of sweat on his brow.

Drindle growls something to the Korean, who hands her a pair of black leather gloves before putting on a pair himself. Romella's face goes chalk white and Findhorn feels his own going the same way.

They trudge up through the snow, Drindle leading and the Korean taking up the rear. Drindle looks through a window, tries a door. Then the Korean is shouting from the side of the house. He is holding a heavy axe. There are wooden steps down into a cellar. In the cellar, there is a pyramid of wood, and trestles, and the smell of sawdust, and a door. They stand back as he smashes at the door repeatedly, the noise painfully loud in the confined space. Then he has an arm through and is fiddling with an inside key, and they are into a short corridor and through another door.

They are met by warmth.

The kitchen has a high stone roof, vaulted in the Italian style. An alcove contains a four-oven, pewter coloured Aga stove. A shiny copper pot is suspended from the ceiling by a big-hooped black chain. Copper pans are hooked onto nails at various points around the white-washed walls. The furniture is pine, antique and solid. It is highly polished. Chairs are scattered around as well as little tables on which are vases with yellow, red and pink flowers. Little decorative cups in odd places contrast with the solidity of the furniture. There is a smell of stew, presumably simmering in one of the four ovens.

Through to the living room, which is doubling as a dining room. Here there is a smell of beeswax and scent, and an air of obsessive neatness. Near the centre of the room is a heavy table with white tablecloth. The table has been set for dinner: there are six places. Crystal wine glasses sparkle in the Christmas-tree lights. The air is warm from a wood-burning stove set in an inglenook. There is an old-fashioned pendulum clock over the fireplace; its steady tick-tock gives a sense of harmony to the room, of solidity and domestic contentment.

It also makes Drindle's voice that much more jarring. 'Every Swiss household has a rifle. Find it.'

Findhorn, Romella and the Korean climb the wooden stairs. There are three bedrooms off. Findhorn follows Romella into a bedroom. 'This is madness. What are we doing here?'

'Do you think I'm delirious about it?'

'Have you thought about the gloves?'

Her face is grim. 'Yes.'

'You know what it means?'

'I'm not stupid, Fred. They're not bothered if we're caught.'

Findhorn whispers, 'But if we were caught we could talk. They'd be at risk.'

'I know. Therefore they intend to kill us.'

'What are you people whispering about up there? Have you found it?'

The Korean shouts triumphantly and appears on the landing with a long-barrelled rifle which looks as if it is polished as regularly as the copper pans.

'What can we do?' she whispers.

'Come down here where I can see you.'

Ms Drindle's fur coat, hat and wig have been tossed on a chair and he has his feet up on the dining table. His hair is close-cropped and grey. He is examining, almost caressing, the gun. It has a wooden stock with a fist-sized hole in it, and a short, stubby dark barrel. The Korean tosses him the rifle and disappears.

Findhorn looks at Drindle. 'I suspected it.'

Drindle smiles. 'To confuse witnesses. And there are so many security cameras these days.'

'Maybe you just get a kick out of dressing in women's clothes.'

Drindle unclips the rifle's magazine, empties the bullets into a vase, replaces it and tosses the rifle to Romella. 'Put it back.'

The Korean shouts something. They go through to a large study. The man is still in trenchcoat and hat, but his sunglasses are off and he is grinning hugely. There is a safe, about three feet tall, in the corner of the room. Drindle drops to his knees, plays with the handle of the safe. He turns to them, a strange expression on his face. 'It's in here, isn't it? The trillion dollar secret. And all we need is the key.' He runs his gloved fingers round the base. 'It's on a concrete plinth, and we would need a small crane to move it. But no matter, the key will arrive shortly.' He stands up and grins ghoulishly. Then he snaps something to the Korean, who scowls and heads out. There is a brief gust of cold air as he leaves.

Drindle waves his gun at Romella and Findhorn, directing them towards the living room. He waves it again and they sit on chairs away from the window. He throws a couple of heavy logs onto the fire and opens the stove's air vent. Then he sits across from them, while a red glow flickers through the room as the sky darkens outside.

The Korean is back in fifteen minutes, during which

time not a word of conversation has been uttered in the room. He looks like a snowman. He tosses his black trenchcoat and hat on the floor next to the Christmas tree and holds his hands to the fire, shivering and cursing. To Findhorn, the man in the firelight looks demonic.

Then the Korean, warmed up, sits back on a low leather armchair with a pistol on his lap, grinning for no obvious reason.

And they wait.

34

Petrosian's Secret

The Saab has snowchains, which is just as well given the steadily falling snow and the steepness of the road. Peering through a crack in an upstairs shutter, Drindle spreads out five fingers of one hand.

There is the rattle of a key in a lock and a brief gust of wind as the front door opens. The voices are in German; two of them are female. Findhorn recognizes one of the male voices.

He tries to visualise what is about to unfold but can't take it in. His legs are shaking. Drindle and the Korean, on the other hand, are showing no emotion. They are standing still, quiet and alert, two predators poised to kill.

Somebody has moved into the kitchen. Pots are being slid onto hotplates. Others are drifting into the living room. There is the sound of logs being thrown on the fire. A collective laugh. Glasses clinking.

And now somebody is plodding heavily up the stairs.

The Korean steps back from the door, an ugly little pistol in his hand. The door opens. Drindle points his squat shotgun at arm's length, straight at the man's head. The man is fortyish and bearded. He drops the suitcases he is carrying. Drindle raises a finger to his lips, then points, and they follow the terrified man down the stairs. Drindle steers him into the living room, and the Korean turns into the kitchen.

A man and woman are lounging back on the leather sofa, glasses in hand. They do not immediately realize what is happening. Then the woman gives a startled 'Ach!' The man next to her gapes, pop-eyed, and spills red wine onto his white sweater and slacks. Two other men, in armchairs, sit bolt upright. One is formally dressed in a white dinner suit and black tie. The other is Pitman, and Findhorn wonders whether there are any limits to human duplicity.

The Korean joins them, pushing an ashen-faced, middle-aged woman in front of him. He pushes her into a chair next to the Christmas tree. Drindle strolls casually towards Albrecht and stops, just outside arm's length. He points the gun at the quivering woman on the couch next to him. 'You have been naughty, Herr Albrecht, alias Tati. Your Temple was to deliver the diaries to my employer, not steal it for your own profit. I fear that punishment is called for.'

There is dead silence.

Drindle continues: 'You will recognize the weapon as a Russian VEPR 308 carbine. Indeed you have done business with the Vyatskie Polyani machine plant where it is produced. I do not need to tell you that it is autoloading, and you will understand its effects on the human body at this range.'

The woman screams. Drindle throws her an irritated

431

glance and continues, 'The position is simple. You will either deliver up the Petrosian document or I will give a practical demonstration of its effects on this woman. Then, if this has not persuaded you, I will repeat the process with another of your guests. If, when I have run out of guests, you still have nothing to say, then it will be your turn.'

Through his fear, Findhorn almost feels admiration for Albrecht's nerve. He is silent for about ten seconds, during which time the woman begins to hyperventilate and Findhorn increasingly expects the gun to fire. Then Albrecht is saying, almost calmly, 'And what happens to us if I give you the document?'

'We will disable your cars and telephone, tie you up and leave you. By the time you have freed yourselves and called the police we will be out of Switzerland.'

'I can't deliver the document. It's in Davos.'

Drindle looks at the woman and smiles. He speaks softly: 'That is unfortunate.'

She looks as if she might faint. 'Please. I have two children.'

'Two misfortunes, then.'

The Korean has moved behind and to the left of Findhorn, near the door, a position from which he can view the whole room. There is a gap of about five feet between him and Findhorn. Findhorn has a desperate momentary vision of diving for the man's gun, using it to shoot Drindle. Almost immediately, he rules it out. It is a schoolboy fantasy, a quick route to suicide.

Again that amazing nerve. 'If I do not give you the

document, you will not kill us. The small gain of doing so would be outweighed by the risk of spending your remaining days in a cage. But if I give you the document you will kill us. This is because its value is so large that murder becomes a risk worth taking. After all, we can identify you.'

The Korean actually speaks. His voice is guttural, coming almost from his chest, and English is clearly a poor second language. 'Shoot the bitch. Show him we serious.'

Albrecht says, 'But if you shoot Elsa there is no point in giving you the document. This is because we would all be witnesses to murder. You would have to kill us all.'

'Your logic is flawed, Albrecht. For one thing, we are professionals. The risk of capture is very small and does not enter into the equation. For another, I can cause pain.' The bang of the carbine irrupts savagely into the quiet room. Blood and fragments of white bone spray from around the woman's shins, along with hunks of polystyrene foam from the sofa. She collapses onto the floor, writhing and shrieking.

Albrecht jumps up. He raises his hands as if to ward off further shooting. He looks down at the screaming woman. His expression is one of pure horror. 'Wait!'

Over the woman's screams, Drindle is saying, 'I fear your Christmas Eve is turning out brutal, Albrecht. And it is going to get worse. But give us the document and you will not be killed. That is a promise. *Sie verstehen?*' He points the gun at the man in the dinner suit, and smiles again. The man pales and speaks rapidly to Albrecht in some Schwitzerdeutsch dialect, his voice brimming with terror. Pitman is sitting quietly, but alert like a cat.

'It's upstairs, in a safe.' Albrecht can scarcely talk.

'I know it is. Get it. *Beeilen Sie sich*.'

Albrecht stumbles out of the room, Drindle following.

The bearded man and Romella are on their knees, trying to stem the flow of blood with table napkins, but the woman is writhing too much, screaming with every touch of her shin. The man in the armchair is gripping its arms and shaking uncontrollably. His eyes are wide with terror. The woman next to the Christmas tree has her eyes closed and is mumbling under her breath. The Korean watches dispassionately from a corner, arms folded and pistol in hand. Findhorn judges the five foot gap, but he knows it is hopeless. The Korean glances at him and grins, as if inviting him to try. A pool of bright red blood is spreading across the wooden floor.

Albrecht appears a minute later, Drindle following with his carbine in one hand and a thick document in the other. The pages are stapled together and look slightly yellow with age. He tosses the document to Findhorn and with his free hand pulls at the cover on the dining-room table. Glasses, candles, cutlery and crockery crash onto the wooden floor in a heap. He pulls a dining-room chair back and motions to Findhorn with his head. 'Verify its authenticity, if you please.'

Findhorn sits down. There are about twenty pages. It is single-sided, handwritten in Armenian, with half a dozen diagrams. Names like Bethe, Bohr and Einstein are written in English. The equations use the familiar alphabet and the diagrams are also annotated in English. Findhorn suspects that, with an effort, he might be able to grasp what is going on through the mass of equations alone.

'I need my translator.'

Drindle snaps his fingers at Romella.

'Fuck off.' She is up to her elbows in blood. The table napkins are now saturated with blood and the woman is moaning, slipping in and out of consciousness.

Drindle stands over the groaning woman, points the gun at her head. Romella looks as if she wants to grab the gun and ram it down Drindle's throat. The frozen tableau seems to go on and on.

Findhorn, sensing catastrophe, says, 'Romella, better not,' and she stands up and heads angrily for the door.

'Where you go?' the Korean demands, pointing his gun, but she pushes past him roughly, blood from her hand staining his shirt.

She is back in a minute, drying her hands with a white towel. She sits down beside Findhorn at the table. She is breathing heavily and white with rage.

The woman is now unconscious. The bearded man says, 'Her pulse is rapid. I can hardly feel it.'

Findhorn hands the document to Romella. 'Let's make it quick.'

She nods, tight-lipped. 'Okay.' She flips through the pages. 'Right, it's entitled *Energy from the Vacuum*. It's in four sections. Section One, Introduction; Section Two, Thermodynamics of energy extraction; Section Three, A new view of gravity and inertia; Section Four, Practical energy extraction.'

'Section One: it's about the Casimir effect?'

'Well, yes. But there's a lot more. Here's this HMS *Daring* you talked about, and Foucault's Pendulum. He's tying it in to something called the Ylem—'

'Never mind, there's no time. What sort of energy is he talking about extracting? What's he saying here?' Findhorn points to a sentence with a number.

' "... the energy density of the vacuum is therefore estimated to be of the same order as the Planck energy, with an extractable fraction of perhaps 10^{21} ergs per cubic millimetre" – is that a lot?'

A Hiroshima bomb in every cubic millimetre of space. 'It's enough. What's his punch line? Give me the last para of the Intro.'

She translates verbatim, speaking in a low, rapid voice inaudible to anyone but Findhorn: ' "In Section Two I show that there is no inconsistency between the principle of conservation of energy and the extraction of unlimited energy from the vacuum. Section Three meets the objection that the energy density of the vacuum would curve space to a degree contradicted by observations. The point here is that the virtual radiation has such a fleeting existence that no gravitational mass is associated with it. Indeed, I show that inertia and gravity can be viewed as the reactions of mass to an asymmetric radiation field in an accelerated frame ..." '

'Her pulse is almost gone. If we don't get her to a hospital she may die.'

Drindle says, 'She assuredly will if Albrecht is not playing straight with me. You two, why have you stopped?'

Section Three amounts to a new theory of gravitation. Findhorn suspects that he is staring a Nobel Prize in the face. He says, 'There's no time for this. The woman may be dying. Skip to Section Four.'

Section Four. The sorcerer's trick.

Romella reads the words rapidly and quietly, not understanding any of it, Findhorn asking her to skip as many paragraphs as he can. And as she translates, Findhorn almost forgets where he is. The concept is utterly strange, an approach to vacuum engineering unlike anything he had visualized. It is a symbiosis of biology and physics. It is also stunningly simple.

In 1952 Chase and Henshal discovered the structure of viruses. It was a dual structure, like a golf ball. A soft inner core of RNA carried the information the virus needed to replicate itself. Protection of this vital core came in the form of a hard outer layer, a protein molecule, a long string of atoms folded round the RNA, its thousands of constituent atoms densely packed. This protective shell – the capsid – is an enormously complex crystal. A golf ball with legs.

The virus is a fraction of a micron in size. Its atoms shimmer and shake in the quantum vacuum; they feel the zero point energy, the vibrations of distant galaxies.

Coat a little plate, a centimetre on a side and machined as flat as technology will allow, with a thin layer of virus. Put this plate in a vacuum, and surge a huge electric current through it. The plate disintegrates into a cloud of microscopic platelets. The energy of the galaxies – the zero point energy – forces the little plates together. For a tiny handful, flatter than the average, the Casimir force is large enough to create X-rays, the pressure from which compresses neighbouring platelets together, creating more zero point pressure and hence more X-rays . . .

And now Petrosian cleverly exploits the dynamics of the viral crystal. It is small enough to feel the vacuum fluctuations and big enough to absorb them, extracting energy from the tiny vacuum between the plates and allowing reactions to take place which would be impossible in the macroworld; time moves at a different rate; light moves faster; causality is violated; high-energy electrons and positrons are created out of the void. The virus crystal now behaves like a single giant atom; its quantum levels are squashed closely together; the relativistic electrons crash through these, penetrating the nucleus, sinking into the shadowy depths of the energy ocean. The vacuum is now unstable; and it cannot be emptied.

A childhood memory flashes through Findhorn's mind, a story about a miller who wished for more flour but the process couldn't be stopped and the stuff poured out of his mill and flooded the countryside.

Petrosian is vague about where it will end but makes speculative remarks about matter annihilation.

Once triggered, there is no more need for an electric field: the immense pressure created in the process is enough. There is an appendix. For some reason Petrosian has typed it in Russian. Romella says she reads Russian, translates in a quiet voice which is seething with rage. There are engineering drawings. Small virus-coated plates are being fired into a giant titanium chamber (a hundred metres across in Petrosian's sketch, with walls three metres thick); they maintain an incandescent fireball, fuelled by gamma rays pouring out of empty space, drawing on incomprehensible cosmic energies.

All this Findhorn and Romella skim through in a couple of minutes. The text is backed up by a second appendix of densely argued mathematics that Findhorn doesn't even attempt. However, he notes the virus that Petrosian has identified as suitable. The tobacco mosaic virus, which Findhorn assumes is a source of disease in tobacco plants.

Another thirty seconds: the problem, admitted by Petrosian in a footnote, is the cut-off point for the energy generation. It depends on unknown properties of the vacuum at unexplored energies. It is all untested theory. It may go as Petrosian thought, giving a sort of controlled fireball from which endless energy can be safely tapped. Or a few powers of ten may be missing and a laboratory and the surrounding countryside may disappear when the switch is thrown. Or a few more powers of ten, and oceans will boil and the planet will be sterilized.

Or the whole process could be a dud. Petrosian's machine might be a nonsense, a fantasy thing which would yield nothing. Findhorn remembers Bradfield's words: *we get a lot of crank science in our field.*

Findhorn thinks of that sweaty day in MacDonald's Ranch where the bits of plutonium had to be pushed together almost to the point of criticality. He thinks of Petrosian's recurring nightmare, that the nuclear fireball might be hot enough to ignite the atmosphere. And he thinks of his own fears about instability, of the polar meltdown waiting to happen, and at last his mind becomes one with Petrosian's, and he understands his fear about the dark corners of the vacuum process, and his wish to hide it away until some future utopia when the pirates were gone and the risks could be assessed in a responsible and open marketplace. Petrosian, Findhorn realises, was the classic naive academic.

Drindle's voice brings him back to harsh reality: 'Have you finished?'

Findhorn blows out his cheeks. 'The document is authentic.'

The Korean grins. He points the gun at Findhorn and says, 'Boom boom!'

35

The Kill

Findhorn is nauseous. He is shaking, and almost choking with stress. He knows the answer but tries it anyway: 'These people know nothing about the process. You can let them go.'

Drindle smiles. 'You are so naive.'

What happens next spans no more than three seconds.

The woman at Drindle's feet moans. He points his carbine down at her and fires. The bang is deafening. A fountain of red spray shoots into the air. The bearded man, still trying to stem the blood from her legs, looks up in astonishment, his face dotted with little red spots, but there is another deafening bang and he falls back in slow motion, his chest a mangled red hole. Albrecht opens his mouth to speak but there is a third bang and his eyes roll back and he flings his arms out like a preacher and collapses lifeless on the sofa. The woman at the Christmas tree still has her eyes closed and she is praying in a wild, frightened voice, and Drindle is pointing his gun at her but now Findhorn is on his feet and screaming at the top of his voice, 'It's going out on the Internet! It's going out on the Internet!'

Drindle pauses, curious, his finger squeezing the carbine's trigger. Findhorn's ears are singing from the bangs.

'It's going to the Chairmen of Fiat SpA and Otto Wolff. It's going to Goldman Sachs International and Chase Manhattan. It's going to Aerospatiale Matra and Siemens Defence. It's being e-mailed to Haisch at Lockheed Martin and Rueda in California and Longair at the Cavendish and Puthoff in Texas. It's going to Nobel prizewinners in Princeton and computer geeks in Idaho. Most of all it's going to electronic bulletin boards. From there it'll spread like wildfire.' He stops, gasping for breath.

The man in the white dinner suit is sobbing noisily. Findhorn, his voice raw from the sudden yelling, continues more quietly, taking deep gulps of air: 'Twenty-four hours from now the biggest secret on earth, the one you've been paid to obliterate, will be the most talked-about item on the planet.'

Drindle doesn't blink. The Korean is a statue.

'I can stop it. But not if I'm dead.'

'An ingenious lie,' suggests Drindle.

'I've put a time lock on it. If I don't reach a computer terminal by a specific time, and punch in a password, the message goes out automatically. You'll have failed. Do you want to explain that failure to Mister Matsumo? Or do you think you can spend the rest of your life one step ahead of Matsumo Holdings?'

The man falls onto his knees, bawling and pleading for his life. The Korean steps over corpses towards him, snarls fiercely, and snaps back the hammer of his weapon.

Drindle shouts, '*Yamero!*' The Korean shouts, 'You be quiet!', whether to Drindle or the man is unclear. The man falls silent, but his shoulders are heaving in terror.

'Contact your paymaster,' Findhorn continues, breathing in cordite and wood smoke. 'Tell him I need access to the Internet every month for the rest of my life. Tell him to hope that I never fall out of a window, never die in a car crash, never have a heart attack, never die of pneumonia or cancer, never drown at sea. I must never, never go missing. Tell him all of that. Tell him that in my good health and happiness lies his own. And my misfortune is his. I expect a man in his position has colleagues who reward success well and punish failure harshly.'

'I am sure you are right, Mister Findhorn. High rewards do entail high risks. I am equally sure that you are lying.'

'That's not your call to make.'

'I will make my call. Sit down.' Drindle gives some curt order to the Korean and leaves the room smartly. Sweat is beginning to run down Findhorn's face and neck. The woman is still praying, quietly, in German. The Korean sits down at the dining-room table. His eyes flicker between Romella and Findhorn.

Drindle is back in less than a minute, tapping numbers on a cordless phone while holding his carbine. He speaks fluent Japanese into the telephone.

'Directory Enquiries,' Romella volunteers to Findhorn. She is grey-faced and trembling. The Korean barks angrily, waving his gun.

Another number. This time the conversation is concentrated, prolonged, with a serious edge. Findhorn is almost overcome with a sort of light-headedness; the room is warm from the log fire, but he is shivering with cold. Colour, on the other hand, is slowly returning to Romella's cheeks. She looks defiantly at the Korean and turns coolly to Findhorn. 'He's phoned a secretary at home. It's about four a.m. in Kyoto.'

The conversation ends. Drindle sits down at the table, directly opposite Findhorn. He is framed by the Christmas tree. He places the carbine and the phone on the table and sits back, arms folded. Findhorn's eyes are locked hypnotically with Drindle's. He hates him more than anything else on the planet.

The silence goes on, broken only by the quiet crackling of burning logs. One crashes in the fire. Findhorn starts and Drindle smiles contemptuously. The smell of overcooked stew is beginning to drift in from the kitchen, mingling with that of wood smoke and fresh blood. It is a mixture that Findhorn knows, if he survives, he will never forget.

Ten minutes pass.

From somewhere far down in the valley, the ponderous Oompah-da-Oompah-da of a brass band drifts up. Church bells, almost on the limit of hearing, ring out eight o'clock.

The phone, when it finally cuts into the stillness, is to Findhorn like an executioner's summons. He feels himself going white. Drindle slides his right hand onto the stock of the gun, finger round trigger, and picks up the telephone with his left. The conversation is almost one-sided, Drindle interjecting no more than the occasional '*Hai!*' Findhorn can't take his eyes from the assassin's; but he can read nothing in them.

Finally Drindle takes the phone from his ear, resting the mouthpiece on his shoulder. 'Are you brave?'

'Go to hell.'

Drindle nods. 'A brave answer in the circumstances. Courage, however, will merely prolong your agony without affecting the final outcome. You are to be tortured to the point where you will scream the password and the location of your electronic file even if it means your death. Medical expertise will be on hand to ensure that your heart does not give out. If you wish, we can demonstrate our skill in these matters by working on your translator friend. Once you have seen what we can do, you will tell us what we want to know. We will of course require to verify your information before we dispose of you. Please believe that I personally will not relish this process. But I cannot answer for my colleague.'

From the corner of his eye, Findhorn sees a broad grin spreading over the Korean's features. Romella has frozen, eyes wide with fear.

Findhorn says, 'You won't touch us.' He says it with an air of confidence but there is a solid lump in his stomach.

Drindle seems amused, raises sceptical eyebrows. 'No?'

'Because if you do I'll scream the password, you'll kill me, and delete the file.'

'Forgive me, but fear is making you confused. That is the object.'

Findhorn continues: 'And then you'll find that hidden away in some distant machine there's a second file, a duplicate. Maybe there's a third such file. Maybe a fourth. But how can you ever verify this? How many Romellas can you torture? Can you resurrect me to kill me all over again?'

For the first time the assassin's suavity is replaced by a darker look. 'That was naughty.' He speaks again into the telephone, his eyes never leaving Findhorn's. Then he slides the phone across the table.

Findhorn doesn't know what to expect. He picks it up. Yoshi Matsumo's voice comes over as clearly as if he is sitting at the table. 'Very clever, Mister Findhorn.'

Findhorn keeps trying for a confident tone. 'You have nothing to fear from me. So long as I outlive you.'

There is a tiny delay. The signal is, after all, travelling from Switzerland to a point twenty-four-thousand miles above the earth, relaying back down to a distant country, and the reply is traversing the same immense journey in the opposite direction. 'You claim you already had the secret before you entered the chalet?'

'I do.'

'Why then did you join my Friendship colleagues?'

'I told you. Your interests and mine coincide on this matter. I didn't want Albrecht's people getting a patent.'

'You stretch credulity to breaking point. But even if what you say is true, how can I let you go, to sell the secret?'

Findhorn puffs out his cheeks. The Korean is frowning angrily. 'Why all talk talk? Just finish the job. Two seconds.'

'Think about it, Matsumo.'

'I think, Mister Findhorn, that you are a principled man. Your principles have forced you to kill the innocent in order to hide the secret. These same principles will not allow you to make this devastating thing public even to save your life. Therefore your Internet files do not exist. Therefore you can safely be executed. Purely, you understand, as a precaution, in case on some future date poverty or greed should overcome those strong principles of yours.'

Drindle is watching Findhorn with quiet interest: a lion studying an antelope.

The telephone is now slippery with sweat. 'You've misread the situation. I killed these people for two million US dollars, one for me, one for my assistant.' Now he senses Romella staring at him. 'Don't you see, with these guys gone, I'm the only person on the planet who knows the process. You're my market, Yoshi. Silence me. Stuff my mouth with gold.'

Unexpectedly, the silence at the end of the line is broken by a peal of laughter. Findhorn holds the receiver away; startled faces around the table stare at the phone. When he has stopped laughing, Yoshi Matsumo says, 'What a magnificent liar you are, Mister Findhorn! I congratulate you on your ingenuity.' There is another long silence. Findhorn begins to wonder if the line has gone dead. Then: 'However, you do present me with an interesting quandary. Suppose that I kill you. Then if, as I believe, there is no message waiting to be broadcast, your death solves my problem. But now suppose that, implausible though it is, you are telling the truth. Then I fear that your death would quickly be followed by my disgrace, perhaps even my demise.'

'So make your pre-emptive sale and let us go.'

'Unfortunately, having sold the secret to me, you might then sell it all over again to someone else. Someone who might use the process and ruin my company. Therein lies my dilemma: alive or dead, you are a risk.'

Findhorn wipes an irritating drop of sweat from an eyebrow. The Korean, sensing an atmosphere, is now grinning and nodding, taunting Findhorn by pretending to shoot him with the gun. Matsumo continues: 'An idealist, or a clever buccaneer? That is the question. Return the phone to my assistant.'

Findhorn is beginning to feel a terrible tightness in his chest and jaw. He slides the telephone across the polished table back to Drindle. There is a brief conversation in Japanese and then, again, silence.

Drindle touches the barrel of the carbine. 'Still warm. It comes with telescopic sights but I removed them. They are just a nuisance at this range. He's consulting colleagues.'

Children's voices.

Stille Nacht, Heilige Nacht . . . The carol drifts faintly up from another world, a world of innocence and love and goodness, of solid values and moral certainties. Findhorn looks into Drindle's eyes, tries to see through them into the man's soul, gives up.

Alles schläft . . .

Big snow flakes are falling thickly past the window: soon they will all be snowed in, trapped together in the chalet. The logs are crackling quietly.

Einsam wacht . . .

They could be in a scene on a Christmas card, were it not for the three corpses, eyes half shut, mouths open, their blood staining the polished wooden floor.

And in the warm dining room, the living are as still as the corpses, sleeping in Heavenly peace. *Schlaf in himmlischer Ruh, Schlaf in himmlischer Ruh . . .*

A voice on the telephone. Drindle listens, his eyes expressionless, for some minutes. Then, again, he slides the telephone across to Findhorn, his face grim. Matsumo speaks like a judge pronouncing sentence: 'Mister Findhorn, I am convinced that you have put nothing on the Internet.'

Dive for the kitchen. Romella might get to the Korean.

'But then, why should I take even a slight chance with that? There is another way forward. Two million dollars is miniscule in relation to what is at stake. On some future occasion, when the money runs low, you might be tempted to talk. I must therefore make you a very rich man, in order to substantially reduce that temptation. I have opened an account for you in the Hofbahnstrasse in Zurich and arranged for twenty million dollars to be paid into it. You will be able to draw on this tomorrow morning when the bank opens.'

Findhorn has trouble taking it in: his mind is being hit simultaneously from several directions. He forces himself to speak calmly. 'Money like that would look like a drug transaction. What about the Swiss Banking Commission? Or even Interpol?'

'Do not concern yourself with such matters; we have mechanisms. Telephone my secretary at noon, Japanese time, that is in eight hours. Understand that, should you ever reveal the secret, or discuss our transaction, I will arrange to have you hunted down and exterminated even from beyond my grave. But that risk is one which, as a rich man, you will find no need to run. Does the solution strike you as satisfactory?'

'I think we have an understanding.'

There is a brief pause, longer than the travel time of radio between them. 'So, I have enjoyed our little game of kendo, Findhorn-san. We are both winners. You are now rich, and I have suppressed the energy secret. The game has been played with our wits rather than *shinai* – forgive me, I do not know the English word—'

'Bamboo sticks?'

'—and if you were Japanese rather than a *gaijin*, I would salute you as an equal.'

Stuff you, Findhorn thinks. He puts the telephone down and turns to Romella. 'We're out of here.'

The assassin's urbanity is becoming frayed. 'If I had my way things would go differently.'

'It's a matter of making the right call. Which is why Matsumo pulls the strings up above while you jerk about down below.'

Drindle picks up Petrosian's document. 'Your witty little barbs don't penetrate my skin, but my partner is a different matter. I can best describe his temperament as volcanic. And, since he is a stupid man, the issues are beyond his grasp.' He opens the front of the wood fire, throws the document onto the logs. The Korean says something in an angry voice. The pages curl, catch fire at the edges. Irrigated deserts, cheap superbombs, fertilizers from the air, social and financial chaos, roads to the back of beyond, all go up in flames. 'Get out. Take the Saab and leave it at the railway station.'

'What about you?' asks Findhorn, standing up. His legs, he finds, are hardly able to support him.

'We have a lot to do here. There are enough DNA samples in this house to gladden the hearts of policemen from the North Cape to Hong Kong. Now go, quickly.'

'May you die horribly some day soon,' Findhorn says.

The man in the white suit stands up, fearfully, edges towards the door, and then runs out; it would be comical in less deadly circumstances. Pitman follows, walking steadily. He seems about to say something to Findhorn, but then leaves without a word. The woman at the Christmas tree has opened her eyes but is sitting, motionless. She seems not to know what is happening. Romella walks over to her, takes her by the elbow, tries out a smile.

At the door, Findhorn glances back. Drindle has opened the cocktail cabinet and is pouring himself a red Martini. The Korean's eyes are flitting between Findhorn and Drindle. His fist is tightly clenched around the pistol. He is jerking it up and down as if it is a hammer. His face is almost comically angry.

The volcano is about to erupt.

36

Brass Bands

Keys on hall table, marked by Saab logo; front door, heavy pine, already open. Pitman and the other man have run ahead of them, vanishing into the dark. Freezing air and snow, billowing into the hall.

Say nothing. Don't stop. Don't look behind.

Outside, the snow is already a foot deep. Romella hastily steers the dazed woman ahead of her. The Saab is a mound of white. Findhorn waves his arms frantically over it, brushing snow off door and windscreen, while Romella bundles the woman into the back of the car. They jump in. He fumbles with the key, the engine starts and he quickly puts the automatic gearbox into reverse. There is a single loud bang from the direction of the chalet.

Romella opens the car door and jumps out, sliding and falling. Findhorn stands on the brake and the car starts to crab sideways. The rear mirror shows only snow and blackness. He knows he is close to horrendous precipices. Romella disappears into the black, crouched and running.

The door of the chalet swings open. The Korean's

squat frame is silhouetted against the hall light. He is clutching Drindle's carbine. Findhorn says 'Christ,' spins the steering wheel. The car spins but he is now utterly disoriented.

Something punches the car's windscreen and half of it disappears. Findhorn is sprayed with little squares of safety glass. He ducks his head and feels the car spin some more; he takes his foot off the accelerator but there is a heavy thump, the car tilts on its side. He thinks he is going over the edge. Airbags explode into the passenger compartment, enveloping him. Throughout this, the woman in the back makes not a sound. Findhorn thinks she might be praying.

The car is on its side. The driver's door is below him, compressed snow pushed up against his side window. He is coccooned in safety belt and airbags. He unbuckles, fights his way in panic through the enveloping bags, scrambling up towards the passenger door. He stands on the steering wheel, thrusts the door up against its own weight and clambers half out of the car. The door thumps down on his back. The pain is excruciating and for some awful moments he cannot move his legs. The Korean is now about thirty yards away, ploughing heavily through knee-deep snow. Findhorn scrambles over the side of the car, falls head first into the snow, picks himself up and finds himself staring at the carbine.

The Korean's face is distorted with rage; he is a man almost out of control.

Findhorn hopes it will be quick.

And then the Korean is performing a sort of pirhouette,

like a ballet-dancing gorilla, the gun flying from his grasp and disappearing into the deep snow. He says 'Oof!' and falls onto his knees, clutching his thigh.

Romella is bounding down the driveway with a rifle, her strides lengthening. She falls face first and snow-ploughs down the slope, pushing up a mound of snow ahead of her. The Korean is on all fours, frantically scrabbling like a dog searching for a mouse.

'Get the gun!' Romella yells, her face snow-covered.

Findhorn scrambles clumsily forwards, almost falling. Within yards of the Korean he sees the long hole in the snow where the carbine has disappeared. The Korean sees it too and lunges towards it. Findhorn reaches it first, snatches the weapon up by the barrel, falls backwards, picks himself up. Romella is on her feet, her face and hair covered in white. 'Kill him!' she shouts.

'*What?*' Findhorn shakes his head dumbly as Romella's instruction sinks in.

'Kill him! If you let him live he'll come after you. He'll find you, torture you for the secret, and kill you. Is that what you want? To go the way of Captain Hansen? To spend the rest of your life listening for sounds in the dark?'

'What about the police?' he calls out.

'For God's sake, Fred! Get real!'

The Korean is limping into the darkness, holding his leg.

'I can't.'

'Fred! You have to!'

The Korean vanishes behind a curtain of snow, limping

swiftly down the road. Findhorn takes off, following the man's tracks. He catches up with him within fifty yards. The man is wondering whether to run off the road. The lights of a village, far below, come and go through dark patches. He turns and faces Findhorn. His head and arms are thick with snow and he is no longer clutching his leg. Findhorn raises the gun and points it at the Korean's heaving chest. The man shakes his head. Findhorn fires once; snowflakes around him are briefly illuminated yellow in the flash from the gun. He has never fired a gun before and his shoulder is snapped painfully back by the recoil. The Korean pitches backwards, face up, on the edge of a precipitous drop. Findhorn approaches, stands over the man. The Korean's face can just be discerned in the light scattered from the snow, and it is distorted with pain and fear. A dark stain is spreading over his right sleeve. He raises a hand protectively, says, 'Please. I leave you alone.'

This time Findhorn holds the carbine firmly with both hands. Blood and bone spurt from the Korean's chest. Findhorn is aghast, not by the sight but by the elation which surges through his body at the moment the Korean dies.

He stands at the edge of the precipice and looks down into a blizzard-filled cauldron. He glimpses house lights far below. Then he sits down in the deep snow and heaves at the Korean's body with both feet. The man is surprisingly heavy. Findhorn keeps pushing and edging forwards until the body slides down a few feet, gathering speed like a sledge, and then disappears noiselessly over the edge in a flurry of snow. Then he tosses the carbine into the black void and ploughs back towards the chalet. His mind is empty and he keeps it that way.

The Saab is in a ditch. Its headlights are pointing up at the snow-filled sky, wipers rubbing roughly over the remaining windscreen. Its engine is still running, little wisps of steam drifting up from the hot exhaust. Romella has opened the back door and is looking in. Findhorn joins her: the woman's body is crouched in a corner, her head barely attached to the rest of it. He thinks about her two children but is unable to speak.

Romella turns and plods back into the house. She re-emerges with keys.

In the Merc, Findhorn manages to fasten his belt, but the heating controls are beyond him; his mind and trembling hands cannot cope. The snow is now about two feet deep. Romella takes the car onto the narrow track. Soon it is nose-down and Romella is starting to negotiate hairpin bends. He thinks it would be dumb to go over the edge after a night like this.

Then they are in the village and passing houses with Christmas trees glittering in their windows and deep snow on their roofs. Somebody is shovelling snow from the front of his house. He pauses to wave and Findhorn waves back.

They are about halfway down to Brig before he is able to speak. His mouth is dry. 'What happened in there?'

Romella is still breathing heavily. 'The Korean took the back of Drindle's head off and then came after you with the carbine. When he left the chalet I slipped into it. I got the Swiss rifle and reloaded the magazine.'

'Why did you go back?'

'I anticipated him. You saw his face. He saw his chance of a fortune slipping away. He didn't intend to kill you, Fred, not until he had squeezed the secret out of you. Don't worry, the trembling will go away.'

Findhorn is silent awhile. They are below the cloud level now, and Brig is spread out below them like an illuminated map. Then he said, 'A massacre.'

'For the greater good.'

'I keep thinking about that woman's kids.'

'Don't. We did our best.'

'Do we go to the police?'

'Fred, switch on again. You killed a man tonight.'

'Romella, I enjoyed killing that man. It was a glorious experience.'

She is taking the car at a snail's pace round a hairpin bend but still it is skidding. The headlights point into black space. 'A natural reaction. You were getting rid of a threat. We all have crocodilian brain stems.' She has negotiated the bend.

'I should have run away.'

'For the rest of your life? And what if he caught up with you some day, forced you to talk? You'd risk evaporating the planet so that you could feel cosy and legal?'

'The police—'

Romella's voice is pained. 'You'd re-open the whole can of worms.'

'I wonder what the law says. I kill a man in cold blood,

knowing that if I don't the consequences could be horrend-ous. Some day I'll ask my old man about that.'

'Fred, stop torturing yourself. The situation transcended legalities. There was nothing else you could do.'

After twenty minutes the road finally levels out, and they turn into Brig. The trembling has now extended to Findhorn's whole body and he marvels that Romella is capable of driving. The main road has already been cleared of snow, although a slippery, compacted layer remains and heavy flakes are still falling. Romella follows a ski-loaded Volkswagen, full of teenagers, through the town. Brig is a blaze of light, defying the brooding mountains around it, Christmas lights festooning the streets, which are bustling with late-evening shoppers. A band of snow-men is pounding out 'Rudolf the Red-Nosed Reindeer'. The conductor is dressed like Santa Claus and mulled wine is being passed around the orchestra.

Romella cruises past, and then they are clearing the town, the range of the car's headlights steadily decreasing as the snow gets heavier. She takes it past Ried-Brig on a broad, climbing highway.

'The Simplon Pass?' he asks.

'Yes. We must get out of Switzerland before Frau House-keeper turns up.'

But the Simplon Pass is *Geschlossen*. A young soldier with a Cossack hat and a rifle on his shoulder looks at them curiously, and then turns them back to Brig.

Romella says, 'I expect the Grimsel will be closed too. We'll head west for Geneva, drive through the night.'

'Surely we'll never be connected with the massacre?'

458

'Dear Fred. He thinks traffic cameras are for traffic control.' She glances at Findhorn's baffled face and shakes her head. 'You need a babysitter.'

37

Steel Drums

Findhorn woke with a start. The car clock was showing 3.30 a.m. In the confined space, the smell of leather and Romella's perfume was strong. But the hot and cold sweats, the nausea, the blinding headache, all had gone.

As had the snow. Romella was taking the car along a lane which opened out into a cobbled square surrounded by an arcade. Shuttered windows looked down on them. It was all very French, apart from the purple and red lights from a very unFrench 'All-Nite Diner' which shone out like a beacon in the dark. She drove slowly across the square towards the light and parked next to a dozen gleaming motorbikes.

From the momentary lull in conversation, Romella had made a dramatic entrance. The bikers occupied three tables and were washing down platters of entrecôte steak and chips with tumblers of dark red vin ordinaire. Findhorn's nose was assaulted by Gaulois smoke, wine, garlic and herbs. It was plain delicious and he tried to remember when he had last eaten. A woman with spiky yellow hair, heavy black eye-shadow and a ring in her nose was skilfully tapping pool balls into pockets as her

460

bearded companion grunted. Tom Jones was declaring that 'It's not unyoosual to be lonely' from a juke box whose chrome veneer was hanging down in long strips.

They sat on hard chairs as far as possible from Tom Jones. The yellow Formica table had shaky legs. Findhorn ordered 'doo shockola' in schoolboy French and the stout proprietor squinted at him, and then at Romella, and then back to Findhorn, through Gaulois smoke. He shambled off.

'Where are we?'

'France. This is Dijon.' She was smoking a black, gold-tipped Balkan Sobranie.

'I didn't know you smoked,' Findhorn said.

'Only at celebrations, like Christmas and birthdays.'

Findhorn played with the salt cellar. After the night's events, he was having problems making a connection with the real world around him. 'What are our chances?'

The *deux chocolats* arrived in cups the size of soup plates. Romella stirred her chocolate. 'You mean together?'

'I mean on the run.'

She studied him through a thin trickle of smoke. 'In my opinion, so long as you have Petrosian's secret, the full apparatus of several powerful corporations and states will be deployed to apprehend you.'

Findhorn took a thoughtful sip at his chocolate. Romella looked at him through cigarette smoke, eyes like Marlene Dietrich. 'The only way you'll avoid a lifetime on the run is to deliver up Petrosian's secret. If you did that, nobody would bother you.'

'Matsumo Holdings would. They'd send in their ninjas.'

'There's a golden way out of that. Say the secret was independently discovered by some third party,' she suggested slyly.

'Forget it. That one per cent chance of boiling the oceans.'

The spiky-haired girl was potting a solitary black with a satisfied smile while her bearded friend made obscene gestures with his pool cue.

Findhorn looked at Romella. For some reason she was smiling. In the harsh light of the diner, her dark features had an enigmatic quality. He wondered if he would ever know her well enough to be sure of exactly what she was thinking. He said, 'We're really about to become fugitives?'

'You are.'

Findhorn waved for the bill, but the bikers were crowding round the till, and the proprietor was counting their money.

There was an outburst of noisy argument. Someone was being short-changed, or thought they were, or said they thought they were.

'Did I tell you Matsumo's opening a bank account for me tomorrow, and he's putting twenty million dollars into it? A little sweetener to ensure my enduring silence.'

'Twenty million dollars.' She stubbed out her little black cigarette.

'Let me see, Dougie and you get twenty per cent each, that's four million dollars apiece, and Stefi gets two million. Leaving me with ten.'

'Stefi deserves as much as the rest of us.'

'Okay. She gets four, leaving me with eight.' Findhorn

462

marvelled at the breathtaking casualness with which he had just given away two million dollars. But then, he thought, it's natural justice.

Romella was saying, 'I've always liked nice round numbers. I could never understand fractions. We can make Paris by daybreak.'

'Surely we won't be connected to the mayhem in Blatten. Albrecht was an arms dealer as well as the leader of a doomsday religious cult. He must have had dozens of enemies.'

'You're the man with the secret. And we've gone through quite a few traffic cameras.'

Findhorn said, 'Eight million in the bank and I feel gutted.'

Romella smiled. 'We ought to get a move on.'

Back in the cobbled square, the bikers had jumped red lights and vanished. Romella waited patiently. Findhorn contemplated the traffic camera. Then the lights were green, Romella was moving swiftly through the gears, and in minutes they were on to a fast autoroute through the flat French countryside.

Findhorn glanced at the speedometer. Telegraph poles were whipping past and the autoroute, at an illegal 160 kilometres an hour, was like a winding country road. 'Why Paris?' he asked.

'I have a friend in the Fifth Arrondissement. It's a place to stay until we sort ourselves out.'

A cluster of red tail lights appeared ahead: the bikers, straddling the carriageway and hunched over their machines. She overtook them effortlessly.

'And beyond Paris?'

'I saw something in a travel brochure years ago, when I was a girl. It's stuck in my mind ever since. It was a place called Treasure Beach. Where snow is unknown, and you celebrate Christmas with a midnight beach party, and if you want you can hear poetry readings at the full moon.'

'You can travel anywhere openly. Without a passport, I'm stuck.'

'Your brother's clients —'

Findhorn laughed, and realized it was his first laugh for a long time. 'Yes, no doubt Dougie can fix something while keeping himself pure as the driven snow.'

They drove on in silence for some minutes.

Findhorn broke it: 'It'll take some time to trickle in.'

'What?'

'The enormity of the events. The fortunes we've made.'

Romella said, 'All from empty space.'

A police car hurtled by on the opposite carriageway, light flashing. She said, 'I think Stefi and Doug are made for each other.'

Findhorn nodded in the dark. 'Yes. United by mutual lust and greed. I'm sure they'll be happy together.'

There was a light smell of perfume in the air, and the warmth of the car was soporific. The cat's eyes on the road were flicking past at a satisfying rate. Their achievement was beginning to sink in. He felt a bewildering mix of emotions; an immense relief, as if he had just shed a huge load; something like pride in a dirty job carried through for the greater good. But there was something else, a tingling anticipation whose nature he found hard to identify. He tried to sound casual. 'This Treasure Beach. I'd love to come along.'

'What?' She laughed. 'Does Findhorn of the Arctic finally trust me?'

'No way, Ms Grigoryan.'

'Anyway, what would a polar explorer do with Caribbean sunshine?'

'You've no idea how often I've longed for it.'

'But your Arctic studies?'

'We're an interconnected whole, remember? If I bring my knowledge of what's happening in the Arctic to El Niño and hurricanes, who knows what might come of it? I could join the climate group in the University of the West Indies, paying my own salary. I might even chase Category Five hurricanes in the best macho tradition while you sit on the porch and knit cardigans for our babies.'

She threw back her head and laughed again. 'By the way, *did* you put Petrosian's secret on the Internet?'

'Would I lie?' Findhorn asked. He added, 'And are you going to extort it from me?'

In the half-dark, her smile was enigmatic. 'I have ways of making you talk.'

Findhorn watched her elegant hands manipulate the steering wheel, listened to the melodious voice, detected the slight body odour underlying her expensive perfume. He settled back in the leather chair, listening to the purr of the big engine. His head was filled with a romantic jumble of pirate coves, treasure chests, hurricanes, Caribbean rainforests and mountain hideaways. He thought about

two falls, two submissions and a knockout, rested his
hand lightly on her slim thigh. 'When can you start?'

38

Byurakan

In the summer the big thistles burned brown and there was a lot of fruit to be picked. Flies were everywhere.

Down in the Yerevan hollow, in the summer, it was stifling, and Mount Ararat had always disappeared into the blue by mid-morning. But summer weekends were good. Weekends were when Grandpa had expected his son Yerev, his lazy wife Asia, and their boy Piotr, to come and help with the orchard and the sheep. Early on Saturdays, they would pile into the Skoda and head for the mountains, where the air was cool and you could still see the white-topped cone of the biblical mountain.

But the routine had been upset following Grandpa's strange death. Yerev had gone off by himself more than once, on business, he said. He had rented out the orchard to another shepherd. The sheep had been sold off. I'm a teacher, Yerev had explained to a distraught Piotr. It's just not possible to be a schoolteacher in the city and a shepherd in the hills, both at once. Asia had expressed her satisfaction and thought maybe weekends could now be spent replastering the ceiling which had collapsed during the last earthquake.

Then, one Sunday night in July, Yerev had come home, wearily climbed the seven flights of their noisy high-rise and declared that he had found a buyer for Grandpa's house. Asia had gone out and returned with a bottle of good cognac. Fourteen-year-old Piotr, conscious that the final link with his grandfather was being broken, had wept quietly that night in his bed. While Asia snored at his side, Yerev had listened to his son in the dark, but had been too weary to comfort him.

Things were a little brighter in the morning. A colleague from school turned up with a truck borrowed from his road-sweeper brother, Asia filled bottles with wine and water, and plastic bags with fruit, grated carrots, beetroot and folded sheets of the Armenian bread *lavash*, along with vodka and home-made beer, and they set off for the hills before the sun was too high.

Within half an hour the truck had transported them up out of the polluted air, and they were moving along a steep climbing road which would take them to the Roman temple and the fluted basalt columns of Garni. The road was all but deserted. After another half-hour they reached a bumpy track which ended at a single-storey house after about fifty yards. The house was on the ridge of a hill overlooking dry, parched countryside. Down below, Piotr could see a man and a boy carrying long scythes over their shoulders; in fact, the boy's scythe was taller than the boy.

It took no more than half an hour to load the back of the truck with Grandpa's possessions. While Yerev's friend was securing the load with string, and Asia was preparing sticks of *shashlyk* for grilling over a charcoal fire, Yerev and Piotr went in for a last look round. Piotr pointed to a small trapdoor in the kitchen ceiling, and Yerev heaved his son up to the tiny roof space.

At first it was dark, but as his eyes adapted to the gloom, the boy became aware of a little metal box. He crawled along a beam. The box had a lid held shut by a loose clasp, and it opened easily. Piotr gasped. Glass marbles! And steel ones! To think that they had nearly missed this! He would be the envy of his friends.

The box was heavy and the boy had to raise himself into a half-crouching position in order to slide it towards the open trapdoor. As his back pushed against the rafters he heard a rustling noise, and a sheet of paper, which had been wedged between rafter and tiles, slid into view. Curious, he put his hand in the space and groped blindly. Feeling a bundle of papers, he pulled them out carefully so as not to tear them; they were old and brittle. Then he lowered the box of marbles to his father, handed down the papers, and let himself back down, brushing dust from his clothes and hands.

Piotr ran outside with the box to show his mother the wonderful collection of marbles. Yerev locked his father's door for the last time, and blinking in the sunlight, sat down at the picnic table and flicked through the papers.

'What have you got, Yerev?' his wife asked.

'It's very strange. Viktor, what do you make of it?'

Yerev's friend looked through the lined pages, torn from a jotter. The writing was in an uneducated hand, someone to whom forming letters was an unfamiliar business.

'Your father's writing?'

'Yes, without doubt.'

'But—'

'Quite, Viktor. Father could barely read and write.'

'But these are equations! And I can hardly understand the text!' This was an understatement: Viktor couldn't understand the text at all. And there were engineering drawings, accompanied by a text in Russian.

'Here are some words.' He flicked through the text and said, 'Electron. Positron. Lithium. Deuterium. Vacuum. Foucault's Pendulum, what's that? And Casimir pinch? And here are people's names. Gamow. Teller. Ah ah! Oppenheimer! Fuchs! I think I have heard these names.'

Viktor screwed up his face. 'Some of them. American scientists.'

'Oh-oh! Oh-oh!' Yerev jumped up from the table and walked up and down excitedly, flicking the pages. He turned to the astonished group. 'And here is something about hydrogen bombs.'

Asia squealed. Her eyes opened in fright. 'Burn that stuff. It's trouble.'

'Papa must have copied this from somewhere, but why?'

'His brother? Lev?'

'Of course,' Yerev said. 'Maybe Lev gave him papers for safe-keeping, and he copied them.'

'Forgive me, Yerev, but did Lev not spy for us?'

'For the Soviets, you mean. Maybe. So that visiting American said. But who knows the truth about these things?'

'Burn the papers, Yerev.' Asia tapped the charcoal grill with a skewer. 'They're trouble.'

Yerev thought about it, contemplated the glowing charcoal, looked at the papers in his hand. Then he said, 'No. They're good news. This stuff might be worth a few drams. We'll take them straight to the Byurakan Observatory. There are people there who know about things like this.' He turned to Piotr, beaming. 'Who knows, we might even get a new Skoda out of it.'

Asia sighed. 'Always dreaming.'

Nemesis

Bill Napier

According to a shock CIA report, Russian cosmonauts
have deflected a giant asteroid onto a collision course
with the United States – presenting the President with
an impossible moral dilemma: either he must wait
passively for almost certain annihilation, or retaliate
first with a massive nuclear strike.

The only hope of averting catastrophe lies with an
elite team of the world's top astronomers and
astrophysicists, gathered secretly at Eagle Peak
Observatory, Arizona. They have five days to identify
the asteroid – codename Nemesis – and stop it. If they
can't, the President will have to assume the asteroid
is going to hit and make his appalling choice.

But as time begins to run out and the search for
Nemesis becomes increasingly desperate, British
asteroid expert Oliver Webb has an extraordinary idea
– that the key lies in the dusty pages of an obscure
seventeenth-century Latin manuscript, a manuscript
which has just gone mysteriously missing . . .

'The most exciting book I have ever read' Arthur C.
Clarke

'Napier has put a lifetime's knowledge into a stomach-
churning thriller . . . a gripping read' *Scotsman*

0 7472 5993 3

Inheritance

Keith Baker

When retired RUC officer Bob McCallan is killed in a gas explosion in a caravan in Donegal, his son Jack inherits an unexpected fortune. He also inherits a key to the past.

The violence in Northern Ireland has been over for two decades, but there are still secrets that could shatter the foundations of peace. Secrets that Bob McCallan's untimely death threatens to bring to the surface. Secrets that some people would do anything to keep buried.

'A gripping read' Michael Dobbs

'Breathtaking . . . if you buy no other thriller this year, buy this one' *Irish Times*

'Gripping' *Belfast Telegraph*

0 7472 5235 1